THE A
OF LIVING
and Other Stories

THE ART
OF LIVING
and Other Stories

JOHN GARDNER

Woodcuts by Mary Azarian

Vintage Books

A Division of Random House, Inc.   New York

First Vintage Books Edition, April 1989

Copyright © 1974, 1976, 1977, 1979, and 1981
by John Gardner

Library of Congress Cataloging-in-Publication Data
Gardner, John, 1933–1982
The art of living, and other stories / John Gardner;
woodcuts by Mary Azarian.—1st Vintage Books ed.
p. cm.
ISBN 0-679-72350-1: $7.95
I. Title.
[PS3557.A712A89   1989]
813'.54—dc19

"The Joy of the Just" was originally published in
The American Poetry Review. "Trumpeter" was
originally published in *Esquire.* "Stillness" was originally
published in *The Hudson Review.* "The Music Lover"
was originally published in *Antaeus.*

Manufactured in the United States of America

10 9 8 7 6 5 4 3 2 1

CONTENTS

Nimram 3

Redemption 30

Stillness 49

The Music Lover 65

Trumpeter 77

The Library Horror 88

The Joy of the Just 101

Vlemk the Box-Painter 136

Come on Back 245

The Art of Living 270

THE ART
OF LIVING

and Other Stories

NIMRAM

Ich bin von Gott und will wieder zu Gott.

[FOR WILLIAM H. GASS]

Seated by the window in the last row of the first-class no-smoking section, his large attaché case edged under the seat in front of him, his seatbelt snug and buckled, Benjamin Nimram drew off his dark glasses, tucked them into his inside coatpocket, and in the same motion turned to look out at the rain on the gleaming tarmac. The dark glasses were his wife's idea, an idea he'd accepted in the way he accepted nearly all her ideas, with affection and a tuck at the corner of his mouth that signified, though his wife did not know it—or so he imagined —private amusement tinged with that faint trace of fatalistic melancholy one might catch, if one were watchful, at the periphery of all he did. Not that Nimram was a gloomy man. When he'd put behind him, at least for public appearances, that famous "Beethoven frown"—once a private joke between his wife and himself but now a thing as public as the mileage of his Rolls, since his wife had mentioned both, in an unguarded moment, to an interviewer—he'd discovered that smiling like a birthday child as he strode, tails flying, toward the light-drenched podium came as naturally to him as breathing, or at any rate as naturally as the second-nature breathing of an oboist. He had mentioned to her—more in the way of trying it out than as sober communication of a determined fact—that it made him uneasy, being recognized everywhere he went these days.

"You poor dear!" she'd said, eyes slightly widening, and he had smiled privately, realizing that now he was in for it. "We'll get a pair of those Polaroid prescription dark glasses," she'd said.

"Good idea," he'd agreed, seeing himself in them the instant he said it—the dark, heavy face, thick eyebrows, large nose, the somewhat embarrassingly expensive suit. "And a shoulder-holster, maybe," he'd thought, but had carefully shown nothing but the tuck at the corner of his mouth.

"Is something wrong?" she'd asked. She stood in the doorway, half in, half out, trowel in hand, a paper bag of some kind of chemical clamped under her arm. He'd caught her on her way out to her gardening. She was smiling brightly, head tipped and thrown toward him, back into the room. It was the look she sometimes got on the tennis court, extravagantly polite, aggressive.

"What could be wrong?" he said, tossing his arms out. "I'll pick up a pair this afternoon."

"Jerry can get them," she said. "I'll phone in ahead." Jerry was their outside man, a grinning young half-Japanese. What he did around the place—besides stand with his arms folded, or ride around the lawn on the huge green mower—had never been clear to Nimram.

"Fine," he said, "fine."

She blew him a kiss and ran out.

Poor Arline, he thought, shaking his head, slightly grinning. "I believe I was destined for this marriage," she had once told an interviewer. Though she was sometimes embarrassed almost to tears by what she read in the interviews she'd given to newspapers and magazines, she continued to give them. She saw it as part of her duty as his wife, keeping his name out there. And though she tried to be more careful, knowing how "different" things could sound in print, to say nothing of how reporters could distort if they were, as she said, "that kind"—turning trifles to tragedies, missing jokes, even suddenly attacking her for no reason (one had once called her "a musical ignoramus")—she continued to forget and speak her mind. Nimram praised her, needless to say, no matter what she said. Certainly there was never any harm in her words. Even her cunning, when she schemed about his "image" or the I.R.S., had the innocent openness of the Michigan fields around her father's little place in the country, as he called it—a house sometimes visited, long before her father had bought it, by the elder Henry Ford.

There wasn't a great deal Arline could do for him in the world, or anyway not a great deal he could make her feel he needed and appreciated—aside, of course, from her elegant company at social gatherings, for instance fund-raisers. She was "a good Michigan girl," as she said; Republican, a member (lapsed) of the D.A.R. Subtly—or no, not subtly, but openly, flagrantly—she had been trained from birth for the sacred and substantial position of Good Wife. She was a quick learner—even brilliant, he might have said in an unguarded moment, if Nimram ever had such moments—and she had snapped up the requisite skills of her position the way a streetdog snaps up meat. She was not a great reader (books were one of Nimram's passions), and music was not really her first interest in life, except, of course, when Nimram conducted it; but she could keep a household like an old-time Viennese aristocrat; she could "present" her husband, choosing the right restaurants, wines, and charities, buying him not only the exactly right clothes, as it seemed to her (and for all he knew she had unerring taste, though sometimes her choices raised his eyebrows at first), but also finding him the exactly right house, or, rather, Brentwood mansion—formerly the home of a reclusive movie star—the suitable cars—first the Porsche, then on second thought, of course, the Rolls—the suitably lovable fox terrier, which Arline had named Trixie. She had every skill known to the well-to-do Midwestern wife, including certain bedroom skills that Nimram waited with a smile of dread for her to reveal, in her open-hearted, Michigan way, to some yenta from *People* magazine or the L.A. *Times*. But for all that, she had moments, he knew, when she seemed to herself inadequate, obscurely unprepared.

"Do you like the house?" she had asked him once, with a bright smile and an uneasiness around the eyes that made his heart go out to her. It was only his heart that got up from the chair; the rest of him sat solid as a rock, with a marked-up score on his knees.

"Of course I like it," he'd answered. "I love it!" When they were alone or among intimate friends his voice had, at times, a hearty bellow that could make Arline jump.

"Good!" she'd said, and had smiled more brightly, then had added, her expression unsure again, "It does seem a solid investment."

Nimram might have said, if he were someone else, "What's the difference? What's a house? I'm the greatest conductor in the world! Civilization is my house!" That, however, was the kind of thing Nimram never said to anyone, even in one of his rare but notorious rages.

Her look of uncertainty was almost anguish now, though she labored to conceal it, and so he'd laid down the score he was fiddling with, had renounced the brief flash of doubt over whether he should leave it there—defenseless on the carpet, where the dog could come in and, say, drool on it—and had swung up out of his chair and strode over to seize her in his arms and press his cheek to hers, saying, "What's this craziness? It's a beautiful house and I love it!"

There had been, apparently, an edge of uncontrol in his heartiness, or perhaps it was simply the age-old weight of the world distracting her, time and the beauty of things falling away, nothing sure, nothing strong enough to bear her up—not yet, anyway, not as quickly as that—not even the strength in her famous conductor's arms. "I'm sorry," she'd said, blinking away tears, giving her embarrassed Midwesterner laugh. "Aren't I a fool?"—biting her lips now, taking on the sins of the world.

"Come," he'd said, "we eat out." It was his standard response to all sorrows no energy of the baton could transmute; a brief arrogation of the power of God—no offense, since God had no interest in it, it seemed.

"But dinner's been—" she'd begun, drawing back from him, already of two minds.

"No no," he'd said, tyrannical. "Go get dressed. We eat out." Candlelight burning through the wine bottle, silverware shining like her dream of eternity, people across the room showing one by one and four by four their covert signs of having recognized the famous conductor, a thing they could speak of tomorrow and next week, next year, perhaps, buoy themselves up on in dreary times, the memory of that dinner miraculously blessed, as if God Himself had come to sit with them. The tuck of private amusement and sadness touched the corner of Nimram's mouth.

He was not a man who had ever given thought to whether or not his opinions of himself and his effect on the world were inflated. He was a musician simply, or not so simply; an interpreter of Mahler and Bruckner, Sibelius and Nielsen—much as his wife Arline, buying him clothes, transforming his Beethoven frown to his now just as famous bright smile, brushing her lips across his cheek as he plunged (always hurrying) toward sleep, was the dutiful and faithful interpreter of Benjamin Nimram. His life was sufficient, a joy to him, in fact. One might have thought of it—and so Nimram himself thought of it, in certain rare moods—as one resounding success after another. He had conducted every major symphony in the world, had been granted by Toscanini's daughters the privilege of studying their father's scores, treasure-horde of the old man's secrets; he could count among his closest friends some of the greatest musicians of his time. He had so often been called a genius by critics everywhere that he had come to take it for granted that he was indeed just that—"just that" in both senses, exactly that and merely that: a fortunate accident, a man supremely lucky. Had he been born with an ear just a little less exact, a personality more easily ruffled, dexterity less precise, or some physical weakness—a heart too feeble for the demands he made of it, or arthritis, the plague of so many conductors—he would still, no doubt, have been a symphony man, but his ambition would have been checked a little, his ideas of self-fulfillment scaled down. Whatever fate had dealt him he would have learned, no doubt, to put up with, guarding his chips. But Nimram had been dealt all high cards, and he knew it. He revelled in his fortune, sprawling when he sat, his big-boned fingers splayed wide on his belly like a man who's just had dinner, his spirit as playful as a child's for all the gray at his temples, all his middle-aged bulk and weight—packed muscle, all of it—a man too much enjoying himself to have time for scorn or for fretting over whether or not he was getting his due, which, anyway, he was. He was one of the elect. He sailed through the world like a white yacht jubilant with flags.

The rain fell steadily, figures and dark square tractors hurrying toward the belly of the plane and then away again, occasionally glowing under blooms of silent lightning, in the aisle behind him passengers still moving with the infinite patience of Tolstoy peasants toward their second-class seats. With a part of his mind he watched their reflections in the window and wondered idly how many of them, if any, had seen him conduct, seen anyone conduct, cared at all for the shimmering ghost he had staked his life on. None of them, so far as he could tell, had even noticed the Muzak leaking cheerfully, mindlessly, from the plane's invisible speakers. It would be turned off when the plane was safely airborne, for which he was grateful, needless to say. Yet it was touching, in a way, that the airline should offer this feeble little gesture of reassurance—*All will be well! Listen to the Muzak! All will be well!* They scarcely heard it, these children of accident, old and young, setting out across the country in the middle of the night; yet perhaps it was true that they were comforted, lulled.

Now a voice said behind him, professionally kind, "There you are. There! Shall I take these? All right?"

When he turned, the stewardess was taking the metal crutches from the young woman—girl, rather—newly planted in the seat beside him.

"Thank you," the girl was saying, reaching down to each side of her for the straps of her seatbelt.

"They'll be right up in front," the stewardess said, drawing the crutches toward her shoulder to clamp them in one arm. "If you need anything, you just sing. All right?"

"Thank you," the girl said again, nodding, drawing up the straps now, studying the buckle. She nodded one more time, smiling suddenly, seeing how the buckle worked, and closed it. She glanced briefly at Nimram, then away again. She was perhaps sixteen.

He too looked away and, with his heart jumping, considered the image of her fixed in his mind. She was so much like his wife Arline—though of course much younger—that he was ready to believe her a lost sister. It was impossible, he knew; Arline's people were not the kind who lost things, much less the kind who had secrets, except on Christmas morning. Yet for all his certainty, some stubborn, infantile part of his brain seized on the idea with both fists and refused to let go. Her hair, like Arline's, was reddish brown, with an outer layer of yellow; hair so soft and fine it was like a brush of light. Their foreheads, noses, mouths, and chins were identical too, or so he'd thought at first. As he turned now, furtively checking, he saw that the girl's nose was straighter than Arline's—prettier, if anything—and more lightly freckled. For all that, the likeness grew stronger as he studied it.

She looked up, caught him watching her, smiled, and looked away. The blue of her eyes was much paler than the blue of Arline's, and the difference so startled him that for a moment —shifting in his seat, clearing his throat, turning to look out at the rain again—he could hardly believe he'd thought the two faces similar. He watched the girl's reflection, in the window eight inches from his face, as she reached toward the pocket on the back of the seat in front of her and drew out a magazine, or perhaps the plasticized safety card.

"I hope they know what they're doing," she said.

Her face, when he half turned to look, showed no sign of joking. Ordinarily, Nimram would have smiled and said nothing. For some reason he spoke. "This your first trip on an airplane?"

She nodded, smiling back, a smile so full of panic he almost laughed.

"Don't worry," he said, "the pilot's in front. Anything happens, he gets it first. He's very concerned about that." Nimram winked.

The girl studied him as if lost in thought, the smile on her face still there but forgotten, and it seemed to him he knew what she was thinking. She was in no condition to pick up ironies. When he'd told her the pilot was "very concerned," did he mean that the pilot was nervous? neurotic? beginning to slip? Did this big, expensive-looking man in the seat beside her *know* the pilot?

"Do you know the pilot?" she asked innocently, brightening up her smile.

"A joke," he said. "Among people who fly airplanes it's the oldest joke in the world. It means don't worry."

She turned away and looked down at the plasticized card. "It's just, with the rain and everything," she said softly, "what happens if a plane gets hit by lightning?"

"I doubt that it would do any harm," he said, knowing it wasn't true. The Vienna Quartet had been killed just a year ago when their plane had been knocked down by lightning. "Anyway, we won't be going anywhere near where the lightning is. They have sophisticated weather charts, radar . . . anyway, most of the time we'll be high above it all. You live here in Los Angeles?"

The girl glanced at him, smiling vaguely. She hadn't heard. The Captain had broken in on the Muzak to tell them his name and the usual trivia, their projected altitude, flight time, weather, the airline's friendly advice about seatbelts. Nimram examined the girl's arm and hand on the armrest, then looked at his own and frowned. She had something wrong with her. He remembered that she'd come on with crutches, and glanced again at her face. Like her hand, it was slightly off-color, slightly puffy. Some blood disease, perhaps.

Now the stewardess was leaning down toward them, talking to both of them as if she thought they were together. Nimram studied the sharp, dark red sheen of her hair, metallic oxblood. Her face, in comparison with the girl's, was shockingly healthy. She addressed them by their names, "Mr. Nimram, Miss Curtis," a trifle that brought the melancholy tuck to Nimram's mouth, he could hardly have told you why himself—something about civility and human vulnerability, a commercially tainted civility, no doubt (he could see her quickly scanning the first-class passenger list, as per instruction, memorizing names), but civility nonetheless, the familiar old defiance of night and thunder: when they plunged into the Pacific, on the way out for the turn, or snapped off a wing on the horn of some mountain, or exploded in the air or burst into shrapnel and flame on the Mojave, they would die by name: "Mr. Nimram. Miss Curtis." Or anyway so it would be for the people in first class. "When we're airborne," the stewardess was saying, "we'll be serving complimentary drinks. . . ." As she named them off, Miss Curtis sat frowning with concentration, as panicky as ever. She ordered a Coke; Nimram ordered wine. The stewardess smiled as if delighted and moved away.

Neither of them noticed when the plane began to move. The girl had asked him if he flew on airplanes often, and he'd launched a full and elaborate answer—New York, Paris, Rome, Tokyo. . . . He beamed, gesturing as he spoke, as if flying were the greatest of his pleasures. Nothing could be farther from the truth, in fact; flying bored and annoyed him, not that he was afraid—Nimram was afraid of almost nothing, at any rate nothing he'd experienced so far, and he'd be forty-nine in June. Or rather, to be precise, he was afraid of nothing that could happen to himself, only of things that threatened others. Once he'd been hit on the Los Angeles expressway, when Arline was with him. Her head had been thrown against the dashboard and she'd been knocked unconscious. Nimram, dragging her from the car, cursing the police, who were nowhere to be seen, and shouting at the idiot by-standers, had found himself shaking like a leaf. Sometimes, lying in bed with his arm around her as she slept, Nimram, listening to the silence of the house, the very faint whine of trucks on the highway two miles away, would feel almost crushed by the weight of his fear for her, heaven bearing down on their roof like the base of a graveyard monument—though nothing was wrong, she was well, ten years younger than he was and strong as a horse from all the tennis and swimming.

In his hundreds of flights—maybe it was thousands—he'd never had once what he could honestly describe as a close call, and he'd come to believe that he probably never would have one; but he knew, as surely as a human being can know anything, that if he ever did, he probably wouldn't be afraid. Like most people, he'd heard friends speak, from time to time, about their fear of dying, and the feeling was not one he scorned or despised; but the fact remained, he was not the kind of man who had it. "Well, you're lucky," Arline had said, refusing to believe him, getting for an instant the hard look that came when she believed she was somehow being criticized. "Yes, lucky," he'd said thoughtfully. It was the single most notable fact about his life.

Abruptly, the girl, Miss Curtis, broke in on his expansive praise of airlines. "We're moving!" she exclaimed, darting her head past his shoulder in the direction of the window, no less surprised, it seemed, than she'd have been if they were sitting in a building.

Nimram joined her in looking out, watching yellow lights pass, the taxiway scored by rain-wet blue-and-white beams thrown by lights farther out. Now on the loudspeaker an invisible stewardess began explaining the use of oxygen masks and the positions of the doors, while their own stewardess, with slightly parted lips and her eyes a little widened, pointed and gestured without a sound, like an Asian dancer. The girl beside him listened as if in despair, glum as a student who's fallen hopelessly behind. Her hand on the armrest was more yellow than before.

"Don't worry," Nimram said, "you'll like it."

She was apparently too frightened to speak or turn her head.

Now the engines wound up to full power, a sound that for no real reason reminded Nimram of the opening of Brahms' First, and lights came on, surprisingly powerful, like a searchlight or the headlight of a railroad engine, smashing through the rain as if by violent will, flooding the runway below and ahead of the wing just behind him, and the plane began its quickly accelerating, furious run down the field for take-off. Like a grandfather, Nimram put his hand on the girl's. "Look," he said, showing his smile, tilting his head in the direction of the window, but she shook her head just perceptibly and shut her eyes tight. Again for an instant he was struck by the likeness, as remarkable now as it had been when he'd first seen her, and he tried to remember when Arline had squeezed her eyes shut in exactly that way. He could see her face vividly—they were outdoors somewhere, in summer, perhaps in England—but the background refused to fill in for him, remained just a sunlit, ferny green, and the memory tingling in the cellar of his mind dimmed out. The Brahms was still playing itself inside him, solemn and magnificent, aglow, like the lights of the city now fallen far beneath them, lurid in the rain. Now the plane was banking, yawing like a ship as it founders and slips over, the headlights rushing into churning spray, the unbelievably large black wing upended, suddenly white in a blast of clouded lightning, then black again, darker than before. As the plane righted itself, the pilot began speaking to the passengers again. Nimram, frowning his Beethoven frown, hardly noticed. The plane began to bounce, creaking like a carriage, still climbing to get above the weather.

"Dear God," the girl whispered.

"It's all right, it's all all right," Nimram said, and pressed her hand.

Her name was Anne. She was, as he'd guessed, sixteen; from Chicago; and though she did not tell him what her disease was or directly mention that she was dying, she made her situation clear enough. "It's incredible," she said. "One of my grandmothers is ninety-two, the other one's eighty-six. But I guess it doesn't matter. If you're chosen, you're chosen." A quick, embarrassed smile. "Are you in business or something?"

"More or less," he said. "You're in school?"

"High school," she said.

"You have boyfriends?"

"No."

Nimram shook his head as if in wonderment and looked quickly toward the front of the plane for some distraction. "Ah," he said, "here's the stewardess with our drinks."

The girl smiled and nodded, though the stewardess was still

two seats away. "We don't seem to have gotten above the storm, do we." She was looking past him, out the window at the towers of cloud lighting up, darkening, then lighting again. The plane was still jouncing, as if bumping things more solid than any possible air or cloud, maybe Plato's airy beasts.

"Things'll settle down in a minute," Nimram said.

Innocently, the girl asked, "Are you religious or anything?"

"Well, no—" He caught himself. "More or less," he said.

"You're more or less in business and you're more or less religious," the girl said, and smiled as if she'd caught him. "Are you a gambler, then?"

He laughed. "Is that what I look like?"

She continued to smile, but studied him, looking mainly at his black-and-gray unruly hair. "Actually, I never saw one, that I know of. Except in movies."

Nimram mused. "I guess we're pretty much all of us gamblers," he said, and at once felt embarrassment at having come on like a philosopher or, worse, a poet.

"I know," she said without distress. "Winners and losers."

He shot her a look. If she was going to go on like this she was going to be trouble. Was she speaking so freely because they were strangers?—travellers who'd never meet again? He folded and unfolded his hands slowly, in a way that would have seemed to an observer not nervous but judicious; and, frowning more severely then he knew, his graying eyebrows low, Nimram thought about bringing out the work in his attaché case.

Before he reached his decision, their stewardess was bending down toward them, helping the girl drop her tray into position. Nimram lowered his, then took the wineglass and bottle the stewardess held out. No sooner had he set down the glass than the plane hit what might have been a slanted stone wall in the middle of the sky and veered crazily upward, then laboriously steadied.

"Oh my God, dear God, my God!" the girl whispered.

"You *are* religious," Nimram said, and smiled.

She said nothing, but sat rigid, slightly cross at him, perhaps, steadying the glass on the napkin now soaked in Coke.

The pilot came on again, casual, as if amused by their predicament. "Sorry we can't give you a smoother ride, folks, but looks like Mother Nature's in a real tizzy tonight. We're taking the ship up to thirty-seven thousand, see if we can't just outfox her."

"Is that safe?" the girl asked softly.

He nodded and shrugged. "Safe as a ride in a rockingchair," he said.

They could feel the plane nosing up, climbing so sharply that for a moment even Nimram felt a touch of dismay. The bumping and creaking became less noticeable. Nimram took a deep breath and poured his wine.

Slowly, carefully, the girl raised the Coke to her lips and took a small sip, then set it down again. "I hope it's not like this in Chicago," she said.

"I'm sure it won't be." He toasted her with the wineglass—she seemed not to notice—then drew it to his mouth and drank.

He couldn't tell how long he'd slept or what, if anything, he'd dreamed. The girl slept beside him, fallen toward his shoulder, the cabin around them droning quietly, as if singing to itself, below them what might have been miles of darkness, as if the planet had silently fallen out from under them, tumbling toward God knew what. Here in the dimly lit cabin, Nimram felt serene. They'd be landing at O'Hare shortly—less than two hours. Arline would be waiting in the lounge, smiling eagerly, even more pleased than usual to see him, after three long days with her parents. He'd be no less glad to see her, of course; yet just now, though he knew that that moment was rushing toward him, he felt aloof from it, suspended above time's wild drive like the note of a single flute above a poised and silent orchestra. For all he could tell, the plane itself might have been hanging motionless, as still as the pinprick stars overhead.

The cabin had grown chilly, and, carefully, making sure he didn't wake her, Nimram raised the girl's blanket toward her throat. She stirred, a muscle along her jaw twitching, but continued to sleep, her breathing deep and even. Across the aisle from them, an old woman opened her eyes and stared straight ahead, listening like someone who imagines she's heard a burglar in the kitchen, then closed them again, indifferent.

Thoughtfully, Nimram gazed at the sleeping girl. On her forehead, despite the cold, there were tiny beads of sweat. He considered brushing the hair back from her face—it looked as if it tickled—but with his hand already in the air he checked himself, then lowered the hand. She was young enough to be his daughter, he mused, pursing his lips. Thank God she wasn't. Instantly, he hated it that he'd thought such a thing. She was *some* poor devil's daughter. Then it dawned on Nimram that she was young enough, too, to be Arline's daughter, from the time before Arline and he had met. Arline was thirty-nine, the girl sixteen. The faintest trace of a prickling came to his scalp, and he felt now a different kind of chill in the cabin, as if a cloud had passed between his soul and some invisible sun. "Don't ask!" Arline would say when he drew her toward the subject of her life—that is, her love-life—before they knew each other. "I was wild," she would say, laughing, "God!" and would touch his cheek with the back of her hand. The dark, infantile part of Nimram's mind seized on that now with the same blind obstinance as it had earlier seized on the idea that the girl was Arline's sister. Consciously, or with his brain's left lobe, perhaps, he knew the idea was nonsense. Arline's laugh had no abandoned child in it, only coy hints of old escapades —love-making on beaches or in the back seats of cars, drunken parties in the houses of friends when the parents were far away in Cleveland or Detroit, and then when she was older, affairs more serious and miserable. She had been married, briefly, to a man who had something to do with oil-rigs. About that he knew a fair amount, though with her Anglo-Saxon ideas of what was proper she hated to speak of it. In any case, the idea that the girl might be her daughter was groundless and absurd; if it remained, roaming in the dark of his mind, it remained against his will, like a rat in the basement, too canny to be poisoned or trapped. Even so, even after he'd rejected it utterly, he found that the groundless suspicion had subtly transmuted the way he saw the girl. He felt in his chest and at the pit of his stomach an echo of the anguish her parents must be feeling, a shadowy sorrow that, for all his notorious good fortune, made him feel helpless.

Strange images began to molest Nimram's thoughts, memories of no real significance, yet intense, like charged images in a dream. Memories, ideas . . . It was hard to say what they were. It was as if he had indeed, by a careless misstep, slipped out of time, as if the past and present had collapsed into one unbroken instant, so that he was both himself and himself at sixteen, the age of the girl asleep beside him.

He was riding on a train, late at night, through Indiana, alone. The seats were once-red plush, old and stiff, discolored almost to black. There was a round black handle, like the handle on a gearshift, that one pulled to make the back recline. Toward the rear of the car an old man in black clothes was coughing horribly, hacking as if to throw up his lungs. The conductor, sitting in the car's only light, his black cap pulled forward to the rim of his glasses, was laboriously writing something, muttering, from time to time—never looking up from his writing toward the cougher—"God damn you, die!" It was so vivid it made his scalp prickle, the musical thrumming of wheels on rails as distinct in Nimram's mind as the drone of the airplane he sat in. The wheels and railjoints picked up the muttered words, transforming them to music, a witless, everlastingly repetitive jingle: *God damn you, die!* (click) *God damn you, die!* (click) . . .

Sometimes he'd awakened in terror, he remembered, riding on the train, convinced that the train had fallen off the tracks and was hurtling through space; but when he looked out the window at the blur of dark trees and shrubs rushing by, the ragged fields gray as bones in the moonlight, he would be reassured—the train was going lickety-split, but all was well. Though it seemed only an instant ago, if not happening right now, it also seemed ages ago: he'd lived, since then, through innumerable train rides, bus rides, plane rides—lived through two marriages and into a third, lived through God knew how many playing jobs, conducting jobs, fund-raising benefits, deaths of friends. He'd lived through warplane formations over Brooklyn; explosions in the harbor, no comment in the papers; lived through the birth and rise of Israel, had conducted the Israel Philharmonic; lived through . . . but that was not the point. She was sixteen, her head hanging loose, free of the pillow, like a flower on a weak, bent stem. All that time, the time he'd already consumed too fast to notice he was losing it—it might have been centuries, so it felt to him now—was time the girl would never get.

It wasn't pity he felt, or even anger at the general injustice of things; it was bewilderment, a kind of shock that stilled the wits. If he were religious—he was, of course, but not in the common sense—he might have been furious at God's mishandling of the universe, or at very least puzzled by the disparity between real and ideal. But none of that was what he felt. God had nothing to do with it, and the whole question of real and ideal was academic. Nimram felt only, looking at the girl—her skin off-color, her head unsupported yet untroubled by the awkwardness, tolerant as a corpse—Nimram felt only a profound embarrassment and helplessness: helplessly fortunate and therefore unfit, unworthy, his whole life light and unprofitable as a puff-ball, needless as ascending smoke. He hardly knew her, yet he felt now—knowing it was a lie but knowing also that if the girl were really his daughter it would be true—that if Nature allowed it, Mother of tizzies and silences, he would change lives with the girl beside him in an instant.

Suddenly the girl cried out sharply and opened her eyes.

"Here now! It's okay!" he said, and touched her shoulder.

She shook her head, not quite awake, disoriented. "Oh!" she said, and blushed—a kind of thickening of the yellow-gray skin. "Oh, I'm sorry!" She flashed her panicky smile. "I was having a dream."

"Everything's all right," he said, "don't worry now, everything's fine."

"It's really funny," she said, shaking her head again, so hard the soft hair flew. She drew back from him and raised her hands to her eyes. "It was the strangest dream!" she said, and lowered her hands to look out the window, squinting a little, trying to recapture what she'd seen. He saw that his first impression had been mistaken; it had not, after all, been a nightmare. "I dreamed I was in a room, a kind of moldy old cellar where there were animals of some kind, and when I tried to open the door—" She broke off and glanced around to see if anyone was listening. No one was awake. She slid her eyes toward him, wanting to go on but unsure of herself. He bent his head, waiting with interest. Hesitantly, she said, "When I tried to open the door, the doorknob came off in my hands. I started scraping at the door with my fingers and, somehow—" She scowled, trying to remember. "I don't know, somehow the door broke away and I discovered that behind the door, where the world outside should be, there was . . . there was this huge, like, parlor. Inside it there was every toy or doll I ever had that had been broken or lost, all in perfect condition."

"Interesting dream," he said, looking at her forehead, not her eyes; then, feeling that something more was expected, "Dreams are strange things."

"I know." She nodded, then quickly asked, "What time is it, do you know? How long before we get to Chicago?"

"They're two hours ahead of us. According to my watch—"

Before he could finish, she broke in, "Yes, that's right. I forgot." A shudder went through her, and she asked, "Is it cold in here?"

"Freezing," he said.

"Thank God!" She looked past him, out the window, and abruptly brightened. "It's gotten nice out—anyway, I don't see any lightning." She gave her head a jerk, tossing back the hair.

"It's behind us," he said. "I see you're not afraid anymore."

"You're wrong," she said, and smiled. "But it's true, it's not as bad as it was. All the same, I'm still praying."

"Good idea," he said.

She shot a quick look at him, then smiled uncertainly, staring straight ahead. "A lot of people don't believe in praying and things," she said. "They try to make you feel stupid for doing it, like when a boy wants to play the violin instead of trumpet or drums. In our orchestra at school the whole string section's made up of girls except for one poor guy that plays viola." She paused and glanced at him, then smiled. "It's really funny how I never make sense when I talk to you."

"Sure you do."

She shrugged. "Anyway, some say there's a God and some say there isn't, and they're both so positive you wouldn't believe it. Personally, I'm not sure one way or the other, but when I'm scared I pray."

"It's like the old joke," he began.

"Do you like music?" she asked. "Classical, I mean?"

Nimram frowned. "Oh, sometimes."

"Who's your favorite composer?"

It struck him for the first time that perhaps his favorite composer was Machaut. "Beethoven?" he said.

It was apparently the right answer. "Who's your favorite conductor?"

He pretended to think about it.

"Mine's Seiji Ozawa," she said.

Nimram nodded, lips pursed. "I hear he's good."

She shook her head again to get the hair out of her eyes. "Oh well," she said. Some thought had possessed her, making her face formal, pulling the lines all downward. She folded her hands and looked at them, then abruptly, with an effort, lifted her eyes to meet his. "I guess I told you a kind of lie," she said.

He raised his eyebrows.

"I do have a boyfriend, actually." Quickly, as if for fear that he might ask the young man's name, she said, "You know how when you meet someone you want to sound more interesting than you are? Well—" She looked back at her folded hands, and he could see her forcing herself up to it. "I do this tragic act."

He sat very still, nervously prepared to grin, waiting.

She mumbled something, and when he leaned toward her she raised her voice, still without looking at him, her voice barely audible even now, and said, "I'm what they call 'terminal,' but, well, I mean, it doesn't *mean* anything, you know? It's sort of . . . The only time it makes me scared, or makes me cry, things like that, is when I say to myself in words, 'I'm going to . . .'" He saw that it was true; if she finished the sentence she would cry. She breathed very shallowly and continued, "If the airplane crashed, it wouldn't make much difference as far as I'm concerned, just make it a little sooner, but just the same when we were taking off, with the lightning and everything . . ." Now she did, for an instant, look up at him. "I never make any sense." Her eyes were full of tears.

"No," he said, "you make sense enough."

She was wringing her hands, smiling as if in chagrin, but smiling with pleasure too, the happiness lifting off as if defiantly above the deadweight of discomfort. "Anyway, I do have a boyfriend. He's the one that plays viola, actually. He's nice. I mean, he's wonderful. His name's Stephen." She raised both hands to wipe the tears away. "I mean, it's really funny. My life's really wonderful." She gave a laugh, then covered her face with both hands, her shoulders shaking.

He patted the side of her arm, saying nothing.

"The reason I wanted to tell you," she said when she was able to speak, "is, you've really been nice. I didn't want to—"

"That's all right," he said. "Look, that's how we all are."

"I know," she said, and suddenly laughed, crying. "That really is true, isn't it! It's just like my uncle Charley says. He lives with us. He's my mother's older brother. He says the most interesting thing about Noah's Ark is that all the animals on it were scared and stupid."

Nimram laughed.

"He really is wonderful," she said, "except that he coughs all the time. He's dying of emphysema, but mention that he ought to stop smoking his pipe, or mention that maybe he should go see a doctor, Uncle Charley goes right through the ceiling. It's really that spending money terrifies him, but he pretends it's doctors he hates. Just mention the word and he starts yelling 'False prophets! Profiteers! Pill-pushers! Snake-handlers!' He can really get loud. My father says we should tie him out front for a watchdog." She laughed again.

Nimram's ears popped. They were beginning the long descent. After a moment he said, "Actually, I haven't been strictly honest with you either. I'm not really in business."

She looked at him, waiting with what seemed to him a curiously childish eagerness.

"I'm a symphony conductor."

"Are you really?" she asked, lowering her eyebrows, studying him to see if he was lying. "What's your name?"

"Benjamin Nimram," he said.

Her eyes narrowed, and the embarrassment was back. He

could see her searching her memory. "I think I've heard of you," she said.

"*Sic transit gloria mundi*," he said, mock-morose.

She smiled and pushed her hair back. "I know what that means," she said.

The no-smoking sign came on. In the distance the earth was adazzle with lights.

In the lounge at O'Hare he spotted his wife at once, motionless and smiling in the milling crowd—she hadn't yet seen him— her beret and coat dark red, almost black. He hurried toward her. Now she saw him and, breaking that stillness like the stillness of an old, old painting, raised her arm to wave, threw herself back into time, and came striding to meet him. He drew off and folded the dark glasses.

"Ben!" she exclaimed, and they embraced. "Honey, you look terrible!" She pulled back to look at him, then hugged him again. "On TV it said there was a thunderstorm in L.A., one of the worst ever. I was worried sick!"

"Now now," he said, holding her a moment longer. "So how were Poppa and Momma?"

"How was the flight?" she asked. "I bet it was awful! Did the man from the kennel come for Trixie?"

He took her hand and they started, moving with long, matched strides, toward the terminal.

"Trixie's fine, the flight was fine, everything's fine," he said.

She tipped her head, mocking. "Are you drunk, Benjamin?"

They veered out, passing an old couple inching along on canes, arguing.

"I met a girl," he said.

She checked his eyes. "Pretty?" she asked—laughingly, teasingly; but part of her was watching like a hawk. And why not, of course. He'd been married twice before, and they were as different, she and himself, as day and night. Why should she have faith? He thought again of the conviction he'd momentarily felt that the girl was her daughter. Sooner or later, he knew, he would find himself asking her about it; but not now. *Scared and stupid*, he thought, remembering, and the tuck at the corner of his mouth came back. He got an image of Noah's Ark as a great, blind, dumb thing nosing carefully, full of fear, toward the smell of Ararat.

"Too young," he said. "Practically not yet of this world."

They were walking very fast, as they always did, gliding smoothly past all the others. Now and then he glanced past his shoulder, hoping to spot Anne Curtis; but it was absurd, he knew. She'd be the last of the last, chattering, he hoped, or doing her tragic act. Arline's coat flared out behind her and her face was flushed.

Almost as soon as she stepped off the plane, Anne Curtis found out from her father who it was that had befriended her. The following night, when Nimram conducted the Chicago Symphony in Mahler's Fifth, she was in the audience, in the second balcony, with her parents. They arrived late, after the Water Music, with which he had opened the program. Her father had gotten tickets only at the last minute, and it was a long drive in from La Grange. They edged into their seats while the orchestra was being rearranged, new instruments being added, the people who'd played the Handel scrunching forward and closer together.

She had never before seen a Mahler orchestra—nine French horns, wave on wave of violins and cellos, a whole long row of gleaming trumpets, brighter than welders' lights, another of trombones, two rows of basses, four harps. It was awesome, almost frightening. It filled the vast stage from wingtip to wingtip like some monstrous black creature too enormous to fly, guarding the ground with its head thrust forward—the light-drenched, empty podium. When the last of the enlarged orchestra was assembled and the newcomers had tuned, the houselights dimmed, and as if at some signal invisible to commoners, the people below her began to clap, then the people all around her. Now she too was clapping, her mother and father clapping loudly beside her, the roar of applause growing louder and deeper, drawing the conductor toward the light. He came like a panther, dignified yet jubilant, flashing his teeth in a smile, waving at the orchestra with both long arms. He shook hands with the concertmaster, bounded to the podium—light shot off his hair—turned to the audience and bowed with his arms stretched wide, then straightened, chin high, as if revelling in their pleasure and miraculous faith in him. Then he turned, threw open the score—the applause sank away—and for a moment studied it like a man reading dials and gauges of infinite complexity. He picked up his baton; they lifted their instruments. He threw back his shoulders and raised both hands till they were level with his shoulders, where he held them still, as if casting a spell on his army of musicians, all motionless as a crowd in suspended animation, the breathless dead of the whole world's history, awaiting the impossible. And then his right hand moved—nothing much, almost playful—and the trumpet call began, a kind of warning both to the auditorium, tier on tier of shadowy white faces rising in the dark, and to the still orchestra bathed in light. Now his left hand moved and the orchestra stirred, tentative at first, but presaging such an awakening as she'd never before dreamed of. Then something new began, all that wide valley of orchestra playing, calm, serene, a vast sweep of music as smooth and sharp-edged as an enormous scythe—she had never in her life heard a sound so broad, as if all of humanity, living and dead, had come together for one grand onslaught. The sound ran, gathering its strength, along the ground, building in intensity, full of doubt, even terror, but also fury, and

then—amazingly, quite easily—lifted. She pressed her father's hand as Benjamin Nimram, last night, had pressed hers.

Her mother leaned toward her, tilting like a tree in high wind. "Are you sure that's him?" she asked.

"Of course it is," she said.

Sternly, the man behind them cleared his throat.

REDEMPTION

One day in April—a clear, blue day when there were crocuses in bloom—Jack Hawthorne ran over and killed his brother, David. Even at the last moment he could have prevented his brother's death by slamming on the tractor brakes, easily in reach for all the shortness of his legs; but he was unable to think, or, rather, thought unclearly, and so watched it happen, as he would again and again watch it happen in his mind, with nearly undiminished intensity and clarity, all his life. The younger brother was riding, as both of them knew he should not have been, on the cultipacker, a two-ton implement lumbering behind the tractor, crushing new-ploughed ground. Jack was twelve, his brother, David, seven. The scream came not from David, who never got a sound out, but from their five-year-old sister, who was riding on the fender of the tractor, looking back. When Jack turned to look, the huge iron wheels had reached his brother's pelvis. He kept driving, reacting as he would to a half-crushed farm animal, and imagining, in the same stab of thought, that perhaps his brother would survive. Blood poured from David's mouth.

Their father was nearly destroyed by it. Sometimes Jack would find him lying on the cow-barn floor, crying, unable to stand up. Dale Hawthorne, the father, was a sensitive, intelligent man, by nature a dreamer. It showed in old photographs, his smile coded, his eyes on the horizon. He loved all his children and would not consciously have been able to hate his son even if Jack had indeed been, as he thought himself, his brother's murderer. But he could not help sometimes seeming to blame his son, though consciously he blamed only his own unwisdom and—so far as his belief held firm—God. Dale Hawthorne's mind swung violently at this time, reversing itself almost hour by hour, from desperate faith to the most savage, black-hearted atheism. Every sickly calf, every sow that ate her litter, was a new, sure proof that the religion he'd followed all his life was a lie. Yet skeletons were orderly, as were, he thought, the stars. He was unable to decide, one moment full of rage at God's injustice, the next moment wracked by doubt of His existence.

Though he was not ordinarily a man who smoked, he would sometimes sit up all night now, or move restlessly, hurriedly, from room to room, chain-smoking Lucky Strikes. Or he would ride away on his huge, darkly thundering Harley-Davidson 80, trying to forget, morbidly dwelling on what he'd meant to put behind him—how David had once laughed, cake in his fists; how he'd once patched a chair with precocious skill—or Dale Hawthorne would think, for the hundredth time, about suicide, hunting in mixed fear and anger for some reason not to miss the next turn, fly off to the right of the next iron bridge onto the moonlit gray rocks and black water below—discovering, invariably, no reason but the damage his suicide would do to his wife and the children remaining.

Sometimes he would forget for a while by abandoning reason and responsibility for love affairs. Jack's father was at this time still young, still handsome, well-known for the poetry he recited at local churches or for English classes or meetings of the Grange—recited, to loud applause (he had poems of all kinds, both serious and comic), for thrashing crews, old men at the V.A. Hospital, even the tough, flint-eyed orphans at the

Children's Home. He was a celebrity, in fact, as much Romantic poet-hero as his time and western New York State could afford—and beyond all that, he was now so full of pain and unassuageable guilt that women's hearts flew to him unbidden. He became, with all his soul and without cynical intent—though fleeing all law, or what he'd once thought law—a hunter of women, trading off his sorrow for the sorrows of wearied, unfulfilled country wives. At times he would be gone from the farm for days, abandoning the work to Jack and whoever was available to help—some neighbor or older cousin or one of Jack's uncles. No one complained, at least not openly. A stranger might have condemned him, but no one in the family did, certainly not Jack, not even Jack's mother, though her sorrow was increased. Dale Hawthorne had always been, before the accident, a faithful man, one of the most fair-minded, genial farmers in the country. No one asked that, changed as he was, he do more, for the moment, than survive.

As for Jack's mother, though she'd been, before the accident, a cheerful woman—one who laughed often and loved telling stories, sometimes sang anthems in bandanna and blackface before her husband recited poems—she cried now, nights, and did only as much as she had strength to do—so sapped by grief that she could barely move her arms. She comforted Jack and his sister, Phoebe—herself as well—by embracing them vehemently whenever new waves of guilt swept in, by constant reassurance and extravagant praise, frequent mention of how proud some relative would be—once, for instance, over a drawing of his sister's, "Oh, Phoebe, if only your great-aunt Lucy could see this!" Great-aunt Lucy had been famous, among the family and friends, for her paintings of families of lions. And Jack's mother forced on his sister and himself comforts more permanent: piano and, for Jack, French-horn lessons, school and church activities, above all an endless, exhausting ritual of chores. Because she had, at thirty-four, considerable strength of character—except that, these days, she was always eating—and because, also, she was a woman of strong religious faith, a woman who, in her years of church work and teaching at the high school, had made scores of close, for the most part equally religious, friends, with whom she regularly corresponded, her letters, then theirs, half filling the mailbox at the foot of the hill and cluttering every table, desk, and niche in the large old house—friends who now frequently visited or phoned—she was able to move step by step past disaster and in the end keep her family from wreck. She said very little to her children about her troubles. In fact, except for the crying behind her closed door, she kept her feelings strictly secret.

But for all his mother and her friends could do for him—for all his father's older brothers could do, or, when he was there, his father himself—the damage to young Jack Hawthorne took a long while healing. Working the farm, ploughing, cultipacking, disking, dragging, he had plenty of time to think—plenty of time for the accident to replay, with the solidity of real time repeated, in his mind, his whole body flinching from the image as it came, his voice leaping up independent of him, as if a shout could perhaps drive the memory back into its cave. Maneuvering the tractor over sloping, rocky fields, dust whorling out like smoke behind him or, when he turned into the wind, falling like soot until his skin was black and his hair as thick and stiff as old clothes in an attic—the circles of foothills every day turning greener, the late-spring wind flowing endless and sweet with the smell of coming rain—he had all the time in the world to cry and swear bitterly at himself, standing up to drive, as his father often did, Jack's sore hands clamped tight to the steering wheel, his shoes unsteady on the bucking axlebeam—for stones lay everywhere, yellowed in the sunlight, a field of misshapen skulls. He'd never loved his brother, he raged out loud, never loved anyone as well as he should have. He was incapable of love, he told himself, striking the steering wheel. He was inherently bad, a spiritual defective. He was evil.

So he raged and grew increasingly ashamed of his raging, reminded by the lengthening shadows across the field of the theatricality in all he did, his most terrible sorrow mere sorrow on a stage, the very thunderclaps above—dark blue, rushing sky, birds crazily wheeling—mere opera set, proper lighting for his rant. At once he would hush himself, lower his rear end to the tractor seat, lock every muscle to the stillness of a statue, and drive on, solitary, blinded by tears; yet even now it was theater, not life—mere ghastly posturing, as in that story of his father's, how Lord Byron once tried to get Shelley's skull to make a drinking cup. Tears no longer came, though the storm went on building. Jack rode on, alone with the indifferent, murderous machinery in the widening ten-acre field.

When the storm at last hit, he'd been driven up the lane like a dog in flight, lashed by gusty rain, chased across the tracks to the tractor shed and from there to the kitchen, full of food smells from his mother's work and Phoebe's, sometimes the work of two or three friends who'd stopped by to look in on the family. Jack kept aloof, repelled by their bright, melodious chatter and absentminded humming, indignant at their pretense that all was well. "My, how you've grown!" the old friend or fellow teacher from high school would say, and to his mother, "My, what big *hands* he has, Betty!" He would glare at his little sister, Phoebe, his sole ally, already half traitor— she would bite her lips, squinting, concentrating harder on the mixing bowl and beaters; she was forever making cakes—and he would retreat as soon as possible to the evening chores.

He had always told himself stories to pass the time when driving the tractor, endlessly looping back and forth, around and around, fitting the land for spring planting. He told them to himself aloud, taking all parts in the dialogue, gesturing, making faces, discarding dignity, here where no one could see

or overhear him, half a mile from the nearest house. Once all his stories had been of sexual conquest or of heroic battle with escaped convicts from the Attica Prison or kidnappers who, unbeknownst to anyone, had built a small shack where they kept their captives, female and beautiful, in the lush, swampy woods beside the field. Now, after the accident, his subject matter changed. His fantasies came to be all of self-sacrifice, pitiful stories in which he redeemed his life by throwing it away to save others more worthwhile. To friends and officials of his fantasy, especially to heroines—a girl named Margaret, at school, or his cousin Linda—he would confess his worthlessness at painful length, naming all his faults, granting himself no quarter. For a time this helped, but the lie was too obvious, the manipulation of shame to buy love, and in the end despair bled all color from his fantasies. The foulness of his nature became clearer and clearer in his mind until, like his father, he began to toy—dully but in morbid earnest now—with the idea of suicide. His chest would fill with anguish, as if he were dreaming some nightmare wide awake, or bleeding internally, and his arms and legs would grow shaky with weakness, until he had to stop and get down from the tractor and sit for a few minutes, his eyes fixed on some comforting object, for instance a dark, smooth stone.

Even from his father and his father's brothers, who sometimes helped with the chores, he kept aloof. His father and uncles were not talkative men. Except for his father's comic poems, they never told jokes, though they liked hearing them; and because they had lived there all their lives and knew every soul in the county by name, nothing much surprised them or, if it did, roused them to mention it. Their wives might gossip, filling the big kitchen with their pealing laughter or righteous indignation, but the men for the most part merely smiled or compressed their lips and shook their heads. At the G.L.F.

feedstore, occasionally, eating an ice cream while they waited for their grist, they would speak of the weather or the Democrats; but in the barn, except for "Jackie, shift that milker, will you?" or "You can carry this up to the milk house now," they said nothing. They were all tall, square men with deeply cleft chins and creases on their foreheads and muscular jowls; all Presbyterians, sometimes deacons, sometimes elders; and they were all gentle-hearted, decent men who looked lost in thought, especially Jack's father, though on occasion they'd abruptly frown or mutter, or speak a few words to a cow, or a cat, or a swallow. It was natural that Jack, working with such men, should keep to himself, throwing down ensilage from the pitch-dark, sweet-ripe crater of the silo or hay bales from the mow, dumping oats in front of the cows' noses, or—taking the long-handled, blunt wooden scraper from the whitewashed wall—pushing manure into the gutters.

He felt more community with the cows than with his uncles or, when he was there, his father. Stretched out flat between the two rows of stanchions, waiting for the cows to be finished with their silage so he could drive them out to pasture, he would listen to their chewing in the dark, close barn, a sound as soothing, as infinitely restful, as waves along a shore, and would feel their surprisingly warm, scented breath, their bovine quiet, and for a while would find that his anxiety had left him. With the cows, the barn cats, the half-sleeping dog, he could forget and feel at home, feel that life was pleasant. He felt the same when walking up the long, fenced lane at the first light of sunrise—his shoes and pants legs sopping wet with dew, his ears full of birdcalls—going to bring in the herd from the upper pasture. Sometimes on the way he would step off the deep, crooked cow path to pick cherries or red raspberries, brighter than jewels in the morning light. They were sweeter then than at any other time, and as he approached, clouds of sparrows would explode into flight from the branches, whirring off to safety. The whole countryside was sweet, early in the morning—newly cultivated corn to his left; to his right, alfalfa and, beyond that, wheat. He felt at one with it all. It was what life ought to be, what he'd once believed it was.

But he could not make such feelings last. *No*, he thought bitterly on one such morning, throwing stones at the dull, indifferent cows, driving them down the lane. However he might hate himself and all his race, a cow was no better, or a field of wheat. Time and again he'd been driven half crazy, angry enough to kill, by the stupidity of cows when they'd pushed through a fence and—for all his shouting, for all the indignant barking of the dog—they could no longer locate the gap they themselves had made. And no better to be grain, smashed flat by the first rainy wind. So, fists clenched, he raged inside his mind, grinding his teeth to drive out thought, at war with the universe. He remembered his father, erect, eyes flashing, speaking Mark Antony's angry condemnation from the stage at the Grange. His father had seemed to him, that night, a creature set apart. His extended arm, pointing, was the terrible warning of a god. And now, from nowhere, the black memory of his brother's death rushed over him again, mindless and inexorable as a wind or wave, the huge cultipacker lifting—only an inch or so—as it climbed toward the shoulders, then sank on the cheek, flattening the skull—and he heard, more real than the morning, his sister's scream.

One day in August, a year and a half after the accident, they were combining oats—Jack and two neighbors and two of his cousins—when Phoebe came out, as she did every day, to bring lunch to those who worked in the field. Their father had been gone, this time, for nearly three weeks, and since he'd left at the height of the harvest season, no one was sure he would return, though as usual they kept silent about it. Jack sat alone in the shade of an elm, apart from the others. It was a habit they'd come to accept as they accepted, so far as he knew, his father's ways. Phoebe brought the basket from the shade where the others had settled to the shade here on Jack's side, farther from the bright, stubbled field.

"It's chicken," she said, and smiled, kneeling.

The basket was nearly as large as she was—Phoebe was seven—but she seemed to see nothing unreasonable in her having to lug it up the hill from the house. Her face was flushed, and drops of perspiration stood out along her hairline, but her smile was not only uncomplaining but positively cheerful. The trip to the field was an escape from housework, he understood; even so, her happiness offended him.

"Chicken," he said, and looked down glumly at his hard, tanned arms black with oat-dust. Phoebe smiled on, her mind far away, as it seemed to him, and like a child playing house she took a dishtowel from the basket, spread it on the grass, then set out wax-paper packages of chicken, rolls, celery, and salt, and finally a small plastic thermos, army green.

She looked up at him now. "I brought you a thermos all for yourself because you always sit alone."

He softened a little without meaning to. "Thanks," he said.

She looked down again, and for all his self-absorption he was touched, noticing that she bowed her head in the way a much older girl might do, troubled by thought, though her not quite clean, dimpled hands were a child's. He saw that there was something she wanted to say and, to forestall it, brushed flying ants from the top of the thermos, unscrewed the cap, and poured himself iced tea. When he drank, the tea was so cold it brought a momentary pain to his forehead and made him aware once more of the grating chaff under his collar, blackening all his exposed skin, gritty around his eyes—aware, too, of the breezeless, insect-filled heat beyond the shade of the elm. Behind him, just at the rim of his hearing, one of the neighbors laughed at some remark from the younger of his cousins. Jack drained the cup, brooding on his aching muscles. Even in the shade his body felt baked dry.

"Jack," his sister said, "did you want to say grace?"

"Not really," he said, and glanced at her.

He saw that she was looking at his face in alarm, her mouth slightly opened, eyes wide, growing wider, and though he didn't know why, his heart gave a jump. "I already said it," he mumbled. "Just not out loud."

"Oh," she said, then smiled.

When everyone had finished eating she put the empty papers, the jug, and the smaller thermos in the basket, grinned at them all and said goodbye—whatever had bothered her was forgotten as soon as that—and, leaning far over, balancing the lightened but still-awkward basket, started across the stubble for the house. As he cranked the tractor she turned around to look back at them and wave. He nodded and, as if embarrassed, touched his straw hat.

Not till he was doing the chores that night did he grasp what her look of alarm had meant. If he wouldn't say grace, then perhaps there was no heaven. Their father would never get well, and David was dead. He squatted, drained of all strength again, staring at the hoof of the cow he'd been stripping, preparing her for the milker, and thought of his absent father. He saw the motorcycle roaring down a twisting mountain road, the clatter of the engine ringing like harsh music against shale. If what he felt was hatred, it was a terrible, desperate envy, too; his father all alone, uncompromised, violent, cut off as if by centuries from the warmth, chatter, and smells of the kitchen, the dimness of stained glass where he, Jack, sat every Sunday between his mother and sister, looking toward the pulpit where in the old days his father had sometimes read the lesson, soft-voiced but aloof from the timid-eyed flock, Christ's sheep.

Something blocked the light coming in through the cowbarn window from the west, and he turned his head, glancing up.

"You all right there, Jackie?" his uncle Walt said, bent forward, near-sightedly peering across the gutter.

He nodded and quickly wiped his wrist across his cheeks. He moved his hands once more to the cow's warm teats.

A few nights later, when he went in from chores, the door between the kitchen and livingroom was closed, and the house was unnaturally quiet. He stood a moment listening, still holding the milk pail, absently fitting the heel of one boot into the bootjack and tugging until the boot slipped off. He pried off the other, then walked to the icebox in his stocking feet, opened the door, carried the pitcher to the table, and filled it from the pail. When he'd slid the pitcher into the icebox again and closed the door, he went without a sound, though not meaning to be stealthy, toward the livingroom. Now, beyond the closed door, he heard voices, his sister and mother, then one of his aunts. He pushed the door open and looked in, about to speak.

Though the room was dim, no light but the small one among the pictures on the piano, he saw his father at once, kneeling by the davenport with his face on his mother's lap. Phoebe was on the davenport beside their mother, hugging her and him, Phoebe's cheeks stained, like her mother's, with tears. Around them, as if reverently drawn back, Uncle Walt, Aunt Ruth, and their two children sat watching, leaning forward with shining eyes. His father's head, bald down the center, glowed, and he had his glasses off.

"Jackie," his aunt called sharply, "come in. It's all over. Your dad's come home."

He would have fled, but his knees had no strength in them and his chest was wild, churning as if with terror. He clung to the doorknob, grotesquely smiling—so he saw himself. His father raised his head. "Jackie," he said, and was unable to say more, all at once sobbing like a baby.

"Hi, Dad," he brought out, and somehow managed to go to him and get down on his knees beside him and put his arm around his back. He felt dizzy now, nauseated, and he was crying like his father. "I hate you," he whispered too softly for any of them to hear.

His father stayed. He worked long days, in control once more, though occasionally he smoked, pacing in his room nights, or rode off on his motorcycle for an hour or two, and seldom smiled. Nevertheless, in a month he was again reciting poetry for schools and churches and the Grange, and sometimes reading Scripture from the pulpit Sunday mornings. Jack, sitting rigid, hands over his face, was bitterly ashamed of those poems and recitations from the Bible. His father's eyes no longer flashed, he no longer had the style of an actor. Even his gestures were submissive, as pliant as the grass. Though tears ran down Jack Hawthorne's face—no one would deny that his father was still effective, reading carefully, lest his voice should break. "Tomorrow's Bridge" and "This Too Will Pass" —Jack scorned the poems' opinions, scorned the way his father spoke directly to each listener, as if each were some new woman, his father some mere suffering sheep among sheep, and scorned the way Phoebe and his mother looked on smiling, furtively weeping, heads lifted. Sometimes his father would recite a poem that Jack himself had written, in the days when he'd tried to write poetry, a comic limerick or some maudlin piece about a boy on a hill. Though it was meant as a compliment, Jack's heart would swell with rage; yet he kept silent, more private than before. At night he'd go out to the cavernous haymow or up into the orchard and practice his French horn. One of these days, he told himself, they'd wake up and find him gone.

He used the horn more and more now to escape their herding warmth. Those around him were conscious enough of what was happening—his parents and Phoebe, his uncles, aunts, and cousins, his mother's many friends. But there was nothing they could do. "That horn's his whole world," his mother often said, smiling but clasping her hands together. Soon he was playing third horn with the Batavia Civic Orchestra, though he refused to play in church or when company came. He began to ride the Bluebus to Rochester, Saturdays, to take lessons from Arcady Yegudkin, "the General," at the Eastman School of Music.

Yegudkin was seventy. He'd played principal horn in the orchestra of Czar Nikolai and at the time of the Revolution had escaped, with his wife, in a dramatic way. At the time of the purge of Kerenskyites, the Bolsheviks had loaded Yegudkin and his wife, along with hundreds more, onto railroad flatcars, reportedly to carry them to Siberia. In a desolate place, machine guns opened fire on the people on the flatcars, then soldiers pushed the bodies into a ravine, and the train moved on. The soldiers were not careful to see that everyone was dead. Perhaps they did not relish their work; in any case, they must have believed that, in a place so remote, a wounded survivor would have no chance against wolves and cold weather. The General and his wife were among the few who lived, he virtually unmarked, she horribly crippled. Local peasants nursed the few survivors back to health, and in time the Yegudkins escaped to Europe. There Yegudkin played horn with all the great orchestras and received such praise—so he claimed, spreading out his clippings—as no other master of French horn had received in all history. He would beam as he said it, his Tartar eyes flashing, and his smile was like a thrown-down gauntlet.

He was a barrel-shaped, solidly muscular man, hard as a boulder for all his age. His hair and moustache were as black as coal except for touches of silver, especially where it grew, with majestic indifference to ordinary taste, from his cavernous nostrils and large, dusty-looking ears. The sides of his moustache were carefully curled, in the fashion once favored by Russian dandies, and he was one of the last men in Rochester, New York, to wear spats. He wore formal black suits, a huge black overcoat, and a black fedora. His wife, who came with him and sat on the long maple bench outside his door, never reading or knitting or doing anything at all except that sometimes she would speak unintelligibly to a student—Yegudkin's wife, shriveled and twisted, watched him as if worshipfully, hanging on his words. She looked at least twice the old man's age. Her hair was snow white and she wore lumpy black shoes and long black shapeless dresses. The two of them would come, every Saturday morning, down the long marble hallway of the second floor of Killburn Hall, the General erect and imperious, like some sharp-eyed old Slavonic king, moving slowly, waiting for the old woman who crept beside him, gray claws on his coat sleeve, and seeing Jack Hawthorne seated on the bench, his books and French horn in its tattered black case on the floor beside him, the General would extend his left arm and boom, "Goot mworning!"

Jack, rising, would say, "Morning, sir."

"You have met my wife?" the old man would say then, bowing and taking the cigar from his mouth. He asked it each Saturday.

"Yes, sir. How do you do?"

The old man was too deaf to play in orchestras anymore. "What's the difference?" he said. "Every symphony in America, they got Yegudkins. I have teach them all. Who teach you this? *The General!*" He would smile, chin lifted, triumphant, and salute the ceiling.

He would sit in the chair beside Jack's and would sing, with violent gestures and a great upward leap of the belly to knock out the high B's and C's—*Tee! Tee!*—as Jack read through Kopprasch, Gallay, and Kling, and when it was time to give Jack's lip a rest, the General would speak earnestly, with the same energy he put into his singing, of the United States and his beloved Russia that he would nevermore see. The world was at that time filled with Russophobes. Yegudkin, whenever he read a paper, would be so enraged he could barely contain himself. "In all my age," he often said, furiously gesturing with his black cigar, "if the Russians would come to this country of America, I would take up a rifle and shot at them—*boof!* But the newspapers telling you lies, all lies! You think them dumb fools, these Russians? You think they are big, fat bush-overs?" He spoke of mile-long parades of weaponry, spoke of Russian cunning, spoke with great scorn, a sudden booming laugh, of Napoleon. Jack agreed with a nod to whatever the General said. Nevertheless, the old man roared on, taking great pleasure in his rage, it seemed, sometimes talking like a rabid communist, sometimes like a fascist, sometimes like a citizen helplessly caught between mindless, grinding forces, vast, idiot herds. The truth was, he hated both Russians and Americans about equally, cared only for music, his students and, possibly, his wife. In his pockets, in scorn of the opinions of fools, he carried condoms, dirty pictures, and grimy, wadded-up dollar bills.

One day a new horn he'd ordered from Germany, an Alexander, arrived at his office—a horn he'd gotten for a graduate student. The old man unwrapped and assembled it, the graduate student looking on—a shy young man, blond, in a limp gray sweater—and the glint in the General's eye was like madness or at any rate lust, perhaps gluttony. When the horn was ready he went to the desk where he kept his clippings, his tools for the cleaning and repair of French horns, his cigars, photographs, and medals from the Czar, and pulled open a wide, shallow drawer. It contained perhaps a hundred mouthpieces, of all sizes and materials, from raw brass to lucite, silver, and gold, from the shallowest possible cup to the deepest. He selected one, fitted it into the horn, pressed the rim of the bell into the right side of his large belly—the horn seemed now as much a part of him as his arm or leg—clicked the shining keys to get the feel of them, then played. In that large, cork-lined room, it was as if, suddenly, a creature from some other universe had appeared, some realm where feelings become birds and dark sky, and spirit is more solid than stone. The sound was not so much loud as large, too large for a hundred French horns, it seemed. He began to play now not single notes but, to Jack's astonishment, chords—two notes at a time, then three. He began to play runs. As if charged with life independent of the man, the horn sound fluttered and flew crazily, like an enormous trapped hawk hunting frantically for escape. It flew to the bottom of the lower register, the foundation concert F, and crashed below it, and on down and down, as if the horn in Yegudkin's hands had no bottom, then suddenly changed its mind and flew upward in a split-second run to the horn's top E, dropped back to the middle and then ran once more, more fiercely at the E, and this time burst through it and fluttered, manic, in the trumpet range, then lightly dropped back into its own home range and, abruptly, in the middle of a note, stopped. The room still rang, shimmered like a vision.

"Good horn," said Yegudkin, and held the horn toward the graduate student, who sat, hands clamped on his knees, as if in a daze.

Jack Hawthorne stared at the instrument suspended in space and at his teacher's hairy hands. Before stopping to think, he said, "You think I'll ever play like that?"

Yegudkin laughed loudly, his black eyes widening, and it seemed that he grew larger, beatific and demonic at once, like the music; overwhelming. "Play like *me?*" he exclaimed.

Jack blinked, startled by the bluntness of the thing, the terrible lack of malice, and the truth of it. His face tingled and his legs went weak, as if the life were rushing out of them. He longed to be away from there, far away, safe. Perhaps Yegudkin sensed it. He turned gruff, sending away the graduate student, then finishing up the lesson. He said nothing, today, of the stupidity of mankind. When the lesson was over he saw Jack to the door and bid him goodbye with a brief half-smile that was perhaps not for Jack at all but for the creature on the bench. "Next Saturday?" he said, as if there might be some doubt.

Jack nodded, blushing.

At the door opening on the street he began to breathe more easily, though he was weeping. He set down the horn case to brush away his tears. The sidewalk was crowded—dazed-looking Saturday-morning shoppers herding along irritably, meekly, through painfully bright light. Again he brushed tears away. He'd been late for his bus. Then the crowd opened for him and, with the horn cradled under his right arm, his music under his left, he plunged in, starting home.

STILLNESS

It would be a strange thing, Joan Orrick often thought, to have second sight, as her grandmother Frazier was supposed to have had. It occurred to her, for instance, one day when she was forty, when Martin stopped the car to wait for a light at the corner of Olive Street and Grand, in St. Louis. They were just passing through. Martin had delivered a paper at Urbana, and now they were heading for Norman, Oklahoma, where he was to serve on the jury for something called the Newstadt–Books Abroad Prize. "What is it?" she'd asked when first the invitation to Oklahoma had come. "Actually," he'd said, and had put on his pompous look, then changed his mind, "God knows." "Maybe we should drive through St. Louis," she'd said. He'd agreed at once, generous and expansive as he always was when preparing a lecture he thought impressive. She'd been less impressed than she'd pretended, but that was in the past now. And when they'd left Highway 70 and nosed past the arch into the city, she wasn't much impressed by St. Louis either. Beyond the stadium, the scrubbed, unconvincing show of government buildings, the husk of the grand old railroad station where she'd met him all those birthdays and Christmases—the years before he'd gotten his motorcycle—everything was gray, windblown, burnt out. Riding down haunted streets, brooding on the thought of second sight, she was sorry she'd come.

What would she have thought, though—sometime in the late 1940s, standing on this corner, on her way to her part-time accompanist's job at the Duggers School of the Dance—if she'd suddenly had a vision of what downtown St. Louis would be like just twenty-five years later? What would she have thought, what would she have felt, standing on that crowded, noisy corner, if the crowd had suddenly thinned to just three or four hurrying figures and the buildings had gone solemn, like prison or mausoleum walls?

She imagined the vision coming as pure image, like a photograph or drab documentary film, with no hint of explanation—saw herself, in her 1940s schoolgirl's clothes, pleated skirt and short-sleeved sweater, dark green coat and light green head-scarf, bobbysox and loafers, her hair in a permanent, shiny and curly and a trifle stiff, books in her arm—since she came in directly from school on the bus, or on a chain of buses that shuttled her from Ferguson to Normandy to Wellston to downtown. There had been—was it on this corner?—a wonderful ice-cream place, the Park Plaza, where for a dollar you could get a parfait two feet high, and all around this section there were magnificent theaters, as colorful as circuses, with high, bold marquees on which yellow, red, blue, purple, green, and white lights (lightbulbs, she remembered, and even then the few that had burned out weren't replaced) went racing around tall, urgent titles—*Rope*, *The Purple Heart*, *The Return of Frank James*—and inside, the theaters were like palaces: great gilded lions; red-velvet-covered three-inch-thick ropes on golden posts; majestic wide stairways that made everyone an instant king or queen; ushers in uniforms from the days of Empire (God knew which empire); and in the great domed theater itself a hush that was patently religious, the boom of voices from the people on the screen coming from all sides and from within, or so it seemed, oracular.

All the great stores had been downtown then, Famous-Barr, for instance, glittering, high-ceilinged, richly ceremonious inside its towering gold-framed revolving doors—the aisles choked with shoppers, most of them white, the counters and high walls revealing wonders, coats and sombre-toned stately dresses with the sleeves pinned straight out, extended for flight far overhead like hovering angels, and—everywhere—draped artificial-pearl necklaces or ruby-red or pool-ball-green or -blue or -yellow costume baubles, bracelets the color of copper in flame, and everywhere the scent of perfumes and talcums, newly printed books, the leather of new shoes, a smell as exciting and at the same time cloying as a vault of roses in one of the big downtown flowershops, or the thick, sweet incense in a Catholic church. Suppose in the twinkling of an eye, Joan thought, that whole world had vanished, and the girl on the corner, herself at fifteen, looked, stunned and afraid, at a city gone dark and empty: suppose a silence had fallen, as if all the gay sounds of the world had been abruptly turned off, like the music and static on a radio, and there came the same instant a visual stillness, as if a heart had stopped—no motion but three or four hurrying Negroes, strangely dressed, dangerous, with hair grown long and alarmingly puffed up, nothing else stirring but two pigeons overhead and a newspaper blowing along the pavement. "I'm in the future!" the imaginary Joan would finally have realized, "and there's been some terrible war, or a plague, and everything's been ruined."

Who'd await the future if she could see it in advance? No use to tell the girl on the corner, "We're happy, Joan. Don't be afraid! There are beautiful places, though this one may be gone." She'd have backed away, frightened and betrayed—yes, terrified, of course. What else could she be, addressed by a strange, wild woman in dark glasses such as Negroes wore then in the most dangerous parts of East St. Louis, a fur coat that looked as if the lynx had died of terror, adrenaline exploding, every hair on end—a woman whose beauty was like fine cutlery, hair falling plain as an Indian's, except red, as brightly burnished and fiery as her own—leaning from the window of a dark blue Mercedes Benz driven by—how weird!—a sorrowful, baggy-eyed man with silver hair that swept down like angelhair to his heavy, hunched shoulders—a monster who was, she had a feeling, suddenly, someone she was meant to recognize.

The girl would have stepped back in fear and anger, raising her hand to the braces on her teeth, and the real Joan would have called to her, shouting past the dead years in pity and anguish, "Child, child, don't be silly! We're as harmless as you are, we've betrayed nobody, nothing! *Look* at us!" Now the child did look, and recognition came: the rich, wildly eccentric lady (who had beautiful teeth, Joan thought, and smiled, feeling a surge of affection for the big-nosed innocent on the corner), the lady in the fur, with emeralds and a ruby and a diamond on her fingers, was herself—her own "child," Wordsworth would say—and the driver was Buddy Orrick, grown sadder and crazier, but still alive, and married to her: so they'd made it, they'd survived! She came a step nearer, her face eager, full of questions (*We could drive her to Duggers*, the real Joan thought; *it's only a few blocks*) and her small hand came cautiously toward the real Joan's hand on the Mercedes' wing-window, both hands equally pale and solid, the child's and the woman's, until suddenly the child's hand was gone and Joan Orrick was gazing at a cracked sidewalk, a piece of dirty cardboard: Fragile.

Martin glanced over and saw her tears. "Hurting?" he asked.

Yes, she was hurting, as she nearly always hurt these days, sometimes such pain that she passed out for a moment—hurting even when the drugs were at work, as now, causing visions, or almost-visions—but she said, "No," and gave him a reassuring smile, "just thinking."

He reached over, touched her hand. The light changed, and the car glided forward without a sound.

She said, "The Duggers School of the Dance was just up ahead. Remember?"

"Which building?" He ducked down over the steering wheel to look.

She pointed as the car came abreast of it. It had been gutted by fire, like most of the buildings in this neighborhood. He scanned the boarded-up, blackened storefronts. She could see he wasn't sure which one she meant.

Jacqui Duggers was tiny, the classic teacher of ballet but in perfect miniature, hair so tightly drawn back you might have thought from a distance that it was paint, as on a Japanese doll. She spoke with the accent all ballet teachers use, even those raised in Milwaukee or St. Louis, wiped her forehead with the back of her wrist like an actress, called Joan "dahling" with perfect seriousness and unfeigned affection, though one failed to notice the affection at first, since she was always hurried, always slightly tense, as if in half an hour she must catch a plane for Munich or Paris. She was—or so it seemed to Joan —a superb dancer, though Joan never saw her dance more than a few steps. Her old photographs seemed to confirm the impression: the Jacqui Duggers in the pictures had that authority one sees at a glance in professionals, and they proved she had danced with good companies of the so-called second rank in both the United States and Canada. "Ah *wone*," she would say, and Joan's hands would move automatically on the keys of the piano.

Her husband, Pete Duggers, taught tap-dance in the mirror-walled studio below. He was nearly as small as she was, but thicker, almost stout, in fact, and he looked and moved like some Disney cartoon of a tap-dance teacher. He had a red face and wonderfully merry blue eyes, wore vests and old-fashioned arm-elastics. If he ever touched the floor when he walked (and he did), Joan had been prepared to believe that he did so by whim. Jacqui's movements at the barre had a look not of lightness, cancellation of gravity, but of eloquent, powerful control, as if her muscles were steel and could no more speed up or slow down against her will than the hands of a clock could escape the inclinations of its mainspring. Rising on her toes in the middle of the room—a brief jerk and click as the heel and ankle locked, a brief trembling like a spasm, then the firmness of an iron wedge—she gave the impression that touching her calf or thigh would be like touching a wall. Pete's dancing feet moved, on the other hand, as if swinging by themselves, as if his body were suspended like a puppet's from invisible wires. His taps were light and quick, as if he never put his weight down with either foot, and they rattled out around him as gaily and casually—and as unbelievably fast— as the fingers of his Negro piano player, a tall, flat-haired boy who sat sprawling in his chair with his head laid far over so that he seemed to be always, except for his forearms and fingers, fast asleep. The speed and lightness with which Pete Duggers danced were amazing to behold, but what was truly miraculous, so that it made you catch your breath, was the way he could stop, completely relaxed, leaning his elbow on empty air and grinning as if he'd been standing there for hours, all that movement and sound you'd been hearing pure phantom and illusion. That was unfailingly the climax when he danced: a slow build, with elegant shuffles and turns, then more speed, and more, and more and still more until it seemed that the room spun drunkenly, crazily, all leading—direct as the path of an arrow—to nothing, or everything, a sudden stillness like an escape from reality, a sudden floating, whether terrible or wonderful she could never tell: an abrupt hush as when a large crowd looks up, all at the same moment, and sees an eagle in the sky, almost motionless, or then again, perhaps, the frightening silence one read about in novels when a buzz-bomb shut off over London. He stood perfectly still, the piano was still, his young students gaped, and then abruptly reality came back as the piano tinkled lightly and he listlessly danced and, as he did so, leaned toward his students and winked. "You see? Stillness! That's the magic!"

Olive Street was already going down at that time, so the storefront was shoddy, solo dancer and dance-class pictures on the windows, big, vulgar stars, the glass around the pictures crudely painted dark blue, as if the Duggers School of the Dance were some miserable third-rate establishment not worth breaking into or stealing from, though the door was not locked. But that was a trick—the dancing Duggers had trunkfuls of tricks: artists to the marrow of their chipped and splintered bones. The scuffed, unpainted door in front opened into a scuffed, unpainted entryway with a door to the left and a knotty, crooked stairway leading upward. On the door to the left, a sign said "TAP DANCE STUDIO," and above the worn railing at the side of the stairs, a sign, cocked parallel to the railing, said "SCHOOL OF THE BALLET ☞." When you opened the door to the tap-dance studio for the first time, you did a mighty double-take: there were glittering mirrors with round-arched tops and etched designs of the sort Joan would occasionally discover years later in the oldest London pubs, and above the mirrors there were walls of red and gold and a magnificent stamped-tin ceiling. In fact she'd never completely gotten over her surprise at the elegance inside, though she'd worked there four years, into her college days. It was a large building, at one time a theater. The tap-dance studio—and the ballet studio directly above it—took up the first thirty feet; then there was a railing, also red and gold, from which one looked out at the long, wide ballroom floor, at the front an enormous stage boxed off by ratty, stiff wine-colored velvet curtains, along the side walls candelabra between high, painted panels—dancing graces, Zeus in majesty, nymphs and satyrs, peacocks and fat reclining nudes done in highly unsuccessful imitation of the late style of Rubens.

She'd walked there once with Martin—in those days

"Buddy"—when he'd motorcycled in from his college in Indiana and had offered to drive her to work in her father's De Soto. He'd driven fast, as usual, his eyes rolling up to the rearview mirror, on the look-out for police cars, and had gotten her to work much too early.

"Care to have an interesting experience?" she'd said.

Their footsteps echoed. The ballroom was half dark. They could just make out the carved figures on the ceiling, two storeys up, circling around the empty spaces from which once had hung huge chandeliers.

"It's like a church," he said. He had a crewcut. Leather jacket. He hung his cigarette off his lip like Marlon Brando. Already he'd written two novels—unpublishable; terrible, in fact, though of course she hadn't said so. She was convinced, in spite of them, that he'd someday be famous, someday when he'd given up James Joyce.

She'd squeezed his hand and they'd stopped and, after a moment, kissed, then walked on, up to the front of the ballroom and up onto the stage, where the Duggers students gave their dance recitals. They looked up at the shuttered lights, ropes, catwalks—it was darker here, spooky, as if the stage machinery belonged not only to a different time but to a different planet. Again they paused to kiss, and he put his arms around her and after a minute she moved his hand to the front of her sweater, then under the sweater to her breast. With his usual difficulty, for all his practice, he unsnapped her bra. She felt her nipples rising, and he pressed closer to her. With a grandiose sweep of his free arm in the direction of the dim, ghost-filled hall, he whispered, "Lady, how would you like to be fucked, right here in front of all these people?"

"Hmm," she said. After a moment, still with his hand on her breast, her hand keeping it there, she led him toward the further wing and the small door opening on a room she'd discovered weeks earlier, half filled with crates, electric wire, old tools, cobwebs, the rotting frames of old sets. Here and there stood old pieces of furniture—chairs, tables, couches—protected from the dust by tarpaulins. "Maybe we need a rehearsal," she said. They passed under a high window through which a single crack of light came and she glanced at her watch. Fifteen minutes. She stood looking around, both his hands on her breasts, until he finally noticed the couch and went over and pulled away the tarpaulin. As he came into her, huge and overeager, as always —but so was she, so was she—she said, "Isn't this an interesting experience?"

She glanced at Martin—Buddy middle-aged. He stared past the steering wheel, professional, absentminded. They'd slipped from his thoughts already, those years, the Duggers. His hands on the wheel were soft, almost fat, though still strong. She looked at his face. "What are you thinking?" she said.

Martin flicked his eyes open, half apologetic. "Nothing," he said. "Something Athene tells Odysseus. Nothing." He looked suddenly embarrassed.

She glanced out the window again, then reached for her purse, opening it, fumbling for a pill.

"Hurting again?"

Her mouth tightened in annoyance at that "again." "Just tired," she said.

"We should have taken a plane," he said, and ducked to look up past the buildings.

The sky was gray, luminous and still, like Lake Erie from one of those hushed, abandoned beaches. She thought of Jacqui Duggers.

"There's still a little coffee in the thermos," Martin said.

"Coffee?"

"To help swallow the pill."

"Oh. No, it's done." His helplessness cheered her. "Odysseus," she thought. Homer had been the subject of his lecture at Urbana. She smiled a little sadly. So he was wishing, as usual, that he might talk about himself. Not that he would do it; he had far too much taste. And she, for her part . . . She shook her head and smiled again.

The whole left side of the building, as you entered from the street, was the Duggers' apartment. It was the most beautiful apartment she'd ever seen, though not as original or even as spectacularly tasteful as she'd imagined at the time. She would see many like it in San Francisco, and far more elegant examples of white-on-white in London and Paris. Everything was white, the walls, the furniture, the chains holding up the chandeliers, the wooden shutters on the windows. Against all that white, the things they'd collected stood out in bold relief: paintings, presumably by friends, all very curious and impressive, at least to Joan—smudges, bright splashes of color, one canvas all white with little scratches of gray and bright blue; sculptures—a beautiful abstraction in dark wood, a ballet dancer made out of pieces of old wire, museum reproductions, a mobile of wood and stainless steel; books and records, shelves upon shelves of them. Their record-player was the largest she'd ever seen and had a speaker that stood separate from the rest. Once when Jacqui invited her in, to write Joan her check for her week's work, Jacqui, leading the way to the kitchen, stopped suddenly, turned a ballerina's step, and said, "Joanie, I must show you my shoes, no?" "I'd like to see them," Joan said. Jacqui swept over to the side of the room, her small hand gracefully flying ahead of her, and pushed open a white sliding door. Joan stared. On tilted shelves that filled half the room's wall, Jacqui had three hundred pairs of tiny shoes. She had all colors—gold and silver, yellow, red, green, some with long ties as bright as new ribbons, some with little bows, some black and plain as the inside of a pocket. "Where'd you *get* all these?" Joan said. Jacqui laughed. "Mostly Paris," she said. She gave Joan a quick, appraising look, then laughed again. "Dahling, Paris you are going to love. There is a store, a department store, Au Printemps. When you go there, blow a kiss

for Jacqui!" She rolled her eyes heavenward. "Ah, ze French!"

Years later, the first time Joan shopped at Au Printemps, she would remember that, and would do as she'd been told. And she would remember Jacqui too a few years later when, at Lambert Field in St. Louis, deplaning with her family from a European trip, she was approached by a news crew of very cool, very smart blacks from KSDF-TV, carrying camera and wind-baffled shotgun mike, who asked if she had any suggestions for improvement of the airport's services. "Way-el," she said thoughtfully, smiling prettily, batting her lashes and speaking in her sweetest Possum Hollow drawl. (Martin and the children had fled into the crowd.) She tapped her mouth with a bejewelled finger and gazed away down the baggage area, then said pertly, as if it were something she'd been thinking for a long, long time and rather hated to bring up, "Ah thank it would be nice if awl these people spoke French." Her performance was included in that night's local news. Her parents missed it, as was just as well. Relatives telephoned to report with pleasure that Joanie had been on television. No one mentioned that anything she'd said was peculiar.

"I wonder if I'll ever get to Paris," she'd said that afternoon in Jacqui's apartment.

Jacqui had laughed like a young girl, though she was then over forty. "Keep playing the piano and don't theenk twice," Jacqui said. "If you don't go to Paris, then Paris will have to come to you."

Where would they have gone, Joan wondered now, when the neighborhood had grown too dangerous to live in? Were they still alive? It came to her suddenly, for no apparent reason, that Pete Duggers had looked like the hero of her favorite childhood book, Mr. Mixiedough, in the story of the whole world's slipping into darkness. It was a book she'd wanted for Evan and Mary, but there seemed to be no copies left anywhere; not even the book-search people from whom Martin got his rare old books could find a trace of it. Had it been the same, perhaps, with Pete and Jacqui Duggers—swallowed into blackness? She'd asked about him once at the Abbey, on Thirteenth Street in New York, when she'd gone—three times—to a show called *The Hoofers,* which had brought back all the great soft-shoe and tap men. On the sidewalk in front of the theater afterward, while she was waiting for Martin to come and pick her up, she'd talked with Bojangles Robinson and Sandman Sims—they'd shown her some steps and had laughed and clapped their hands, dancing one on each side of her—and she'd asked if either of them had ever heard of Pete Duggers.

The Sandman rolled up his eyes and lifted off his hat as if to look inside it. "Duggers," he'd said, searching through his memory.

"You say the man worked out of San Looie?" Bojangles said.

"I played piano for his wife," Joan said. "She taught ballet."

"Duggers," said the Sandman. "That surely does sound familiar."

"White man married to a *bal*let teacher," Bojangles said, and ran his hand across his mouth. "Boy, that surely rings a bell, some way."

"Duggers," said the Sandman, squinting at the lighted sky. "Duggers."

"He used to go faster and faster and then suddenly stand still," she said. "He was a wonderful dancer."

"Duggers," Bojangles echoed, thoughtful, staring at his shoes. "I know the man sure as I'm standing here. I got him right on the tip of my mind."

At the motel that night, sixty miles past St. Louis—it was a new Ramada Inn, as new as the concrete and dark-earth slash through what had lately been farmland—Joan sat up after Martin was asleep, unable to sleep herself, waiting for the Demerol to start working. On the mirror-smooth walnut formica desk lay Martin's paper, "Homeric Justice and the Artful Lie." Though he'd delivered it already, it was a maze of revisions. He'd been "working it over a bit," as he said, before he'd at last given up in despair, as usual, kissed her on the cheek, and gone to bed. Eventually, no doubt, he'd include it in some book, or make it the plan of some story or novel. He was forever revising, like her stern-jawed, icy-eyed grandmother's God—or like God up to a point. Joan Orrick thought for an instant—then efficiently blocked the thought—of the doctor in New York who had spoken to them, incredibly, of psychiatric help and "the power of prayer." She slid Martin's paper toward her with two fingers, glancing at the beginning. "In Attic Greek," he'd written—and then came something in, presumably, Greek.

She looked for perhaps half a minute at the writing, tortuous, cranky, as familiar as her own but more moving to her: it contained all their years—they'd been married at nineteen, had been married for more than half their lives—and she found herself thinking (she was not aware of why) of her grandmother Frazier's sternly Southern Baptist attic: old *Christian Herald*s full of pictures of angels, stacked tight under cobwebbed rafters; small oak-leaved picture frames as moldy as old bread; a squat deal dresser with broken glass handles; tied-up bundles of music as brown-spackled and brittle as her grandmother's hands; and on the attic's far side, trunks of clothes—dusty black and what she thought of as Confederate gray. The old woman's predictions had been terrible and sure, or so legend had it. Her brother, Joan Orrick's great-uncle Frank, would stand on the porch of his cabin by the river when a tornado came roaring like a thousand trains, and would fire at the wind with a shotgun.

The cabin was long gone, like her grandmother's house, like her grandmother, like Martin's beloved Homer. She touched the pulse in her throat with two fingers and looked at her watch. Normal, and yet she felt drained, weary. Not entirely an effect of the wine they'd had at dinner, though also it was not yet the drug. She slid away the paper, rose quietly, and moved past the wide, still bed where her husband lay sleeping, his broad, mole-specked back and shoulders uncovered, motionless as marble except for his breathing, exactly as he'd always slept, winter and summer. She was slightly surprised for an instant by his lighted gray hair. Outside, the parking lot was dusty with the still, cold light of lamps half hidden among maples the bulldozers had left. She looked hastily back into the clean, noncommittal room.

When she'd crawled into bed with him, carefully not waking him, she lay for a time with her eyes open, eyes that might have seemed to a stranger, she knew, as cold and remote as her grandmother's. As she drifted toward sleep it crossed her mind—her lips and ringless right hand on Martin's arm—that sooner or later everyone, of course, knows the future.

THE MUSIC LOVER

Some years ago there lived in our city a man named Professor Alfred Klingman, who was a music lover. He was a professor of Germanic philology or something of the sort—or had been before his retirement—but he never spoke with anyone about his academic specialty, nor did anyone ever speak with him about anything but music or, occasionally, the weather. He'd lost his wife many years before this story begins and had lived alone in his dingy downtown apartment ever since, without pets, without plants, without even a clock to attend to. Except in the evenings, when he attended concerts, he never went out but sat all day listening to orchestral music on the radio, or, on Saturday afternoons, the opera. His solitary existence made him—as no doubt he'd have admitted himself, since he was by no means a fool—peculiar. One might have thought, to look at him, that he lived alone for fear of giving other creatures offense. Even in the presence of lapdogs, you might have thought, Professor Klingman would feel inferior. He walked with his shoulders drawn in and his raw, red face stuck out, anxiously smiling, timidly bowing to everyone he passed, even cats and, occasionally, lampposts.

This story makes use of parts of Thomas Mann's "Disillusionment," all slightly altered.

But every man who survives in this world has at least one area in which he escapes his perhaps otherwise miserable condition, and for Professor Klingman this area was music, his wife having been a piano teacher. Whenever there was a concert—which was nearly every night except in summertime, since our city had a famous school of music, a professional symphony, an amateur philharmonic orchestra, and innumerable choirs—Professor Klingman would dress himself nervously and meticulously in his old brown suit, his rather yellow white shirt, and black bow tie, and would pull on his long brown overcoat, fit his brown hat on his head, take up his cane, and, after inspecting himself for a moment in his mirror, exactly as an orchestra conductor might have done, or a featured soloist, he would hurry, his near-sighted, smiling face thrown forward, looking terrified and slightly insane, to the civic auditorium. As soon as he entered the hall he would look in panic at the clock above the ticket window and would check it against his gold pocketwatch. Though he was invariably some twenty minutes early, his look of furious anxiety would remain until he'd checked his coat and hat, climbed the wide red-carpeted stairs (helping himself with his crooked brown cane), and made his way to his accustomed seat in the front row of the balcony, right-hand side, the area his wife had found acoustically most pleasing. Then he would relax to a certain extent, sitting motionless except for a minuscule tremble, his pale eyes glittering and darting as the theater filled. He had bushy red eyebrows and a large, lumpy nose. His ears were extraordinarily large and as pink as flowers. In his nostrils and ears he had tufts of red hair (and in one ear a large gray hearing aid), and there was yellowish fuzz on the backs of his fingers. The hair on the top of his head was white.

Sometimes before the orchestra came on he would push his program toward the person beside him and whisper timidly, pointing to some item, "Excuse me, what's this? What's this piece? Do you know it?" The question was abrupt, one might even say frantic, since Professor Klingman had lost, in the years since his good wife's death, the technique of polite conversation. It was she, of course, who had done all their talking. One might not unnaturally have gotten the idea that, despite his smile, the professor fiercely disapproved of the item which was about to be performed (perhaps he imagined it immoral, or fascistic) and was merely checking to make sure the piece was what he thought it was before steeling himself and rising to cry out, in his piping voice, challenging and halting the performance. If, as sometimes happened, the person beside him was familiar with the piece and could hum a few bars, Professor Klingman would brighten, crying "Yes, yes! Thank you!" in a voice embarrassingly cracked by emotion. Strangers could not know that in former years, attending concerts with Mrs. Klingman, the professor had always been advised by his wife what tunes he was about to be favored with. No charitable person, observing his curious concert behavior, could doubt that Alfred Klingman's feelings were deep and sincere, but he was, no question about it, something of a nuisance, even for an elderly person. Also people noticed that he was singularly uninformed about music, for a concert devotee. He could not identify by number and key any symphony but Beethoven's Fifth, and even in that case he could never recall the key.

On the other hand, no one could be more responsive to the anguished wellings and sweet palpitations of the music itself. When Mahler was played, or even the coolest, most objective of Bruckner, tears would run streaming down Professor Klingman's nose, and sometimes he would sob audibly, so that everyone around him was made uncomfortable. At musical jokes he would sometimes guffaw, though how a man so ignorant could know that the musical jokes were jokes was hard to see. And even when the music was neither tragic nor comic, merely sang its way along, in a manner of speaking—one of Mozart's less dramatic concertos, for instance—Professor

Klingman could manage to disgruntle his neighbors. Sometimes he tapped his feet, sometimes he nodded (slightly out of time), and sometimes, especially to Kabalevsky or Liszt, he would thump his rolled-up program. People touched him on the shoulder, whispered politely but sternly in his ear. His contrition, at such times, was touching to see, but it lasted for only a few minutes. Charitable people ignored him and said, when the subject of his concert behavior came up, "Well, music is all the poor man has, you know," or, "Well, he feels things deeply, you know; too bad *more* people don't." All our concert-hall ushers knew him, and the leader of the music school's string quartet would always look up and smile if he was present. Not that he was loved universally, of course. Sometimes children who were not well brought up—and sometimes even college students—mimicked him cruelly, thumping their programs, bobbing their heads, and pretending to swallow back agonized sobs. To such mockery, of course, Professor Klingman was oblivious. From the first note to the last, even if the concert was abysmal, Professor Klingman was in heaven.

One evening in late autumn, Professor Klingman attended a School of Music concert which was advertised as offering "three contemporary pieces." He would never have attended had he any idea what he was in for. Professor Klingman, it should be mentioned, was by no means a man of conservative taste. He had disgraced himself by literally whooping his emotion at Janáček's Slavonic mass and had once sat, enraptured and stunned, unable to applaud, at a performance of Bartók's Concerto for Percussion, which he later remembered as Stravinsky's greatest masterpiece. But this particular departure from musical tradition—this so-called "three contemporary pieces"—was a new and terrible experience for him. It opened with a cello concerto in which the soloist used not a bow but a saw, a fact Professor Klingman missed at first, because of his eyesight. By the end of the piece, which was distressing enough in any case, the cello had been sawed in two. The second piece featured two radios tuned to different stations and a violinist expressing his musical impressions of a life-sized photograph of an ape.

Timid as Professor Klingman was in life's more ordinary situations, he reacted to this music with the unselfconscious abandon that had made him mildly notorious among concert-goers in our city. He wrung his fingers, groaned, covered his eyes, and on one occasion cried out loudly, "Oh my God! My God!" On each side of him and behind him, embarrassed fellow sufferers labored to shush him—to no avail. He caught the pale hand of the lady beside him (Mrs. Phillips, the wife of Reverend Irving Phillips, who plays second clarinet in our philharmonic orchestra) and whispered, violently shaking, "Insane!"

"Be still!" she whispered, cold as ice, though it was clear she was not in complete disagreement. She was tall and stately, with a pale blue face, a face almost exactly the color of her pearls. She was breathing like a person who is about to experience a heart attack—whether from anger at the musical outrage or from anger at the mad old man beside her, no one could say.

Mrs. Phillips' words had no effect on the professor, but a moment later he became aware, as one could see by the anxious craning of his neck and the darting of his eyes in their thick-lensed glasses, that he was surrounded by mimics, all wringing their fingers, twisting their faces into masks of agony, and moaning and groaning, driving their timider friends into shuddering lunes of demonic giggling. Professor Klingman clung to Mrs. Phillips' hand, feeling sick at heart with shame and anger, and squeezed his eyes shut, waiting in silence for the intermission. He could not notice, in his misery—or perhaps did not notice because of his eyesight—that a man in the box to the left of the stage was watching all he did with a queer fascination, watching as a scientist might study an insect, never shifting his gaze for an instant toward the stage.

At last (incredibly, from Alfred Klingman's point of view) the intermission did arrive, the houselights came up, and he was able to scramble, or, rather, stagger, to the aisle and up it, toward the exit sign, pushing through the crowd in a way quite unlike him, apologizing right and left to faces he probably could not see, since he was weeping. He somehow reached the cloakroom and retrieved his hat and coat, then pushed toward the street door. There, however, he found he could go no further because of the violent pounding of his heart. He leaned on the wall, wide-eyed, pink-nosed, clutching his chest as if aware that if he did not calm himself, this excruciating night might be his last.

"Monstrous!" he whispered over and over, probably more loudly than he knew. "Monstrous! Blasphemous!"

Then, as men will do in such desperate situations, Professor Klingman tried to reason with himself. "Yet what harm, after all?" he said loudly, his red-lidded eyes squeezed tight shut. "No doubt an inexpensive, even worthless cello. A harmless little joke. What harm in that?" But his heart, it seems, was thudding more violently now than ever, and, judging from his face, some sorrow vast and plangent as the sea was threatening to drown him. He opened his eyes as would a drunken man to steady himself by the solid lines of furniture and vistas of neatly patterned carpet.

A small, anxious crowd had gathered around him, largely composed of people he knew, fellow regulars, though apparently he couldn't focus any faces. And now one of the crowd moved forward, extending his hands toward him.

"You've had a shock, my good man," the stranger said kindly, taking hold of the professor's trembling hands. "Come with me, I beg you. Let me buy you a drink."

Professor Klingman accepted—being, of course, in no position to resist, though not a drinking man. Little did he know what man he was putting his trust in. Slowly—to the crowd's considerable relief—the two men went through the foyer, the

professor leaning on the younger man's arm. They entered the lounge, where the younger man guided Alfred Klingman to a table by the window looking out on a river and park. The night was tranquil, dark except for an occasional streetlamp. On the grounds of the park, which were safer in those days, one could see, here and there, pairs of lovers walking, and over by the golfcourse a woman with a dog. The younger man brought drinks of some kind, then took a chair opposite Alfred Klingman's and sat watching him fixedly, much as he had watched from the box to the left of the stage.

Gradually the professor regained his composure.

"The music disturbed you deeply, I see," the stranger said.

"I'm afraid so," Professor Klingman confessed. "I'm afraid I behaved like a dreadful old fool." He made an effort to smile, but blushed instead, a slow blush, remarkable on a man so old, that rose to his hatbrim. "A harmless little joke, harmless little trick on the audience—" He broke off abruptly. His eyes filled with tears which he made no effort to explain, if, indeed, he knew their explanation. He removed his thick-lensed glasses and wiped them on his handkerchief.

The younger man continued to study him. He was a thin, sallow person of thirty-five or forty, dressed in a black suit with a black waistcoat and black bow tie. His forehead was high and queerly narrow, like the forehead of a horse, and his eyes, which blinked continually, were unnaturally bright and alert, like a chicken's.

"Perhaps the music was not a joke," the young man said, and smiled in a way that might have been malicious.

Professor Klingman merely looked at him and raised his right hand to his hearing aid.

"Perhaps you alone, in all that fat, complacent audience, understood tonight's music," the young man said.

"Yes, perhaps," the professor said tentatively, slowly lowering his hand. He cautiously waited for things to become clearer.

"Let me explain myself," the young man said. He leaned forward, vaguely aggressive, still rapidly blinking, placing his strikingly long white fingers on each side of his glass. "I grew up in a clergyman's family, in a very small town not many miles from here. There reigned in our home a punctilious cleanliness and a pathetic, bookish optimism. We breathed an atmosphere of dusty pulpit rhetoric—large words for good and evil which I have learned to hate, since perhaps they are to blame for all our human sufferings."

Professor Klingman touched his chin, considering.

"For me," the young man hurriedly continued, "life consisted entirely of those grandiose words, since I knew nothing more of it than the infinite, insubstantial emotions they called up in me. From people I expected divine virtue or hair-raising wickedness; from experience either ravishing loveliness or consummate horror. I was full of avidity for all that existed, and full of a passionate, tormented yearning for True Reality, whatever form it might take, intoxicating bliss, undreamt-of anguish.

"I remember my first disillusionment. There was a fire one night in my parents' house. It spread insidiously until the whole first floor was in flames, and soon the stairs would be on fire. It was I who discovered it. I went rushing through the house shouting, 'Fire! Fire!' I know what emotion underlay those cries, though at the time it may not have come fully alive to my consciousness. 'So this,' I thought, 'is a fire. This is what it's like to have a house on fire. Is this all there is to it?'

"Heaven knows, it was serious enough. The whole house burned down; only with difficulty was the family saved, and I myself got some nasty burns. It would be wrong to say that my fancy could have painted anything much worse than the actual burning of my parents' house. Yet some vague, formless idea of an event that was even more frightful must have existed somewhere within me, by comparison with which the reality seemed flat. This fire was the first great event in my life.

"I need not go on to recount all my various disappointments in detail. Suffice it to say that I zealously fed my magnificent expectations of life with the matter of a thousand books. Ah, how I have learned to hate them, those poets who chalk up grand words on all the walls of life—because they had no power to write them on the sky with penpoints dipped in Vesuvius! I came to think every large word a lie and a mockery.

"Ecstatic poets have said that speech is poor: 'Ah, how poor are words!' they bleat. But no, sir! Speech is rich, extravagantly rich compared with the poverty of actual life. Pain has its limits—physical pain in unconsciousness, mental pain in torpor. The same is true of joy. Our human need for communication has found itself a way to create sounds which lie beyond these limits.

"Is the fault mine? Is it down my spine alone that certain words can run so as to awaken intuitions of sensations which do not exist?"

There was no question now of the malevolence in the young man's smile. But old Alfred Klingman, who'd spent a lifetime teaching the young and outraged, watched him with a look that seemed more bafflement than horror. He may have felt even a touch of admiration for the man's rhetoric.

The young man said, leaning even nearer: "But you, my friend, as a music lover, must understand that the disappointment I've thus far delimited is nothing by comparison with the disappointment I have yet to describe. The moment my father first saw me in the crib, with these fingers that reach out like tentacles, he cried out, 'A pianist! The Dear Lord has sent us a pianist!' I could reach a full octave at the age of seven. And I was rhythmically talented, and had perfect pitch. I amuse acquaintances by telling them the frequencies of pistol shots, car crashes, screams for help. The point is this: what are a poet's lying words to the rich and the secret intimations of a piano chord, a great pipe organ, an orchestra, a voice? I've searched the globe for some firm reality that could give me even the shadow of a hint that our musical intuitions are not madness. I've stood before the greatest works of sculpture, and I've thought, 'Yes, it's beautiful. Is that all there is?' I've looked up from Zermatt at the Matterhorn and thought, 'Very like the postcards.' I watched a friend die. It was just as I'd expected."

The young man smiled as if consciously laboring to make his smile ferocious. "That is why I compose as I do, my dear music lover."

Professor Klingman said, "You, then, are the composer of—" He said it almost casually, as if merely checking an earlier conclusion.

"I am," the young man said fiercely, and waited.

Perhaps as much as a minute passed. At last Professor Klingman took off his glasses to wipe them again. He did this slowly and carefully, his fingers trembling. He hooked the glasses back over his ears, folded his handkerchief, then changed his mind, unfolded it, and blew his nose. He noticed that he still had his hat on, and removed it, carefully setting it down on the table. "I'm flattered that you should tell me all this," he said softly, tentatively.

The young man waited. He seemed to be growing more angry by the minute.

Professor Klingman sat nodding slowly and thoughtfully, nervously smiling. Finally he said, as if he had no idea what else to say, "My wife was a pianist."

He began then, slowly and patiently, to explain what she had meant to him, though of course his feeling was impossible to put into words.

TRUMPETER

Queen Louisa's dog, Trumpeter, was nobody's fool, which is one of the reasons he kept mostly out of sight, taking care of himself, harmlessly chasing a rabbit now and then, soaking up the sun in the cemetery—where no one ever went—one eye half open, on the watch for trespassers, sometimes wandering through the alleys of the village, peeking in through windows when the sun had set, observing how shopkeepers counted up their money unaware of the servants who peered from every curtain and hungrily eyed those stacked silver coins, and then again sometimes pausing by old shanties where cutpurses met, filling the night with their blasphemous obscenities, and where there were smells, everywhere, of bile and perspiration and unwholesome drink, still other times trotting to the foul black wharf, where old merchant ships bumped against the water-logged planks and young sailors snored and whistled in the arms of drunken maidens and sometimes a pirate slipped silent as a reptile from fog-wisp to fog-wisp, wetly smiling, carrying his parrot and rum. Sharp ears lifted, burning eyes narrowed into needle-thin slits, Trumpeter would listen to whatever un-righteousness came drifting his way, and then he would lift his leg, leave his warning, and move on.

Trumpeter knew, as no one else did, all that was afoot in the

kingdom of mad Queen Louisa. Not that he took undue pride
in this. It was his nature, as a dog, to keep track of things, to
be a jealous guardian, eternally alert. Even when, unbeknownst to them all, he lay in a corner of Queen Louisa's
room, or slept with his head on his paws behind the stove, or
bared his fangs to keep the cat on his toes—for the cat was an
old one and weary of mice—Trumpeter's mind was on one
subject: the welfare of the kingdom. This was, so to speak,
what he was paid for. Not that Trumpeter could really be
called *paid*. But Trumpeter was no haggler, never one to stand
on ceremony. It is true, he would admit, that the people of
the castle almost never spoke to him and, once they'd grown
used to him, hardly looked up when he went gliding like an
angel of death through the room; but sometimes when he
rubbed against Queen Louisa's shoulder she would give him a
brief, absentminded pat, and on rare occasions, for no discernible reason, she'd say, "Sit, Trumpeter," or, "Down—for the
love of *God*, boy!" or, "Outside!" As for the others, they paid
to Trumpeter no attention whatsoever, merely obeyed him as
they obeyed the King or Queen, without thought or hesitation.
When he stood by the door, they opened it. When he stood by
the cupboard, they filled his dish. When he barked, they went
over furtively and peeked out the window.

He was nobody's fool, but he had, it is true, his limitations,
and the chief of them was this: ponder as he might—and ponder he did, hour on hour and year on year, his black head
lowered into the carpet's scents, his eyes rolled up—he could
never penetrate the reason (for presumably there *was* some
reason) for the curious behavior of Queen Louisa and her
court. It was said, and Trumpeter in his way understood, that
at times Queen Louisa, to rest her mind, would transform herself suddenly into a large greenish toad. This habit was notorious, reported far and wide; everyone who knew her had seen
the thing happen quite frequently. Everyone, that is, except
Trumpeter. It was not, in his opinion, a case of the Emperor's

Clothes. Trumpeter was no innocent: man's ways are not dog's, he knew. He had seen the whole court sit erect for hours, dead silent except for an occasional whisper, an occasional cough, listening to people on a bright raised platform howl. He, when he tentatively joined them, had been kicked and sent outside. On that same raised platform he'd seen a man in black creep up cunningly on another, a dagger in his hand, and when he, Trumpeter, had hurtled to the rescue, he'd been beaten and seized by five knights and had been chained behind the buttery.

The oddities of man were inexhaustible, and this change that came over the Queen—a change Trumpeter could not see except by the reaction of the others—was merely one of them. He had learned to accept, simply to watch and consider, stretched out half hidden behind the curtains or under the table, offering no comment. One moment the court would be walking toward the chapel all in solemn array, bearing high white candles, Queen Louisa at their head in her long sky-blue gown, her red hair gleaming, her expression sweet and sad— they all had sad expressions as they moved toward the chapel, and their bodies were rigid, as if ritually so, slightly trembling with each step—and the next they'd all be leaping, or darting their tongues out—even King Gregor, with a pained expression, his black beard bristling—and the princesses and princes would suddenly begin croaking, ludicrously grinning, and their eyes would bug out. Trumpeter would let out a sigh and shift his position slightly, and when Queen Louisa came down like an avalanche inches from his nose, he would thump his tail once, courteous, showing her he'd noticed. "Goo-boo!" she'd say. This was not, strictly speaking, his name, or the right time of day, but he accepted it.

Whatever the reason for this strange behavior on the part of the Queen and, after her, the court, it was a peaceful kingdom, no one could deny it. King Gregor and King John, who for years had been at war, were now, because of the general confusion, the best of friends, squatting on some garden path arm in arm, or, in another mood, debating at the tops of their voices, jabbing their fingers at the writing in a book. "Saintly, my ass!" King John once yelled. (Trumpeter had no trouble understanding words. It was merely sentences that befuddled him.) "Saintly, my ass! Do you wash your peasants' feet on Maundy Thursday?" King Gregor's eyes widened. "God forbid!" he said.

If all this was strange, there were other things still stranger. No one seemed to remember anymore, except for Trumpeter, that the Princess had gone away. Not the Princess called Muriel, whom the Queen had discovered and declared to be her own dear long-lost child, and not the numerous princesses and princes she'd found later and joyfully recognized and brought to the castle, Djubkin and Dobremish, Pretty Polly, and the rest. For all these, Trumpeter had no hostile feelings; and he understood—dimly, yet clearly enough—that in making them her children, as perhaps they were indeed, since the life of a dog is but a heartbeat, so to speak, in the long span of man, the Queen had brought happiness to a kingdom that had suffered, before that, grave troubles—peasants against royalty, "madness against madness," as the minstrel said: an obscure saying; but Trumpeter, in his heart, understood it.

He remembered, nonetheless, that another princess had lived here once in the days before Queen Louisa was mad— she had vanished one morning like dew into the blind blue air. Her hair was yellow. He would lie beside the fireplace, an old slipper in his mouth—he was not always, in those days, wide awake—and he would feel a certain pressure bearing down on his shoulder, and when he opened his eyes and turned his head, there the Princess would be, her hair falling over him, her cheek on the flatness between his shoulder and back, using him as a pillow, and he would moan and she would mimic him, harmlessly mocking.

This was no flickering memory but steady as the floor.

Whether or not he understood the details, he understood the importance of a kingdom at peace. Vrokror, that terrible grudge-bearing fiend, had no supporters now. The words with which Queen Louisa had undone him—"All error," she'd said, "begins with soreheads"—were now common slogan in King Gregor's realm. It was part of a verse for skipping rope to. Trumpeter, travelling far and wide, had seen the extent to which Vrokror had been undone. Vrokror was a monk again, as he'd been in the first place, but a monk in absolute and terrible isolation: he saw nothing sentient—certainly not God—but lived all alone on the top of a mountain, eating tundra plants.

All was well, all was well. Travelling through alleys, Trumpeter saw that the servants were afraid of their masters and would do them no harm, hunger as they might for those coins stacked like pillars in the palace. Watching the cutpurses, studying every smile, he saw that they were miserable, whatever their pretenses. There are never, of course, enough purses to go around. And Trumpeter saw that the merchants all cheated fellow merchants, and the pirates all stole from them, and no one was distressed; they were used to it. Trumpeter began to feel a strange discomfiture.

"Bad dog," she'd say, this real Princess whom only Trumpeter remembered, and she'd shake her finger ferociously, and he would duck his head. But it was a pleasure, he would admit, that attention she gave him; and he partly understood—sometimes fully understood—that she did it for the absolute absurdity of the thing. Here was he, four, five, six times her weight, with jaws that could cut through the thighbones of a steer; and here was she, who with a word could lay him flatlings.

Sometimes lately, in the middle of the night, Queen Louisa would sit bolt upright in her bed. She would be atremble all over. He lay perfectly still, ready to spring to the defense, but there was nothing to defend her from. "We must have," she said one drizzly, miserable dawn, "a royal ball. I must marry off my princes and princesses."

There followed a period of intense preparations; dressmakers came, and cooks and carpenters and pirates disguised as wine merchants, eyeing the silverware. The palace was transformed. King Gregor paced furiously back and forth, stroking his black beard, snatching at the arm of his friend King John. "We've forgotten something," he cried out, "but *what?*" Trumpeter rushed with renewed intensity from the cemetery to the alleys of the village to the foul black wharf. All was well, all was well. On every lamppost and wall he left his warning.

She'd grown pale as marble and quick to be exhausted. Nevertheless, all was well, it was obvious. King John and King Gregor met daily for war, and their armies came home bleeding—or King Gregor's came home bleeding and King John's army went—and there was dancing till midnight and poetry speaking and courtly love—and the Princess would shake her head and smile: "They're all mad, you know, Trumpeter. Stark raving mad." He would hold out his paw, and she would take it and solemnly make acquaintance.

"She seems pale," Queen Louisa said, pulling at her lip.

"She needs to eat more beefsteak," said King Gregor, and never moved his eyes from the map. "Ha!" he said suddenly. "He'll creep up on us from *here*"—he jabbed down his finger on some lines on the map—"and little will he guess . . ."

Since the palace was filled to overflowing with princes and princesses, none of them the pale one whom Trumpeter remembered, King Gregor and Queen Louisa held their royal ball. The orchestra played merrily, waltz after waltz, and by midnight all the merchants and the merchants' servants had found themselves some princess, and each and every prince had found some daughter of a merchant who was exactly to his liking, and the peace and serenity of the kingdom were more wonderful than ever.

When the ball was long over and everyone in bed, Queen Louisa sat bolt upright and said, "Trumpeter! What's that?"

It was nothing, he knew. If there were anything there, he'd have heard it or smelled it or felt it in his bones. But he dutifully rose, head turned to yawn, and mournfully went over to the window to look out. It was nothing: emptiness. Poor Trumpeter had no imagination.

"Something must be done," said Queen Louisa, "about the pirates and parrots, not to mention the cutpurses." She leaped from the bed, her white legs bowed, presumably presuming she'd been changed into a toad, and stared past Trumpeter's shoulder deep into the night. Absentmindedly, she stroked his head, and he moaned. "That's it," said Queen Louisa, as if it seemed to her he'd spoken. "We must show them we love them and think of them as equals. What can we do?" She began to pace, bowleggedly hurrying back and forth, wringing her fingers and biting her lip. Trumpeter sat, ears cocked, head tilted.

A queer expression stretched Queen Louisa's face. "Do we really need the royal treasury?" she said.

Though the sentence was difficult, Trumpeter understood, and, hardly knowing what else to do, he covered his eyes with his right paw. Queen Louisa, however, was too excited to notice. "That's it!" she cried. "We'll invite the cutpurses, pirates and parrots to guard the royal treasure. They'll steal it and never be miserable again!"

A dog has no power. His only hope was that in the morning the Queen would have forgotten her plan.

Morning came, and she had not. "Gregor," she said, "I have a brilliant idea."

Trumpeter slunk off. He rushed to the cemetery, where no one ever went, and kept careful watch for an hour or so. But no one trespassed, not a rabbit stirred, so he hurried on, though it wasn't yet dark, to peek through windows here and there in the village, but no one was in sight—the merchants and their servants were all away celebrating with their new royal wives—then he rushed, quick as lightning, to the foul black wharf. But it was empty as a rum bottle lying in the sand, and then, with a heavy heart, Trumpeter returned to the palace.

"Dear God!" the King was yelling, though he was in on the plan, "the royal treasury has been depleted!"

Trumpeter lay down.

All was well; all was well.

She, this Princess whom only he remembered, had grown increasingly pale, increasingly quick to weary. He'd insisted on lying at the side of her high bright platformed bed, waiting, on the theory that sooner or later, inevitably, given the span of human time, the sun would rise and she'd abruptly sit bolt upright, and they would walk out again into the fields to pursue silly rabbits. Then, for reasons not discernible to him, five knights had come and had cajoled and coaxed him and had finally seized him with their iron gloves and had dragged him by a chain to the place behind the buttery. When they released him days later, the Princess was gone.

"We've done it! We've done it!" Queen Louisa cried wildly, startling him awake. As far as Trumpeter's eye could see there were people dancing.

"Ah, peace!" cried King Gregor.

"Ah, justice!" cried King John.

There stood Vrokror the Terrible, looking shy as a maiden, holding Muriel's hand; and Djubkin, Dobremish, Pretty Polly, and the rest were throwing rose petals over them, their faces bright with tears. Queen Louisa was laughing with a beautiful lilt, for the king of the pirates was offering her a treasure chest crammed to the gunnels with silver and gold, kissing her fingertips and squinting his eyes like a man who intended to steal it all back again; and King John and King Gregor were agreeing, all smiles, that both of them were certainly, in their own small ways, saints; and the parrots were crying, all, "Cracker! Pretty cracker!"

The palace was full of light—beyond the windows, thick darkness. Nothing was wrong; nothing could go wrong. It was a balanced kingdom, the only kingdom in the world where art reigned supreme.

Trumpeter crept from beneath the dark curtain of the table-cloth and glided to the door. He stood waiting. It was opened. He hurried away from the dancing and light, away from the joyful celebration of things that he knew to be quite proper, and when he reached the depths of the forest, he began to howl.

THE LIBRARY
HORROR

I had been troubled for days—odd sounds, objects out of place, all the pitiful and mundane symptoms of a disordered mind, symptoms I know all too well, coming as I do from a family of lunatics, as everyone knows—when a few odd phrases in a book on aesthetics threw everything into sharp new perspective. I had been reading along in my usual fashion, simultaneously urgent and desultory, one hand pressed to my chest, a faint uneasiness in the back of my mind, a sort of floating anxiety like a shape moving furtively from window to window—never mind the reason (I had missed an opportunity to drop in on my father at the asylum outside the village, or, rather, I had thought of several reasons I could not possibly go, and then, not having gone, I had suddenly seen everything in a new light and had realized that my reasons were all trivial and absurd, I should certainly have gone; nor was that all, but never mind)—when suddenly I came upon these curious observations on "living form" in art.

I no longer recall what I read, exactly, or even the general outline of the theory. There was some talk, I remember—very interesting at the time—about "virtual time and space" in music and painting, and something . . . you must forgive my haste . . . about "organic forms." My wife—this much I remember distinctly—was working in the kitchen, banging the cooking utensils around, turning the water on and off with a violent suddenness I could only interpret as critical of my sitting in the livingroom, reading while she worked. All her acquaintances have maids, and she feels, she has told me, that a man as well off as I am could surely afford that small luxury. It wasn't so bad when my father was still at liberty, dropping by every night or so and helping with her chores. But my father has been put where he belongs—no fault of mine—so now she talks about having at least a maid. I've explained to her many times why a stranger in the house would be, to a man like myself, anything but a luxury. Even a stranger *near* the house is deeply upsetting to me, so that, inconvenient as it may be, I walk wherever I go (I seldom go out except for my rare official visits to the bank), since to own an automobile would inevitably involve me with a mechanic for the engine, a chauffeur, and heaven knows what else. But I am straying from my point.

I had been hearing for several days and nights now strange noises from the library. (It took me some time to pinpoint the noises as coming from the library, but I must hurry past all that; my time, as you will see, is limited.) Now, at the sound of a particularly loud crash, I jumped up from my chair, closed the book of philosophy on my finger to keep my place, and moved carefully—I was wearing my slippers—to the library door. With my hand on the knob and my ear against the panel, my body bent over like an old man's—like my father's, for example—trying with all my might to make out what it was that was happening inside, I suddenly found myself—suddenly and surprisingly, as when a man wakes up in a different room from the one he went to sleep in—staring with ferocious concentration at the title on the book: *The Problems of Art*. It came to me with a jolt, such a jolt that I found my knees were trembling, that all this while, when I'd thought I'd been listening with all my wits, I'd been mulling over those ideas I'd just encountered, ideas I at that time recalled with the greatest exactitude.

The philosopher wrote—this much I can still make out—of how in paintings, as in mirrors, we see "virtual space," that is, space that seems as real as any other until the moment we try to enter it, at which time it proves an apparition. In the same way, reading novels, we move through virtual landscapes watching virtual human beings, people who speak and act as do real human beings until they vanish, or, rather, snap magically into words on a page. The implications, I hardly need tell you, are staggering!

Perhaps, though time is short, I should try to dredge up one or two more details of the argument, to make the larger implications a little clearer. These "apparitions" that come to us in music or, say, fiction are not at all mere imitations, like the figures in a mirror. On the contrary, they are created expressions of life itself. They function in the same ways as do other living things; that is to say, they are pushed and pulled by the same laws that push and pull me or, for instance, my wife, Greer. I speak only, of course, of such works as we call successful, works that have "vitality" or "autonomous life." It was of course this idea—this *fact*, I should have said, for so it seems to me—that made my knees tremble.

Heaven knows what force it was that caused me to act. I myself was amazed, watching my hand as, with a will of its own, it closed more firmly on the large brass doorknob and turned it. Then, in the pocket of my jacket, the same hand closed around my gold-plated penknife and drew it toward the light. With my shoulder—hardly knowing what I was doing, abandoning my senses—I pushed open the huge old door and stepped in.

The world is aclutter with mysteries, as everyone knows. The sane Newtonian universe has proved more illusory than your face in the mirror or the "solid" oak floor. We must somehow imagine, it seems, black holes and white holes, wormholes through which Time makes astounding jumps, even some subatomic particle, I read, which is approximately the weight of an electron and two light-years broad! We're stuck, if you believe our more outlandish physicists, with the real possibility of dying of asphyxiation because the oxygen has all piled up in a corner of the room where we happen not to be.

We take these things for granted, or at any rate for probably true, and though we glance left then right before crossing a street, as if Newton's universe were still in operation, or even Moses' universe ("I know I have sinned, therefore it is likely that I'll be hit by a car"), we know we have no choice but to make do with the universe we're caught in. I could say more on this subject—I'm a voracious reader and, as you'll see, no fool—but as I've said, my time is limited.

My library—*our* library, for the house is in my wife's name as well as my own—gives at first the impression of being nothing but books: books from floor to ceiling on all four walls, more books on the five free-standing stacks, three feet apart, which stretch from the east wall of the room to the west with only a four-foot-wide passageway tunneling through them, like a series of entrances to a crypt. These shelves too rise from floor to ceiling. One ducks one's head, moving to the heart of the library; above the eighth shelf—the roof of the tunnel through the stacks—the shelves run straight across the room. One feels, in our library, buried in books, entombed. It is partly for this reason that I avoid the place.

Yet the impression from the doorway that the room contains nothing but books is an illusion. Beyond the low passage through the free-standing stacks one sees—or, rather, I saw as I came in—that the heart of the library is flooded with moonlight, so that there must be large windows or (as happens to be the fact) French doors. Then one notices a glow in a part of that light, and one deduces (or knows) that in the heart of the library there is a fireplace where not long since there was a roaring fire. Every night around dusk I make a fire in the library fireplace. I never read there—the place makes me uneasy, all that gloomy weight of learning, ton upon ton of contradictory opinion, as if right to the center of things reality is moot—but the truth, I'm afraid, is that if I didn't make a fire there my wife would complain that we need servants. For the same reason I work frantically in the garden, trim the hedges, pick up the droppings from our high enclosing walls of blue spruce. . . . But enough.

There was not a sound now. I groped for the lightswitch to the right of the door and flicked it three times until finally, as if grudgingly, slightly arcing, it turned the lights on. The room was hardly lighter than before; in fact, it was only the quality of the light that changed. Cautiously, I moved my right slipper forward, then my left, soundlessly heading toward the hearthlit center of the library. I opened the penknife as I went.

Well, no point making high drama of it. Suddenly, there in front of me—leaping out so quickly from behind the third bookshelf that I hardly knew at first where he'd come from— stood a man with an axe. He was a small man, no more than four feet tall. Why this should be I have no idea, but small he was, a perfectly formed midget with terrified, rolling, somewhat slanted eyes, more terrified of me than I had time to be of him, a ferocious little Russian—a student, I imagined—crazily muttering to himself. Dim as the room was I saw everything with dreadful clarity, like a man about to die. His eyes were sunken, his lips wildly trembled, his coat came almost to his ankles. On the blunt side of the axe there was blood and what might have been gray hair. I tried to speak, but it was as if all the air had gone out of me. My knees banged crazily together. He drew back the axe, blunt side forward, to strike me, but that very instant a young woman in English Victorian dress appeared behind him and cried out, "Lord in heaven! Have you gone loopy?" He turned his head, or, rather, threw it around, to look at her, and his axe waggled downward a little. She too was a midget, though now it was less obvious; something was beginning to happen to my sense of the scale of things. The books on the shelves had grown larger, and the people the same. He looked at the girl with a terrified fixity, as if—in the word's profoundest sense—he'd never seen anyone like her.

With a part of my mind I was so afraid of the little man I could think nothing at all, but with another part, or so it seems to me now, I sensed what he was thinking. Raskolnikov—for of course it was he—had never seen an English schoolgirl and had no way of knowing she was, so to speak, an "outlaw" English schoolgirl; but he knew, it seemed to me, that she was somehow an outlaw, as he was, theoretically; and what had shocked him so badly that he had lowered his axe was philosophical: this girl in dark ringlets, with the slightly puffy eye-sacs, the petulant mouth, the stance he could not judge as obscene or unobscene, not knowing her culture, but knew to be somehow or another defiant and by the standards of her own time and place almost certainly unacceptable, this girl was, like him, a moral outcast, but outcast from a morality so different from his own world's as to cast the idea of "universal human nature" into the trash-heap of ancient *pseudodoxia*. As he dropped the axe and crazily stared at her, she paid attention. He was astonished by this and reached for the axe again but merely touched it with the tips of his fingers then changed his mind and let it lie. It seems pointless to analyze, but it comes to this: his standards of good and evil—the standards by which he defended and condemned himself—were so different from hers, or her society's, that he abandoned all sense and followed her, like a sexually aroused animal, into the dimness beyond the fourth shelf.

I can hardly bear to tell you the trivia that followed. It seemed to me at the time astonishing, even wonderfully interesting, but on reflection I see that it was neither. I could recreate my state of mind for you perhaps, by trickery and rhetoric, but I refuse to descend to such foolishness. Suffice it to say that I saw Ahab, split by lightning from head to toe, who argued with Boswell's Dr. Johnson, boringly—sometimes threatening to hit Dr. Johnson "a good one, right smack in thy face," to the latter's dismay, of course—about immanence and transcendence; saw Scrooge and Bunyan's Pilgrim, who sounded to my ears remarkably alike; talked with Jane Austen's Emma, who was not at all as pretty as I'd imagined her to be and seemed oddly bigoted on almost everything we touched . . . etc.

I will leap to the heart of the matter, which is this: when I had been in my library for several hours, arguing with these dreams or apparitions or realities, my wife came to me dressed in her nightgown—she is generally said to be quite beautiful— and said, "Winfred, are you coming to bed?" I knew this was a threat and a proposal. "Soon," I said, twisting my head around to look at her, "I'm not quite finished." She stood waiting. By now the beauty of her breasts and flanks, well defined under the nightgown, had become, I thought, slightly comic. If one sits looking long enough at mere actuality it becomes, well, obvious. She pivoted away, swinging her rear end in a way that an actress might call cliché, and disappeared through the low-slung entrances or, in this case, exits. From the door she called back, "Remember, tomorrow is visitors' day at the asylum. I know you're busy, of course. . . ."

At this moment, as if summoned by her words, something came charging from the books, terribly shrieking. It came straight toward me. I couldn't make out what it was, at first. It was brighter than the light from a bursting star, coming straight at me with a clatter and roar like a lightning-ball. At the last instant, I saw the apparition with absolute clarity: the hero of my youth—I was sixteen when I first read a version of his story—Achilles! Without a word, without an instant's hesitation, he raised his sword and struck. In amazement, I watched blood rush down my chest from the deep wound in my neck. I stared at him in horror—more horror than disbelief.

It was incredible! He was the hero of absolute justice, God-sent doom, terrible purgation, and I was—I screamed with all my might—"Not guilty!" He stared at me, baffled. Perhaps he spoke no English; or perhaps he was amazed that, wounded as I was, I could still speak. He raised his huge sword to strike again.

My wife cried, from somewhere far away, "Winfred!" And then again, from somewhere nearer, "*Win*fred!"

He turned, listening, more baffled than before. Slowly, carefully, eyes somewhat confused, he raised that huge, gleaming knife.

Now she was behind me. "You were screaming! Have you gone crazy?" she demanded. He stood teetering the knife, as if he imagined I was moving, like a chicken who nervously twists its neck on the block.

"Winfred," she whispered, "what's come *over* you?"

Achilles, lover of justice and truth, glanced past his shoulder as if for invisible support, then swung again, this time softly, uncertainly, though his blade nonetheless cut the tendon that held my neck to my right shoulder.

"Winfred!" cried my wife. "Say something! What's the *matter* with you?"

I sat hunched forward, hiding my condition as well as possible. Abruptly, seeing that I would not speak or turn, she left me, furiously whispering to herself.

Not to make too much of it, I knew then and there that I was dying.

Though time is running out—each word I write is more shaky than the last—let me pause to discuss this peculiar situation. If my sentence ends in the middle, so it ends. Goodbye, God bless you. So I pray while I still have the strength.

Let us say, for the sake of argument, that I'm not dying but going mad. (I'm obviously rational, but no one's more rational than a maniac, this I know. My wife, you may say, does not seem to see Achilles; but my wife is no test of reality. She too comes from a long line of lunatics, all people of substance in their day, like myself.) Very well, let us say, for argument's sake, that I am mad. Here sits character x, a madman, struck a mortal blow by character y, a fiction. What can x do, mad as he is, but struggle to maintain justice, normality?

Perhaps my father is unjustly accused. The judge who committed him is afraid of black cats. Even the testimony I myself gave may not have been quite fair, though to the best of my knowledge it was true. My wife also may be unjustly accused, insofar as I accuse her of imbalance. But this much, at least, seems certainly true: if a fictional character, namely Achilles, can make blood run down my chest (if it is indeed running down my chest), then a living character, or two such characters—my father and my wife—can be made to live forever, simply by being put in a fiction.

For this reason—though possibly it makes no sense, possibly I'm making some outlandish mistake—I sit at my desk in this library, writing while the blood runs out of me, the moon hides in clouds, and the fire in the fireplace burns down to ash—Achilles, five feet tall, rather larger than the others, hacking and chopping at my shoulders and spine, while Tom Jones, Gulliver, Hamlet, and many others stand cheering, booing, or complaining in the shadows, taking note of my demise or ignoring it, involved in their own huge affairs. For this reason I construct the following, which I'll pursue as time allows.

"Ah, Greer, what a good, gentle woman you are," says my father.

She shakes her head, gloomy, and with her long fingers turns the cup handle north. The table runs east and west. "You're babbling," says my wife.

Her irritation surprises him, and he glances up at her, then down again at his knees. "That's not what I meant," he says.

She rises suddenly, goes over and opens the icebox door, and, like a child, stands looking inside. "Christ," she says.

"No cheese?" he asks. He has no idea why he thinks she's looking for cheese.

"*Cheese?*" she asks, more irritable than before. She looks at him. He can see that she thinks he's crazy. He could make a fire in the sink, she wouldn't think it more crazy than his assumption that she's looking for cheese. She comes back to the table with the milk pitcher and a glass.

My father feels pain, a light ticking exactly in the center of his chest. Once, years ago, riding with my mother, he had to stop the car—she'd been bawling him out about his failure to press charges against someone who had robbed him—he had to stop the car and run down the road pell-mell to keep from having a heart attack.

"All I meant . . ." says my father, and lets it trail off. With enormous effort, he reaches across the table and takes her hand.

Tears burst into my wife's eyes and spill down her cheeks. "Never mind," she says. "I'm sorry." She thinks about it, then slowly lowers her head to the tabletop. My father, after carefully thinking about it, raises his crooked, calloused hand and lowers it to touch her soft hair.

"Dear God, if I were Winfred's age," my father complains. He moves the stiff hand to the side of her face and brushes the barely perceptible fuzz on her cheek. He does not touch the tears.

"You're crazy," she says, and laughs, half crying. "Has it ever struck you that if you and I were normal people, like Winfred, for instance, in there turning the pages, one, two, three—"

"Now now," says my father. "When you're my age you've thought about everything, more or less." His hand moves slowly, gently, over her hair. He's eighty-two. She's thirty. No one would think him insane except that he once backed his truck through the plate-glass window of my bank.

The hair prickles on the back of my neck, as if an ice-cold wind has touched it. Achilles, Lord of Justice, is standing in the doorway, dressed in a drab, neat suit, like a Jehovah's Witness. I see that he has grasped the situation between my wife and my father.

I snatch at his elbow. "No justice," I plead, "enough of justice!"

None of this is possible, I realize. My father is in the asylum, Achilles does not exist. I focus hard, trying to read what I have written. The desk is all blood.

My head is filled with planets and stars. Achilles moves slowly toward my father, raising his knife.

"Dear Heavenly Father," I whisper with all my might, for any good fiction will serve in hard times—I clench my eyes against the tumbling of the planets—"Dear Heavenly Father," I whisper with all my might

THE JOY
OF THE JUST

1

There's all kinds of justice, I suppose you might say. But give me the justice of Aunt Ella Reikert, the time she got run off the road by the Preacher's wife, down on Boskydell Road, this side of Makanda. By the time she got, for the second time, to the diner that her niece's husband ran—one of her real nieces, not one of the hundred, maybe two hundred kids that imagined "Aunt Ella" was her natural designation—she was hopping mad. She pulled that half-demolished old square-framed black-and-yellow Dodge up in front of the gaspumps and pushed open the only door that still worked. The car had rolled just once. The sticky red gumbo in the creekbed stopped it. The only real damage was to the tires and roof and sides—the whole right side of the roof was caved in so it looked like a chicken coop or hog-shed on wheels—or that was the only real damage unless you counted (and she did) the damage the Hume boys had done with their tractor, pulling it out of the mud and up onto the road. They'd broken off both bumpers with their chain, one after the other, and then they'd looped the chain around the right-hand windshield post and broke that. When they'd started hitching onto the runningboard she'd made Ralph get out of the car, cast and all, and make them stop. He looked sadder than usual when she made him get out in that mud. He was sure he'd broken his leg all over again, which he had. But he got at least one crutch out the door, and all of his wide pink nose, and he said, looking as if he might cry, "Come *on* now, Gib, you mind Aunt Ella." She'd told them and told them they ought to use mules, they pulled easier; but they wouldn't try it, or not till they thought of it themselves. When it worked they grinned at her and said, "Now didn't we tell you we'd lug you out, Aunt Ella? There it is, setting in the sunshine as good as new, almost." If she hadn't been so angry at the Preacher she'd have given them a switching apiece, big as they were.

She got out nimbly for a woman of her years, considering the trouble she had with her knees, and she slammed the car door, forgetting Ralph would be coming out behind her since the door on his side wouldn't open. The window hit him squarely, high on the forehead, and he sat still a minute, wincing so hard you could see most of his gums, and he was rubbing his pink bald spot with both pink hands. Then he opened the door again and got his crutches under his armpits and started for the diner.

"Leon," she said to her niece's husband, "I been run off the road."

"Again?" he said.

He stood there tall as a pinetree, grinning at her, wiping his hands on a dishtowel. Darthamae came into the doorway behind him, holding the baby. The dog was with her.

"No, the same time," Aunt Ella said. "Wasn't it bad enough once?"

"But that was three days ago, Aunt Ella," Darthamae said. It was Leon who'd put on four new tires for her and straightened the fenders so the wheels would turn. She'd come into the Dew Drop Inn on the rims, the tires cut to ribbons and flopping, one of them completely gone, the whole car screaming like a cow the slaughterer's maul had glanced off too lightly. He'd bent the fenders into shape by hand, as if easily. For the roof he was going to need tools, though; and Aunt Ella was too angry and impatient to leave the car.

She said now, "It don't make a particle of difference how many days ago it was." Both her hands and her head were shaking, and her false teeth barely kept rhythm with her tongue. "I been shamed and humiliated and there'll not a soul lift a finger in my behalf."

"Now Aunt Ella," Leon said.

"I been to the lawyer and I've got no legal recourse, that's what he said."

"Vengeance is mine, saith the Lord," Leon said sadly.

"Now don't you mock, young man," she said. She shook her finger. "He that saith unto the wicked, Thou art righteous, him shall the people curse, nations shall abhor him; but to them that rebuke him shall be delight, and a good blessing shall come upon them."

"The meek shall inherit the earth," Leon said.

"Leave not thy place, for yielding pacifieth great offenses," she said.

"And the greatest of these is charity," he said.

"Leon, *stop* it," Darthamae broke in. The dog looked up at her to see if she meant him too.

"Come on in and sit down, Aunt Ella," Leon said, timid all at once, ashamed of himself—as he usually was when Darthamae came down on him. He pulled off the army cap he always wore and led Aunt Ella to the middle booth, poor Ralph hopping along behind. It came to Leon too late that with her gimpy knees she couldn't comfortably get into the booth, and neither could Ralph with his leg in a cast. He brought over chairs for them and set them down facing out the window to talk to the gaspumps and the highway. It was a bad arrangement, he saw right away. With the wrecked car sitting in front of her—the car she'd taken care of all these years like the child of her own she'd never had—she couldn't forget her indignation for a minute. Leon squeezed into the booth himself and sat wedged there, hands folded, trying to look sympathetic. "Darthamae," he said, "bring over some tea for Aunt Ella." She got the tea, carrying the baby on her hip. The baby kept his eyes on them, especially on Ralph. Neither Leon nor Darthamae thought of getting tea for Ralph too.

"Boo!" Ralph said to the baby. The baby looked at him.

"It was the Preacher's wife," Aunt Ella said.

"*We* know that, Aunt Ella," Leon said. "That's what you told us before."

Nevertheless, she said it again. "It was her, it wasn't him at all. As I hope for Glory there wasn't a soul in that blessed car but her." She was outraged, which made her palsy worse. Her eyes were big as saucers, and her nose twitched. She told them the whole story again, fighting her teeth over every third word —it must be fifteen times she told it by now—and they shook their heads and nodded and agreed.

It was Monday. She was only going over to Henry Hawkins' for milk and eggs, not a two-mile drive and all country road, as sunny a day as you'd hope to see. She'd been driving herself because she hadn't any choice, Cousin Gordon was over to the market with his turkeys, and Ralph was laid up with a broken leg from Sylvester Lipe's running him over with the buckrake. Ralph had no license anyway, but the sheriff allowed him to drive the truck between fields, as long as he kept it in low-low and off on the shoulder. It was wrong, her driving an automobile with her eyes not what they used to be (from the front pew she couldn't see whether the Preacher was bowing or looking at the ceiling). But a person had to eat, and there was Ralph to think of, her own dead sister's son. And so she was inching around the corner, not yet three rods from the foot of her driveway, heading up toward the church, when there was the Preacher's car heading straight toward her, way over on the wrong-hand side of the road, and she'd had to take the ditch. When they were sitting down there in the creekbed and the Preacher's car jacked up on the shoulder

from when it had started to follow them down, who should they see climbing out of that car but the Preacher's wife, all painted up with rouge and lipstick, running up the hill for her house. ("It was *her*," she said fiercely. "I told them and *told* them who it was. Who was it, Ralph?" "It was her," he said.) And then pretty quick down comes the Preacher, still wearing his black-and-white cowboy shirt from riding that palomino horse, and he came down to the cattails where the mud began and leaned toward them, saying, "You all right, Sister Reikert?" "Don't you sister *me*," she said. "Your wife run me clear off the road." "My wife?" he said. "Why, Sister, my wife hasn't even got a driver's license."

And he'd stuck to it. He'd told the deputy how sorry he was, Sister Reikert had been over on his side of the road and hadn't seen him till the last minute and he'd surely be glad to help defray the expenses of fixing her car. "Why that's a blessed lie," she'd said, "it was his wife driving. Ralph, tell them it was his wife." "It was his wife," Ralph said. But they didn't believe her, nor Ralph either. He was the Preacher, and she was half blind, and Ralph would say anything she told him. He'd say it was Grover Cleveland, if Aunt Ella said to. He'd even believe it. "Are you saying I'm bearing false witness?" she said. The deputy said (no more than a youngster; he was one of the Howard children), "We just think you might be mistaken, Aunt Ella, what with your eyesight. We'll look into it, you can be sure." Yes indeed. Shortly after Doomsday. She'd said to Ed Hume, "Ed Hume, he was never in that car at all. He was up on that palomino horse he bought with people's tithes." "That may be so," Ed Hume said, "and then again it may not be so." "Well I *saw* him," she said. "If I never saw him the Lord strike me dead on this spot." Ed Hume took a puff from his cigar and looked at his shoes and said, "Anyways, I'll send down the boys to try and lug you out."

Leon shook his head sadly.

"He never believed me," Aunt Ella said. "I nursed him

through scarlet fever when he was no more than a little thing, but he never believed me now."

"It's criminal," Darthamae said. She shifted the baby to her other hip, and Aunt Ella looked at him. After a minute she patted the baby's shoulder, her hand as stiff as wood. The baby rolled his eyes down to look at the fingers and smiled, drooling. "Bless him," she said, but only from habit; she was still thinking of the Preacher's wife. The dog lay next to the foot of Ralph's cast, sniffing at it.

Leon James tapped the tips of his fingers together. "Aunt Ella," he said, "let's try and be reasonable about this. It was a bad thing for the Preacher to do, we all admit. . . ."

"Preacher!" she said. Her mouth worked as if she were lining up her teeth, getting ready to spit.

"Ain't much of a preacher," Ralph said, speaking slowly, concentrating on getting the sounds right so they'd understand him. He shook his head.

"Let's look at this thing from the Preacher's side," Leon said. "He's a young man yet, you've got to remember. He's not mature in judgment." He sighed, once more tapping his fingers together. He was moved for a moment, thinking of judgment. Then he was moved by the thought of youth. (Sometimes looking at Darthamae sitting at the window with the baby, light falling into the nearly-one-year-old's delicate new-grown hair and into Darthamae's, rich and full and warm as ripe wheat or an orchard in August—or looking at the flawless smoothness of their faces, the child's still innocent and undefined, Darthamae's blooming and too easily wise—the heaviness of his middle age, the indignity of his baldness and, worse, his monstrous, gangling, ridiculous height seemed more than he could carry. He could envy Ralph, a man still innocent at forty, kicked by a cow at the age of six and transformed to a kind of earthly angel, his baldness a halo, the lines at his eyes mere weather marks like the cracks in a smooth old rock.) "It's his first call, this job here, and everything's gone well for him so far. The people all like him. He gives good sermons. He's found himself a pretty wife—"

"A Jezebel," Aunt Ella said. Her teeth clicked. "She's like apples laying in the hay."

"Well, *she's* young *too*," Leon said.

"They're not either one of 'em as young as all that. If a ten-year-old that was kin to me tried a stunt like that I'd thrash 'em to an inch of their life."

He sighed and looked out at the car. Smashed, black and yellow, it made him think of a crushed yellow-jacket, and his mind wandered vaguely to the differences, not yet quite clear in his mind, between hitting a grown-up, a child, and a bee. He'd had a tendency to strike out at people himself, once; a bad tendency in a man as big as he was. The doctors at the university claimed that he was a bona fide giant; some glandular disorder. He tried to think whether he'd stopped for any reason. He realized he couldn't remember what they'd been saying, and he concentrated.

"Aunt Ella," he said firmly, when he'd caught the thread, "the Preacher was upset, that's all. If he'd had time to think he might've done something different. You can't really blame him. Then too, he was protecting his wife. He might have had better sense if it was just himself."

"She's a vixen besides," Darthamae said. "You know what she does if he doesn't do every last thing she asks him to? I know people that's friends with her . . ."

Aunt Ella wasn't interested. "Man seven foot tall can handle a flabby little hussy."

"Now Aunt Ella," Leon said, "she's no hussy, and he's not—"

"Seven foot tall and not one inch under or the Lord strike me dead on this spot."

Ralph looked at the ceiling.

Darthamae said, "He may be eight-six for all I know, but that's no help in the bedroom."

Aunt Ella looked around her, shocked at her coming out with it in front of Ralph and Leon. But after she'd thought about it a minute she smiled. She was beginning to like the Preacher's wife.

Darthamae leaned over closer to Aunt Ella. "I wouldn't be a bit surprised if she married him in the first place just to torment him. Betty Jane always was a tease. She'd come to Sundayschool in those white frilly dresses, and she'd smile and smile till every boy for half a mile around had his eye blacked and his clothes torn to pieces fighting for her, and when somebody won, oh *my* but she was cooled! She doesn't really *like* boys, that's my opinion."

Aunt Ella smiled, looking at the baby again, and this time she was conscious of it when she patted him and said, "Bless you." Then she looked back out the window and saw the car. "I want justice," she said fiercely. She clenched both fists. "I just want satisfaction, and not a soul will lift their finger in my behalf!"

"Now Aunt Ella," Leon said, "put on charity."

She drew herself up. "To every thing there is a season, and a time to every purpose under the heaven: a time to be born and a time to die, a time to plant, and a time to pluck up that which is planted."

Darthamae's eyes widened. "Are you thinking of plucking up the Preacher, Aunt Ella?"

Leon said, "It is better to dwell in the wilderness than with a contentious and an angry woman."

"It is a joy to the just to do judgment," she said, "and destruction shall be to the workers of iniquity." She stood up. She felt more cheerful now. There was nothing she liked better than quoting the Scriptures. Also, she had a plan.

"God help the Preacher," Leon said.

He watched them go out to the car. Ralph got in before her, sliding in back end first, Aunt Ella hanging on to his leg. Then Aunt Ella got in and drove.

2

He wasn't out riding, as she'd somehow expected him to be (though it was dark). He was sitting at the round table in the diningroom, writing. He was less than six feet from the window she watched through, and she put off knocking. It was the first really good look at him she'd gotten. The light over the table was the only one they had on in the house, as near as she could tell from the porch. His wife must have gone to bed. He had on a clean blue workshirt with the sleeves rolled up, and horn-rimmed glasses she'd never seen on him before. There were papers scattered all over the table, and books lying open. He'd been at it for a long time, she could see, and the way he was working—writing a sentence, reading a page from one of the books, writing two more words, scowling and chewing on his pencil, reading some more—she knew he was going to be at it for a while yet. Working on next Sunday's sermon, she guessed. His sermons were humdingers, that was the truth. They could make you perspire.

He was a nice-looking preacher, really. He was tall as a stalk of fieldcorn, though not as tall as Leon, of course. He had big broad shoulders and a chest like a stove; nice tanned skin; a handsome face with a cleft in the chin. It wasn't a weak face or the usual kind of liar's face (Aunt Ella trusted her judgment in these matters), and it wasn't the face of a stupid person. The face of a young man too tall for his grade all the length of his childhood, a mother's pride and joy too often praised—for his voice, a big bass voice that could fill the whole church; for his marks in school; for his hearing the call of the Lord; for his height and for his weird gray-blue eyes, and for the lock that fell over his forehead, suspiciously casual, from his otherwise straight hair.

"What's he doing?" Ralph whispered, just audible over the

clicking of the crickets and the rustle of the maple leaves.

"I don't know," she whispered. "Writing something."

"Oh," he said.

"*Shhh!*"

The Preacher put down his pencil and got up. He arched his back and stretched, pulling his chin into his neck. Then he picked up the cup from beside his papers on the table and walked toward the kitchen. When he reached the door Aunt Ella heard the Preacher's wife calling, "You coming to bed, Bill?"

He looked cross. "Pretty soon, honey," he said. He was too far away for her to see his features clearly.

His wife's voice said, "All you care about is your preachin."

"Now Betty Jane, that's not so."

She said nothing more, and his blurry shape stood undecided. He went on standing in the doorway a long while, his hands around the cup, but then at last he went into the kitchen.

"What's he doing?" Ralph asked.

"Shh." She raised one finger to her lips. "Gone for some coffee."

Ralph tried to get closer, to help her watch, but the porch wasn't wide enough—not a proper porch at all but a concrete square with wrought-iron ornamental supports on each side and a roof over it. He couldn't get both crutches up onto it at once, and when he did he couldn't get his feet on it right. He stood with one crutch on the cement and one in the grass, hovering precariously between them like a beetle with some of its legs missing.

The Preacher came back in and set the cup on the table. He stood a minute listening for something more from the bedroom, then pulled out his chair and brushed his hair back and sat down. It was true, Aunt Ella reflected, uneasy at heart, that the Preacher was a worker. It was a piece of luck when a country church like the Ebenezer Baptist got a man like that.

Mostly they either got old men that ought to be retired years ago or young men not smart enough to get called to a church in town. Why he'd come had been a puzzle to them all until the day that horse appeared. *Then* they knew. Pretty soon he'd put up a white fence made out of boards and had barrels for the horse to run between. You might have seen him riding along anywhere between here and the other side of Cobden. But she had to be fair, the Preacher got his work done. He put on the best weddings the church had ever seen, and he went and prayed with the sick and decrepit, and he built up church attendance till they hardly knew what to do with the offering. If he had his way, they'd be putting up a new brick church before long, and he'd probably fill it, too.

He looked like no more than an overgrown boy, she thought, feeling still more uneasy. She'd looked after she didn't know how many young ones just like him—but not so tall. She could see as well as Leon James how he must have felt, that first minute, when his wife came in and told him she'd run some old lady off the road, maybe sent her to Glory. Maybe if Ed Hume and the Howard boy had believed her when she told them the truth, if they'd gone along with him only because he was the Preacher, knowing all he said was lies . . .

"Aunt Ella," Ralph whispered.

"Hush," she said.

"Aunt Ella, I'm cold," he said. He was shaking like a leaf, trying to balance on the crutches and hug himself.

"Won't be long now," she said. She was about to knock. She stood with her fist raised near the door, hesitating not from curiosity now but because she wasn't sure she wanted to go through with it. That very second the Preacher's wife came in from the bedroom. Quickly, Aunt Ella got in front of the window again so Ralph wouldn't see.

The Preacher's wife had nothing on but a pale blue nightgown that didn't hide one thing. She came over and stood beside him, with one hand on the nape of his neck, and she said very sweetly, "Billy?"

Just then, like a house tipping over, Ralph fell down. Aunt Ella got her face back out of the window as quick as she could and knocked at the door. She got a glimpse of the Preacher's wife running for the bedroom. Ralph couldn't get up.

The Preacher was white as a sheet when he came to the door. "Who is it?" he said. He bent down a ways, squinting, holding his glasses in his two hands.

"Ella Reikert," she said. "I'm sorry to call so late."

"Good evening," the Preacher said. He looked past her. "Evening, Brother Ralph."

"Evening," Ralph said. He was trying to pull himself up on the crutches. His mouth was twisted all out of shape from the effort, and his eyes were crossed, but he made a quick snatch at his hatbrim.

The Preacher said, "Won't you come in?" He showed Aunt Ella into the parlor, and when Ralph didn't come he went outside to help. When finally they were all sitting down, Aunt Ella said, "I owe you an apology, Brother Flood. I ought not to been so stubborn."

The Preacher smiled, but a trifle vaguely, looking at his interlocked fingers. "We all make mistakes," he said.

She studied him.

He said with more spirit, "Leg giving you any discomfort, Ralph?" Just talking he sounded more musical than the basses in the choir when they sang.

"I'm all right," Ralph said. "Your wife did it." He shaped the words with extreme care, and every one of them came out clearly. When he finished he smiled with pleasure and crossed his eyes on purpose.

"I was sinfully proud," Aunt Ella said. "Better is the end of a thing than the beginning thereof, and the patient in spirit is better than the proud in spirit."

"Well, then too," the Preacher said, smiling kindly, "our eyes play tricks on us."

Again, longer this time, she studied him. That man was truly obstinate. His neck was an iron sinew and his brow was brass. Except that it was worse than just stubbornness; it was as though he was an invisible man and could do whatever he pleased against her. If one of them was blind or confused or crotchety, if one of them was slipping back into petulant childish fibbing, it had to be her. She wondered in sudden panic if even Leon and Darthamae believed her. "Put on charity," he'd said. Well enough for *him*. You could choose to step on an ant or not, but the ant had no say about it. No sir! She was shaking so badly she had to keep her hands folded.

Ralph said something neither of them caught and began to say it again more slowly, but Aunt Ella interrupted. She felt a rush of wicked pleasure the instant she knew she was actually going to say it. "That's not what we came here to talk about, Brother Flood. I'm here to see about buying your palomino horse."

His eyebrows went up, and a second later he laughed. "Sister Reikert, that horse is worth two hundred dollars."

"I'm willing to pay, if I look at him and see it's fair."

Now it was the Preacher's turn to do the squinting. "Golly," he said finally, "I'm sorry, Sister. I'm really not thinking of selling him. Star's like one of the family." He laughed again.

"Well, you think about it," she said. "Call me if you change your mind."

"I'm afraid that's not likely," the Preacher said.

And so it was done, or would be done pretty soon now. She felt light, as though she were sitting in empty air. She said, "Ralph, we better go home now." Ralph opened his mouth and eyes wide, reaching over the chair arms for his crutches. And so they left.

At the door the Preacher said, puzzled-looking, "What did you want him for, Sister Reikert?"

"Oh, you know how it is," she said. She took Ralph's right elbow, jutting out from the crutch. "Evening, Brother Flood."

He seemed to consider, then nodded.

When he closed the door Aunt Ella took a quick look in through the window. Already the Preacher's wife Betty Jane was coming from the bedroom, but things were different now. She had on a heavy brown bathrobe and her hair was in pink plastic curlers. It wasn't hard to see Brother Flood was in trouble for sitting up all that while while she was waiting.

Six rods down the road, a third of the way to her own house, Aunt Ella stopped the car and turned off the lights, and Ralph got out. She watched him hobble through the tall grass and apple trees toward the Preacher's horse-barn, the other side of the graveyard. In fifteen minutes Ralph was back.

"I feel ten years younger," Aunt Ella said thoughtfully, smiling at her reflection in the cracked windshield.

"Yes'm," Ralph said, scrunched down level with the dash, ducking the low roof on his side. The horse had stepped on his good foot, and he believed the toe was broken, which it was.

3

"There's just no satisfaction," Aunt Ella said. That was three days later, at Leon's. The baby was sitting on the floor cooing, picking up a soupspoon and putting it down again, and the big part-collie dog was sitting opposite, looking at him with his head tilted and his ears straight up. Ralph sat half-heartedly watching them, the crutches lying in his lap, the broken leg going out to his right, the leg with the broken toe going out to his left. He was sunk in gloom, but sometimes he would remember to lean down toward the child, the muscles of his face contorting with the effort, and say "Boo!" The child showed a hint of a smile.

Leon said, "What happened?" He wished Darthamae

would come in from the pumps (she was filling up Leonard Avery's dumptruck). He hated to be the only one to hear what Aunt Ella had done. She was Darthamae's relative, after all; he only called her "aunt" the way other people did, because after all those years of her nursing people and taking care of children while their mothers worked (with Ralph at her heels, forever wailing "Aunt Ella! Aunt Ella!") it had turned into part of her name. It was Darthamae's responsibility more than his. She ought to be hearing it anyway, because it was something.

It was the old gypsy pea trick, and if the Preacher had just called in Doc Coombs, the way other people did, and not some real veterinarian from town, it would never have worked. ("The Lord resisteth the proud," said Aunt Ella.) It ought to have taken at least three days, but the Preacher was hasty as well as proud. The vet gave the horse a shot of tranquilizer, and when he was wiping off the needle, he said, "I hate to tell you, Reverend, but your horse has gone crazy." Even after the tranquilizer had taken effect, the horse went on jerking his head up and down and rolling his eyes back, trying to get the pea out of his ear. ("I'd rather have given him spavins," Aunt Ella said. "You can run a piece of his tail's hair between the two bones in his foreleg and clip off the ends. You'd swear he was crippled for life, but then you measure up and take that hair out and he's just as good as ever, sometimes improved. That's what I'd done if I wasn't worried Ralph would measure wrong and we'd never find the hair.")

It took the Preacher about fifteen minutes to get down to Aunt Ella and say he'd thought it over and maybe he'd let his horse go after all. He'd had some unexpected expenses.

"Vetinary bills?" Aunt Ella said. Inside, she was jumping up and down with glee. She felt ten years old again. She felt the way she'd felt the time she broke out all the schoolhouse windows, seventy years ago now. After a while she talked the Preacher into driving her up for a look at the horse. He was asleep in the stall—he had enough tranquilizer in him to kill any ordinary horse. The Preacher said he'd been riding him hard all morning. "Hmm," Aunt Ella said. She opened up the horse's eye. It could have been perfectly normal, for all she knew. But she squinted at the Preacher and said, "Well, I can give you twelve dollars." He looked like she'd knocked all the wind out of him, and for a minute she was sure he'd had a heart attack, and she was going to have some explaining to do to Leon and Cousin Gordon. He said, "What are you talking about?" She thought a minute, or pretended to (looking up at the new-timber rafters above the stall, and the hay that lay in the shaft of sunlight, as green as dry evergreen boughs). "Well then, fourteen," she said. "I can't stand dickering." He looked like she'd whipped him in front of his playmates. Finally he said, "All right." He was so mad he could hardly talk. She followed him into the house and paid him, and that night she took the pea out and walked the horse down to her place and staked him in the yard like a goat.

"Surely you gave the horse back to him later," Darthamae said—standing at Aunt Ella's elbow now. She still had Leonard Avery's money in her hand.

"Certainly not," Aunt Ella said. "I sold him for glue."

"You what?" Darthamae said.

Leon said, "A two-hundred-dollar riding horse?"

"I needed the money," Aunt Ella said, pouting. "And he owed it to me, for the expense of fixing Ralph's toe."

"They don't *take* horses for glue anymore," Leon said.

"Down at Elizabethtown they do."

"That's seventy miles."

"Well, Bobby Hume drove us down in the truck," Aunt Ella said. "It was the only decent thing to do. It wouldn't be right to make a profit off it." She folded her hands.

Darthamae leaned her knuckles on the table. "Aunt Ella," she said seriously, "you've committed a crime. Do you know that?"

"Judge not that ye be not judged," Aunt Ella said.

"You tell the jury that," Darthamae said.

But Leon was gazing up at the fan, musing. At last he said, "And you still weren't satisfied? Aunt Ella, how can that be?"

She slapped the table. "That man had *in*surance," she said. "Now you tell me, Leon James, would a man that trusted in the Lord go out buying *in*surance?"

"The Lord helps those that help themselves," Leon said.

She scowled, the palsy moving her head. "Lay not up for yourselves treasures on earth, where rust corrupts, and thieves break in and steal."

"The poor is hated even of his own neighbor," Leon said, "but the rich hath many friends."

"Be strong, fear not," Aunt Ella said, "the Lord will come with a vengeance, even God with a recompense."

Leon couldn't think of one.

After a minute Aunt Ella said, "Not only that, the congregation's buying that man a new riding horse. They had a meeting last night. There's no justice this side of heaven."

"Well now that beats everything," Darthamae said. She straightened up, shocked (also, she hadn't been informed of the meeting, and she couldn't think who would have done it to her). It was easy to see she was inclining to Aunt Ella's side. The dog was trying to bite off a string from Ralph's cast, and Ralph was wincing. The baby was hitting at Ralph's other foot with the soupspoon.

Aunt Ella sat with her hands folded and her lips closed flat. At last she said, "Well, I got a plan."

4

Sunday was the Preacher's hardest day, with two sermons in the morning and another one at night, so at first, above and beyond any suspicions he may have had about Aunt Ella, he wasn't sure he could accept her invitation. She'd thought he might speak of her breaking the Sabbath, but if that ever entered his mind he kept from mentioning it. She liked him for that. There was no surer sign of small-mindedness, in Aunt Ella's opinion, than a love of the letter of the law. His religion had imagination in it: she'd seen that the first time she'd heard him preach. It made your heart light, it was all so fine. When he spoke of the fires of torment it was purest poetry. It was by means of the Preacher's imagination she intended to undo him.

Even though Sunday was his hardest day, he'd decided to come, in the end. As she'd known he would. She'd merely waited him out, sitting at the telephone table with the phone in her left hand and the receiver in her right, looking up over the rims of her glasses at the velvet sign over the calendar, BLESS THIS HOUSE. She'd said merely, "You have to harvest the grapes when the Lord sees fit to send them, Brother Flood." She saw the marker ribbons coming out of the limp old Bible on the table before her and was inspired to add, "I knew you'd be interested in how we do it, for your understanding of the Lord's Word. But of course it's true, a Sunday's your hardest day."

She gave him a show. She was out to undo him, but she wasn't going to be small about it. She normally set up the grape press on the kitchen sink and the bottle-capping machine on the kitchen table, but this time she moved the press and capper out to the barn and built a kind of platform for them and nailed up a two-by-four frame around them like a booth at the fair or an immersion closet, to make it all more impressive. When it still looked small she nailed a board against the wall and put hooks on it, and built another little platform and put a washtub on that: instead of using the same straining sack over and over, as anyone would normally do, she'd use ten different sacks and wash each one out and hang it up to dry after every use. It might ruin the grapejuice—she wasn't sure—but it made the operation something to look at. He'd appreciate that.

Since Brother Flood came to Ebenezer Baptist, the worship had gotten so complicated they had to write down the directions on a program. After that she swept the barn floor till you could eat off it and brought in a table and some kitchen chairs and some glasses. The morning of the day the Preacher was to come she drove into Cobden and hired some drunkards from the Appleton Hotel, and then she drove back to teach her Sundayschool class and invited the girls to come over to her place right after lunch and join in the grapejuice making. A little after noon, after she'd put them all to work (and shortly after the Preacher had arrived), she got the Preacher to drive her down to Cobden again, for the parable's sake, and hired herself two more drunkards.

When they got back, the place was humming like a hive, and if you didn't know better you'd have sworn it was a real operation. The drunkards were all sweating like they hadn't sweated in three, four years, walking around bumping into each other, slipping into the shade of the burdocks sometimes for a pull at the bottles they'd brought, getting more cheerful and more dignified as the day wore on, sometimes missing the grapes completely and snipping off the vine instead, sometimes tipping their wheelbarrows over or falling off the plank coming into the barn. One of them was already asleep, lying under the wagon in the corner. Two of the girls from Aunt Ella's class ran the press, one cranking, one stirring sugar in, and two more ran the capper. Most of the sacks hung on the wall drying, getting bits of straw and cobweb on them. The Preacher's wife sat with Ralph and three of the girls at the table. She had on her white hat and gloves.

The Preacher stopped in the doorway and put his hands on his hips and looked at it all. He still had on his black Sunday suit. He was a happy man. He could understand the drunkard problem. In this day and age, you took what hired labor you could find. When Aunt Ella finished her explanation of the work she gazed worriedly at the four rows of grapevines, picked clean a good half hour ago, and said, "We may need more men before sunset." "Mmm," the Preacher said. He too was worried. "I can drive you back to Cobden if you think—" "We'll wait and see," she said. And now it was time. She said, "Shall we try a taste?" He would like that very much. She led him to the table.

The crockery jug stood behind the door, right where she'd hidden it. She caught it up and carried it over to the wooden tub under the press. She turned the spigot. Her hands were beginning to shake again; her head too. At the look of mysterious joy on her face, Carol Ann Bowen, standing by the press, was startled.

She let about two cups of juice run in, then turned off the spigot and swirled the jug a time or two to mix the juice and the gin. She went back to the table and poured a glass for the Preacher and one for his wife. She watched him taste it, suspecting it tasted like hell's last torment, and for a second she was sure it was all up. The Preacher lowered his eyebrows, disappointed, but before he could speak his wife said, "Say, that's *good*." Her glass was empty. The Preacher took another swallow, and he liked it better this time. "It waters your eyes," he said. "It's not at all what I expected." Aunt Ella said she wasn't surprised. She carried back the empty jug and filled it with plain juice and poured glasses for Ralph and the girls and the four drunkards she'd been able to persuade. Then she slipped back into the sheepfold for more gin. When she poured the second glass for the Preacher and his wife they hardly noticed she was there. The Preacher was speaking slowly and thoughtfully of friendship versus brotherhood. He could say he felt love for Aunt Ella, for instance, yet in all honesty he didn't believe she felt actually *friendly* toward him, in the ordinary sense. He looked up at her sadly. *She* would understand what he meant. And yet she could see the position he was in. A man made certain moves, with certain intentions, and these moves had certain results, if she followed his thought. . . .

One of the drunkards who'd been out in the burdocks patted the Preacher's shoulder, leaning on him a little. Things were going faster than Aunt Ella had expected.

"Girls," said Aunt Ella, "it's time you all ran home now. You've been a wonderful help, and each of you take a bottle of grapejuice to your mother."

They thanked her, and in a matter of seconds she had them out of there.

She got more juice for the Preacher and his wife and sat down to observe her work. The Preacher was speaking very slowly, very solemnly, of the difference between the love of God and the love of man. His voice was loud, and he winced from time to time, making fine distinctions. His wife gazed deep into Aunt Ella's eyes and brooded. She was a pretty child, Aunt Ella reflected. Perfectly lovely in her blue flowered dress, white hat, white gloves. In spite of the make-up, her face was as soft and innocent as a baby's. She was feeling terribly sad, for some reason, and Aunt Ella's heart went joyfully out to her. She smiled, and as if the girl had been waiting for that sign, she spoke.

"Why do they all call you *Aunt* Ella?" she asked.

"Oh, you know how it is," Aunt Ella said. "After all these years—"

The girl burst into tears and clutched Aunt Ella's hand. "Yes," she said. "Yes! Oh, beautiful, *beautiful!*" Aunt Ella returned the girl's grip and felt somewhat uneasy. The girl leaned her head onto her arm (carefully slipping her hat off first, for fear of spoiling it) and let the tears run, still clinging to Aunt Ella's hand. The Preacher rubbed the small of his wife's back while he spoke to Ralph and the drunkard about the inability of women to love, truly love, God for Himself. He could mention certain situations—*they* would know pretty well what he meant—in which a man and a woman stood in a certain relationship to one another and to certain matters of an *exterior* kind . . .

"Yes," Ralph said, squinting, working his mouth. His eyes lit up, and it hit Aunt Ella like a thunderbolt that Ralph was drinking straight gin. "Yes," he said. "Yes!"

"Good heavens," Aunt Ella said, "the evening service starts in twenty minutes!" She started to get up, but Betty Jane Flood was still holding her hand.

"Aunt Ella," she said, "could *you* learn to love *me*?"

5

He stood, his head and shoulders lowered, filling up her doorway like the Angel of Death, in his solemn black coat and hat. It was an awesome sight: beyond him there was still red, and the smell of smoke was sharp as brimstone in her nostrils. He had on his steel-rimmed glasses, and there was a smudge mark on his cheek. "*Now* are you satisfied?" he said.

"Leon James," she said, shaking her finger, "if I burned that church may the Lord strike me dead on this spot!"

"Hah!" he said, curling his lip in his righteous scorn. But the next second he was unsure of himself. She was shaking badly, and there were still signs of her nervous crying. When he came into the kitchen his look of terrible avenger was gone; he looked merely large and foolish. Darthamae came in behind him carrying the baby. The screendoor shut with a clap as Darthamae stepped away from it, and Aunt Ella had a brief, surprisingly clear view of the sky, black with smoke, and, against the mountain, the embers of the church. It all made her think of a Biblical engraving.

"Don't slam the door, Darthamae," she said, knowing it was unnecessary, the bang of the screen would be enough to remind her. Darthamae shut the door without a sound, the way she'd done as a little girl coming over on a Sunday afternoon.

The baby was wide-eyed and watchful, as always. When Aunt Ella clucked at it, it smiled.

"All right," Leon said, "what happened?" He slid his hat onto the kitchen table and sat down. Before she answered she went to the toy room and brought back a plastic duck for the baby. Darthamae put him down on the floor. Ralph was still on the couch in the parlor, out.

"Well," Aunt Ella said finally, "he was drunk."

"What?" Darthamae said.

Leon said, "Go on." His eyebrows sagged like the lines at the sides of his mouth.

"We made grapejuice today." She stopped. "Would you care for some grapejuice?" They wouldn't.

And so she told them how she'd hired some drunkards, since she wasn't as young as she'd use to be and Ralph was laid up, and how unbeknownst to her they'd brought liquor with them and one way or another the Preacher had gotten ahold of something, and his poor wife too, and when he'd gone up to the church for the evening service he'd been so bad he'd forgotten his car. It was still out there in the driveway; they must have seen it.

Leon could see how it had been, pretty well, but he kept his suspicions to himself. "He did the evening service drunk?" he asked. He could see how that must have been, too. All those people who admired him so much—who'd take his side against even Aunt Ella, who'd passed the hat to buy him a new horse and negate the power of Aunt Ella's vengeance—all those people would gradually have understood there was something wrong, he wasn't himself. Darthamae's sister, sitting at the organ prim as a pincushion, would be one of the first to catch the scent, and then the ushers would have caught it, bringing up the offering plates, and soon the choir would have smelled it too. And all the while his speech would be getting more labored, his gestures slower, the pauses for emphasis longer and longer, until somebody whispered, and then someone else:

"He's drunk!" It might be that minute or it might be days later that it would occur to them that maybe Aunt Ella had been telling the truth. If a preacher could take to drink—there was no telling.

But Aunt Ella was shaking her head, staring at the center of the table. "No he didn't," she said. "Not a soul in that whole church saw him, far's I know."

Leon mused, studying her. "How unsearchable are His judgments," he said. "His ways are past finding out."

"Leon," Darthamae warned.

Aunt Ella said calmly, "There's no satisfaction."

"What happened, Aunt Ella?" Darthamae said.

She and Ralph had driven up the hill right behind where the Preacher and his wife were walking. They walked with their arms around one another's waists. Her dark hair fell to the middle of her back. She'd forgotten her hat. When they got to the churchyard most of the cars were there already, and most of the people were waiting inside. There were two or three older boys on the porch, and they waved at the Preacher and his wife when they saw them, and the Preacher and his wife waved back. They walked on toward the rear of the church—the Preacher had to get into his robe—and Aunt Ella pulled the car up under a maple tree and parked. She left Ralph in the car. She couldn't have him seen that way, and yet she hadn't dared leave him home alone either. He didn't mind staying. In fact when she said, "You stay here, Ralph," he never answered. She walked along the side of the church, keeping to the shadows by the graveyard fence.

When the Preacher had his hand on the knob of the narrow back door, he paused a moment and looked at his wife. (She saw all this more or less clearly. She was too far away to see what kind of expressions they had—for which she was grateful: she was old, and such things could be tiresome—but the light over the door was on, making their figures unnaturally sharp against the drab white of the church. She could see as much as she'd have seen at any other time.) After he'd thought about it first, he leaned down and kissed her. Aunt Ella looked away, and when she looked back again they were hugging. She felt pleased for an instant, thinking it was she who had brought them together, had made them see by the simplest and most ancient of tricks how trivial, really, were all the eternal differences between women and men—not differences of wish at all, mere differences of pride. The next instant she remembered she was here for vengeance, and she felt confused and unhappy. When she looked again the Preacher's wife was looking at the moon and the Preacher had gone inside. For a time there was no sign of him. Then she saw him going past the window with his robe on and his hands out in front of him, holding something. She couldn't see what he was holding, and yet she knew, instantly, even before she was aware of the glow high on the window. He was carrying a lighted candelabrum, just like a Catholic. It seemed to her now that she'd understood from that first second what was going to happen. She went for the church as fast as her stiff knees would carry her, and by the time the people in the front started shouting she was already in the hallway, the Preacher's wife beside her, and they were dragging him away from the burning drapes and toward the back door.

"What will we do?" the girl was yelling. She seemed to believe he was dead already, and it made her cold sober.

There was no time to think, certainly no time to unscramble the confusion of her feelings about them, but Aunt Ella knew for certain it wasn't anything like this she'd intended for the Preacher and his wife. "Get him over in the weeds," she said. And so, each of them pulling one leg, they dragged him into the high weeds by the graveyard fence, and she told the girl to stay there with him, out of sight. "Aunt Ella," she said, "do you think he'll be all right?" "Don't be silly," she said, "he hasn't hurt a hair of his head. You just stay here."

And so the Preacher's wife stayed, lying in the weeds with

her arms around him (and Aunt Ella could guess what would come of that, too). Aunt Ella went back to her car.

By that time the whole inside was afire, and she woke up Ralph, because it was something he wouldn't want to miss. There were people running around every which way, throwing buckets of water on the outside walls and running back to the well in front, and there were boys pushing cars back out of the way, and lights going on in the house across the road, the Poleham place, and Lucy Poleham yelling, "Ma, you better put some cocoa on!" It had come to Aunt Ella suddenly, like a thundering voice out of heaven: *The Preacher's going to get his new brick church.*

"Aunt Ella," Darthamae said, "you've really gone far enough. You've got to stop now."

She was so serious Aunt Ella couldn't meet her eyes.

"Think, Aunt Ella," Leon said, and he too was so serious she felt like a scolded child. "Suppose somebody'd gotten killed in that fire. You want a thing like that on your conscience?"

"*I* never started that fire," she said. But she knew herself how feeble it was. She remembered standing in the woodshed, infinitely long ago, her father towering above her scolding her though she was already sorry and helplessly miserable and too small to make him stop. (What had she done, that time? She tried to remember. It wouldn't come. Perhaps it was the time she'd murdered the cat.) *You get old*, she thought, *and you go into your second childhood.* And maybe that was all it had been from the beginning. She had a feeling she'd be crying in a minute. A feeble old woman, nobody left that cared about her, nobody to lift a finger in her behalf. She folded her hands tightly and clamped her lips.

Darthamae said softly, looking at her in a motherly way which so outraged Aunt Ella she wanted to scream, but a way which was insidiously comforting as well, "Fighting's no real answer, Aunt Ella. That's what you always used to tell us yourself."

"It was *her*," Aunt Ella said. "I told them and told them." Again she saw clearly—more clearly than she'd seen anything for the last fifteen years—the Howard boy looking down at the dirt, moving a pebble with the side of his boot, waiting patiently for her to give up. The sky was deep blue and enormous behind him, falling away over the blue of the hills toward Kentucky. It was as though neither of them could hear her— neither the Preacher nor the Howard boy—they merely stood on their side of the glass and saw her shaking her finger and stamping her foot. She said again, violently, "It was *her*, Leon." Tears blinded her.

"You want them to put her in prison?" Leon said. "Aunt Ella, is *that* what you want?"

She was confused, hounded half to her grave. "If preachers commence to bear false witness, what's to become of the world?"

"You've got to stop brooding on it," Leon said. "You're supposed to be a Christian woman. You act like the kind of Christian wants to burn somebody."

And this time it was Darthamae who did it, the only verse she knew. "Aunt Ella," she said, "remember what you taught us? 'Whatsoever things are true, whatsoever things are honest, whatsoever things are pure, whatsoever things are just, whatsoever things are lovely, whatsoever things are of good report; if there be any virtue, and if there be any praise—think on these things.' "

Tears streamed down Aunt Ella's cheeks. "That's wrong," she said. "The *just* comes before the *pure*."

It checked her for only an instant. "All the same," Darthamae said. She took Aunt Ella's hand. "All the same."

For two minutes Aunt Ella cried and Darthamae held her hand. While she cried, it all seemed clear to her: she didn't want the Preacher's wife in prison, of course not, nothing of the kind. She wanted her to be happy, have children, be a good preacher's wife. And she wanted good for the Preacher too. They ought to *know* that, hadn't she wanted good for people all her life? But she wanted vengeance, it was right.

Leon said, "Aunt Ella, you need to get some sleep. Let's talk about it later."

After a minute Darthamae helped her up and they went down the long hall to the bedroom off the parlor, and Darthamae helped her into bed, still in her clothes.

"Why couldn't he just have apologized?" Aunt Ella said.

"Shh!" Darthamae said, lifting her finger to her lips. The instant before she snapped out the light, she stood smiling kindly, for all the world like some gentle aunt of half a century ago, and Aunt Ella felt in the same rush of emotion loved and crushed. The light went off then. But inside Aunt Ella's head the light had come on at last, a radiant joy like revelation: she knew what she had done wrong.

6

When Aunt Ella woke up in the morning, Darthamae was still in the house. Leon had gone home, and the baby with him. Darthamae offered to comb Aunt Ella's hair for her, and Aunt Ella thanked her meekly and got up. Her knees were so stiff she could hardly walk, but she refused to be troubled today. The Lord was with her. She sat still in front of the dresser mirror, deliciously conscious of the lightness of Darthamae's combing, and she tried to think how old Darthamae was, whether she was old enough to remember when the yellow-white hair had been red. Darthamae began to roll the bun and slip in the amber pins. All quickly, quickly.

"I've been thinking," Darthamae said.

Aunt Ella looked at Darthamae's face in the mirror and waited.

"About Brother Flood," Darthamae said. "It doesn't really matter that he won't admit what he did. That is, it doesn't hurt *us*."

Aunt Ella smiled docilely and waited.

"And of course it *does* hurt *him*, you know? I mean, how can his wife respect him, knowing what she does? And how can other people—those of us who know the truth, that is? How can he even respect himself?" Her hands hesitated a moment. She said, "You know, Aunt Ella, I feel sorry for him. Really."

"You're a wise girl for your years," Aunt Ella said, smiling. "Bless you." She felt light as a bluejay, warm and sweet and old as summer fields.

Darthamae's glance was sharp, and Aunt Ella looked down at the dresser doily. "I've been foolish," she said with sincere humility. "Leon was right from the beginning. I should have put on charity."

When she glanced up into the mirror again, Darthamae was looking at her harder than ever.

"Aunt Ella," she said, "I want to know what you're thinking."

"Why, Darthamae!" she protested sweetly. Outside her window there were butterflies playing over the grass. The lightest of them was not as light as she was.

"I *warn* you, Aunt Ella," Darthamae said. She clenched her teeth.

Ralph moaned, in the parlor, and Darthamae went to him. His head was splitting, poor boy. Aunt Ella thought sadly, *Poor Ralph, poor dear child*. It was Ralph who'd gotten the worst of it, right from the start. It was all her fault, and no one else's. And the greatest of these is charity. Yes. Oh yes.

"Ralph's got a headache, Aunt Ella," Darthamae said. "What should I do?"

"It's going to be all right," she said. "There's aspirin in the medicine closet in the bathroom." On second thought she said, "Perhaps if you run cold water over his head it will help. Run it for three, four minutes." As soon as Darthamae was gone she got up, still light, despite the sharp pains in her knees, found her cane in the closet, and went as quickly as she could out onto the porch. Slowly, slowly (and yet quickly, for all that, borne aloft on the mighty wings of charity), she slipped around to the barn.

The white hat was right where Betty Jane Flood, poor dear, had left it, hanging on the chair. She made her way back to the corner of the house with it and stood there a moment, head cocked craftily, listening. When she heard water running, she hurried as fast as she could to the Preacher's car and got herself up in behind the steering wheel. Merely by releasing the emergency brake she was able to back the car fifteen feet down the driveway. She got out and planted the white hat on the ground beside the driver's door. Then she went back in the house, listened at the door, then went in and sat down by the window, meek as a dove, to watch. She heard Darthamae helping Ralph to his bed.

At lunchtime Darthamae said, "Aren't you going to eat, Aunt Ella?"

"No thank you, dear," she said. (Outside there were swallows, light as feathers blowing.)

Darthamae stood thinking, her forehead troubled. "You just keep looking out the window," she said.

"I'm praying," Aunt Ella said, smiling sweetly. "You run along and eat."

Darthamae said, "Are you praying *for* somebody or *against?*"

"Have charity, child," Aunt Ella said. "Do unto others . . ."

She pretended to be satisfied.

It was midafternoon when Aunt Ella saw the Preacher walking down from the manse for his car. Darthamae was in the kitchen cleaning beet greens. Aunt Ella got up as quietly as possible and went out onto the porch and down, slowly, to the driveway. He hadn't yet seen her, though she made no effort at secretiveness, knowing the Lord watched over her. Six feet behind the car, on a span she'd backed over earlier, she smoothed the pebbles away and eased herself down onto her back. It wasn't as comfortable as she'd expected. She closed her eyes, and stretched one arm out awkwardly in a gesture oddly humble, like a broken wing. It seemed a long time before she heard his footsteps coming up the drive, the sound loud under her ear, far away, then closer and closer. Perhaps ten feet from where she lay, the footsteps stopped. She resisted the urge to peek. He'd be looking at the car, his heart beating slightly faster now—poor dear, poor dear!—remembering it wasn't where he'd parked it. Now he would have seen the hat. Now he came closer, his feet moving very slowly, his reeling wits knowing without any need of evidence that she was dead. He whispered, so close that she almost jumped, "My God." Then poor Darthamae was out on the porch, screaming in terror, and the Preacher was exclaiming, "I never saw her. She came out of nowhere. Call Dr. Coombs, quick." They went up on the porch and she waited until the door slammed, then opened her eyes. She couldn't see them or hear what was happening inside, and she could have kicked herself for forgetting to leave that blessed window open. Then she heard the door open again, and she snapped her eyes shut tight. It was Darthamae, running to her, weeping and bending over her. Aunt Ella opened her eyes and winked. Darthamae's face froze, first amazement, then outrage. "Aunt Ella!" she whispered. But by the very act of whispering she'd turned herself into an accomplice. Aunt Ella closed her eyes. "I called Leon," Darthamae whispered. "And we called Doc Coombs, too. And the sheriff. Oh, Aunt Ella, *really!*" Aunt Ella said nothing.

Then the Preacher was with her. Darthamae said, "Don't touch her! Wait for the doctor!"

"My God," the Preacher said.

Darthamae said, "What will we do with Betty Jane's hat?"

He said again, as though his voice were stuck, "My God."

"It was bad enough when she ran Aunt Ella off the road," Darthamae said, "but *this*."

"God," he said.

There was a long silence. Then Darthamae said, "Why don't we just hide her?" She began to speak more rapidly. "We could stuff her under some hay in the barn."

He moaned.

"The poor thing," Darthamae said. "Your wife, I mean. How will she ever *live* with it?" Suddenly she was laughing wildly and Aunt Ella opened her eyes for a moment. But he thought it was hysterics.

"You mustn't tell it was her," the Preacher said. "She's only a child."

"That's right, we've got to lie for her," Darthamae said eagerly. Again the laughing took her. She loved it all—sinfully. Poor child, God forgive her.

Then Aunt Ella heard the siren, far away, and almost the same instant another sound that she couldn't identify for a second. It came to her at last. The door banged shut. She thought, *No*, knowing the rest already. She opened her eyes. She saw them looking toward the porch, and she heard the crutches hurrying toward the steps. "Ralph, be careful!" Darthamae yelled. But it was too late. They listened to the racket of his fall. *There's no satisfaction*, Aunt Ella thought. She sighed.

Now the police car was turning into the yard. Half from weariness of heart, Aunt Ella went on lying where she was. She heard the Preacher explaining to the deputy, "I never knew she was there till I felt the bump."

At last Aunt Ella opened her eyes and, little by little, shaking from the exertion of it, sat up. Ralph, too, was sitting up, over by the steps. Up the hill toward the burned-down church she saw the Preacher's wife running between the tombstones in a white dress, coming down to see what was happening. They too had seen her by now. And now they saw that Aunt Ella was sitting up, dusting off her hands and the sleeves of her dress. The Preacher stared. After a second he came over to her. Behind where the deputy's car was parked, Leon's car was just turning in.

"How could you?" the Preacher whispered, astounded.

Then the deputy was looking at her, and Leon was beside him.

"Aunt Ella," Leon said. She had made him old before his time.

"What a childish thing to do," the Preacher whispered. He was sweating.

"Of such is the kingdom of heaven," she said.

"It's mean and spiteful, that's all there is to it," the Preacher said. He was pale as a ghost.

"Do onto others as you would have others do onto you," she said smugly, knowing it was smug and feeling delighted about it.

"Terrible is thy wrath, O Lord," Leon said.

"It wasn't wrath," she said. "I did it for his correction, out of pure charity. Bless him."

"I have seen Thy mercy, show me then Thy thunder, O Lord," said Leon.

"What's going on here," the Howard boy said.

Darthamae said, "Someone should help poor Ralph."

Ralph was looking sadly up the hill toward the graveyard.

"Cheer up," Leon said, "he's going to inherit the earth."

VLEMK
THE BOX-PAINTER

1

There once was a man who made pictures on boxes. Snuff boxes, jewel boxes, match boxes, cigar boxes, whatever kinds of boxes people used in that country, for keeping their treasures in or giving as presents to friends and loved ones, the people would take their boxes to this man, who was called Vlemk the box-painter—or they'd buy one of the boxes the man had made—and he would paint pictures on them. Though he was not old and stooped, though old enough by several years to grow a moustache and a beard that reached halfway down his chest, he was a master artist, as box-painters go. He could paint a tiny picture of a grandfather's clock that was so accurate in its details that people sometimes thought, listening very closely, that they could make out the noise of its ticking. He painted flowers so precisely like real ones that one would swear that they were moving just perceptibly in the breeze, and swear that, pressing one's nose to the picture, one could detect a faint suggestion of rose smell, or lilac, or foxglove.

As is sometimes the way with extremely good artists, this Vlemk the box-painter was unfortunately not all he might be when it came to matters not pertaining to his art. When he was painting, up in his bright, sunlit studio that looked down over the houses and streets of the city, he was a model of industry and good sense. He kept his brushes, paints, glazes, and thinners as carefully and neatly as a fussy old widow keeps her dishes and spoons, and he worked with the deep concentration of a banker or lawyer studying his books in the hope of growing richer. But when his work was finished, whenever that might be, since sometimes he worked all night, sometimes all day, sometimes for an hour, sometimes for a week and a half without an hour out for rest—this Vlemk changed completely, so that people who had seen him at work would swear now that he was not the same person, surely not even that person's brother, but someone else entirely.

When the artist wasn't working, it was as if some kind of demon got into him. He would go to the tavern at the end of his street, where he talked very loudly and waved his arms wildly, knocking over beerpots and sometimes tipsy old men, and though many people liked him and were interested in his talk, since none of them had the knack of painting pictures as he did, sooner or later he was too much for even the most kindly and sympathetic, and they would call the police or throw him out into the alley by the collar of his shirt and the seat of his trousers. Sometimes he had dealings with unsavory characters, drunkards, pickpockets and pilferers, even a certain murderer who took his axe with him everywhere he went.

The artist was not proud of himself, needless to say. Often, sitting up in his studio high above the city, he would moan and clutch his head between his hands, saying, "Woe is me! Oh, what's to become of me?" But moaning was no solution. As soon as he'd finished his work for that day, or that week, as chance would have it, down he would go into the city again, and his fall to dissolution would be as shameful as before. "What a box I'm in!" he would cry, looking up from the gutter the next morning. It had long been his habit to think in terms of boxes, since boxes were his joy and occupation.

One morning when this happened—that is, as he was crying "What a box I'm in" and struggling to get himself up out of the gutter, where he was lying among bottles, old papers, and the remains of a cat—a carriage was passing, driven by a uniformed man in a top hat. The driver was elegant—when his boots caught the sunlight they shone like polished onyx—and the carriage on which he sat was more elegant still, like a splendid box of black leather and polished golden studs. When the carriage was right alongside the poor artist, a voice cried out "Stop!" and at once the carriage stopped. A small hand parted the window curtains, and a pale white face looked out. "Driver," said the person in the carriage, "who is that unfortunate creature in the gutter?"

"That, I am sorry to say," said the driver, "is the famous box-painter Vlemk."

"Vlemk, you say?" said the person in the carriage. "Surely you're mistaken! I once visited his studio, and I'm certain I'd know him anywhere! That creature in the gutter is some miserable, pitiful wretch without a talent in the world!"

"I assure you, Princess," said the carriage driver sadly, "that the filthy thing you see in the gutter is Vlemk the box-painter."

In horror, Vlemk covered his face with his hands and arms, for now he recognized that the person in the carriage was indeed the Princess, soon to be Queen of the Kingdom, people said, since her mother had been dead for years and her father was declining. Vlemk was so ashamed to be seen by such a person in his present condition that he fervently wished himself dead.

"Shall I throw the poor devil a coin?" asked the driver. "I assure you he can use it, for if rumor be believed he squanders all he earns by his art on his life of dissolution."

"Heavens no!" said the Princess, parting the curtains more widely in order to get a closer look at Vlemk. "What earthly good would a coin do him? He'd spend it on further debauchery!" So saying, she closed the window curtains and ordered the driver to drive off.

"Heartless monster!" cried Vlemk, clumsily rising and staggering a few steps in the direction of the swiftly departing carriage. He was so angry he raised both fists to the sky and shook them.

But secretly, Vlemk did not blame her for her words. All she'd said was true, and if he was wise, he knew, he would thank her for her righteous severity. "Woe is the kingdom," he said to himself, "whose rulers are dismayed by every sniffle." Besides, when she'd parted the curtains wide, he'd gotten a very clear look at her face, and with the force of a knife in the back or an arrow in the chest it had struck him that the Princess was the most beautiful creature he'd ever set eyes on.

When he returned to his studio that day he found he was incapable of painting. His brushes had a malevolent will of their own, dabbing too deeply, as if angrily, into the paints, so that every stroke he made in the picture was slightly off its hit and inefficient, like the work of an amateur, so that he had to wipe it off and start over. By midafternoon he understood that his case was hopeless. He'd lost the will to do perfect paintings of animals or flowers or rural landscapes, paintings of the kind that had made him famous. Indeed, he'd lost the will to paint at all. Carelessly, irritably, he put away his materials, hardly noticing that the brushes were less clean than usual, the paints not well capped, one bottle of thinner tipped sideways and dripping on the floor. "What a box I'm in!" he said, but dully, without feeling.

In the tavern he discovered that nothing the establishment had to offer was exactly what he wanted. The wine, he knew without tasting it, was bitter, the beer too full of froth, the brandy too sugary and thick. "What *is* it I want?" he thought, sitting with his mouth open, hands clasped in front of his chin, eyes rolled upward, staring without interest at the cracks in the old, sagging ceiling. All of the regulars of the tavern threw puzzled, slightly irritable glances in his direction, perplexed at his seeming so unlike himself. By this time, people grumbled, he should be singing, if not kicking up his heels or starting arguments. One might have thought they would be pleased, since Vlemk could be a nuisance when behaving in his normal way, but in general this was not the case. Even the laziest and most base of the regulars—not including three who were all in some sense artists themselves—were simple people who led complicated lives, and Vlemk's disruption of what little routine they could persuade themselves they kept was distressing.

"What *is* it I want?" Vlemk asked over and over, inaudibly, sitting by himself at his table by the window.

"Why doesn't he drink?" grumbled the regulars, or all except the three. "Why doesn't he *do* something?"

The three or, rather, four—the barmaid and three glum men who wore their hats low and went about armed—said nothing, hardly noticing. The flaxen-haired one, formerly a poet, was fast asleep with his eyes open. The one in the glasses, an ex-violinist, was picking the pocket of the laborer just behind him. The third one only stared, like a cat before a mousehole. He was the axe-murderer.

Secretly, of course, Vlemk had known from the beginning what it was that he wanted, and when he came to full awareness of what that something was, he was filled with such misery that he could no longer stay indoors. He rose without a word to anyone, not so much as a glance at the sullen, fat barmaid, and with his hands thrust deep into the pockets of his painter's frock, which in his misery he'd neglected to leave behind in the studio, he walked to the door and, after a moment's hesitation, out onto the street.

He walked quickly, like a man with some urgent purpose, though in fact he had nowhere in particular to go and nothing much in mind. If someone had asked of him the time of day, he would have had to look around to determine that it was evening, almost nightfall. He walked from street to street and from bridge to bridge in this dejected state until, to his surprise, as the last glow of sunset was fading from the clouds, he found himself standing at the gates of the royal palace.

The Princess, as it happened, was at just that moment returning from walking her greyhounds on the palace grounds. At sight of the box-painter, the greyhounds set up a terrific rumpus and jerked fiercely at their leashes in an attempt to get at him and scare him away, with the result that the Princess was drawn, willy-nilly, to where Vlemk stood gazing in morosely at the palace door. When they reached the iron gates between Vlemk and themselves, the dogs leaped and snapped, dancing on their hind feet and lunging at the bars, all to so little avail that the painter hardly noticed. At last, at a word from their mistress, the dogs fell silent, or, rather, fell to whimpering and sniffing and running around in circles. The Princess, cautiously keeping well back lest Vlemk be some dangerous anarchist, leaned forward at the waist and, holding the leashes with one hand, shaded her eyes with the other, trying to make out whether she knew him. Suddenly she gave a start and cried, "Vlemk the box-painter!" Whether or not she had actually recognized him Vlemk could not tell. At very least, she had recognized his frock.

Vlemk sadly nodded. "Yes, Your Highness," he said, "it's Vlemk."

"For heaven's sake what are you doing here?" asked the Princess. "Surely you don't think we give hand-outs!"

"No," said Vlemk, "I have no reason to think that."

"What is it, then?" asked the Princess, a little more kindly.

For a long moment Vlemk said nothing, so sunk in misery that he could barely draw a breath. At last he pulled himself together and said: "I will tell you the truth, since then at least I will have it off my chest. It's not that I expect any good to come of it."

"Very well," said the Princess, and abruptly, as if at a premonition, dropped her gaze and went slightly pale.

"I have come," said Vlemk, "to ask for your hand in marriage." He was so abashed at having said the words, though he couldn't help saying them, that he wrung his hands and stared fixedly at the knobs of his shoes.

To her credit, the Princess did not laugh. "That is an exceedingly odd request," she said, and glanced up at him, then away. "As a man who's had dealings with wealthy aristocrats, you must surely be aware that it's unusual for members of the royal family to marry box-painters."

Even the dogs seemed to notice that something was taking place. They abruptly stopped their antics and stood motionless, their heads raised crookedly, like the heads of jurors.

"Yes," said Vlemk, "I'm aware of that."

"No doubt you're also aware," the Princess continued, her voice slightly husky, as if her heart were beating too fast, "that I saw you this morning in the gutter with some bottles and papers and the remains of a cat." Now she too cocked her head, studying him. Whether or not she was smiling Vlemk could not be sure in the enfolding darkness.

"Yes, I'm aware of that too," Vlemk said. The memory so abashed him that he was unable to say another word.

But as luck would have it, the Princess took over his argument for him. "I suppose you will say," she said, "that you are nevertheless an aristocrat, in your way, and worthy of any princess alive, since no one in the world is your equal at painting little boxes."

Poor wretched Vlemk could only nod and wring his hands and make his knuckles hurt. In the palace behind the Princess the windows were now all lighted—so many lighted windows it was like snow in the air. Above the highest tower, the moon was just breaking free of clouds.

"An interesting argument," the Princess said, though the argument was her own. She touched her forehead with the tips of three fingers and gave her head a queer, just perceptible jerk. "But I'm afraid I'm not persuaded. How can I know that, living as you do, you haven't lost all your former ability?"

At this, Vlemk's gift of speech rushed back. "Believe me," he said recklessly, "I could paint you a picture of your face so real it seems to speak!"

"Interesting," said the Princess thoughtfully. "Make it actually speak, and I'll permit you to talk with me again about these matters." So saying, giving him a mysterious smile—perhaps mocking, perhaps affectionate; in the frail moonlight and the glow of the palace not even a wizard could have decided for sure—she turned from him, gave a little tug at the leashes, and walked away toward the arched palace door with her greyhounds.

"Make it actually speak!" thought the artist, his heart beating wildly. It was hopeless, of course. Though a man had ten times the talent of poor Vlemk, no amount of care and skill could make a painting so true to its original that it could speak. If he couldn't make a painting so perfect that it could speak the Princess would never again talk to him. And if he couldn't find some way to talk further with the Princess—bask in that beauty that had struck him like an arrow in the chest this morning—how was he to paint? He was boxed in for certain, this time!

On the other hand, he thought, walking more rapidly down the hill toward the city, perhaps it *was* possible. It was, after all, an effect he'd never before attempted. The idea grew on him, and when he reached the city limits he was running full tilt, his long white artist's frock flying out behind him, his hat mashed down on his head under one long hand.

"Ah, he's himself again," said the regulars at the tavern as Vlemk ran by. The four—the barmaid and the three who carried arms—said nothing.

He ran full tilt, as if devils were chasing him, until he came to his house, paused only long enough to jerk open his door and slam it shut behind him, then ran full tilt up the stairs to his studio in the attic, overlooking the city. He sorted through his boxes, took the best he had on hand, and began on his project that same night.

2

When Vlemk had worked for six weeks without sleeping, he began to get morbid, unsettling ideas. Sometimes it crossed his mind that what the Princess had said to him might be nothing but a grim, unfeeling joke, that she had no intention whatsoever of marrying him, indeed, that her purpose in giving him the seemingly impossible task was simply to make sure that he never again spoke to her. As an artist, he had difficulty believing such things, for if one gives in to the notion that visions of extraordinary beauty are mere illusion, one might as well cut off one's hands and sit on street-corners and beg. With all the strength of his carefully nourished and trained imagination he cast back in his mind to that morning when he'd seen her in the carriage, peeking out through the curtains, and with all his dexterity and technical trickery he labored to set down that vision in paint. He could not doubt the intensity of the emotion that had surged in him or the accuracy of the vision he set down line by line. Every flicker of light in her pale blue eyes was precisely correct; the turn of the cheek, the tilt of the nose, the seven stray hairs on her forehead—all, insofar as they were finished, were indisputable.

Nevertheless, he was bedeviled by misgivings. It occurred to him for instance that the paint was controlling him, creating not an image of the Princess but something new, a creature never before seen under the sun, the painting growing like a plant under his brushes, faithful to the form of its parent but unique, evolving to singularity by sure, ancient laws—the white of the earlobe calling to the white in the lady's eyes and demanding from the painter infinitesimal changes not true to the actual lady but true, instead, to the natural requirements of the picture on the box. It alarmed him to discover that the throat was taking on, slowly but inexorably, a greenish tint very rare if not unheard of in human beings. "Yet why am I so fretful?" he rebuked himself. "Is it not true that the emotion I feel when I look at the painting is precisely the emotion I felt when I looked at the lady, except for certain small mistakes which can easily be fixed, such as the cock of the nostril and the false glint of the eyelid?" He stood back and looked at the painting to see if it was true. It was. "Then all is still well," he said, moving the brush again, his left eye closed; "let the throat be green as grass, so long as it feels right!"

But that was the least of his misgivings. It struck him that the feeling that had surged in him that morning was mere chemistry, nothing more. "I'd drunk a good deal the night before," he said aloud, bending over his table, mixing paints. "Just as now if I straighten up suddenly, tired as I am and tending toward dizziness, the room will strike me differently than it would if I rose slowly, so that morning—dehydrated, soaked to the bone with dew and gutter wash—I must undoubtedly have seen what I would not have seen at some other time, in some other physiological condition. Is it possible that I'm painting not the Princess but, say, my own uric-acid level? my blood pressure?" The question vexed him, but even this misgiving he was able to quiet, to some extent, with the thought—which burst out of him when he was standing at the window looking down at the old crooked streets of the city— "Very well, my condition was abnormal that morning; but the abnormality was one very common among mortals—or anyway human beings—so that the vision can hardly be called freakish or divorced from reality." If the answer was not as comforting as the painter of boxes might have liked, it was nevertheless an answer, and Vlemk for a time went on painting.

But the greatest misgiving of all was this: the character of the face taking shape on the box was not altogether admirable. One saw faint but unmistakable hints of cruelty, vanity, and stinginess. He did his best, as any honest artist would have done, to undo them or overcome them, but the faults seemed ineradicable; they went, literally, to the bone. Vlemk stood patting his beard, pondering. It was not the first time he'd had this experience. Indeed, more often than not when he'd set out to capture some image which had given him pleasure, he'd found as he painted that the image, under scrutiny, proved slightly less appealing than he'd imagined. This had not much troubled him on those earlier occasions, because his purpose then had been simply to paint a pretty box. As a public minister unobtrusively rephrases the remarks of an irate king, fixing up the grammar, dropping out the swear words, here and there inserting a line or two that the people will perhaps find more memorable, so Vlemk had offhandedly edited Nature, straightening crooked stems, giving life to drooping leaves, suppressing all traces of dog manure. In the project at hand, that was, of course, impossible. He began to perceive clearly the fact that he'd known all along but had never quite confronted: that Beauty is an artist's vain dream; it has, except in works of art, no vitality, no body.

Abruptly, Vlemk found himself profoundly depressed. Slowly, meticulously, as if going through empty motions, he cleaned his brushes and carefully capped his paints, saw to it that his oils and thinners were exactly as they should be, removed his painter's frock and hung it on its hook, then poked his arms into his overcoat, stepped out of the studio, and locked the door behind him.

At the tavern, things were just beginning to hum. The regulars were singing and arguing politics; the sullen, fat barmaid was pretending to smile in the arms of an old drunken seaman. Old Tom was, as usual, asleep under the stove.

"Ha!" cried one of the regulars as Vlemk came through the door, "it's Vlemk the box-painter!"

Instantly, everyone smiled, delighted, for it was a long time since they'd seen him. "Vlemk!" they shouted, "where have you been? Pull up a chair!"

Soon poor Vlemk was as drunk as he'd ever been in all his days, riding on a horse with a milk wagon behind it—where he'd gotten the horse he had no idea—milk bottles crashing on the cobblestone streets at every jolt or sudden turn, bringing cats from every doorway; trees careening by, looking drunker than he was; people on the sidewalks going flat against the walls at his approach. Then, sometime later, he had no idea how long, though he dimly remembered sitting in some woman's apartment, staring with drunken fixity at the birthmark on her throat, he found himself chatting with an old, bony monk in a graveyard. They were sharing a bottle of some fennel-flavored drink.

"Ah yes," said the monk, "Beauty is momentary in the mind, as the poet saith." He handed Vlemk the bottle. After a moment he continued, "I'll tell you how I got into this business in the first place. It had to do with women."

Vlemk tipped up the bottle and thoughtfully drank. The graves all around him tilted precariously then righted themselves.

"By the highest standards I am able to imagine, I have never known a beautiful woman," said the monk, "or even a good woman, or even a relatively good mother." He sighed and tapped the tips of his fingers together. "It occurred to me early on that since we can *conceive* of a beautiful woman, or a good woman, or even a relatively good mother, though we find none in Nature—always with the exception of Our Saviour's Mother—" He cleared his throat as if embarrassed, and a quaver came into his voice as he continued, "It occurred to me early on that Nature is not worthy of our attention. Even the best we mortals can conceive, if we believe old books, is but a feeble reflection or ethereal vibration of the beauty God sits in the midst of, millennium to millennium."

Whatever more he had to say, Vlemk did not hear; he was fast asleep.

Sometime much later, as the sun was rising, Vlemk found himself standing at the door of his house, studying the doorway with tortuous attention, noting every stipple on the wall, every crack in the wood, making sure it was indeed his own doorway. He had never examined it quite so carefully before, which was perhaps the reason that, the more he looked, the more uncertain he was that the doorway was his own. What he did know, with certainty, was that the doorway was extremely interesting, as these things go. He ran his numb fingertips over the stone and cement and then, carefully, for fear of splinters, over the wood. He thought, for some reason, of the arched door of the palace where the Princess lived, and suddenly there welled up in him an emotion as curious as any he had ever experienced: pity for the Princess's doorway. It was not that there was anything wrong with that grand, solemn arch. Its proportions were perfect—though more appropriate, per-haps, for a church than for a palace. Its elegance was properly understated, its craftsmanship inspired though not original— the quatrefoils, the lozenges, the mournful beaked face that formed the keystone were all done to perfection. Yet the fact remained that, like his own humble doorway, it was obscurely ridiculous. No sooner had he thought this than he was am-bushed by another thought more curious than the first. If he were to be granted, like Saint John in the Bible, a vision of heaven, he would certainly feel this exact same emotion, a faintly ironic amusement mixed with pity. Let all the archi-tects of heaven and earth work together on the project, the result would be the same: not disappointing—nothing at all like that—but touchingly ridiculous.

Say heaven's gates were of pearl, and its streets pure gold. How could one look at those effects, however grand, without drawing back a little, with charitable amusement, thinking, "Ah, how labored! how dated!" One would recognize in a flash that the dragons on the pillars were Ming Dynasty, or Swedish, or French Imperial; that the structures were Mayan, or London 1840s, or Etruscan. Suppose to avoid this God made Himself a heaven as humble as a shepherd's hut. "How artfully simple," one would say, as one said of a thousand such creations. Or suppose God chose in His infinite wisdom to make something brand new, unheard of on earth or on any other planet. "How new!" one would cry, and a billion billion other risen souls would cry the same, in antique harmony.

Thinking these thoughts, more pleasant than grim, for if they ruled out the ultimate value of all art, they gave mud beetles, humankind, and God a kind of oneness in futility, Vlemk opened the door and entered, hoping the house was indeed his house, still waiting for some sure sign. He found the stairway more or less where he'd expected he might find it, carefully avoided two sleeping cats, and began to climb. The bannister was as smooth as dusty, dry soap, like the bannister in his own house, which perhaps it was. When he came to the door to the studio, locked, he was virtually certain that this must be the place. He tried his key. It worked.

The first thing he saw when he entered the studio was his painting on the box, the Princess's face. With a start he realized that the picture was essentially finished. The lines he had doubted—the lines suggesting a touch of meanness in her character—were exactly right, no question about it, not that these were the most obvious of her lines. There was kindness too; generosity, a pleasing touch of whimsy. Indeed, an ordinary observer might never have noticed these slightly less pleasant qualities, though certainly they were there.

Vlemk sighed, pleased with the world in spite of its imperfections if not because of them—and made himself a large pot of coffee. The city below his window was still fast asleep except for, here and there, a garbage cart. He thought of the bony old monk in the graveyard, the woman with the birthmark. He poured himself coffee and sat looking at the painting on the box, smiling. Though she was a princess, she was no better, it seemed to him—though he knew that it might well be the alcohol—than the barmaid, the monk, the woman with the mark on her throat. Wherever the life-force could find a place to push it pushed, he mused—into barmaids, princesses, dandelions, monks, even box-painters. He laughed.

He was conscious of looking at the world as from a mountaintop. Yet even as he thought these serene, fond thoughts an uneasiness came over him. *Make the picture speak*, the Princess had said, *and I'll permit you to talk with me again about these matters*. It was true that she was beautiful, for all her faults, more beautiful than he'd ever before realized. If it was true that all the universe was one in its comic futility, it was also true that certain comically imperfect expressions of the universal force were for some reason preferable to others to any given life-expression, such as Vlemk. Having come to understand the Princess, both the best and the worst in her, poor Vlemk had fallen hopelessly, shamelessly in love. It was not some vague, airy vision now, it was something quite specific. He wanted to be in bed with her, talking, earnestly but in full detail, as if they had years to get everything right, about questions of Life and Art. He glanced down at his coffee. Did she perhaps prefer tea? He studied the painting. It told him nothing.

Abruptly, urgently, hardly knowing what he was doing, Vlemk uncapped his paints and seized a paintbrush. He painted furiously, with nothing in his mind, putting in without thought every beauty and deformity, working almost carelessly, almost wildly. Soon the painting was so much like the Princess that not even the Princess's mother could have told the two apart.

The picture began to speak. "Vlemk," it said, "I put a curse upon you. You shall never speak a word until I say so!"

Vlemk's eyes widened and he tried to protest, but already the curse was in effect; he was unable to make a sound.

3

Now began a terrible period in the life of the box-painter. He had achieved what no artist before him had achieved, had succeeded in the most arduous love-task ever dreamt of, but the victory was ashes; he was as mute as a stone. If the picture remained stubborn, and Vlemk had no reason to doubt that it would, he would never in all his life say a word to the Princess, his love and inspiration.

He made feeble attempts at adjusting to his fate. Occasionally he'd take an order for a snuff box with pansies on it, or a quill box with a picture of the owner's house, but his work was inaccurate and shoddy; his heart had gone out of it. People began to haggle and try to put off paying him, even local doctors and bankers who could easily have afforded to pay if they'd wished to—a sure sign, as all box-painters know, that the work was no longer giving pleasure—and as the weeks passed business grew worse and worse; fewer and fewer people climbed the narrow stairs to his studio. That was just as well, in fact, for these days and nights Vlemk worked slowly or not at all. Even if he put in long hours, as he sometimes did in a fit of anxiety or anger turned inward, he got very little done. Ever since he'd finished his painting of the Princess, all other kinds of painting seemed beneath him, a betrayal of his gift. He found that he literally could not paint what was asked of him, and even if by dint of superhuman stubbornness he got through a given job, no one any longer praised his work, not even the stupidest oaf who came up off the street.

His fall was dramatically underscored, in Vlemk's mind, when occasionally, to his annoyance, some customer would glance unhappily from the painted box Vlemk had just finished for him to the box, nearby, on which he'd painted his portrait of the Princess. Sometimes they would say, "It looks real enough to speak!" "It does," the painting on the box would pipe up, and the customer would stare, disbelieving. Soon there were rumors that Vlemk had made a pact with the Devil. Business got still worse and eventually dropped away entirely.

"Woe is me," poor Vlemk would think, sitting alone in his studio, pulling at his knuckles. And as if he didn't have troubles enough these days, the painting would start speaking again, complaining and criticizing, trying to offer helpful suggestions. "How can you call yourself a painter?" it would say in its ringing little voice, a voice not much louder than an insect's. "Where's your dedication? Is this what your disorderly habits have at last brought you down to?"

Vlemk would put up with this—or would leave for the tavern to get away from it—though it seemed to him brutally unfair, to say the least, that the masterpiece of his life should prove his curse and his soul's imprisonment. At times, throwing dignity to the winds, he would plead with his creation, imploring her in gesture—even going down on his knees to her—that she give him back his voice.

"No!" she would say.

"But why?" he would ask with his hands, fingers splayed wide and shaking.

"I don't feel like it," she said. "When I feel like it I will."

"You have no mercy!" he wailed in gesture, raising his fist and sadly shaking his head.

"*You* tell *me* about mercy!" cried the box. "You created me, you monster! Do you know what it's like, stuck here in one place like a miserable cripple, owning nothing in the world but a head and two shoulders—not even hands and feet?"

"Forgiveness is the greatest of all virtues," Vlemk would signal.

"No," the box would say. "The curse is still on!"

Vlemk would groan and say nothing more, would get up

stiffly from his thick knees, and to punish the box in the only way he could, he would put on his hat and coat and descend to the street and make his way to the tavern.

Except for the inconvenience his poverty caused him, Vlemk could not honestly say he was sorry that his business as a box-painter had failed. It had never been a highly respected occupation, though people were amused by it. It had none of the prestige of gargoyle carving or stained-glass-window making or the casting of bells, and to Vlemk, who believed himself vastly superior to those other, more respected artisans, it was a relief to become, for all practical purposes, a simple citizen, no longer an artisan looked down on by artisans he despised. His inability to speak, his inability even to whimper or grunt, soon made his anonymity complete. He spent more and more of his time at the tavern, cadging the few coins he needed by holding out his hand and looking pitiful. His landlady was a problem, but only in the sense that it embarrassed him to meet her. The rumor of his friendship with the Devil kept her civil and distant.

It was winter now, picturesque in Vlemk's city if you were a rich man or only passing through. Icicles hung glittering from the eaves of every shop; snow put pointed hats on every housetop and steeple; horses in their traces breathed out hovering ghosts of steam. He was not altogether indifferent to all this. He observed with interest how shadows changed color behind a steam cloud, how the droplets on the nostrils of a horse gleamed amber in the sunlight. But his interest was tinged, inevitably, with gloom and anger. To Vlemk and those like him, cold weather meant misery and humiliation. His clothes were thin and full of holes to let in every wandering chill. "On *my* wages," thought Vlemk, bitterly joking—as was more and more his habit—"I'm lucky I can still afford skin." It was a joke worth saying aloud, he thought, but the curse prohibited it, so he stared straight ahead, living inside his mind, raising his glass with the others in the tavern, now and then joining in a fistfight if the cause seemed just.

Day after day, day after day, he would walk to the tavern as soon as it opened, trudging with great, gaping holes in his shoes over ice and through slush, hunched in his frayed old overcoat, snow piling up on his hat and shoulders, his fists clenched tight in the pockets that no longer held things. "What a box!" he would think, then would quickly shake his head as if the voice were someone else's, for he grew tired of his thoughts, now that he had no one to vent them on—tired and increasingly critical, for it had struck him, now that he must listen and not speak, that an immense amount of what was said in the world was not worth saying.

As the cold settled in and the snow deepened, fewer and fewer strangers were to be found in the streets of Vlemk's city, and begging became increasingly difficult. Sometimes whole days went by when Vlemk couldn't gather enough coins for a single glass of wine. On these days Vlemk walked bent double from hunger pains—not surprisingly, since wine was now almost all he lived on. If he was lucky one of his unsavory friends—the petty thieves and marauders who gathered at the tavern every evening—would give him some of their wine; but the generosity of thieves is undependable. Sometimes their mood was wrong; sometimes they'd found nothing to burgle for weeks, so that their stomachs were as empty as Vlemk's.

"What am I to do?" his friend the ex-violinist would growl at him. "The rich have nothing but their money on their minds. They walk around the city with one hand in their billfold and the other on their pocketwatch." And with a stubborn, guilty look, he would drink his cheap wine, if he happened to have any, himself.

"Don't look at *me* with those mournful eyes," his friend the ex-poet would say to him. "Solomon in all his glory was not guarded and zipped like one of these!"

The axe-murderer—or rather, would-be axe-murderer, for

so far he'd never found the perfect occasion, the aesthetically perfect set of murder victims, and he was nothing if not a perfectionist—the axe-murderer would sit staring at the table with his icy stare, lost in thought—perhaps thoughts of killing Vlemk for his belt and shoelaces—and would let out not one word.

"I must do something," thought Vlemk. "Life is not fit to be endured if a man's cold sober!"

One night as this was happening—that is, as he was sitting at his table in the tavern with his misbegotten friends, clenching his belly against the hunger pains and shivering from the cold he had no wine to drive away—he saw the fat, sullen barmaid serve wine to a customer, a stooped old man with a white goatee, and leave his table without asking him to pay. In great agitation, Vlemk poked the poet with his elbow, pointed at the old man, and splashed his hands open to show he had a question. The poet studied him, managed the translation, then turned around to look at the old man.

"Oh, him," said the poet. "She always serves him free." He returned his attention to his drinking.

Again Vlemk poked him and splashed open his hands, this time raising his eyebrows as well and jerking his head forward, showing that his question was urgent.

" 'Why?' " said the poet, translating.

Eagerly, Vlemk nodded.

"The old man is a composer," said the poet. "Years ago he wrote the barmaid into an opera. She's showing her gratitude."

The axe-murderer slowly closed his eyes in disgust. So did the tomcat beside him. The ex-violinist looked depressed.

Abruptly, Vlemk stood up, said goodbye with his hands, and hurried, bent over with hunger, to his freezing-cold studio. He painted all night like a man possessed, grimly ignoring the comments of the picture of the Princess, which stood watching, objecting in its piping little voice to every stroke he set down. He painted quickly, easily, as he'd painted in the old days, perhaps because his project, however suspect, was his own idea and had a certain morbid interest. In the morning, when his new painted box-lid was finished, he went to curl up in his bed until the paint was dry. As soon as it was safe, he wrapped the painted box in a scrap of purple satin, which he'd stolen from the laundry chute weeks ago, and carried his gift through the slanting, soft snow to the barmaid.

When he set it on the bar, nodding and smiling, pointing from the box to the barmaid and back, the barmaid for a long time just stared at him. She had never really liked him—she liked almost no one, especially men, for she'd been badly used. Sometimes (Vlemk had noticed it only as he painted) she would come in bruised and battered from a night with some sailor who had strong opinions, or some farmer who knew only about cows. Sometimes—and this too he had remembered only when his brush reminded him—her eyes would suddenly fill with tears as she was pouring a glass of ale.

But at last the barmaid accepted the present, seeing that only if she did so would she ever be rid of him, and with a look oddly childlike, fearful and embarrassed, she removed the purple cloth. When the barmaid saw the painting she gave a cry like a brief yelp of sorrow and her lips began to tremble; but before you could count ten, the tremble became a smile, and she reached out with both plump hands for Vlemk's bearded face, drew it close, and kissed it.

Vlemk was bitterly ashamed, for nothing was ever less deserved than that kiss, but he forced himself to smile, and he smiled on, grimly, as the barmaid ran from table to table with her gift, showing it to the regulars one after another, all of whom heartily praised it.

No one seemed to know except the ex-poet, the ex-violinist, and the axe-murderer that the painting on the box was a lie, a fraud, an outrage. He'd given the barmaid a childlike smile, though it was as foreign to her sullen, lumpy face as Egypt to an Eskimo. He'd given her the eyes of a twelve-year-old milkmaid, though her own eyes had nothing but the exact same brown of the irises in common. He'd reddened her chin and removed certain blemishes, turning others—for example the birthmark on her throat, which he paid close attention to only as he painted it—to beauty marks. He'd lifted her breasts a little, tightened her skin, raised a sagging eyebrow, increased the visibility of her dimple. In short, he'd made her beautiful, and he'd done it all so cunningly that no one but an artist could have told you where the truth left off and the falsehood began.

"Wine for the box-painter!" cried one of the regulars.

"Wine whenever he wants it!" cried the barmaid, and abruptly, as if changed into some other person, she smiled.

The troubles of Vlemk the box-painter were over—or at any rate Vlemk's most immediate trouble. From that night on when he went to the tavern he got all he asked for, wine, beer, and whiskey until only with the help of a friend could he find his way home, and sometimes not even then. As for the barmaid, a curious thing happened. She became increasingly similar to the fraudulent painting, smiling as she served her customers, looking at strangers with the eyes of an innocent, standing so erect, in her foolish pride, that her breasts were almost exactly where Vlemk had painted them. The success of her after-hours business increased, so much so that Vlemk began to worry that perhaps she would get married and leave the bar, which would throw him back on begging. Sometimes to his distress, he would catch her stealing a little look at the box, which she kept prominently displayed, and once—far worse for Vlemk's sense of honor—she gave him a look that made him think for an instant that she *knew* what he had done. Why not, of course. Wasn't she also a dabbler in visions, a creator and destroyer? She said nothing, however; for which Vlemk was profoundly grateful.

With other people, Vlemk was all too often less fortunate. Because he was a mute now, people began telling him things,

all of them eager to share their troublesome and shameful secrets, yet concerned that their secrets remain unknown.
Women, looking into his gray, all-seeing eyes, and assured that
he was voiceless, as safe as a boulder, would reveal to him
such horrors of frustration and betrayal, remorse, inexpressible
indignation, and despair, that his sleep would be troubled for
weeks by alarming dreams. Gentle old men told him stories of
rape and arson, cruelty to animals, and heaven knows what
else. Vlemk the box-painter became a walking cyclopedia of
the sins and transgressions of humanity—more scapegoat than
priest, alas, since he was powerless to forgive or condemn.

He learned, among other things, why the poet no longer
wrote poetry and the ex-violinist had turned in disgust against
music.

"My audience," said the poet, lips trembling, eyebrows
twitching, "has, collectively, the brains of one pig." He pursed
his lips. "Perhaps that's unfair," he said. "Perhaps I under-
estimate pigs." This the poet said in Vlemk's studio, where no
one could hear him but Vlemk and the painting of the Princess
on the box, who said nothing. "What good is it," the poet
asked, pacing up and down, flaxen hair flying, "telling my
audience things they can never understand?" He puffed at his
pipe, sending up angry little clouds, and continued, jabbing
with his pipestem and pacing again, "*We* know, you and I, the
sad truth of the matter: to fools, nothing *can* be said; to the
wise, nothing *need* be said. Take all the wisdom of Homer and
Virgil. We knew it in our hearts when we were four, you and
I— No, I'm serious, my friend!" He raised his hand as if Vlemk
might find his voice and object. "Who learns anything—I say,
anything—from poetry? Say I describe all the agony of love
with magnificent precision, showing true and false, revealing
the applications for the priesthood and men engaged in business. If I'm right, exactly and precisely right, what do you
say—you, the reader? 'That's right,' you say, if you're wise and
not a fool. What have I taught you, then? Nothing, of course!

Nothing whatsoever! I have said, with a certain elegance, exactly what you know. And what does the fool say? Why, nothing, of course. 'I never really cared much for poetry,' says he. 'I like a man to say what he means.' Poetry's a trinket, then, a luxury and amusement, a kind of secret handshake between equals. Nothing wrong with that, of course. It's an occupation no worse than, say, being a cook"—his lips twisted to a sneer—"a cook, ha ha, a man whose art is consumed and goes sliding back to earth!" He heaved a deep sigh. "I have therefore abandoned that paltry mistress poesy." He stood now angrily gazing down at the crooked little streets. "I have put my intelligence to more interesting uses," he said quietly, glancing past his shoulder. "I steal people's jewelry. I kidnap people's children. That surprises you?"

Vlemk shrugged.

"I do not kill people," said the poet; "that's against my principles! I merely upset them a little—teach them values, like Goethe and Schiller."

Vlemk nodded. It crossed his mind that if his friend the ex-poet was really a jewel-thief and kidnapper of children he'd be a good deal better off than he was; but Vlemk let it go. Poetic license. It was true—Vlemk knew because he'd seen it—that the man picked pockets and stole eggs.

The violinist said, not many nights later, sitting in the abandoned railroad car which was his temporary home, "I have only one real ambition in life: getting even."

Vlemk splashed his hands open and lifted his eyebrows.

" 'With whom?' you say," said the ex-violinist, translating. His spectacles flashed, catching a little light from the candle on the crate between them. "Audiences, composers, conductors, violin makers . . . Everyone's my enemy! Why should I make exceptions?" He passed Vlemk the crackers and Chianti, for in small things he was generous, and the Chianti had turned. The ex-violinist sat grinding his teeth, his fingertips trembling, then continued very softly, "You have to understand how it is for us performers. Some fool writes a piece and we interpret with all our hearts, but there's nothing to interpret, just the noises a fool makes, or if there's something there the conductor gets the tempo wrong, or the audience dislikes it because they've heard on good authority that all Slavs are sentimental. At best, a string on the violin breaks." Loudly, he cracked his knuckles, all ten of them in rapid succession, so that a shudder ran down Vlemk's back. Though the light in the railroad car was dim—too dim for Vlemk to make out what the creatures were, moving now and then in the corners—it seemed to Vlemk that as he spoke there were tears in the ex-musician's eyes. "Thousands of dollars' worth of music lessons, thousands of hours of arpeggios and scales—for that! Very well!" He sucked in breath. "There are other uses for dexterity like mine!"

Vlemk raised his eyebrows and opened his hands.

The musician leaned forward, confidential, trembling violently. "I steal valuables from purses in coatrooms," he said. "There's no real money in it, but the response of the crowd is tremendous."

Vlemk had long made a point of never being alone with the third of his unsavory friends, the axe-murderer, but one night in January, when he ducked into a doorway to avoid an icy rain, that too happened. The axe-murderer was a dour man with thick, hairy forearms, short, thick legs, and a neck as big around as a large man's thigh. He had a mouth made unpleasant by small, open sores, and eyes that seemed never to fix on anything but to stare with fuming discontent in whatever direction his small, shiny head was turned. He rarely spoke, but tonight, pinned shoulder to shoulder beside Vlemk in the doorway, waiting for the rain to stop—the street full of shadows, the lamps not yet lit—the murderer abruptly, for no reason, broke his rule. "Vlemk," he said, in a voice as low and gravelly as a frog's, "the trouble with you is, you're insensitive to the power of evil."

Vlemk nodded, shuddering, and made an effort to look

thoughtful. He craned his head forward, thinking the rain was perhaps lighter than he'd imagined, but the shoulder of the murderer pinned him tightly against the doorjamb, and he soon realized that the pressure against him was intentional; he was meant to stay, hear the murderer out, listen attentively, as if his life depended on it, for indeed, conceivably, it did.

"You have a strange point of view," said the axe-murderer. "It seems to you quite normal, because the herd of humanity generally shares it; but believe me your view is in fact both strange and irrational."

Again Vlemk nodded.

"You look for Beauty in the world," said the axe-murderer. "You formulate impressions in the archaic vocabulary of Grace. This is a mistake. What the intelligent man looks for is *interest*. Look at our friends the ex-poet and the ex-musician. They started out as pursuers of Beauty, devotees of supernatural premises. What are they now?" He laughed so deep in his throat it might have come from a well. "They are retired, my friend. And even in retirement they have no more understanding of the truth than a pair of fat ducks." He turned his sorespecked, expressionless face, allowing the eyes to bore coldly into Vlemk. "I, on the other hand," he said, "am not retired. Actually, strictly speaking, I haven't yet begun. Many people say I will never begin, but I spit in their eyes." He glanced downward, indicating that Vlemk should do the same, and from under the skirt of his overcoat showed the blade of an axe.

Vlemk swallowed and quickly nodded. The rain was beginning to let up now, but still the firm pressure of the murderer's shoulder boxed him in.

"You're an idealist, Vlemk," said the axe-murderer. "Reality, you think, is what might be, or what peeks from behind what is. What evidence have you for this shadow you prefer to the hard, smelly world we exist in? Look again!" Again they looked down, both of them, at the axe. "Reality is matter in all its magnificent complexity," said the murderer, "the sludge of actuality in infinite mechanical aspiration. Break the machine and you begin to know its usefulness! Close off the view of the mountains with a curtain and you begin to see the glory of the view." He pressed harder against Vlemk and asked with a sneer, "You imagine you search out Reality, painter of little boxes?" He laughed. "You're an evader and avoider! I give you my assurance—experience is the test—chop off the heads of a family of seven, let the walls and the floors be splashed with their blood, let the dogs howl, the cats flee, the parakeets fly crazily in their filthy wicker cages, then ask yourself: *is* this or *is this not* Reality?—this carnage, this disruption of splendid promise? Take the blinders from your eyes! Death and Evil are the principles that define our achievements and in due time swallow them. Ugliness is our condition and the basis of our interest. Is it our business to set down lies, or are we here to tell the Truth, though the Truth may be unspeakably dreadful?"

Vlemk nodded slowly and thoughtfully, and pursed his lips.

The murderer's face grew more unpleasant than usual, and when he spoke again his grumble was so low and disheartened that Vlemk could barely hear him. "Admittedly all this is as yet still a little theoretical. The police are everywhere, and how is one to get proper coverage? The newspapers suppress things, edit things. I'm like you, my friend Vlemk, if what I hear about the picture of the Princess is true: a genius who's never reached his audience." He chuckled, miserable as a snake. Suddenly the murderer drew in one sharp breath and became still all over, his hand clamped firm as a vise on the box-painter's arm. "Perhaps this is it!" he whispered. A family of five was entering the old empty church across the street, ducking in out of the rain, perhaps. As soon as the door closed behind them, the murderer stepped softly from the doorway, tipping up his coat-collar and pulling down his hat, then hurried away through the rain to the farther curb. At once, before the murderer could change his mind, Vlemk set off, almost running, in the direction of the tavern. He need not have hurried. When he met the axe-murderer the following night he learned that, as usual, he'd done nothing. Nothing, as usual, had been quite as he required. For some arts, the difficulties are all but insurmountable.

4

So Vlemk's life continued, day after day and week after week. Insofar as possible, he kept himself drunk. In due time, were it not for the picture, he might have forgotten his unhappiness and learned to be content.

But the talking picture of the Princess would give him no rest. It complained and nagged until he was ready to throw it out the window; yet complaint and unpleasantness were by no means all that the picture was capable of. Sometimes when Vlemk was so sunk in gloom that it took him all his strength to raise his chin from his fists and his elbows from his knees, the picture would speak to him so kindly, with such gentle understanding, that he would burst into tears. At such moments it grieved him that he'd abandoned his profession, that all order had gone out of his life, all trace of dignity. He wrung his hands and ground his teeth and looked longingly at the brushes laid in shabby disarray on the table.

"Well, why don't you paint, then?" said the picture on the box, who had been watching him narrowly for some time. "It can make you no more miserable than you are!"

"Ha!" Vlemk thought, "you know nothing!" He wished with all his heart that he could say it aloud, but owing to the curse he could speak not a single syllable, even to the box. "*No* one knows anything!" he wanted to say, for the opinions of his friends had persuaded him. "We artists are the loneliest, most miserable people in the world, misunderstood, underestimated, scorned and mocked, driven to self-betrayal and dishonesty and starvation! We're masters of skills more subtle than the skills of a wizard or king, yet we're valued less highly than the moron who carves out stone statues with no reference to anything, or sticks little pieces of colored glass together, or makes great brass bell-molds in endless array, the first one no different from the last one!"

"Does it help," asked the picture, "to stand there shaking your fists like that?"

Vlemk the box-painter whirled around, furious, intending to shout obscenities at the picture on the box, though of course he could shout nothing. His face became red as a brick and his eyes bulged, and his breathing was so violent that it seemed he would surely have a heart attack. But at once he changed his mind and put his hands over his face, for he'd seen again, staring at the picture, that the Princess was too beautiful for words.

"What is it?" asked the picture. "What is it that so upsets you?" She spoke with great kindness and what seemed to Vlemk sincere concern, so that he could only assume that she'd forgotten she'd put the curse on him. (In this he was mistaken.) He tried mouthing words at her, but the picture only stared at him as if in puzzlement, and at last Vlemk gave up in despair and turned sadly away. Tears began to brim up in his eyes and drip down his cheeks.

"It's nothing strange," thought Vlemk, clenching and unclenching his fists. "She fills me with sorrow for what I might have had but lost, this vision of extraordinary beauty I've painted on the box." He ground his teeth and wiped away the tears, but at once his eyes were filled again. "Vision," he thought woefully, and began to shake his head like a child. "Vision, yes, nothing but a vision—a romantic illusion!" Suddenly he bent over, sobbing.

"Poor Vlemk!" cried the box in its piping little voice. "Oh poor, poor Vlemk!" If he'd turned around to look, he might have seen to his astonishment that the box was crying too. But he did not turn. He sobbed for a long time, deaf to the peeping sobs behind him; then at last, with a great, broad shudder and a grinding of his teeth, he got hold of himself. What a fool he was being! There was no way on earth she could have forgotten that it was she who'd put the curse on him. She was a charmer, his pretty little picture, but mean as a snake! And if the picture had no heart, what of the Princess?

"I've been a dolt," he thought. "The murderer's quite right. I must rid myself of idiotic visions!"

With eyes like a maniac's he went over to the hook where his artist's frock hung, carefully took it down, and poked his arms in. He went back to the table where his brushes lay, uncapped a bottle of thinner, poured just a little into a dish, unbuttoned and rolled up his sleeves, then, more meticulous than a surgeon over his knives, began the exceedingly delicate business of cleaning and trimming his brushes. Then he squeezed paint onto his palette and poured oil and glaze into their containers. When all this was ready, he chose a box—a beautiful one of rosewood—and began to paint.

The picture of the Princess watched with interest. "Another picture of me?" she asked after a time.

"Every painter," thought Vlemk, in lieu of giving answer, "has his own proper subject. Some are best at cliffs, some at trees and flowers, some at boats, some at cows crossing a stream, some at churches, some at babies. *My* proper subject—the subject which for some reason engages me heart and soul—is the Princess's face."

For several hours, Vlemk painted with such intensity that it seemed he might explode.

Suddenly the picture said, "*I* don't look like that!"

Vlemk turned, nodded with a mysterious dark smile at the picture on the box, then coolly turned away again, back to his work.

He was painting as he'd never before painted in his life,

gazing, unflinching, into the abyss. Every hint his memory of her face provided him, or his increasingly sure knowledge of her perfect twin, the picture he'd earlier painted on the box— the face now watching him in dismay and indignation—he pursued relentlessly, as a surgeon edges into a cortex, following a cancer with the tip of his knife. He softened nothing, gave in nowhere, but set down the Princess's flaws in bold relief. Nothing escaped him: the fullness of the lower lip which only now, as it helplessly submitted to his brush, did he recognize for what it was, a latent sensualism that, if pushed as he pushed it now in paint, fulfilling its dark potential, might be the Princess's ruin; the infinitesimal weakness of one eyelid, its barely perceptible inclination to droop; the even less perceptible but nevertheless real inclination toward hairiness on her upper lip and chin, should her diet fall into disorder, her hormones lose balance. It was a terrible experience, painful and alarming, yet at the same time morbidly thrilling. Both about seeing and about finding new ways to give expression to what he saw, he was discovering more in a single night, it seemed to him, than he'd discovered up to now in all his life.

"That's stupid," said the picture on the box behind him, crossly. "You've missed the likeness. I'm not like that at all!"

"Well, you know, it's just *Art*," Vlemk answered inside his mind, ironically joking, playing fool in the ancient way of angry artists. Deny it as she might, he thought—and heaven knew she was stupid enough; it was visible in the eyes—she would perhaps not miss it entirely, but feel, at some animal level, rebuked. Behind and to the left of the lady he was painting, he fashioned a small monkey at a pulpit, reading a Bible and shaking his finger, a blazing arched window behind him, obscuring his outlines. Her case, the image was meant to say, was not quite hopeless. If she turned, she might yet receive instruction, if only from a monkey.

The painting that could speak was saying nothing. She had

closed her eyes and put on, to punish him, a bored look, or worse than bored: a bored person frozen alive. He felt a brief flash of anger and impatience, then suddenly a kind of joy, though dark and subterranean: she'd given him inspiration for another painting. This time, he decided, he would work more purely, in absolute isolation; that is, outside the influence of her judging eyes. Carefully, as if fondly, he lifted the box with the painting that could speak and carried it to the darkest corner of his studio, where he set it down on a chair and covered it with a black velvet cloth.

"What are you doing?" the picture protested. "Take me back where I was! I don't like it here!"

Vlemk, of course, said nothing but returned to his paints.

It was morning now. Light was streaming in, and chickens and dogs in the city below were calling from street to street like peddlers, their voices bouncing over the ice. Vlemk made coffee, thought briefly of getting a little rest, then settled down on his stool, at his slanted table—methodically, neatly, with controlled but white-hot concentration—to begin on his new work, "The Princess Looking Bored." The lines seemed almost to fall from his brush, the idea taking shape with the natural-ness and ease of a flower's opening—though a terrible flower, needless to say: a bloom almost certainly poisonous. As with the painting he'd worked on through the night, he pursued the Princess's worst potential with the reckless abandon of a lover in a fury, a husband betrayed. It was an eye-opener. Who would have guessed (who did not know her as Vlemk knew her) what depths of deceit and self-deception she was capable of, how pitiful and self-destructive her stratagem, or the mea-sure of panic and self-doubt behind the mask of disdain? No wonder she held out on him, refused to lift the curse! He could understand now the dream of the axe-murderer, standing in the midst of his butchery, and he at the same moment recog-nized with immense satisfaction that his art was as much above that of the murderer as was the murderer's above that of the man who carved bestial fantasies in pious stone. Vlemk painted quickly, fanatically, yet precisely, like a virtuoso violinist scattering notes like leaves in a wind. Not that he worked, like his friend the ex-violinist, to get even. Nothing could have been farther from the box-painter's mind. His work was absolutely pure; it had no object but knowledge—and Ah! thought Vlemk, what knowledge he was getting! "Princess, how well I know you," he said inside his mind; "you have no idea!" From the chair in the corner came occasional peeps of distress. He ignored them.

He painted all day, finished the second of his Reality boxes, as he jokingly called them, rested for an hour, then went down —his head full of new ideas—to the tavern. As in the days of his innocence (so he thought of them now), his unwinding was like a frenzy. Though he'd meant to remain fairly sober and eat some food, since his heart was full of plans and he was eager to get back to his studio, he'd forgotten his intentions by the second drink. He was painting, after all, as no other box-painter in the world could paint, making discoveries as rare as any scientist's. He was coming to such a grasp of life's darkest principles—and at the same time discovering, as he chased his intuitions, such a wealth of technical tricks and devices—that not a dozen fat books could contain what he had learned in one day. He was achieving, in a word, such mastery of his art, and he was filled with such pleasure in what fortune had granted him, that he could not possibly sit quietly for just one drink, then quietly trudge home. He held the barmaid on his lap and patted her knee, made scornful faces at the poet, whose poverty of wit he despised, mocked the ex-musician by pretending, voicelessly, to sing to him, even once recklessly shook his fist at the axe-murderer.

He awakened the following morning in a cellar—he had no idea how he'd gotten there—his trousers smelling powerfully of duck manure, as if he'd walked through some pond, his head pounding fiercely, his hands so shaky it would be hours, he knew, before he could steady his fingers sufficiently to pick up a paintbrush. Swearing at himself inside his mind, he got up, found his bearings—for he'd wandered to the squalid lower rim of the city—and went home.

"So you've decided to leave me here hidden under a cloth for the rest of my natural days? Is that your intention?" called the picture that could talk.

Grudgingly, Vlemk went over and lifted the cloth away.

"Good heavens!" cried the picture, eyes wide. "Are you all right?"

Vlemk scowled, pulled at his beard, and went to bed.

Again that night he painted until dawn, made coffee, then worked on yet another box all through the day. Each box was more sinister than the last, more shamelessly debauched, more outrageously unfair in the opinion of the picture that could talk, which she now did rarely, too angry and too deeply hurt to give Vlemk the time of day. When his work was finished he again went to the tavern, where he again got so drunk he had no memory of what happened and staggered home as the milkmen were beginning their rounds.

For several weeks this frenzy of painting and drinking continued, and then one day in March—standing in his roomful of boxes with pictures of the Princess on them, each picture meaner and uglier than the last, some so deformed by the painter's rage to tell the truth unvarnished that you could make out no face—Vlemk abruptly stopped. Why he stopped he could hardly have said himself. Partly it was this: whether or not it was true that his work was magnificent, as he sometimes imagined, no one came to see it, and when he carried a box with him to the tavern, no one liked it, not even the axemurderer.

"How can you not like it?" Vlemk asked angrily with his hands.

"Borrrring," said the axe-murderer, and turned his head away, staring through the wall.

"Ha," thought Vlemk, hardly hiding his scorn, "*your* work is interesting, *my* work is boring."

But Vlemk, being no fool, understood the implications. It was exactly as the half-wit ex-poet had said: we learn nothing from Art, merely recognize it as true when it happens to be true; no law requires that we be thrilled by it. Not that he would have said Science is any better. "What are the grandest proofs of Science," Vlemk thought, "but amusements, baubles, devices for passing time, like the game of quoits? 'Science,' you may say, 'improves life, even when it makes it longer.' Yes, that's true. Let us be grateful to Scientists, then, for their valuable gifts to us, as we are grateful to cows for milk, or pigs for bacon. As the brain's two lobes work dissimilar problems, Science and Art in dissimilar ways try to work out the truth of the universe. This activity the Scientist or Artist finds comforting to his ego, and it provides him with Truths he can make as gifts to the world as a gentleman gives his lady a locket. And what if the Truth about the universe is that it's boring?"

So Vlemk gradually came to the conclusion that his joy in his work, like his earlier vision of extraordinary beauty, was delusion. It was not that he denied having enjoyed himself, learning the techniques by which he nailed down his, so to speak, vision—his perception, that is, of the fragility and ultimate rottenness of things. So one might enjoy learning the technique of the mandolin, but when one finished one was only a mandolin player. One might as well have studied the better and worse ways of sitting on a porch.

So Vlemk, with bitter little jokes to himself, stopped painting. The talking picture sulked as much as ever, and from time to time it crossed Vlemk's mind that perhaps if he looked he could find some tourist who might buy it of him; but for one reason or another, he did not sell it. He settled down now to a life of serious, uninterrupted dissolution, never washing his face or changing his clothes, never for a moment so sober that he remembered to feel regret. Days passed, and weeks, and Vlemk became so changed that, for lack of heart, he gave up all his former rowdiness, and often not even regulars at the tavern seemed to know him as he groped his way past them, bent and glum as the Devil in his chains, on his way to the bathroom or to the alley. He forgot about the Princess, or remembered her only as one remembers certain moments from one's childhood. Sometimes if someone spoke of her—and if it was early in the evening, when Vlemk was still relatively sober —Vlemk would smile like a man who knows more than he's telling about something, and it would cross people's minds, especially the barmaid's, that Vlemk and the Princess were closer than one might think. But since he was a mute and declined to write notes, no one pressed him. Anyway, no one wanted to get close to him; he smelled like an old sick bear.

Things went from bad to worse for Vlemk the box-painter. He no longer spoke of life as "boxing him in," not only because the expression bored him but also, and mainly, because the box had become such an intransigeant given of his existence that he no longer noticed.

Then one May morning as he was lying in a gutter, squinting up bleary-eyed and exploring a newly broken tooth with his tongue, a carriage of black leather with golden studs drew up beside him and, at a command from the person inside, came to a stop.

"Driver," said a voice that seemed as near as Vlemk's heart, "who is that unfortunate creature in the gutter?"

Vlemk turned his head and tried to focus his eyes, but it was useless. The carriage was like a shadow in a fire too bright to look at, a gleam of sunlight on a brilliantly glazed, painted box-lid.

"I'm sorry, Princess," said the driver. "I have no idea."

When he heard it was the Princess, Vlemk thought briefly of raising one hand to hide his face, but his will remained inactive and he lay as he was.

"Throw the poor creature a coin," said the Princess. "And let us hope he's not past using it."

After a moment something landed, plop, on Vlemk's belly, and the carriage drove away. Slowly, Vlemk moved one hand toward the cool place—his shirt had lost its buttons, and the coin lay flat on his pale, grimy skin where at last his groping fingers found it and dragged it back down to the ground where it would be safe while he napped. Hours later he sat up abruptly and realized what had happened. He looked down at his hand. There lay the coin, real silver with a picture of the King on it.

"How strange!" thought Vlemk.

When he'd gotten to his feet and moved carefully to the street-corner, touching the walls of the buildings with the knuckles of one cupped hand, he found that he had no idea where he was, much less how he'd gotten there, and no idea which direction to take to reach his house. When he waved to hurrying passers-by, looking at them helplessly and silently moving his loose, mute mouth, they ducked their heads, touching their hats, and hurried around him as they would if he were Death. He edged on alone, hunting for some landmark, but it was as if all the streets of the city had been moved to new locations. He shook his head, still moving his mouth like some mechanical thing, not a living man, wholly unaware that he was doing it. An old sick alleycat opened his mouth in a yawn, showing teeth like needles, then closed it again and lowered his head. In his right hand Vlemk clenched—so tightly that the rim of it bit into his flesh—the coin with the picture of the King on it.

5

Three days later, having carefully considered from every point of view, having bathed away the filth and trimmed his beard and washed his old black suit in the sink in the studio, and having dried it on the railing of the balcony, Vlemk the box-painter started across the city and up the hill toward the royal palace. Tucked under his arm, he carried the box with the talking picture. In his pocket he had a carefully folded note which he'd meticulously lettered, intending to put it in the Princess's hand as he gave her the box. "Dear Princess," the note read, "Here is the gift I said I would try to make for you, a picture so real it can speak. I release you from your promise to talk with me, since misfortune has made me a mute, perhaps for my impertinence. I hope this finds you well. Respectfully, Vlemk the Box-Painter."

He arrived at the palace, as he had planned to do, just at the time when the Princess would be coming in from walking her dogs. The last of the sunset was fading from the clouds, exactly as last time; the moon was bright; here and there pockets of fog were taking shape, intruding on the smoothly mown slopes from ponds and woods. He approached exactly as he'd approached before, but to Vlemk's dismay, first one thing was different and then another, so that in the end the palace seemed changed entirely. The outer gates of iron had been thrown wide open and there were no guards in sight, and he wondered for a moment if the greyhounds, when they saw him, would not tear him to bits; but all around the front of the palace stood carriages and large outdoor lanterns, dozens and dozens of them, flickering merrily, as if vying with the stars, and near the arched front door he had once felt pity toward, aristocrats stood talking and laughing, drinking champagne in their splendid dress. It was unlikely, he thought, that they would stand there and watch the dogs kill him—though on the other hand Vlemk had learned enough from people's secrets to be aware that in these matters nothing is ever quite certain.

But the dogs, he thought the next instant, were the least of it. How could he walk in, in the middle of a party of lords and ladies, and give the Princess his present? How would he even find her? As he drew nearer, moving slowly now, he saw that the lords' and ladies' clothes were all of the finest material, with clasps and buckles, buttons, epaulettes, and swordhilts of gold and silver. He looked down at his knobby brown shoes, white worksocks, and baggy black trousers, then at his vest, riding like a saddle on his pot-belly. It had only three buttons —two gray ones and a blue one. His coat had no buttons at all. He stood staring, with the box clamped tightly under his elbow, thinking what a fool he'd been, seeing himself as the Princess and her highborn friends would see him: gray-streaked unmanageable hair to his shoulders, a number of veins in his face broken, the slope of his shoulders and the bend of his back the realized potential of a life of disorder and dissolution. "I had better go back home," he thought. "I'll catch her sometime when she's not busy."

From under the black velvet cloth the picture called, "What's the matter? Why are we stopping?"

Vlemk brought the box out from under his arm, held it in front of him, and, like a waiter unfolding a napkin with the back of his hand, tipped off one corner of the cloth so that the picture could see.

For a moment the face on the box only stared, abashed. At last, in a piping voice smaller than usual the picture said, "The Princess must be having a party."

If he'd been hoping the picture would resolve his dilemma, Vlemk was disappointed. He should hardly have been surprised. She might look like the Princess, might have the very same intelligence and emotional make-up, but all that those painted blue eyes had ever seen before this walk was the box-painter's studio.

"What shall we do?" she asked.

As Vlemk stood irresolute, the answer was thrust upon them. The ground began to tremble and a sound like distant thunder began to rise from behind a dark clump of trees. A moment later six or seven horses came bounding over a hill into the light of the lanterns, on their backs young highborn men and women in capes and riding hats, returning, with the greyhounds at their heels, from a gallop over the grounds. Not far from where the others stood drinking their champagne, the riders reined in and the horses came trotting up, docile as sheepdogs; then, before the first of the horses had stopped, the greyhounds saw Vlemk and, barking like devils, came shooting out, bounding like deer, toward him. Instantly the horsemen wheeled after them, hurrying to the rescue—or so Vlemk prayed.

The greyhounds came flashing through the darkness like knives, with astonishing speed and clarity of purpose, but the horsemen were close behind, shouting stern orders at the dogs and hurried good advice to Vlemk, if only he could have heard what they were shouting. It was a horseman who reached him first; the dogs held back at the last minute. The rider was a tall young man with a moustache, his cape like midnight except for the gleaming pure white of the lining, thrown back jauntily past his shoulder like a wing. He shouted something which Vlemk could not make out, then shouted it again. Now the others came swerving and slanting up around him—one of them, he saw, the Princess. He was suddenly conscious of the late-June warmth and wetness in the air. She did not look at all as she'd looked before, but even with his heart pounding wildly in his throat from the scare they'd given him, Vlemk knew at once what the changes were—the make-up, the hair, the padded square shoulders, the startling spring paleness of skin and the hollowness of her cheeks. Fasting? he wondered. He tried to recall if some religious holiday was at hand. Two of her friends were on the ground now, quieting the dogs. The tall young man with the moustache bent down from the saddle. "Who are you?" he shouted to Vlemk. "What are you doing here?"

Vlemk threw a look at the Princess for help, but she kept back, remote and cautious, almost ghostly. Her horse pranced and turned, eager to be gone, and from time to time the Princess glanced back at the people who'd been drinking by the door, now all hurrying in a crowd to find out what was happening. Seeing that there was no other way, Vlemk reached into his pocket and drew out the note, unfolded it with badly shaking fingers, and handed it to the man. The man came close, apparently having difficulty reading it in the moonlight. He half smiled, then wheeled around and trotted his horse to the Princess. "It's for you," he said.

The Princess did not reach for it. "What does it say?"

"You think I read your mail?" he said, smiling like a lover, and held it nearer, insisting that she take it. Vlemk glanced down, full of gloom and a curious detachment, as if the Princess were an acquaintance from some other life and they had both changed completely. His gaze happened to fall on the box. The face was watching the Princess and the man in the moustache with sharp, almost virulent disapproval.

The Princess did take the note at last, giving the man a little smile, half cross, half playful. When she had finished reading she glanced sharply at Vlemk. "You are Vlemk the box-painter?" she asked, displeased. He nodded. She seemed to make out, now, the box under his arm. She looked around—the people with the champagne glasses were drawing near—and at last she said, "Bring him where it's light," and, without another glance, assuming their obedience, she set off at a trot toward the lanterns. "I don't like her," said the picture on the box, emphatically. Vlemk covered the tiny painted mouth with

his hand. Now the moustached man was bending down again, reaching to offer Vlemk a lift up and ride. Vlemk stared a moment before he saw what was intended, then shook his head in alarm and hurried on foot after the Princess. When she reached the lanterns she stopped again for a moment and looked back at him, then nodded, as if telling him to follow, and rode straight on to the enormous, arched front door. There she dismounted, gave the reins to a servant, and stood waiting for Vlemk to catch up with her. As soon as he did, panting from exertion and hastily covering the face with the cloth, the Princess said, "Won't you come inside?" Without waiting for an answer she started up the wide marble stairs.

Vlemk was by this time well aware that by bringing the box to the Princess he had made a mistake. There were social implications he hadn't bothered to think through, implications that now, too late, he recognized as painful to the Princess. Either she must curtly and crudely dismiss him, a poor harmless mute—which was not in her nature—or she must place herself in a position to be laughed at—not a pleasant prospect for a lady so concerned about appearances. Painted boxes were often, in those days, love-gifts, and from the first moment he'd seen her with her friends, Vlemk had known that, even if he had in some sense once loved her, he could not say he loved her now and could hardly imagine recapturing that emotion, though some things about her—the tilt of her head—recalled it, teasingly and faintly, heightening the shock of their mutual change. And so, clearly, he had no business here, certainly no business offering a gift that, given in front of others, had nuances of insult and entrapment, as if one were to offer a lady a dead infant in its coffin, declaring it her own. Even if, as a professional painter of pictures on boxes, he could carry it off—avoid the implications of sentiment that displeased her— there was the matter of the box itself, or, rather, the picture: she, the imitation of the Princess, would not be happy here, God knew. How much responsibility should one have, he wondered, for a feeling creature that was not, strictly speaking, a creature? Whatever the right answer, the fact remained that feel she did, and her pain and indignation were not easy matters to ignore. Even now as he walked up the marble stairway, followed the Princess and her gathering friends down the long, blue-carpeted, chandeliered hallway, and turned in, behind her, to a room filled with mirrors and figures wrought in gold—a room she had chosen, he recognized at once (knowing her as he did) for the irony it imparted, an irony that defused the effect of his coming and put limits of a kind on the scene she feared (he had forgotten, of course, that she was afraid of his art, afraid of the idea of a painting so perfect it could smile or cry or talk, though of course he had known it, had seen, while exploring her with his brush, that fear of what whimsy might lead to, her terror in the face of the unexpected) —even now, as he sat at the low glass table in the center of the room, obedient to her command, the muffled voice under the cloth was complaining, berating him, insulting the Princess.

"I want to go home," the tiny voice wailed. "You've all gone crazy! I don't look like her at all!"

Vlemk raised his eyebrows, closed his eyes, and pressed one finger down gently to stop the painted mouth. He set the box on the table, still in its black velvet cloth, and waited for the guests to gather and the Princess to take her place. It was not strictly true, apparently, that the moustached young man had been too scrupulous to read Vlemk's note. On every side of him Vlemk could hear whispered speculations on whether or not the painted picture would talk. At last a servant pulled back the Princess's chair, his head bowed in the way people bow when they quickly and casually say grace, and the Princess seated herself, unsmilingly, opposite Vlemk. When the room had quieted, Vlemk, with infinite weariness, scorning himself for this obedience to mindless ritual but seeing no way out, boxed in by the illusory infinity of mirrors, bent forward and removed the black cloth. The Princess for an instant looked not at the box but at Vlemk the box-painter, as if assuring herself that, like her, he meant harm. Then her gaze dropped to the box, and she seemed to pale. The room was faintly humming. After a moment she looked up at the man at her left, the old servant. "Do I actually look like that?" she asked quietly, her voice so sweet that Vlemk's heart wrenched. The servant seemed to muse, bending closer, two fingers on the corner of his spectacles—for all one could tell, he was sincere and honest. At last he said, "I'm not sure, Your Highness. I don't really see the resemblance."

Vlemk smiled.

"Stupid, stupid, stupid," whispered the picture, making sure that no one heard but her maker.

Now the Princess was looking hard at Vlemk the box-painter. "You say it talks?" she said.

"She talks if she wishes to," he wanted to say, but being unable to speak, Vlemk simply nodded.

Then, to Vlemk's horror, the picture said crossly, with undisguised contempt, "So you're the famous beautiful Princess."

A gasp went through the room, and the Princess's face went blank. People began whispering; here and there someone laughed; others began shushing them for silence, hoping to hear more from the box.

When everything was still again, the picture said: "You find your image unflattering, Princess?" The painted face paused, waiting for full attention. "Perhaps you've been painted too often by people who 'respect' you." The picture smiled.

The Princess, to her credit, was as calm as stone. To Vlemk she said, "Is the picture always so insulting?"

Vlemk nodded, then in fairness shook his head, then shrugged. He rolled his eyes in the direction of the box and hoped that it would soon learn resignation and, if only for his sake, make peace.

At this moment there was a commotion, and, looking up,

Vlemk saw—guided by the eyes of all the others—that on a balcony high on the wall behind him, a balcony he'd failed to notice before, a golden door was opening. After a moment a man in a wheelchair came carefully through the door, assisted beyond his need by eager servants. Vlemk knew the face at once, ravaged and sorrowful, infinitely patient yet capable of flying into rages over trifles, the face of a man of keen intelligence, plagued by some constant, nagging pain and bearing up as well as he's able. It was the King, whose picture was on the coin. He seemed at death's door. His eyes were slits, his body so wasted beneath the splendid clothes that a small child might have carried him in her arms like a doll. He tipped his head—he wore no crown—as if gazing down at the company, then feebly waved his bejewelled hand as a sign that the business of the evening, whatever it might be, should go on as before. The people bowed and bent their knees to him, some with tears in their eyes; he solomnly nodded back; and then, gradually, all eyes returned to the box.

The Princess said, "Vlemk, my friend, whatever the personality of this toy you've created, there can be no denying that you're an amazing painter of boxes. We accept your gift with pleasure."

Vlemk sadly nodded, ignoring the look of wild outrage from the box, the tiny wail of "Toy indeed!" If he closed his eyes, he knew he would see his friend the Princess as she'd looked that day when she'd refused, out of kindness, to throw him a coin from the carriage. All that was a long time ago, and Vlemk (so he told himself) had no regrets. Nevertheless, he was careful to keep his eyes open, and pressing his hands on the arms of the chair, he prepared to get up and leave.

But the picture on the box was not so pleased with the way things were going, and spoke again: "If you find me unflattering, you should look at the pictures in his studio. He's painted you again and again, Princess. Perhaps in one of the others you'd find something to your taste."

The strength went out of Vlemk's arms, and he sat as he was.

"Is this true?" asked the Princess, both interested and uneasy.

Like images in a nightmare, Vlemk's dreadful pictures of the Princess rose up before his eyes. It was not that he believed them false, exactly—indeed, the drooping eyelid he had predicted was now an actuality, at least when the Princess was angry. Nevertheless, the pictures were not things he desperately wanted her to see. He tried to think whether to nod or shake his head, and at last he pretended he hadn't heard her.

"I must admit," said the Princess almost apologetically, as if admitting that the fault might indeed be her own, "though I'm naturally impressed by the picture you've brought me, I'm not quite sure I see the likeness."

A noise came from the balcony, and instantly everyone looked up. "It speaks," cried the King in a wheedling, childish voice, banging his tiny fist on the arm of the wheelchair. "Think about that, girl! It's real enough to speak!" Instantly a terrible coughing fit took him, blood fell from his nose, and his servants rushed him—shuddering and shaking and snapping his teeth—from the room.

6

Though she hadn't admitted it the Princess was disturbed by the picture Vlemk had left her, and as the spring days passed, her discomfort in its presence increased. She would have had it destroyed if she could bring herself to do so, but the thought nagged at her that facing the whole matter squarely might somehow be important. Moreover, the idea of destroying the picture, even when it attacked her with its vulgar little tongue, made her tremble with superstitious alarm. If she threw it in the fire, might that not be a kind of murder, even though the substance of the creature she destroyed was just paint? And there was this, though she hardly dared think of it: as the flames leaped up around the picture, destroying it, might not she suddenly feel an onslaught of mysterious heat—might she not, in fact . . . She refused to let the thought complete itself.

Sometimes, if she was lucky, she was able to catch the picture in its sleep, and could gaze at the image thoughtfully for long periods, as she could never have gazed at her image in the mirror, for then the eyes were of course always open and every flicker of thought was reflected, so that nothing was to be trusted, she could never get inside herself. It had struck her as true of many people—the man with the moustache was only one—that what they saw as most interesting or charming in themselves was never in fact what was best in them: their finest expressions, their most beautiful aspects, were things unknown to them, because never shown in any mirror. She could see that the man with the moustache, for example—a prince who was considered by the kingdom's chief ministers to be an excellent match—had been persuaded by his mirror that his noblest expression was the one in which he lifted an eyebrow in ironic amusement. Personally she found that supercilious look downright offensive. She could imagine how tiresome and stupid it would look when he was eighty. What drew the Princess's heart to the man—despite her displeasure at being treated as a brood mare, an ambush piece in a political chess game—was the look of childish perplexity that sometimes came over him, a look she was sure he'd never seen on himself and would have done almost anything to avoid.

Though at first she'd been convinced that the box-painter's image was nothing at all like her—a surprising lapse in the box-painter's art or a proof that his manner of living had done damage to his brain—she had gradually begun to revise her opinion, examining the image when the eyes were closed. She saw blue lights in the temples that vaguely frightened her: she was more mortal than she thought. She saw, in addition to the many things that pleased her, little troublesome hints of cruelty, vanity, and stinginess. She began to think the portrait was accurate, and she was filled with a feeling like moths fluttering in her chest.

It was worse, of course, when the picture on the box was awake. It would sit watching her, smug as a cat, or it would say things she never would have dreamed of saying; that is, things she would never have said to herself even in a dream. By the slightest twist of a phrase, the picture on the box could make her heart turn to ice. The most innocent remark—"You do have your little ways, don't you?"—spoken in her own unmistakable voice (unmistakable to her), with her own secret ironies ringing down and down, could emotionally disable the Princess for a week. Her anguish at such moments was so bewildering and complex she could hardly make out what it was that she felt; she could only go to bed and weep. What the box said to her was for one thing so infuriatingly stupid, which meant, she knew, that she, the Princess, was for all her fine airs stupid, tiresome, in fact worthless. Though she was outwardly young, the tedious clichés with which the box attacked her— her own clichés, her own forms of attack—revealed to her that nothing was any longer new about her, the prettily painted box might as well have been her casket. At the same time, what the box said was true, however monstrously unfair— undeniably true. The picture on the box hated her; that was the gist of it. She hated herself. She needed healing, needed the touch of some loving magician who would transform her, return her to her childhood innocence, but who could love her? And if anyone did—the Prince, for example—could an intelligent woman give her heart to such a fool? There were plenty all around her who were willing to give her praise, plenty to whom she could play the Good Princess like a skillful actress, hating herself all the more as she played the role. But there was no one who could silence the voice of the truth-telling box. Even when the picture on the box was quiet, like a watchful animal, a murderer biding his time, it seemed to the Princess that it could fill all the high, square room with its crackling contempt. The picture hated her; if that was all there was to it, she would have been ruined, and that would have been that.

But the picture on the box had another side to it. Sometimes it spoke its emotions without thinking, forgetting its hatred and simply responding to the warmth of the sunlight pouring through the window, the music of the songbirds, or the beauty of the wheatfields sloping away toward the river to the west of the palace. She, the Princess, would feel herself splaying anew to the warmth of the summer, or noticing again, as she hadn't in years, how lovely the wheatfields were, yellowing into season. That voice too, the voice that gave her unthinking and unstinting praise, was unmistakably her own, and the Princess was in those moments as pleased with herself— however briefly and unsurely—as a child who's been given some wonderful gift for no reason.

The feeling was not all sweetness. It inevitably heightened in the Princess's mind the disparity between what she felt to be her best self and knew to be her worst. One day, for instance, walking in the garden with the Prince who wore the moustache, pointing out to him the glow of a blooming tea-rose, she was suddenly overwhelmed by anxiety, wondering which was the truer feeling, the innocent delight which had sprung the remark or the manipulative instinct that had turned it to a ploy in their game of political-romantic *approchement*.

"As lovely as your eyes," said the Prince, idiotically.

"Are my eyes red, then?" asked the Princess, lowering her lashes and giving him a smile.

"I was really thinking of your cheeks," said the Prince, with that look of childish vexation and befuddlement she usually liked on him. Today she was only annoyed by it—annoyed partly, if she told herself the truth, by the virginal innocence it revealed in him, an innocence she could not match. "Is it not true," she asked herself angrily, "that the Prince's remark *was* stupid and manipulative?—aesthetically stupid, a floundering metaphor, and both politically and sexually manipulative? Why should a woman's cheeks (or eyes) be celebrated for their redness, as would a child's, and not a man's?"—for her Prince would be insulted beyond words, she knew, if she should seek to flatter him by praise of his pretty, red cheeks. (They *were* red, in fact, and for a manic instant she thought of trying it.) Yet alas, both the stupidity and the attempt at manipulation came bubbling from the Prince in the moustache as innocently as water from a well, as unconsidered and open-hearted as grapes on a grapevine or pink and blue hollyhocks blooming beside a farmer's brick house.

"Are you all right?" asked the Prince with a look of alarm. Her face was flushed—as red as a rose, he might have said if he'd thought of it—and for no clear reason there were tears in her eyes.

"My dear, dear Princess," he said, in panic now, "is it something I said?"

"It's nothing," said the Princess, and put the tips of her fingers to her forehead.

"Perhaps we'd better go inside," said the Prince, and gave an irritable glance up past his shoulder, as if the heavens' over-brightness were at fault.

"Yes, perhaps we'd better," the Princess said.

At the door to her room they parted with a touch of hands, the Princess promising to be out again soon, as soon as she'd had a little rest. The minute the door was closed, she hurried to her bed and lay down with her head on the pillow, one hand draped limply across her forehead.

The picture on the box was feeling talkative. "Have a nice time?" it asked, ironically putting on the voice of an old woman.

At once, in a fury, the Princess sat up again.

"Not the quilt! Not the quilt!" cried the picture—for of late it was the Princess's habit to cover the box with a heavy yellow quilt in hopes of silencing it. "I'll be good! I'll be nothing but sweetness and light! You have my promise!"

The Princess lay back again and closed her eyes, not resting, ready to spring if the box started in again.

After a long time the box asked, trying to sound innocent, "Did he talk dirty?"

The Princess groaned.

"It's not that I *mean* to be troublesome," said the picture hastily, thinking of the quilt. "And of course it's none of my business what your suitors say to you. It's just that life's not very interesting for a person who's not real, if you know what I mean. Has it ever occurred to you that all I have is a head and neck and shoulders? I can't even play with my—"

"Stop it!" cried the Princess, sitting up again. "Where in heaven's name do you get those vulgar, obscene, unspeakable . . ." She did not finish, but put her hands to her face and bent forward like a person in pain. "Why do you hate me?" she whispered. "What is it you *want* of me?"

"I don't hate you, really," said the picture, then abruptly went silent, thinking her own thoughts.

After a long time the Princess said, "You told me once that Vlemk the box-painter made other pictures of me."

The picture on the box let the sentence hang in the air a moment, then brought out, in a voice strangely quiet, "Yes . . ."

"What are they like?" the Princess asked.

The picture on the box said nothing.

"Well?" asked the Princess.

"You'd have to see them," said the picture, again in that quiet, reserved voice that might mean anything.

"Perhaps I will," said the Princess thoughtfully, and dropped her hands to her knees, one hand on the other, her eyes staring vacantly at the farther wall. After a moment she said, "I'm told the box-painter is very poor. Perhaps if I went with a few friends to his shop, people who could afford to pay him well if he happened to have something that struck their fancy . . ."

Again the picture on the box said nothing.

"I don't mean we'd give him charity," said the Princess. "It's just that I thought . . ."

The picture on the box said, "I'm sorry I don't please you. I don't blame you for being angry, I've been thinking of no one but myself, I admit it. Perhaps if we both could try harder—especially me, I mean—"

The Princess frowned. "You don't *want* me to see the other boxes!"

"Oh, it isn't that!" the picture exclaimed. But the Princess knew her own voice too well to be fooled.

"That settles it!" said the Princess. She rose quickly and crossed to the door to call a servant and send a message to her driver. The Prince, who had been standing with his hands behind his back, looking at the pictures of nobility on the walls, saw the Princess talking with her servant and came to greet her.

"Are you better, then?" he asked.

"Prince!" she said, giving him a quick, false smile. "I've thought of something we must do. Will you help me?"

"Anything at all, my love," said the Prince, and shifted his eyes to some point above her head, slightly troubled by that smile.

"We must do something to help the poor box-painter," she said. "There he is, living in abject poverty, though he may well be one of the most brilliant artists in the kingdom!" And she told him her plan.

7

A whisper went through the tavern, and the next thing Vlemk the box-painter knew, the barmaid was leaning down to him, murmuring in his ear. Though he did not quite hear what she said, he turned around and, there at the doorway, saw the man who drove the Princess's carriage, dressed in all his finery, with the boots that shone like onyx.

Vlemk's mind was beclouded—he'd drunk a good deal of wine—and he turned to his friends in hopes of judging by their faces what was wanted of him. The poet was asleep with his eyes rolled up; the axe-murderer was staring dully straight ahead, like a man in a trance. "He's asking to see *you*," said the ex-violinist, and jabbed his long finger in the direction of the carriage driver. Vlemk looked up at the barmaid. She nodded.

Slowly, clumsily, Vlemk felt for and found his shoes—which he'd pulled out of because of the pain they gave him—scuffed his feet into them, and struggled to get up out of his seat. The barmaid took his arm, helping him, saying in his ear, "Don't be afraid! I think it's something good!" and led him across the room to where the carriage driver waited, aloof and displeased by everything around him—the open mouths, warts, and blemishes of the regulars, the stink of stale whiskey, sickness, and tobacco, the barmaid's tomcat lying over by the bar on his back, his eyes rolled sideways, waiting for someone to drop food. As Vlemk approached, the driver gave a kind of smile and a bow that were almost obsequious but constrained, full of grim reservations.

"The Princess," said the driver, "has asked if you might possibly be willing to open your shop."

Vlemk opened his mouth, put his hand on his chin, and thought deeply.

"She is interested in looking at your work," said the driver.

After a time, Vlemk nodded. He felt for the top of his head, seeing if his hat was there, then nodded again. He sensed some awful trouble outside the door, but his drunkenness was unable to place it, and so, at length, he nodded again and moved with the driver toward the entrance.

Outside, four carriages were lined up, filled with people.

Vlemk removed his hat. The door of the black-and-gold carriage opened, and the Princess leaned out to smile at him. "Hello, Vlemk. I'm sorry—we weren't sure about your hours."

Vlemk laughed, then stopped himself, thoughtfully licked his lips, then nodded. "No matter," he tried to say, then remembered the curse and simply shrugged.

"Would you do us the honor of riding with us?" asked the Princess.

He gazed at her in dismay, looked up and down the street, then helplessly shrugged again. With his hat in his hands he moved toward the carriage and, when he reached it, raised one foot, like a blind man. The driver bent down beside him and guided the foot to the shining brass step, then gently helped him in. He could see nothing inside the carriage—he had a sense of white faces gazing at him like moons—and had no choice but to submit to their kindness as they turned him and aimed his rear end toward the seat beside the Princess. "Thank you," said the Princess, leaning past him; and the driver closed the door.

"It's a great honor to meet you again," said a voice Vlemk faintly recognized. A glowing white hand hung in front of him, and after a moment he understood that he was meant to shake it. Clumsily, he did so, then wiped his hand on his trousers. The carriage smelled of flowers or perfume. Vlemk breathed very shallowly for fear of being sick.

"It's a fortunate kingdom," said another voice, "that has artists of such stature and renown!"

"Renown is for gargoyle hackers," Vlemk said scornfully; but luckily no sound came out. His hands lay on his knees. The Princess's glove came down gently on the hand to the right. He was puzzled to find it shaking like the hand of a madwoman.

The carriage swayed, soundless as a boat on the water except for the tocking of the horses' iron shoes on the cobblestones, rhythmical as clocks. Then the sound stopped and, soon after, the swaying also stopped, and the door at Vlemk's elbow fell open. He caught his breath, but all was well. The driver was extending his hand.

It was while he was climbing the stairs that his mind came back to him. A shock went through him, and he glanced down past his arm at the lords and ladies following him up the steps in all their finery. They were smiling like children at a party, expecting presents, and with a turn of the stomach he realized what it was they'd come for, what it was they wanted to see. Without his willing it, his feet stopped and his left hand clamped tight on the bannister as if never to be moved. The Princess, just behind him, looked up at his face inquiringly, waiting, dark circles under her eyes, and after a moment, touching his beard, wetting his lips, Vlemk continued climbing.

As he lighted the candles in his studio, the box-painter hesitated again, wondering if perhaps he might fool them by keeping the place relatively dark. But it was not to be, for the Prince with the moustache, ever eager to be useful, had found phosphor sticks and was hurrying here and there through the studio finding more candles in their old china dishes and lighting them, one after another. Soon the place was glowing like a room in the palace, and Vlemk knew that all was lost. Slowly, deliberately, he brought the little boxes from their various places—first the shoddily painted boxes with landscapes on them, then the boxes with flowers, then the boxes with cats and dogs—but he knew from the beginning that it would not be enough. He stood with his hands in his pockets and his eyes half closed, like some pot-bellied watchman asleep on his feet, and observed as they admired those shameless betrayals of his gift.

"I had heard . . ." said the Princess, and let the words trail off.

She seemed to Vlemk very young, very frightened, just an ordinary child, not a Princess whose father, though said to be dying, had powers like a god's in this kingdom. The Prince with the moustache stood beside her, his hand on her arm, as childlike as the girl, in the painter's eyes, a cocky, good-looking boy who'd never seen trouble, had no idea—unless he'd gotten it from books or the tales of old servants—that in the streets below there were axe-murderers, people who picked pockets, men who crept like rats through cloakrooms. He could say, he thought—that is, he could manage to impart to them by gestures—that he had no more boxes, that the pictures she'd heard of did not exist. But he saw that again she was shaping the question, opening her mouth to speak; and he did not have it in him, he found, to lie to her. He retained, despite his efforts, too much of that original lunatic vision, the shadowy reality peeking out from behind what she was.

Vlemk the box-painter nodded grimly, and brought out the boxes on which he'd painted all her worst potential. When he'd displayed them he turned curtly and went over to stand with his back to them, looking out the window. It occurred to him briefly that he might jump from it, but he was too old, too familiar with misery to be moved by cheap romance. He heard them whispering. No, they were not pleased.

"How tragic!" someone whispered.

Vlemk nodded grimly and smiled to himself. He had forgotten their talent for self-delusion. He put on a doltish look, turned back to them, and opened his hands as if to ask, "What do you think?"

"Beautiful! Just beautiful!" said a lady with silver hair. "How much?"

Vlemk ignored her, watching the Princess. Her lips faintly trembled and she shot a quick look at him, something between confusion and anger. Then she looked down again. The picture on the box she was holding in her hand was one he called, privately, "The Princess Considers Revenge." If anyone had cared to look, it was her mirror image now, the face distorted, short of breath, the lips slightly puffy, the eyes sharp and stupid as an animal's. Eager to press the scene to its conclusion, Vlemk shrugged so broadly, with a look so unspeakably foolish, that the Princess could not help but look up at him. "What do you think?" he asked again with his hands and arms.

She stared straight at him, guessing, he suspected, that he was putting on some act.

"I don't like it," the Princess said. "I don't think I look like that."

A stillness went through them all. She had given them permission to despise him.

"It's true," said the lady with the silver hair, looking at the box she'd just admired, "it's not a good likeness, really."

They looked at each other. Vlemk went on grinning like a fool and waiting. Only the Prince in the moustache seemed not to have noticed what had happened. He was staring with interest at a small, meticulously painted little pill box on which the Princess was shown waking from a dream of terrible debauchery. He turned it slightly—it was no larger around than a coin—making the glaze of the lips catch the light. "I like this one," he said, and held it toward the Princess, then saw her face.

"You should buy it," she said, cold as ice.

The poor boy had no notion of what it was he'd done wrong. His hand lowered as if all strength had suddenly drained out of his arm, and he looked again, critically and sadly, at the picture. The fact, Vlemk saw, was that he *did* like it, that his innocent heart saw no evil in it, and rightly enough, because for him there was no evil there. "I don't know," he said, and his innocence was, that instant, just a little corrupted. He compressed his lips, as if he dimly understood himself what it was that was happening to him; but he was weak, without defenses, and after another quick look at the others, put the box back down on the table where he'd found it. "No," he said, "I guess not. I don't know."

The Princess had turned toward the door. She stood thinking, her features completely expressionless, the look of a woman taking pains to hide her thoughts. Her small fingers picked irritably at her clothes. Vlemk the box-painter, who knew every muscle and bone in that lovely young face, was not thrown for a moment. She would turn—she turned—and would reach almost at random for a painted box, almost certainly a landscape—she reached for a landscape—and would hold it up to ask "How much?"

The Princess looked up, seemed to hesitate an instant, as if reading something in Vlemk's eyes. "How much?" she asked.

Vlemk put on a sad, apologetic look and told her in gestures that unfortunately that one was not for sale. She moved instantly, like a chess player who knows her opponent, putting the box down and picking up another one, not even looking at it. "This one?" she asked sharply.

He must have shown surprise. He covered as quickly as possible; it was better to take her charity than to continue this dangerous game. He raised six fingers, then with one finger and his thumb made a circle the size of the coin with the King on it—an exorbitant price.

Her eyes widened in astonishment, then suddenly she laughed, and then, just as suddenly, she shot him a hard, inquiring look. That too she quickly veiled, lowering her lashes. "Very well, six crowns," she said, and gestured to her servant, who reached with clumsy haste into his purse.

The lady with silver hair was at once struck by another of his landscapes; a gentleman in a wig found himself drawn to a picture of two dogs. The Prince in the moustache let his eyes wander over in the direction of the picture he'd been taken by, then thought better of it and began to look with studious interest at pictures of flowers. Vlemk waited until everyone was occupied, bending over landscapes, flowers, and animals, then slipped "The Dream of Debauchery" from its place, waited for his moment, slapped the Prince on the arm in the age-old pickpocket's way, and dropped the little pill box into his pocket.

"How much?" they asked, one after another. "How much?"

Each price he quoted, holding up his fingers, was more

outrageous than the last. The Princess eyed him coolly, then went over to stand at the window, lost in thought. When it was time for them to leave, the Princess smiled and said, "Good luck, Vlemk. God be with you, you poor man."

"A touch!" said Vlemk inside his mind, taking her hand and kissing it. "A touch! I felt it right here, just under my heart!"

8

However, the Princess was not yet rid of those evil-hearted pictures her friend the box-painter had made. Studying the picture that could talk, in her room, she was more and more convinced that her father had been right. It was indeed her true likeness, much as she hoped it might not be. Might not the others, still less pleasing, be equally true to what she was? She tried to summon them up in her mind, but her memory was fuzzy, or if not, some mechanism distorted the image as soon as it came to her, burned it as an image is burned out of clarity when one looks at it in too much light.

"Why did he paint them, I wonder?" she asked aloud one day, standing at her window, talking to herself.

"I'm sure he meant no harm," said the picture on the box, its voice no louder than the buzzing of a bee.

The Princess tipped her head, not quite turning to the box. After a moment she asked, "Does he hate me, do you think? Is that it?"

"He never spoke of you unkindly, so far as I remember," said the picture on the box.

"You're lying," said the Princess, though in fact she was not sure. For some queer reason she found it harder and harder to know what the image on the box was thinking, even when the tone of voice was most distinctly her own.

"I'm not!" said the picture with a touch of indignation. "The fact is, I never heard him mention you!"

"Well, he certainly must have given me some *thought*," said the Princess. "I mean, my face seems to be an obsession with him!"

"Ah!" said the picture. "So you admit that there is indeed some slight resemblance!"

"I admit nothing!" snapped the Princess. "Stop quizzing me!" Quickly, to avoid further argument, she left the room.

But her doubts would not leave her a moment's peace. Sitting at supper, with the Prince across from her, looking gloomy because he no longer understood her and the time of his visit was nearing its end, the matter between them still entirely unresolved, the Princess, taking a small bite of her roll, would suddenly see Vlemk the box-painter's image of her eating a piece of chicken with a look of insatiable gluttony, her eyes like a weasel's. Or walking in the woods, wringing her hands and tossing her hair back again and again, as if to drive away fierce thoughts or deny unfounded charges made by people she had trusted implicitly, she would suddenly see in her mind's eye, more real than the ferns and trees around her, Vlemk the box-painter's image of her tearing at her cheeks with her fingernails, gone mad.

One night her father the King came into her room, something he had never done before. When the door was closed behind him and his servants had stepped back in the way he required of them, seeming to disappear like September mist into the curtains and walls, the King, clutching at his clothes with a kind of unconscious desperation, as if anything that touched him, any slightest physicality, gave him a scalding pain, almost more than he could bear, raised his head with great difficulty and said: "Daughter, what's the matter with you? I'm told on good authority you're like a woman that's out of her wits."

The Princess went white with fear, for like everyone in the palace she had experience of her father's rages.

"Don't lie!" snapped her father.

"I wasn't going to!" she snapped back, indignant.

His eyebrows lifted, and he studied her, his tiny claws pulling more fiercely at his clothes. "Good," he said. His head snapped back suddenly, as if something invisible had struck him on the chin. And he shook all over, his hands flying out over the wheelchair arms, fluttering like wings, until the fit was over. The servants stood like monkeys, bent forward, prepared to rush to him. When he could raise his head again, sweat streaming down onto his nose and beard, he said, "Tell me what's the matter, then. I haven't much time left—as any damn fool can see." When she said nothing, he said, "Well?"

"I haven't been myself," said the Princess, feebly. She noticed, in horror, that she was picking at the front of her dress, exactly as her father did, though not so wildly.

His head fell toward her, tilted sideways, the lips stretched wide with agony. "Don't waste time!" he cried. "Have mercy!" Again, more violently than before, the old King's head shot back and the trembling came over him. The servants moved toward him, and—with such strength of will that the Princess was thrown into awe of him—his fluttering hands waved them back. "No time for niceties!" he gasped. His nose began to bleed and he tried to take an angry swipe at it.

It was the box that cried out in an agony of love and sorrow, "Tell him! For the love of God tell him and be done with it!"

The King rolled his eyes toward the box, then let them fall upward again.

"Very well!" the Princess said, clutching at her dress, twisting and wrinkling it, then straightening it again. In a rush, she told him all. When she was finished, she sat staring at her knees, weeping and occasionally sniffing, jerking back her head.

The King let his head and shoulders fall forward, his eyelids sinking over his eyes as if by their weight. With what seemed his last breath, he said, "Go to the box-painter. Beg him to remove the curse. Otherwise we're doomed."

"Princess!" cried the picture on the box in a voice unlike any the Princess had ever heard from it, "he's dying! Run to him!"

Without thinking, the Princess obeyed. "Father!" she cried, "Father, for the love of God!" Now the servants were all around her, and it seemed to the Princess in her madness that the walls of the room had caught fire.

"Don't die!" she whispered, but she knew now, flames all around her, that that was why he'd come to her. In the ravening heat, it was as if her mind had flown open and she knew everything everyone in the room was thinking. Then, the next instant, in the blinding whiteness, her mind went blank.

"Princess," one of the servants said softly, lifting her as if she weighed nothing, "we'll take care of him. Rest yourself."

Slowly, the illusion of fire sank away, and she was standing, supported by servants, gazing at something too still, too full of peace to be her father. Now his strange words came back to her: "Beg him to remove the curse."

The day after the King was buried, she went to the box-painter.

9

She could not believe, at first, the change that had come over him. He seemed much older, much sadder, so gentle that the Princess—or, rather, the Queen, since she now ruled the kingdom—could almost have believed she had dreamed their last meeting, when he'd charged those mad prices for the worthless pictures she and her friends had bought, carelessly scrawled landscapes of cows crossing streams, sickly, drab asphodels and forget-me-nots, day-lilies and primroses, or those maudlin little animals, cats, dogs, teddy-bears—not so much box-paintings as angry parodies, at best, of the box-painter's art. He was busy at the same kinds of subjects now, but with such a difference that they seemed not the work of the same hand. His paintings of gardens were so accurate in each detail, even to the occasional weed or insect, so alive with the spirit of whoever it was that had planted them—some old woman, she imagined, or some old man in suspenders, once a farmer or a lawyer, who'd settled down in his final days to make the life he was leaving more comfortable for someone he knew, or perhaps did not know, for the world in general, with all its sorrows—so accurate in their depiction of both the beauty and the sadness of the world as it is, that one believed, if one closed one's eyes, that one could smell the autumn leaves.

Nor was the studio he worked in the same at all. What had seemed a kind of crypt never visited except by the artist's ghost, a bleak place of weariness, misery, and failure, had now become a hive of activity. There were customers who greedily sorted through the boxes, pretending to find fault with them to get an easier price, children and old people, a lean, smiling banker with a terrible worried look flickering around his eyes —he was looking for a box for his wife, he said, and had no idea what might appeal to her ("Bring her in!" said the box-painter with gestures. "Bring her in!")—an angry old woman, a laborer, a midget. . . . Vlemk the box-painter had taken on three young apprentices, two dull, lanky ones and one who was fat and near-sighted—"A master!" Vlemk told the Queen with gestures, "a genius!" She looked at the young man with distaste: plump, pink-cheeked, working with his tongue between his teeth, bending down to watch, almost cross-eyed, as his mallet ticked brads into the eight-sided box he was at work on. When he saw that she was watching he smiled and gave her a wink that seemed vaguely obscene. Quickly, she looked away. How Vlemk had done it all in less than a month was a mystery to her, for the Queen had no idea that she herself was at the heart of the change. Her friends who'd bought boxes had made Vlemk the social *dernier cri*, and they had done so just at the moment when, as chance would have it, he was in a mood to revise his life. That too was of course her influence, though she could not know it. She could know only that he was a changed man, an artist again, though not at all the artist she had come to seek out—and in fact not an artist she approved of. There had been in him, before, something scornful and majestic, the dignity and barely contained rage of a fallen Lucifer, a haughty detachment, unbending pride, even in his abject poverty, that transformed his afflictions, even his muteness, to bends of nobility. Now overnight he had become just another peasant artisan—indeed, a man at ease with peasant artisans: over by the window, timidly peering down with tiny pig's eyes through his thick, thick spectacles, stood a famous stained-glass-window maker called Lefs—her father had often been his patron—and on a stool, half asleep, sat Borm the bellmaker, a thick-nosed, doltish-looking fellow with hair in his ears.

She stood erect, her face half hidden in the cave of her hood, her gloved hand closed on the doorknob. She was half inclined to flee, sick at heart. It was at that moment, looking around her at the tedious goodness that rolled like granulating honey through the box-painter's shop (such was her word for it; she was no longer comfortable calling it a studio), that the Queen understood that the terrible paintings of her were true. She might not like it, she might—knees trembling—feel shocked toward despair by the frightening fact, but she knew that those paintings she had seen were serious, as none of this was, that the mind that had seared through her flesh to the bones, the mind that with the icy indifference of a god had layer after layer torn the sham away, the childish eagerness, the ridiculous pretenses—the mind that had stripped her and used her and dismissed her—was the mind, sublime and cold-blooded, of an artist. Tears sprang to her eyes as she considered the ruin he had become: a man worth, at his best, all the gold in the kingdom, a thousand kingdoms, now reduced, without even knowing it, to this. She remembered with incredulity how once she had refused to let a coin be tossed to him, imagining in her madness that it might lead him to "further debauchery!" Unconsciously she raised her hand to her eyes. The movement was enough to draw the attention of Vlemk the box-painter.

Quickly he came toward her, moving his lips in some remark of dismay, as if he'd forgotten that he'd lost the gift of speech.

"I must go," she said, and opened the door. A warm breath presaging rain came in.

Grotesquely, as solicitous as her moustached Prince, he caught the edge of the door, half closed it, and held it. He gestured and rolled his eyes. Heaven knew what he was saying. His gaze was fixed on her black band of mourning.

"I must go," she said again, this time more sternly.

A calm came over him. A coldness, rather; faintly reminiscent of his greater days. With the look of a man killing an insect while holding a conversation—a brief wince, then no change in his expression—he closed the door. She stared, a little frightened, trying to read his eyes. He simply stood there, queerly smiling, the hum of sweetness filling the room behind him, customers chattering, his apprentices hurrying, now painting, now talking, no one noticing the two of them, herself and Vlemk, as removed as two stars. She jerked at the doorknob. She might as well have jerked at a knob on a wall of stone. She focused on the doorknob, studying the wild leap of feeling inside her. She was angry enough to scream at him, but at the center of her rage lay the mad question: am I in love with this pot-bellied old man?

"I'll come back when you're less busy," she said.

"You've come to see the pictures," he said. Though she knew it was impossible, he seemed to say it with his voice.

"Yes, I have," she said.

Vlemk the box-painter nodded, polite, then took his hand from the door and turned away. He stopped to speak in gestures to one of his apprentices—the young man looked over at the Queen, then quickly back at Vlemk—then, half smiling, nodding to his customers, stepping carefully past his table of boxes, the box-painter went to a covered stack in the corner of the room, lifted off the cover, took a folded sack from the floor beside them, and indifferently dropped the boxes, one by one, into the sack. When he returned to her, the box-painter took her hand as he would a child's, hardly looking at her, opened the door, led her from the room, and softly pulled the door closed behind them. Then, letting go of her hand, he started down the stairway. The Queen followed.

Strange as it may seem, the Queen had never before seen the inside of a tavern. She walked with the false assurance of a blind man pretending he needs no help, pressing forward, stiff and erect, waiting as if impatiently for Vlemk to choose a table, though in fact she had no idea whether or not it was accepted practice for a man and a woman to be seated together in a tavern. She was assaulted by such sensations, such newness and mystery, that she could hardly think, could only see and see, drinking in vision with the wide eyes of a child—indeed, she thought instantly of the way she had seen things at four or five, every surface alive, unnaturally sharp-edged: she remembered when she'd gone to the Fair with her father, servants all around them, looking out with sharp, fearful eyes for anarchists, her father still strong and tall, almost fat, crying "Ho, ho, ho" and shaking hands with his people when he could reach past the circle of guards.

The room was still, the people all pretending not to look at her. She stood, chin lifted, feeling a strange thrill of evil in her veins. What would people say? she wondered, knowing what they'd say, and an image from one of Vlemk's paintings rose before her, what she secretly called "The Queen as Fallen Woman."

Then the barmaid stood before them, more innocent than the Queen had been even in childhood, or so the Queen imagined, the barmaid companionably nodding and smiling, guiding them to a long table close to the front door, a table with candles on it, alongside it six stolid chairs. Vlemk led the Queen to a chair by the wall, went back around the table to the chair directly opposite, and laid the sack on the table while the barmaid silently moved the other four chairs away. Vlemk made a signal, presumably his order, and the barmaid left. Then, without expression, Vlemk opened the sack and took out the boxes, one by one, and slid them across to her. When he'd removed the last box, he folded the sack and put it on his lap like a napkin. He splashed open his hands and smiled disparagingly, eyes remote. The Queen looked down at them.

It was incredible to her that they'd so shocked her the first time she'd seen them. There they were, her possibilities, each more terrible than the last; but they did not seem to her terrible now. It was like reading history books: this king died in battle, this king of syphilis, this one by a fall from his horse. What she felt, more than anything else, was a sense of new freedom, release. It was true, she thought, as if responding to something the talking picture on the box had said to her; this decorous life she'd pursued all her days was trivial, ludicrous. How strange and wonderful to be able to gaze down from the mountaintop, like a soul at last free of its body, and see life as it was. This king died in battle, this one of syphilis. . . .

One of the pictures showed her face tipped so high it seemed her neck would snap. "The Queen Full of Pride," she secretly named it. She laughed. Vlemk the box-painter glanced at her, judgmental, and she laughed again, more openly than she'd meant to. A man with yellow-white flaxen hair and sleepy eyes stopped abruptly in the middle of the room to look at her, then after a moment drew up a chair and sat down beside her. At just that moment the barmaid returned with the drinks Vlemk had ordered, two small, crude glasses that contained something thick and vaguely black. The barmaid looked daggers at the man who had come to sit with the Queen, then looked questioningly at Vlemk, who lowered his eyes and shrugged. With a frightened expression, the barmaid glanced at the Queen. "It's no harm," said the Queen, and mimicked Vlemk's shrug. One casual hand raised to hide her ugly birthmark, the barmaid looked again at Vlemk, who pretended not to notice; then, at last, she reluctantly turned away to go about her business.

"Hello," said the man with flaxen hair, and grinned one-sidedly. His teeth were discolored and tilted, like headstones in an old, old graveyard.

She nodded and glanced at his patched, ragged elbow, too close to her own.

"I," said the man, "am a poet." He tipped his head back, slightly to one side, letting his remark sink in.

"That's nice," she said, and glanced at Vlemk. He was looking at the boxes. She too looked down at them.

"Poets are much disparaged in this moron age," said the poet.

She said nothing, but gave him a noncommittal nod and reached for a candle to give the boxes more light. The poet leaned closer, looking too. She lowered her eyebrows and tensed her forehead, straining to ignore him.

It seemed that any one of the paintings might speak if it wished to, even the ones done most carelessly, as if in disgust. What had he been thinking as he painted them? she wondered again. And how was it that he could sit there so calmly now, two fingers around the stem of his glass, hardly looking at her, beginning to show signs of impatience. She drew away from the poet a little, shooting him a look, and then glanced again at Vlemk. Here in the tavern, with the candlelight making his graying hair glow like newly cut iron, he no longer seemed just one more artisan. In comparison to the poet, he might have been made of solid marble. "I have come to beg you to remove the curse," she thought of saying, and quickly looked down, driving out the image of her father by saying to herself with intense concentration, "It makes no sense."

The poet said, "Your eyes are like curdled cream. Does that offend you?"

She looked at him as she'd have looked at some curious insect.

Instantly, the poet rolled his eyes up and waggled his hand.

He looked exactly like her father, and the breath went out of her. She threw a wild glance at Vlemk for help, but Vlemk had his eyes closed, infinitely patient, burying both the poet and herself in the rot of time. Suddenly she found herself shaking like a machine, and Vlemk opened his eyes. He looked at the poet, so calmly that the whole world changed for her. Yes, she must learn to be like Vlemk the box-painter. Learn to dismiss with absolute indifference the antics of mere mortals! She must live for the imperishable! She'd been wrong about him, she saw now. He had not mellowed, gone soft. In the end he had dismissed even rage and scorn, even the young artist's hunger for Truth. He had moved beyond silence to a terrible kind of comedy, painting nonsense with unholy skill—landscapes, animals, all that dying humanity foolishly clings to.

That instant Vlemk leaned forward, one finger raised as if in warning, and with a stern expression shook his head. Was he reading her mind? she wondered. He must be, of course. He knew her as no one had ever known her before, every spasm and twitch.

The boxes gleamed in the candlelight, a coolly disinterested catalogue of horrors—wretched grimaces, rolled eyes; ten obscene masks of corruption. And it came to her suddenly that the point was *not* that one of them was fated to come true: *all* of them were true. And it was not that he loved her or hated her. She was a specimen, simply, like the rat the biologist happens to come down on with his glove. He could have done it as well with the poet—she could do it herself, if she had his craft! This is the world, he had said. So much for the world! And he'd gone back to painting pretty gardens, where weeds pushed up, merry as crocuses, and insects chewed and were chewed, like gargoyles on a church. This is the world, my children, my moustached princes, coyly smiling ladies. Again Vlemk's eyes were closed, burying all that lived. *I never heard him mention you*, the picture that could talk had said. Even when he was painting her hour after hour, he'd given her no more thought than the biologist gives to the frog he is cutting to pieces, still alive. That was Art. That was the mountaintop. The boxes blurred together in an image of her father's dying face.

She leaned forward, clutching the table, struggling to clear her sight. Her wits reeled, though she hadn't yet tasted the vaguely black drink. She found herself staring now at one of the boxes in particular—perhaps she'd been staring for some time. "The Queen Envious," she thought it might be called. It showed her face almost comically narrowed and peaked, her eyes enormous, the tips of her teeth showing.

Vlemk opened his eyes. "Your health," he said soundlessly, murderously ironic—or so it seemed to the Queen—and raised his glass.

Soon there were two more of them, friends of Vlemk, or so they claimed, and Vlemk accepted it in silence, eyelids sinking again. One maintained he was an ex-violinist. The other maintained nothing at all, staring at her throat a moment, occasionally glancing at the door as if expecting more of these "friends." The Queen could hardly breathe. All her life she had scorned and avoided vulgarity, ugliness: but here, sunk deep in both, she was revising her opinions. She had wanted gardens without insects. She wanted that no longer. She wanted now only to *see*. But her mind was fuzzy. She strained for concentration. There was no feeling in the tips of her fingers.

The poet said things so foolish one had to think about them. "Suppose," he said, floating his head toward her, half-moons of yellow below his irises, "suppose God were a spider!"

She waited. He seemed to have nothing more to say. But when she turned to the ex-violinist for help, the poet broke in quickly, seizing the floor again, violently trembling, "Out of his own *entrails* the spider spins!" He gave a jerk, trying to raise his arm to shake his fist at her, but his elbow struck hard against the edge of the table, making him yelp and bringing tears to his eyes. The ex-violinist shook his head and said, "Listen—" Furiously, wildly, the poet struck out with his narrow left arm, hitting the ex-violinist in the chest. "But also the spider stings!" the poet yelled. The voice, thin and high, reminded her of the voice of the picture that could talk, and abruptly she remembered that the picture was herself. She looked at Vlemk. He was asleep.

The poet, for no reason, was crying. Softly, the ex-violinist said, "He's so full of hate, this man. Who can blame him?"

She looked for help at the man who sat staring at her throat. Something in his look made her blood curdle, and, smiling nervously, lowering her lashes, she asked, "And what do *you* do?" Nothing in his expression changed, but he looked into her eyes, giving her a terrible sensation of endless falling. After a moment he indicated by a shift of his eyes that she should look under the table. She felt herself blushing scarlet; then, biting her lip, she obeyed. In the darkness below, almost touching her shoes, lay the blade of an axe. Instinctively, before she knew she would do it, she touched her throat. The man smiled, then his eyes once again went out of focus. She put both hands over her heart to calm the pounding, like a fire behind her collarbone.

Vlemk the box-painter opened his eyes a little, raised his eyebrows, and looked at his friends. He looked at the Queen, as if to ask what had happened, then down at his lap. He lifted the sack and began to put the boxes in, one by one. She watched them being taken from her with the anguish of a child losing its treasures. Each horror he moved to the sack was like flesh torn from her, but she kept herself from speaking. When he'd put them all inside and had pulled the purse-string that closed the neck, he pushed back his chair and stood up, nodding to her and gesturing. She too pushed back her chair—breathing shallowly, her legs slightly shaking—and stood up. The poet protested. The man who had the axe raised his head as if in distress, looking at her throat. She tried to look away from him but found herself helpless until the box-painter came around the table and offered her his arm. She seized it and clung tightly. Though she looked back, trailing him to the door, still clinging, no one asked for money. She tried to think about it, but her mind was still full of the image of the axe.

Soon they were on the street, where her driver was waiting, the black-and-gold carriage gleaming weirdly in the light of the lamps and the distant moon. The driver held the door of the carriage for her, melting into darkness in the way her father had always liked, and Vlemk the box-painter squeezed her arm, more powerfully than he knew—she would have bruises in the morning—then released her and began to back away. Before she knew she would do it, she reached out, sudden as a snake striking, and seized the bag of boxes. He did not seem surprised but only looked at her, expressionless, as if thinking of another way of painting her.

"Let me take it," she said. She could not look at him. "Sell them to me!"

He said nothing, showed nothing, but after a long moment shook his head sadly, a little sternly, and opened his thick, strong fingers so that the bag was hers.

She stepped into the carriage, the door closed behind her, and almost at once she heard the tocking of the horses' hooves and felt the swaying of the carriage.

10

It was the beginning of a terrible period for the Queen. Whatever the truth might be, it seemed to her unquestionable that she had glimpsed a world more important than her own, gloomy and malevolent but intrepidly alive. In her sleep she would dream of the dark, smoky tavern and see again the tip of the axe peeking out from the skirt of the silent man's coat. Putting on a necklace or walking in a field, she would suddenly find herself not looking at the emeralds or watching the airy pirouette of starlings but gazing, mystified and perhaps a little frightened, at the calm, sleeping face of Vlemk the box-painter, the sum of the earth all around him—the poet who could not write, the violinist who could not play, the grim man who carried an axe and stared at throats.

Strange to say, the boxes, when she laid them out one after another on her table, had no great interest for her now. She looked at them, studied them, but the magic had evaporated. They were pictures, simply—not even very good ones, she occasionally suspected—and though she knew, intellectually, that they were the story of her life or image of her character, she found that something had gone wrong with her; she had no feeling for them. She looked at them each time with renewed disappointment. They might as well have been sick cartoons. They were not just that, she knew, and she struggled to feel their significance. Sometimes, indeed, she could feel a frail echo of the original thrill of alarm—sense herself decaying, know the horror of death. But when she thought, she knew that the feeling did not come from the pictures, it came from the tavern, the silent man's axe. The pictures were boring. It was because of that, because she had lost all feeling, that sometimes she sat with the terrible pictures spread out before her and silently wept.

"Are you all right?" the picture that could talk would say. She would sniff, jerk back her head, and nod.

"You certainly are becoming a bore," the picture that could talk would say. "What ever happened to your fury?"

" 'Fury,' " the Queen would mock, sniffing. There it usually ended. But one night when unaccountably the air smelled of winter, the picture felt cross enough to press the matter. "That's what I mean," the picture said. "Why are you so quick to *pounce* on things?"

"The quilt," said the Queen coolly, rising from her bed.

"Why? That's no fair!" cried the picture. "What did I say?"

But the Queen had no mercy and put the quilt over the picture's face.

It was not quite sufficient; she could hear the picture wailing, like the hum of a mosquito; but she ignored it.

Tiresome as the paintings on the boxes were, or deeply depressing, not for what they showed but for the proof they gave her that she was only half alive, a miserable creature displacing air in the world for no good reason—the thought of the tavern filled her with something like the same alarm she had felt when she first stepped through the door. Perhaps that was the answer, it struck her all at once. Immediately she thought of the man with the axe and felt a tingle of fear. Suppose he should indeed kill her! In her mind's eye she saw it vividly, the sudden moving shadow where she had thought there was only a doorway, his rush toward her, coattails flying, the axe uplifted, the man running just a little sideways, coming without a sound. The vision was so clear that it made her cry out, sudden tears filling her eyes. She clenched her fists, then clutched her head, trying to think clearly. Was that perhaps the curse that had fallen on her—a fear of life because she too much feared death? Surely that was wrong! Surely there was nothing in the world that she feared, pain, sickness, madness. . . . Abruptly, reaching her decision almost without knowing it, she rose and snatched up her cloak, crossed to her door, thinking of calling for her carriage driver, then paused, lips pursed, and, deciding on another course, threw her cloak across a chair. She quietly opened the door, stepped through, and just as quietly closed it; she looked to left and right, then hurried to the chamber of her maid. When she opened the door without knocking, letting light rush in, the maid sat bolt upright in bed and gave a peeping cry.

"It's all right!" said the Queen.

The maid's eyes widened again, and her small gray mouth fell open.

"I need to borrow some clothes," said the Queen.

And so that night the Queen walked down into the city, alone and in disguise.

Not even the stupidest of the regulars were fooled, but they pretended to be. The Queen stood stiff and erect at the elbow of the ex-violinist. "Do you mind if I sit down?" she asked.

The ex-violinist looked at his friends in befuddlement, then back at the Queen, then severely nodded, reaching out with a jerk of his arm for the chair, to pull it back for her.

It was the strangest, most joyful and terrifying night of her life—as much of it as she could remember. It seemed to her that all she had suspected was true: her ordered life was madness, only this wild, unbridled acceptance of whatever the universe might throw, in its glorious indifference, was true and right. Somehow in her innocent dreams of debauchery she had imagined that she would sing like a gypsy and dance, throw her fists like a man, indulge in unspeakable language. That, when she thought of it now, made her toss back her head and shake uncontrollably with laughter. No no, it was nothing like that for the Queen. It was something far more wonderful and vile. It was the smell of the armpits of the ex-violinist as he closed her in his arms, almost falling from his chair beside hers in the tavern, raging against music. It was the coldness of the flesh of the sleeping poet when she kissed him on the cheek—

she would have sworn he was dead—and the heat in the fingers of the axe-murderer as he slowly lowered his hand onto hers, pinning it to the coarse tavern table, his eyes staring through her.

"Very well," she thought, sometime long after midnight—full of cunning, her eyelids so heavy she had to peek out through the slits, "very well, very well . . ." She strained futilely to remember what she'd meant to say. The three men's eyes were all glazed and still, like the eyes of dead animals she'd seen beside the road. "Very well," she said again, with conviction, and raised one finger to shake it at the axe-murderer. She made her face bold and dissolute. "I suppose you're aware that my father died?" The murderer looked at her as before. Yes, she thought, yes! and felt a thrill of aliveness. What was it to artists—a life, a death? She smiled and jerked herself left to look around at the room, pawing abstractedly for her glass and straining hard to clear the blur. Smoke, darkness, people, a tall figure, blurred at the edges, standing by the door. She smiled, head lowered, and swung her face back toward the axe-murderer. "*Well*," she said, her voice gone deep. "I imagine you wonder why I'm here!" She laughed, hearing the girlishness, the sweetness. "Ha ha! Ha ha!" She steadied herself, focusing on the murderer's face, and it occurred to her that it was time to speak truthfully. She took a drink from her glass, not looking down from his eyes. "I suppose you're aware that my father died?" she said. "Well!" she said, coming to her senses—she was making a scene; it was absurd. "Very well!" she said, and smiled. The murderer was leaning down, doing something with the axe, under the table. The tall man at the door came toward them and slowly walked past, his arms folded over his chest. He was a policeman. When he was gone, the murderer wiped his forehead. The policeman sat down in the corner of the room. He got out his pipe and stoked it. After a moment, pursing her lips, the Queen said, "I suppose we all die, don't we." She found she was crying.

For Vlemk the box-painter, it was not easy to believe his eyes when he found her the next morning, gray as a ghost, one shoe missing, her body in the gutter surrounded by old papers, oyster shells, and frost like bits of glass and white hair. He knew from the instant he first saw her exactly what had happened and all that was wrong with her, for strange to say, she looked, right down to the last detail, like a certain one of the cruel, bitter pictures he'd made of her. He gawked, his knees bent, his arms reaching out; then, clamping down his hat with one hand, ran around her, absurdly looked down for a relatively clean place to plant his knees, shook himself in anger at such foolishness, then dropped down to listen—almost dizzy with dread—for her heartbeat. Was it possible that she'd frozen to death? He heard her heart at once, sound as any drum, and joyfully patted her on the cheek, weeping with relief, then rubbed his hands. "Yes, yes," he exclaimed inside his mind, looking up and down the street, "be quick about it!" Tears ran down his cheeks, cold as ice in the wind. He planted his knees more firmly and thought about where to put his hands to pick her up.

It was only when he was halfway up the hill on his way to the palace, huffing and blowing, the Queen a deadweight in his arms, that the box-painter's joy at finding her still alive gave way to worry. What was to become of her? He'd told himself at first that it was grief at the death of her father that had brought on this fling of self-destruction; for indeed, the whole kingdom had reeled and staggered at the death of the old man. But now Vlemk was beginning to remember certain things that disturbed him. He remembered how, when he'd ridden in the carriage with her, her gloved hand, laid on his, had trembled. It had filled him with alarm which he'd have given more thought to, had he not been, at the time, too drunk to think of anything but himself. He remembered, and saw again now, looking down at her—her head falling limply, slightly turned to one side as he carried her in his arms—how hollow her cheeks had looked of late, and how under her eyes she had dark circles. He thought of the glint he had seen repeatedly in her eyes when she was angry, a glint that seemed a little like madness. "Bless me," he said in his mind, and his distress became greater than before. "How beautiful she is!" he thought, and did not notice the strangeness of it, for what he was noticing was quite the opposite, that she had changed for the worse.

Vlemk's arms and legs were trembling and aching—"None of us are as young as we used to be," he thought—and he saw that he must rest before finishing the trek up the hill. Now that the sun was out, the day had become quite warm. A maple tree stood beside the road just ahead of him, and he decided to push that far and set down his burden for a little underneath it in the shade. Shortly before he reached the tree, red-gold and glorious, he saw to his surprise that there was a monk sitting under it. He felt a touch of dismay, for he had hoped he could get her to the palace without anyone's seeing her; but his weariness was not to be denied. If he carried her much farther he would fall; it was no time for niceties. He entered the sparse shade of the maple with the Queen, bowing politely to the monk as he came in, and lowered her to the grass and fallen leaves on the tree's far side, where the monk might not notice who she was. Vlemk dusted a few bits of dirt from her forehead, straightened her arms and legs—as if arranging her for her funeral, he thought woefully, for in fact she looked astonishingly like the cruel painting he called "The Princess Almost Dead of Despair." Then, wiping away all trace of his tears, Vlemk went around to the side of the tree where the monk was, to keep him occupied.

The monk was an old man as bony and wasted as a person

who's lived for years on just air and tea. He sat with the skirts of his cassock hiked up to let the breeze in at his legs—it was a day for picking persimmons or going for one last cool swim in some farmer's pond—and he had his hood thrown back, revealing his large ears and head, as hairless as a darning egg. A stalk of timothy hung down limply from the brown stumps that more or less served him as teeth, and inside his collar, to cut down the scratching, he had burdock leaves.

"Ah! The box-painter!" said the monk, looking up at Vlemk.

Vlemk studied him more closely.

"We met one dark night in a graveyard where I make my home, insofar as I have one," the monk explained.

Vlemk nodded and smiled, remembering now, though only dimly. He also remembered that when he'd last seen the monk the curse of the picture had not yet been put on him. By gestures and winces, he revealed his new condition.

The monk smiled and nodded, utterly unperturbed. "That's the world, my friend," he said. "Sin"—he looked up into the tree as if the notion pleased him—"sin is all around us. The whole of creation is one vast sin." He smiled.

Vlemk scowled to show that he was not in agreement, or that at any rate he did not consider his curse to be a punishment for his sins but, on the contrary, a stroke of blind chance.

"Matter itself is sin," said the monk. "This is a hard lesson, my child." He reached toward Vlemk to pat his foot with one skeletal hand. Not instinctively, but to show how he felt, Vlemk drew his foot back. The monk closed his eyes and smiled as benignly as before. "I know, I know. You don't believe me. No one does. Nevertheless it's the case, I believe. I'm an old, old man, as you can see by these teeth—close to the grave, beyond all desire to make up stories. I can give you my assurance as a Christian ascetic, I was never so happy in all my days as I've been since the night I accepted the proposition that all matter, all earthly physicality, is filth and corruption."

Vlemk sighed irritably, reached down for a stick on the grass beside him, and considered whether he was strong enough to continue on his way up to the palace. His legs were still weak, the strength in his fingers so diminished that he could barely break the stick with two hands. "Very well, I'll sit here a moment longer," he thought. Much as he disliked the monk's opinions, Vlemk joked to himself a little bitterly, the monk did no more harm in the world than, say, an axe-murderer, and Vlemk had tolerated that, though perhaps not with pleasure.

"Ah yes, ah yes," the monk said, nodding. "I understand the pull! That lovely lady there—" He gestured toward the Queen lying still as a corpse on the far side of the tree. Carefully, or so it seemed to Vlemk, the monk avoided looking at her. "Physicality has its beauties, but they're devil-lures and delusions. Take my word for it. Everything passes. That's the one great truth, this side of heaven." He glanced at Vlemk, oddly shy. "Symbols, that's their value," he said. "Signs of what might be. This timothy stalk"—he pointed at the stalk he chewed on even as he lectured—"all the juice has been gone out of it for months now. That's why I chew on it."

As he spoke, a bee, for some reason not flying but buzzing in the grass, struggling along through it, found purchase on his ankle and, still buzzing, beating its small wings with the fury of a damned soul in fire, climbed up on top of his foot and settled, gradually calming itself, between the monk's first and second toes. Vlemk leaned forward slowly, not to alarm the bee, and pointed, imagining that the monk had not noticed it was there.

"Let him rest," said the monk. "He has his troubles too." He shook his head sadly. "A tiny soul trapped in the horror of materiality—sick unto death, it may well be; certainly it *will* be, sooner or later. For him, all the pain in the world is right there in that small body." He pointed at the bee.

"You're not afraid he'll sting you?" asked Vlemk with gestures.

Ever so slightly, the monk shrugged. "Let him sting me. Not that he will, I think. But suppose he does? Who am I to complain? Up there where we can't see them, blinded by daylight"—he pointed up into the tree, or through it—"stars are exploding. Have you ever seen an elephant die?" He rolled his eyes up, then closed them, shaking his head.

Rested, the bee began beating its wings again, and apparently whatever had been wrong before was no longer wrong, for it lifted from its place between the monk's two toes, flying backward, then forward, or so it seemed to Vlemk, and zoomed toward the trunk of the tree. It moved on past the trunk in the direction of the Queen, and suddenly Vlemk's heart floundered. It flew straight to the Queen's lower lip and settled there. Vlemk was up at once, leaping like a flea, and dropped down on his knees beside the Queen and flailed his right hand above her face to drive the bee off. Horrified, too shocked to flail his hand again, he saw the bee lower its stinger into the pink of her lip—slowly, deliberately, it seemed to Vlemk— then fly away. The Queen's eyes popped open and she gave a little cry. She raised her hand to her mouth.

"Oh no!" Vlemk exclaimed without a sound.

"He'll die now," the monk said. "You've killed him; or he's killed himself." He still had his eyes closed. "That's what comes of falling in love with the things of this world. Let them be—let them batter and claw themselves to death, as they will. In the end they'll be better off for it, believe me. Freed souls, pure spirit! The same as they were before matter undid them, with all its serpentine twists and accidents." The monk waved his hand, still with eyes closed. "I know, I know," he said wearily. "You don't believe me."

The Queen rolled her eyes to left and right in panic, poking at her lip with two fingers, trying to make out what had happened and where she was.

"It's all right," said Vlemk with gestures. "A bee stung you."

She stared at him, closed her eyes again, then opened them and touched her mouth with the tip of just one finger.

The monk stretched out on his back, as if dismissing them.

Gingerly, as if her body were as bruised as her dress was torn, the Queen sat up and looked up the hill toward the palace. "What am I doing here?" she asked. Then her eyes widened and she raised her hand to keep him from answering.

Rising, giving a little bow, Vlemk invited her to continue with him if she was ready. She seemed to consider it carefully, then at last nodded.

Until they reached the palace gate, the Queen walking with both hands on Vlemk's arm, putting her feet down one after another with the care of an invalid, occasionally reaching up with a troubled gesture, pushing her hair back or briefly covering her eyes, neither Vlemk nor the Queen said a word. At the gate she hesitated, looking in toward the great, arched door like a stranger, then glanced at Vlemk and, after an instant, bowed her head. With her right foot she abstractedly drew something in the yellow-white pebbles of the road, a small, perfect square like the beginning of one of his boxes. "Will you come in with me?" she asked.

Vlemk sighed, imagining what the servants would say behind their hands, what they would suppose about his bringing her home in this bedraggled condition, long after breakfast time, her lower lip bright red and swollen. She was looking at him earnestly, on the verge of withdrawing her question, and, to save her that further embarrassment, however trifling, Vlemk the box-painter nodded and gave a little shrug.

Now they had another problem. It seemed that the Queen had no key to the gate—if she'd started out with one, she'd lost it somewhere—and so they took two stones from the side of the road and banged on the iron, at first politely, then with all their force. Suddenly the door of the palace opened and the

Queen's greyhounds came bounding out, followed by a stooped old man. Barking noisily, leaping like deer, the dogs charged the gate as if trained to eat intruders alive. There were five of them, lean as eels, their eyes rolling wildly and their teeth like razors, hurling spittle to left and right. "Smakkr! Lokkr! Zmölr!" cried the Queen, but even at the sound of her voice they seemed not to know her, bounding up again and again and biting empty air. She put her hand between the bars of the gate, then snatched it back. "Down, Klauz!" she shouted, furious. "Eerzr! Down, boy!" The old man was still some distance back, moving without hurry, leaning hard on his cane, throwing a shout to the dogs from time to time, but only from a feeble civility. Now, however, the most cunning of the dogs, or perhaps the most suspicious, was showing signs of confusion. He hung back, head slung sideways, still barking as tumultuously as the others but no longer bounding up. The Queen, too, had noticed it. "Zmölr!" she cried, as loud as she could shout, her face red with anger, and now another dog, perking up his ears, showed uncertainty. Suddenly the two dogs were snarling at the others, interfering with their leaps, and in an instant all five dogs had changed their ways completely, whimpering and whistling in their throats like puppies, pressing their narrow noses between the bars, crying for a pat from the Queen. The old man, seeing it, began to hurry.

"Fool!" shouted the Queen when he was near enough to hear, "is this how you manage our watchdogs?"

"Oh, Mistress, Mistress," cried the gatekeeper, tears running down his face, and wrung his hands.

"Look at me!" said the Queen, as if her filthy, torn clothes were the fault of the gatekeeper and his dogs. "Look at me!" she raged, bursting into tears. "You'll pay for this, villain! As sure as I'm standing here you'll pay for this!"

"Oh, Mistress, Mistress," he wailed again, as if it were the only phrase he knew, wringing his hands more fervently than before.

"Undo the gate, you stupid old man!" the Queen shouted. "Must we just *stand* here?" Timidly, Vlemk touched her arm to calm her. She pretended not to notice.

Nearly falling in his haste, the old man got out his key ring, turned the lock, and began pushing at the gate. The five dogs leaped all around him, joyfully yapping.

"Fool," said the Queen, seizing the gate bars in her own two hands, her eyes filled with tears, "can you do *nothing* right?"

That instant, with her hair flying out around her head, crackling with the lightning-bolt charge of her anger, the Queen looked exactly like the picture Vlemk had called "The Princess Gives Way to Wrath." Her cheeks were so bright that Vlemk held his breath.

Almost at once his senses came back to him. He rubbed his hands on the sides of his trousers and stared morosely at the ground. He understood well enough that it was the Queen's fright and feeling of having been betrayed when her dogs turned against her, also her shame at coming home in this condition, looking like a strumpet who'd been run over by a cart, conceivably also a touch of embarrassment over the fact that Vlemk had been witness to it all, had seen with his own eyes how the palace, so well run and orderly even at the height of her father's illness, was now reduced to chaos, when the rule was hers. Even so, her anger seemed excessive, in fact mad, as was the fear he'd seen in her when they'd first arrived here, her desire that he come in with her and protect her from the glances of her servants. He shook his head, hardly knowing he was doing it.

Now, since the gate stood wide open, they went in. She was no less fierce with the servants inside. Vlemk moved away from her while she yelled at them, and occupied himself with the paintings on the walls, family portraits. He saw how the King had looked once, or anyway, how the painter had chosen to see him, tall and elegant but very stern. His hand around the ball of his cane was, for no clear reason, clenched, as if in a moment he might raise it and brandish it, and his hat was cocked forward, not jauntily but somehow fiercely, as if it were intended to cushion the blow if he should suddenly choose to butt someone. Her mother, on the other hand, was the soul of sweetness and gentleness, such gentleness that it verged on feebleness. One wouldn't have been surprised to learn (and indeed it was true) that she'd been dead for years and years.

The Queen's chambermaid came running past him, her hands over her face, weeping.

"A terrible business," thought Vlemk, and shook his head. The Queen's hands, he saw, were jerking and twitching. It was terrible! A tragedy! But what was he to do?

Now servants were running in every direction, weeping and wringing their hands or tearing out their hair. When the Queen had finished with the last of them, she came to him and said, "Wretches! I have half a mind to order them all whipped!"

Vlemk did nothing but stare at the floor with his head bowed.

"Would you care for tea?" asked the Queen.

"Perhaps another time," Vlemk said in gestures. "You should rest."

Quickly, before she could think better of it, she reached out to touch his arm with her trembling hand. "Must you leave so soon?" she asked. "Just *one* cup of tea?"

Vlemk shook his head, then shrugged and nodded.

"Tea!" shouted the Queen, as if expecting the paintings to jump down off the walls in fearful obedience and serve it. Then more quietly she said, "This way," and led him toward another room. Strange to say, eager as she was to have him stay longer with her, she said not a word to him as she led him to the door, opened it and, not quite meeting his eyes, waved

him in. Just inside the door Vlemk stopped short and wiped his
hands on his trousers, utterly at a loss. Though it was true that
there were chairs and tables in the room, it was also true that
the room was the Queen's bedroom; and Vlemk was becoming
more and more, these days, a man of rule and decorum. Perhaps it was the influence of the middle-class visitors who were
of late his main customers, or perhaps it was the influence of
the mellower paintings themselves—or again, conceivably, it
was the queer muttering that for a moment he imagined to be
coming from the sinister paintings he'd made on the boxes,
indifferently scattered around the room. But whatever the reason, Vlemk the box-painter felt wretchedly out of place there
where she slept and did all that is most private, and if he
dared, he would have fled like a rabbit. But too late to worry
about it now, he saw; for that minute a serving girl arrived,
sniffing and hiding her face, bringing the tea-tray.

"Over on the table," said the Queen. When the tea things
were in place the Queen sent the serving girl out again and
invited Vlemk to take a chair. No sooner had he come where
she could see him than the picture that could talk cried out,
"Vlemk! Vlemk!"

Vlemk smiled and threw up his hands as joyfully as an old
man when he sees his son. "My little masterpiece," he cried in
gesture, and in his delight did not even remember that she was
the reason he could never speak aloud.

"Oh, Vlemk," cried the picture, "take me home, I beg you!
She's so cruel I'd die of sorrow if you'd made me of anything
less durable than paint!"

The Queen became still with rage, more angry even than
he'd imagined her in his painting. She was so angry all the
breath went out of her, and her face became as gray as old
snow. "Do take her back, by all means!" she said as soon as she
could speak. "All she does is whine and revile me and complain! Take her back at once and good riddance!"

"I can't do that," said Vlemk in gesture. "She's your own very self, a picture so real it can speak. Surely you can find a way to live with your own very self!"

But the Queen was too angry to be reasoned with, slamming the table with the flat of her hand so that the box made little jumps up and down. "Get it away from me! Take it back! Get it from my sight!" cried the Queen.

"Very well," said Vlemk with gestures, humbly; and then he began to nod up and down like an old philosopher, for an idea was taking shape in his mind. "Perhaps," he said in gesture, "I can change the picture's personality a little, so that when you look at it again you may find it somewhat more acceptable."

"Change it to a spider, for all I care," said the Queen. "Just get it *out* of here, away from my sight!"

"I *like* my personality," said the picture.

"*Will* you shut up?" screamed the Queen, and raised both fists above her head to smash it. But Vlemk was too quick for her, and soon the box was in his pocket and his feet were on the road again, trudging toward the city.

12

Vlemk the box-painter thought long and hard about the idea that had come to him in the Queen's bedroom. Sometimes he thought the idea was stark mad, so that he would clutch his head, eyes wide open, and whisper, "Woe is me! What's become of me?" At other times he thought it magnanimous beyond the wildest dreams of any ordinary mortal, and he would put on such airs that to everyone he met he seemed insufferable. But usually he hung undecided between opinions and could do nothing but pull at his knuckles and rock back and forth on his stool, with his eyes tight shut and his lips between his teeth, like a woman who has a baby that won't stop crying.

The idea that had come to him in the Queen's room was this: that perhaps he could alter the painting here and there, removing those hints of imperfection in its character, so that it was no longer a true-to-life miniature of the Queen but a picture of what she might be if she had no faults at all. Then she would surely like it, he thought—how could she not? especially considering the fact that (but ah, this was the hard part!) it would no longer talk back to her; indeed, since it would no longer be a perfect imitation, it would no longer talk at all. There would go not only the picture's chief glory, the unanswerable proof that no one in the world had ever captured such a likeness in a painting on a box—no small matter, to Vlemk, for he had hardly gotten where he was without a trace of artistic vanity—but also, alas, there would go Vlemk's hopes of regaining his speech, since it was the picture that had put the curse on him, and the picture—the picture or no one!—that must take it off.

The idea of living out his life as a mute was by no means a pleasant one to Vlemk, for though it is true that he'd been mute for some time and had in a way gotten used to it, indeed, had learned secrets about everyone around him, thanks to his affliction, that had enriched his knowledge of the world immeasurably, with no small effect on his box-painting, it is also true that, with the optimism natural to living creatures, however they may resist it or in their worst moods mock it, the box-painter had always gone on hoping in secret that his bad luck would someday change to good and the picture would relent. Now, sitting in his busy studio with the picture that could talk on the table before him, his apprentices sawing, hammering and painting, or sweeping up the sawdust, cleaning brushes, and talking with visitors—the tiny image of the Queen chattering happily, telling him of life at the palace, how the King had died, how the Queen had frequently covered her with a quilt—Vlemk wrung his hands and rocked back and forth and considered the idea that had come to him again and again. He was so abstracted that he hardly looked up when people spoke to him, and so sick with indecision—whether to do this or, on the other hand, do that—that he would sometimes heave such a deep sigh of woe that people would step back from him in fear.

"If I'm really going to do it," he told himself, "I should get out my brushes and start painting." But day after day he did nothing but sit rocking and sighing, weighing the arguments on this side and that. He thought of the picture he'd painted of the barmaid and how it had seemingly changed her life. On the other hand he thought of the incident with the bee, how in his attempt to be helpful he'd done nothing but harm. Though the monk's opinions might offend and annoy him, he couldn't help but see that there was truth in them: what good was it, loving this physical world—gardens and queens, barmaids and poor trembling maniacs? Where would they be in a thousand years? Painting them was one thing—a record for posterity—but throwing away all one's hopes for their sake . . . "No, no!" thought Vlemk. "Absurd!" Also, there was the matter of the feelings of the picture herself. Had he really any right to deprive his creation of speech? Is all life not sacred? Is not the true work of art a thing greater than its maker? Indeed, wasn't it the case that a work of art, once out of the artist's hands—if not before—belonged to no one, or to all humanity? He began to find it hard to meet the eyes of the picture on the box. He could see that she was worried and suspicious, watching him like a hawk. "How queer it is," he thought, "that what ought to be the noblest, most selfless act of my life should be made to seem sordid and inhumane!" Vlemk clenched his fists. He should have known, of course, from the moment the picture first opened its mouth. She was unnatural, a piece of Devil's work! Indeed, had she not ensorcelled him? And hadn't she clung to her meanness through good times and bad times, chattering endlessly, refusing to let Vlemk get out a gesture?

Well, her days of meanness were ended, thought Vlemk with a terrible scowl.

But no sooner would Vlemk reach this sensible decision than the picture would speak up and charm him again with that seeming childlike innocence, and he would feel she was breaking his heart. The terrible truth was that he loved with all his heart that saucy, incorrigible little picture on the box—and no doubt also the Queen, since the two were identical; but *that* he would not think about. However fine the reason, and even though she stubbornly held out on him, refusing to lift the curse, he would rather be dead than change a line on that complicated face.

"Vlemk?" the picture would say, smiling to hide her fear. "A penny for your thoughts?"

Vlemk would shrug guiltily and would realize that among the many other thoughts was this one, shameful as it might be: that if he played his cards right—since the picture was so happy to be home again—he could get her to cancel the curse of silence and *then* perhaps repaint her. At once, at the thought of such treachery, he would become glum—irritable and irritating so that the picture would look put out and hurt, then gradually become crotchety, and in the end fall silent. This went on for days and days, and he seemed no nearer a decision than he'd been in the beginning.

One night when his anger at himself was intense, Vlemk stood up abruptly and put on his hat and coat and went down to the tavern. All the regulars were there as usual, the barmaid smiling and showing her ring, for she was newly engaged to be married. The axe-murderer, the ex-poet, and the ex-musician were seated together in their usual corner, glaring out at everyone like weasels in a henhouse. Vlemk the box-painter stood pondering with his thumbs in his suspenders, then at last went over to them. As he seated himself he signalled to the barmaid, and said in gestures, when she came to him, "Wine, my dear—the best in the house! I'm paying myself, since now my boxes are selling well, and I can't accept your charity any longer." When he was sure she'd understood all this and when he'd dismissed her protests that indeed she must pay, she owed it to him, he added, "Also, the best wine you have in the house for my three old friends."

The barmaid said, "But they already have our best wine— more than they can drink and God knows far more than they deserve. Look!"

Vlemk turned to look and, sure enough, in front of each of them stood a costly bottle of wine not yet half empty. "Well, well," he said to himself, then glanced at the barmaid and shrugged and signalled for wine for just himself. When he turned to his friends again and asked in gestures what accounted for this good fortune, they looked at one another with baneful grins, trembling like leaves in a strong breeze, until at last the poet said, "You don't fool us, pretending you don't know, you sly old fox! But if you think we're ashamed to say it, you're quite mistaken! We too can debauch our art and make it fill our poor stomachs."

Vlemk looked from one to another of them, wounded, then opened his hands as a sign that he failed to understand.

"Ah," said the ex-poet to the ex-violinist, "how we loves to mock, this ex-box-painter!" His cheek muscles twitched and a vein stood out in his temple. The ex-violinist laughed harshly and, from behind his spectacles, threw a wink at the axe-murderer.

The ex-poet pointed one finger at Vlemk, the finger only inches from Vlemk's nose. "You," he said, "paint foolish pretty pictures, exactly what your idiot customers would paint for themselves, if they had wit enough. You're right, of course. Why should men of genius go hungry while stupid little insects eat potatoes and gravy?" He winked at the ex-violinist, who winked at the murderer. The ex-poet pushed his flaxen-haired

face close to Vlemk's, as if daring him to scoff. "I write verses
for a cardboard-container corporation: 'Got troubles? Out-fox
'em! Box 'em!' "

"I write music," said the ex-violinist. "I take themes from
famous symphonies. Soon every time you hear the work of a
famous composer, you'll think 'Cardboard boxes!' "

Vlemk looked sadly at the murderer.

The murderer smiled. "I chop up wooden boxes to make
the phosphor sticks people buy in those little cardboard boxes.
They're getting to be all the rage, these phosphor sticks.
They're easier than a flint. Also, sometimes children burn down
hotels with them. Ha ha!"

Vlemk was so depressed at the thought of the murderer's
chopping up wooden boxes that when his wine came he could
hardly raise his glass. It was as if an enormous weight of snow
lay over him. "So this is what everything comes down to in the
end," he thought, staring at the dirt in the fingernails of the
two fingers closed on his wineglass stem. "All our early promise, all our grand ideals!"

Though he felt a little cross, or worse than cross, as if his
heart had turned to ice—useless to deny it—it was no good
berating his fellow artists. Hunger and poverty are powerful
persuaders, and so was the policeman who'd taken to sitting in
the tavern nights, smoking his pipe and occasionally glancing
at the murderer. Nor could Vlemk deny that he himself had
unwittingly contributed to their decline. In his cynical period,
he had spoken with pleasure and excitement of his work on the
"Reality boxes"—his evil pictures of the Queen. In his mellower period he'd had nothing to say. Indeed, he had nothing
to say even now. It was just one more instance, he told himself,
of spirit weighed down by matter until it no longer knows
itself. He sighed.

"Very well," thought Vlemk, and leaned forward slowly,
bidding his friends good-evening and putting the cork in the

bottle, the bottle in his pocket, then walking up the street to his house and up the stairs to his studio, where he opened up his paints.

"What are you doing?" cried the picture as she saw the brush approaching.

He tried to say in gestures, "I'm hoping to make you even finer than you are," but the picture on the box was in such a wild panic, her little bosom heaving, her eyes opened wide, that in the end he only smiled as reassuringly as possible, sucked in his lower lip between his teeth, and began to paint. He painted for a week without stopping, and when he finished, the painting looked—to Vlemk, at least—exactly like the Queen except with none of her faults. Nearly everyone who looked at it said it was the most beautiful, most angelic face in the world, so true to life—or at least to some barely imaginable possibility—that you could literally hear it breathing. But the picture no longer talked. Not everyone was persuaded, of course, about the picture's perfection. When he showed it to his apprentices they frowned and looked evasive, and at last the fat one said, "It looks sort of the same as before."

Vlemk gestured wildly, as if to say, "I paint for a week— me! Vlemk!—and the painting looks the same as before?"

The fat one ducked his head. "I just said *sort* of," he explained.

Little did they know, he thought sorrowfully. Though it watched him as if on a jury, the picture had become, like himself, as mute as a stone.

13

Cowardly or not, he could not bear to take the picture up himself—and no reason he should, he convinced himself; there was no reason the Queen should have anything to say to him. Nevertheless he was secretly puzzled when for a week after sending the repainted picture by the youngest of his apprentices, Vlemk had still heard nothing. Then a message arrived, brought to him in person by the driver with the top hat and the polished boots. It was a small white card on which the Queen had written, in a feeble hand, an urgent invitation to the palace.

Vlemk frowned and studied the face of the driver for some sign. Behind the driver's head there were low, leaden clouds. The driver showed nothing, standing with his hands folded, gazing solemnly—almost tragically, Vlemk would have said—at the floor. In haste, the box-painter hung up his frock, put on his good black Sunday coat, gave instructions to his apprentices on the business of the day, and went to the carriage with the driver.

At the top of the hill, the gates to the palace were open wide, and the dogs lay still beside the road as if someone had put a spell on them. The gatekeeper made no move to interfere with the entrance of the carriage but stood back, with his hat off, crying out as Vlemk peeked through the window, "God be with you, sir!" Vlemk frowned more deeply.

At the high arched door the carriage stopped abruptly and the driver jumped down from his seat in front so quickly, for all his dignity, that the door was opened for Vlemk before the carriage had stopped swaying. The driver's face, as he took Vlemk's arm to help him down, was so abysmally solemn that Vlemk for an instant hesitated, narrowing his eyes and pushing his bearded face close to the driver's for a better look; but the man's expression told him nothing, and so, with an increasing sense of urgency, Vlemk went up the steps into the palace.

Nothing was at all as it had been before. In fact, so transformed was the palace when he entered that he stopped in his tracks and snatched his hat off in order to think more clearly. First, all the walls had been washed till they shone like new-cut marble, and everywhere he looked there were new, fresh flowers—rising stalks and blooms, shimmering and blazing, ferns and white ribbons, climbing in such profusion toward the sky-light overhead that one might have thought one had shrunk to the size of a ladybug and were standing at the bottom of a florist's box. Second, and more ominous, the servants moved back and forth as quietly as swallows, or stood in doorways, no more talkative than owls. No one anywhere was smiling even slightly, not even the chief butler's grandchildren over by the fountain. "This is bad," thought Vlemk, standing with his shoulders hunched, rubbing his palms together, squinting and pursing his lips.

Then suddenly the door to the Queen's room opened, and, to Vlemk's amazement, out rushed the Prince with the moustache.

"You!" cried the Prince, with an expression so twisted and uncertain one couldn't tell whether it was rage or the hope that, now that Vlemk was here, all might at last be well.

Vlemk bowed and nodded, then tipped his head inquiringly.

"Come quickly," said the Prince, "she's been asking for you since she wakened." Even now his expression was neither one thing nor another but filled with contradictions. He seized Vlemk's arm, but Vlemk stood rooted, still with his head to one side, his hands opened out like a beggar's. At last the Prince understood. "You haven't heard?" he asked. When Vlemk went on waiting, the Prince explained. "The Queen is ill! No one has the faintest idea what the trouble is. I came over from my neighboring kingdom as soon as I heard." His face became more stern and his grip on the handle of his ornamented cane somewhat tightened. "I refuse to let it happen! Believe me, I'll move heaven and earth, if I have to. . . ." Sweat had popped out on his forehead, and he took a swipe at it with his sleeve, then lowered his head and frowned like a goat.

At the news that the Queen was seriously ill, Vlemk's knees turned to rubber, and to keep himself from falling he had to cling to the Prince with both hands.

"In my personal opinion, it's the picture you did of her," said the Prince, and his hand closed still more tightly on the cane. Anger lit his eyes, but then the next instant his expression was full of doubt, panicky. "Then again, perhaps everything's just the opposite of what it seems," he said, and quickly looked away. His gaze went running around the room. As if in hopes that Vlemk might resolve his confusion, he tugged abruptly and rather sternly at Vlemk's arm, moving him in the direction of the door, and Vlemk, after a moment's resistance, gave up and followed.

The moment the Prince and the box-painter entered, the servants and doctors who were gathered around the Queen's four-poster bed drew back the curtains and slipped out of the way like shadows. In this room too there were flowers everywhere, especially around the bed. The Queen's head lay as white on its pillow as a pearl in its crimson casque, her arms above the covers, and in her white, white hands she held the box with the picture Vlemk had altered. As if he didn't mean to but couldn't help himself, the Prince pushed past Vlemk and went up to her first, bent quickly, impulsively, to kiss her on the forehead, then turned away, blushing, signalling urgently for Vlemk to come and help. As soon as he thought Vlemk could not see him, the Prince covered his face with his hands like a man stifling a groan and turned his back.

Somewhat timidly, Vlemk approached near enough to touch her pale cheek. Then he stood looking down at her, drawing his hand back to the other hand, with which he was holding his hat. After a moment, with a feeble flutter, the Queen opened her eyes.

"Vlemk," she said softly, with infinite sadness and more affection than she'd ever before shown him.

Instantly, Vlemk's eyes swam with tears. He nodded, sniffled, and bent forward a little to show that he'd heard.

When she tried to speak again, it seemed that she was too

feeble to bring a sound out; but after a moment she managed to say, "Thank you for coming. I was terrified that I might die without seeing you, to put your heart at rest."

Vlemk, hearing these words, opened his eyes wide to stare at her. "Nonsense," he exclaimed, and then, seeing that she seemed not even to notice that he'd spoken—spoken with his voice—he seized her in both hands.

Angrily, the Prince pushed in beside the painter. "You're not going to die!" he cried, his eyes bright as glass. He turned to look with great fury at Vlemk. All Vlemk could make out was a blur of pinkish light. Turning to the Queen again, the Prince cried out, "You're getting *better*, my dear girl!" To the Queen his guilty concern was touching and amusing, though she was careful to hide what she felt.

"No no, dear Prince," she said, and sighed, looking at the Prince's trembling face. His teeth were grinding and tears were now streaming down his bright pink cheeks—tears of love for her, she knew, such innocent, open-hearted love— though also, she knew he was hiding something—that it seemed to her criminal that she should trouble him so, be so unworthy of his goodness. Not that she was any longer filled with self-hatred. What more atonement could anyone ask of her than the atonement she was making, death for her sins and crimes? Yet how they had stooped and clasped their hands like suppliants! She did like that, no use denying it! The feeling of queenliness it gave her tempted her for a moment to say no more to either of them, to spare them further pain; but then a kind of heaviness came over her—almost, she thought, like a feeling of old age, or at any rate righteousness—and she felt that, quite simply, she didn't have it in her to die without leaving things straight and clear, clean and open as sunlight, let them handle it as they would. For die she must; her heart was set on it.

Vlemk the box-painter stood pulling first at his left hand, then at his right, filled with alarm at the Queen's words "put your heart at rest." It was just as he feared, he saw. It was he who had brought her to this sorry pass; and she, knowing that sooner or later he must see what he had done, was eager, for his sake, to deny him any guilt, rise above all such pettiness to deathly, sweet wisdom. She was smiling like an old mother cat. Anxiously, Vlemk looked from the face of the Queen to the tear-stained, indignant red face of the Prince. But though he wracked his brains, Vlemk could think of no way of preventing her from doing what she intended. Her labor so far had greatly drained her, he saw. Her hands had fallen away from the box she'd been holding, leaving it resting on the covers on her waist.

"Vlemk," said the Queen, her voice growing feebler and feebler, "I was wrong when I told you the original picture on the box was not a good likeness. When I saw the new picture, after you'd made it perfect, I saw with terrible certainty how far I was from the person I imagined myself, how surely I was becoming, from moment to moment, more like those other things you painted."

"New picture?" said the Prince.

The Queen continued, ignoring him, "Seeing the disparity between what I am and what I wish to be, I have come to the only happiness possible for such a wretch as I am, the sad joy of the old philosophers who at least 'knew themselves.' " She lowered her pale blue eyelids and tears slipped warmly from her eyes. "That," she continued, when her voice was in control again, "that is why I can no longer go on living and have purposely declined to this pitiful state. I want you not to feel guilty when I am dead, just as I hope my dear friend the Prince—"

Here the Queen was dramatically interrupted. Neither she nor Vlemk had noticed that at her mention of the talking picture on the box, the Prince had widened his eyes in horror, everything slowly coming clear to him, and in the first wild impulse of his recognition he had snatched the box from where it lay on the covers and had run to throw it into the fire in the fireplace. There he remained, looking sterner and more guilty than ever. Now it seemed to the Queen—and it was partly because of this that her sentence had broken off—that she was, she herself, on fire all over; and the same instant there came a wail of pain and terror from the fireplace—"Vlemk! Tell her it's not my fault! Oh, Master, dear Master, *save* me!"

At the cry of the painting, the curse was lifted—so they all perceived—and Vlemk, running toward the picture, cried out over his shoulder in a loud voice, "You're mistaken, Queen! Spare the picture and spare yourself!" The words rang as loudly as thunder in the room. "She's not an impossible ideal, she's your own very self! Otherwise how could she speak?"

The Prince heard none of this, for the instant the cry came from the fireplace he whirled around without thinking—Vlemk was still three or four paces away—to snatch out the box and sprinkle it with water and save the poor picture's life.

"Is it possible?" cried the Queen, flushing with pleasure and embarrassment, "is it possible that I have become exactly like the picture on the box?"

"Vlemk," cried the picture, coughing a little and blinking soot from her eyes, "I hope you don't think—"

Suddenly understanding, Vlemk hit his forehead with the palm of his hand, so hard he nearly knocked himself over. "Treachery!" he bellowed. "You could talk all the time!"

"I could?" asked the picture in seeming amazement, and shot a glance at Vlemk and the Queen to see how much trouble she was in. "You won't believe it," the picture said, "but—"

"No, we certainly won't!" snapped the Queen. Though she'd been pale as a ghost just a moment ago, she was suddenly as healthy and lively as could be. "Shameless little vixen!" the Queen exclaimed, "you pretended you couldn't talk, just to spite poor Vlemk, and you wouldn't let *him* talk, miserable as he was, until your life depended on it! What a horrible, horrible little creature!"

"Horrible?" cried the picture, bursting into tears. "We're in this together, remember! If I can talk, it's because I'm exactly like you! So who's the horrible little creature?"

The Queen blanched and drew her hand to her bosom. Her face went red with anger, then white. When the words had struck with full force, she was so shocked by the revelation that her eyes rolled up almost out of sight.

The Prince was anxiously pulling at his moustache, waving his cane with his left hand, trying to understand. "Now wait," he said. "If I rightly follow this ridiculous business, you"—he pointed to Vlemk, squinting—"you changed the picture to get rid of the little imperfections, is that right?"

"Exactly," said Vlemk, then looked confused. "At least I thought I did."

The Prince's look became thoughtful. "If it had worked, and if the Queen had failed to come up to the standard of the picture, you'd have been mute for the rest of your life!"

The Queen and the picture looked at Vlemk, then away, embarrassed.

"If it had worked, yes," said Vlemk, frowning and scratching his head. "But somehow the picture was able to outwit me and hang on to her powers. It's a mystery."

The picture looked pleased with herself, and privately, the Queen was smiling a little too.

"Is it really such a mystery?" asked the Prince with a laugh. Suddenly he was enjoying himself, as if some burden had been miraculously lifted. There was no longer any trace of the mingled anxiety and anger. He was standing much taller, not gripping his cane like a weapon but playing with it, balancing it on the tip of one finger while he talked. "Surely," he said, "surely, my dear Vlemk, you painted what you *thought* was a picture of perfection, but it came out exactly as it had been before you started!"

"That must be it," said Vlemk, eyes widening, and he nodded. He glanced at the Queen, then over at the box, and to his surprise saw that both of them were crying. "What's this?" he said. "Did I say something wrong?"

"You loved me!" said the Queen and the box, both at once. "How *could* you?" Neither of them could say another word, because both of them were sobbing.

Vlemk, confounded, looked over at the Prince for help.

The Prince shrugged broadly, grinning. "God help you, Vlemk. For most men *one* such unpredictable creature would be enough!" He gave the cane a little toss, so that it went gracefully end over end and came down onto his fingertip, where he balanced it as before. "Well," he said, "since every-thing seems to be all right again, I'd better hurry home to my wife." He turned to leave.

"*Wife!*" shrieked the Queen and the picture at once.

The Prince's face reddened and the cane fell off balance. He grabbed it. "How was I to tell you?" he said. "You were sick—perhaps dying, for all I knew...."

"You're married?" asked Vlemk.

"Two weeks ago," said the Prince. "Politics, you see. But when I heard that the Queen—"

"You did the right thing," said Vlemk at once. Abruptly, he laughed. "I *thought* you were acting a little strangely!"

Neither the picture or the Queen even smiled. "Oh yes," said the Queen, and angrily rolled her head from side to side. "*You* can laugh. What if I'd gotten better because I thought he loved me and then I'd found out? Say what you like, it's a cruel, cruel world full of falsehood and trickery and delusions!"

"It's true, all too true," said Vlemk, trying not to smile. "All the same, I notice there's color in your cheeks. One way or another it seems we have muddled through!"

In secret, the Queen was noticing the same thing. As a matter of fact she had a feeling that if she put her mind to it, she could jump up out of bed and dance. Nothing could please her more than having the Prince with the moustache as only a good friend—he was a wonderful horseman—and not having to worry about that other business. The difficulty was that any minute now he would leave, and so would Vlemk, and there were important matters not yet decided between Vlemk and herself. The thought of his leaving was like a knife in her heart; she would gladly give up her life, her very bones and flesh, and be nothing but a summery warmth around him, a patch of sunlight on his head, anything at all, but near him. Yet try as she might, she could think of no way to keep him here now except petulance and sulking.

"Well," Vlemk was saying now, fiddling with his hat, stealing a glance at the flowers near the door.

"Oh yes," said the Queen bitterly, "trickery and delusion are just fine with you. They're the stock and trade of an artist."

Vlemk looked at her, then down at his shoes, and sighed.

Her eyes became cunning. It crossed her mind that if she knew how to put some kind of curse on him, he'd figure out some way to be near her till the day she lifted it, which would be never.

"Well, it's getting late," the Prince said.

Vlemk the box-painter nodded.

All the while the box had been watching them with her lips slightly pursed. Suddenly she said, "Vlemk, why don't you marry the Queen and come live with us?"

"Yes, why not?" said the Queen quickly, a little crazily. She felt her face stinging, an enormous blush rushing into her cheeks.

"Me?" Vlemk said, then hastily added, "I was thinking the same thing myself!"

"Wonderful!" cried the Prince. "We can visit each other and go riding!"

Vlemk smiled eagerly. The thought of riding a horse made him faint with terror.

"You mean we—you and I—" stammered the Queen. Her face went pale green, then red, then white.

"If you like," Vlemk said.

"Oh, Vlemk, Vlemk, I'm sorry about the curse!" the picture wailed. "It was just—I mean . . ." Now all at once her words came tumbling. "One has to have something to hold back—a woman, that is. If she just gives the man she loves everything, just like that—"

Vlemk nodded. "I understand." He was thinking, absurd as it may sound, about box-painting, about the risks one ran, the temptations.

"But is it possible?" asked the Queen. "You and I, a box-painter and a Queen?"

"Well, it's *odd* of course," said Vlemk. "No doubt we'll have our critics."

"You won't go back to sleeping in gutters or anything?" the Queen asked.

"I don't think so," said Vlemk, "though life is always full of surprises."

Abruptly forgetting her fears, the Queen reached out her arms to him, smiling joyfully. He bent to her, smiling back, and they embraced, quick and light as children.

Now the servants, having noticed the change in mood around the Queen's bed, crept in nearer to find out what was happening. The Prince too had noticed that everything had changed entirely. "Well," he said, "I must go now, as I said." He made no move to leave.

"You're welcome to stay to supper if you like," the Queen said.

Vlemk, as if the palace were his own, reached out his hand to the Prince. The Prince looked from Vlemk to the Queen. He stood for a long moment staring into space, puzzling things through; then abruptly his face lit up. "No," he said, gripping his cane with a sort of easy firmness, "but I'll come for the wedding. I must go home to my wife."

"And I," said Vlemk, "must go home and make my various preparations."

It was now clear to even the least of the servants that everything had changed and all was well. They seized Vlemk's hands, also the Prince's, kissing the backs and fronts of them and thanking both Vlemk and the Prince for what they'd done. Vlemk beamed, nodding and bowing and telling them on every side, "It's nothing! It's nothing!" moving them along with him to the door as he did so, walking with the Prince, waving his repeated farewells to the picture and the Queen, who'd come out to the bedroom door, the box in the Queen's left hand. In the high front room the driver of the carriage was waiting, more elegant than ever, and on either side of him stood servants with armloads of flowers for Vlemk and the Prince. "Come back quickly," cried the Queen and the picture, both at once.

Vlemk waved his hat.

"Well," said the driver, bowing and falling into step beside Vlemk and the Prince, "things have turned out better than I thought they would."

"So they have," said Vlemk. "It's good to have everything settled at last. It's good to know exactly where we stand!"

They came to the high arched door and the driver stepped ahead of Vlemk to seize the door-handle. As he opened the door, a sharp blast of wintery wind swept in, filling out the female servants' skirts like sails and hurling in fine-ground blizzard snow.

"Oh!" cried the Queen and the picture on the box, astonished.

"It's winter!" cried the Prince, so startled he could hardly believe his eyes. Instantly the flowers in the servants' arms began to tremble and wilt, and the leaves of the flowers inside the room began to blow around crazily.

"Winter," said Vlemk, full of wonder, his voice so quiet that only the carriage driver heard.

They had to lift their feet high, Vlemk, the Prince, and the carriage driver, to make it through the drifts to the black leather, gold-studded carriage. The carriage of the Prince stood just beyond. In every direction except straight above, the world was white and lovely, as if the light came from inside the snow. Straight above—or so it seemed to Vlemk, standing with one hand on his beard, the other in his pocket—the sky was painfully bright, blinding, as if someone had lifted the cover off the world, so that soon, as usual, everything in it would be transformed.

COME ON BACK

Forty-five years ago, when Remsen, New York, was called "Jack" and nearly all the people who lived there were Welsh, my uncle, or, rather, my maternal great-uncle, E. L. Hughes, ran the feedmill. His name is no longer remembered in the village, and the feedmill is in ruins, set back behind houses and trees so that you have to know it's there to find it. There's a big sprawling Agway that already looks ancient, though it can't be more than fifteen or twenty years old, on the other side of town.

I seldom get up to that area anymore, but I used to visit often when I was a child living with my parents on their farm outside Batavia. My grandfather Hughes, whom I never knew except by the wooden chest of carpenter's tools he left my father and a few small, tattered Welsh hymnbooks he left my mother, had originally settled in the village of Remsen, or just outside it, and for years, even past the time of my uncle Ed's death, my parents made pilgrimages back to see old friends, attend the Cymanfa Ganu festivals, visit the white wooden church called Capel Ucca, and keep a casual eye on the mill's decline. At the time my grandfather and his brothers came over, Remsen was generally viewed, back in Wales, as a kind of New Jerusalem, a shining hope, a place of peace and prosperity. There was a story of a Welshman who landed in New York, and looking up bug-eyed at the towering buildings, said, "If this is New York, what must Remsen be!"

In those days it was a sleepy little hamlet beside a creek. Though the Depression was on in the rest of the country, you saw no signs of it in Remsen. On the tree-lined streets with tall houses set back from them, each with its roses, small vegetable garden, and grape arbor, there were shined-up square cars, mostly Model A Fords, and occasional buggies. (My uncle Ed, one of the richest men in town, had a black-and-green Buick.) Milk was still delivered in squarish glass bottles by an orange horse-drawn cart; coal for people's furnaces came on a huge, horse-drawn wagon, black with white lettering: W. B. PRICE & SONS, COAL & LUMBER. The horses were chestnut-colored Belgians, I remember, so immense and so beautiful they didn't seem real. At the end of almost every driveway, back behind the house, there was a two-storey garage with chickenwire on the upstairs windows. If you shouted from the driveway, one or two of the chickens would look out at you, indignant, like old ladies; but however you shouted, even if you threw pebbles, most of them just went about their business. The people were pretty much the same, unexcitable. There weren't many houses, maybe twenty or thirty, a couple of churches, a school, Price's lumberyard, and a combination gas-station and market.

As we entered, from the south, my uncle Ed's high gray mill reaching up past the trees into the sunlight was the first thing we'd see. The mill was to the left of the narrow dirt road, a three-towered, barnlike building set back beyond the lawn and flower garden that rose gradually toward the brown-shingled house where Uncle Ed had lived for years with his wife, my great-aunt Kate. I remember her only dimly, as an occasional bright presence, soft-spoken and shy, in my uncle Ed's kitchen or in his "camp," as they called it, on Black River. She wore thick glasses that made her eyes look unpleasantly large. They shared the house, or anyway the basement, with Uncle

Ed's younger brother, my great-uncle Charley—Cholly, they called him—who helped out at the mill for room and board and a trifling wage. Across the road from the mill and Uncle Ed's house stood a blacksmith's shop, then still in operation, a dark, lively place full of coal smell, iron smell, and horse smell. All day long it rang like a musical instrument with the clanging of iron on iron, just far enough from the house and mill to sound like bells. The creek ran just behind the blacksmith's shop, a bright, noisy rattle. I used to catch tadpoles and minnows there, though it was deep in places, and if my grandmother found out I'd been playing in the creek I got spanked. The building's gone now, and the creek's fallen silent, grown up in weeds. I remember the building as small, made of stone burned black inside, crowded outside with burdocks whose leaves were always wet with the mist from the waterfall that rumbled day and night not far upstream.

I was five or six, still at that age when a day lasts for weeks and everything you see or hear or smell seems vividly alive, though later you can get only glimpses to serve as memories— or anyway so it seems until you start to write. This much comes at once: the large, grinning figure of my uncle Ed, Uncle Charley next to him, timidly smiling, dwarfed beside his brother, and standing not far from them Aunt Kate with a dishtowel and teapot. I get back, too, a little of the sunlit world they inhabited, seemingly without a care, as if forever. On one kitchen wall they had a large black pendulum clock on which the four was written IIII; I could never decide whether the thing was a mistake (I was already aware that the Welsh were prone to make curious mistakes) or something more mysterious, brought down from the ancient, unimaginable time when, according to Uncle Ed, the Welsh lived in caves and trees and couldn't talk yet, but had to get along by singing.

In those days everything was for me—for me more than for most children, perhaps—half real, half ethereal. It was not just the stories Uncle Ed liked to tell. In our farmhouse I slept with my grandmother, and every night before she turned off the bedlamp she would read me something from the Bible or the *Christian Herald*. I don't remember what she read, but I remember seeing pictures of bright-winged angels playing harps and singing—beings she insisted were entirely real, as real as trees or hay wagons. She made my world mythic—her own as well. During the day she would sometimes go out in our front yard with a hoe and kill grass-snakes. It made my father, who was a practical man, furious. "Mother," he would ask, "what *harm* do they do?" "They bite," she would say. Sometimes my mother would try to defend her. Grandma Hughes had lived in Missouri for a time, where there were rattlesnakes, and she was too old now to change her ways. "Even a darn fool *mule* can be reasoned with," my father would say—he was a breeder and trainer of plough-horses—but he wouldn't pursue the argument. To me, though, steeped in her Bible and *Christian Herald* stories, nothing seemed more natural than that my grandmother in her righteousness should be out there in the dappled light below the maple trees, her bright blue eyes narrowed, her hoe-blade poised, every nerve on the look-out for serpents.

"Did you ever really *see* an angel?" I once asked her. Since there really were snakes, it seemed to me probable that there were angels.

"Not that I'm aware of," she said.

I thought it over. "Did my dad?"

"I doubt it," she said, then bit her lips together, trying not to smile.

So I knew on my grandmother's authority, to say nothing of Uncle Ed's, that there was more to the world than met the eye, or rather, knew that there were two worlds, and it came to seem to me that Remsen, like the valley where Jacob saw the ladder, was one of the places where they connected. Perhaps it was Remsen's peculiar, clear light, or the sense of peace my whole family seemed to feel there, gathering with relatives and friends to sing hymns in Capel Ucca those bright Sunday mornings; or perhaps it was simply the otherworldliness of a village that spoke Welsh. It was true that time had stopped there, or at very least had paused. We had no blacksmith's shops in Batavia. Mr. Culver, who shoed my father's horses, came with his equipment in a panel truck. And the mill where my father took his grain, the G.L.F., was like a factory—freightcars on one side of it, track on track of them, and inside, wherever you looked through the billowing white dust, big iron machines and men in goggles. My uncle Ed, when he worked in the old-fashioned mill in Remsen, wore a suit. It was gray with grain-dust, and it was a little dishevelled; but it was a suit. (Uncle Charley wore striped bib-overalls.) Uncle Ed's machinery was mostly made of wood and made very little noise, just a low, sweet humming sound, with rhythmical thumps.

I would sometimes be left over night with the two old men and Aunt Kate while my parents went off with younger relatives to some "sing." There was always a sing on somewhere around Remsen. "Every time three Welshmen meet," people said, "it's a choir." In those days it was more or less true. Everywhere my parents drove, they sang, almost always in a minor key and always in harmony; and every time relatives got together they sang, in almost as many parts as there were people.

I'd be alarmed when my parents began dressing for a sing, telling me in falsely sweet voices that I was to stay with my uncles and aunt and be a good boy. My grandmother, if she was there, would insist on going with them. Though she was nearly eighty, she had a voice like a bird, she claimed. The songfest wouldn't be the same without her. Uncle Charley would shake his head as if disgusted, though everyone said he'd had a wonderful tenor voice when he was younger. In those days, they said, he wouldn't have missed a Cymanfa Ganu or an Eisteddfod—the really big sing, where hundreds and hundreds of Welshmen came together—for all the tea in China. Uncle Charley would blush like a girl when they spoke of his singing days. "Well, a body gets old," he'd mutter. "Pride!" my grandmother would snap. "Sinful pride!"

She was a woman of temper; she'd been a red-head when she was young. But for all her sternness, she loved Uncle Charley as she loved nobody else—her husband's youngest brother, just a boy when she first knew him, all his life the one who'd been of no account. "That voice of his was his downfall," she said once to my mother, wiping dishes while my mother washed. "It gave him ideas."

To me, a child, it was a puzzling statement, though my mother, ruefully nodding, apparently understood. I tried to get my grandmother to explain it later, when she was sitting at her darning in our bedroom—more my bedroom than hers, she would say when a certain mood was on her. Another puzzling statement.

"Grandma," I asked, "how come Uncle Charley's voice gave him ideas?"

"Hush now," she said. That was always her answer to troublesome questions, and I knew how to deal with it. I just waited, watching her darn, making a nuisance of myself.

"Well," she said at last, then stopped to bite a thread. She looked at the end, twirled it between her fingers to make it pointed, then continued: "Singing's got its place. But a body can get to thinking, when he's singing with a choir, that that's how the whole blessed world should be, and then when he comes down out of the clouds it's a terrible disappointment."

I suppose I looked as puzzled as ever, tentatively considering the idea of people singing up in the clouds, like the angels in her pictures.

She leaned toward me and said, "Uncle Charley never found a good woman, *that's* what's wrong with him. Bills to pay, whippersnappers—*that'll* bring you down from your *la-la-la!*"

I gave up, as puzzled as before and slightly hurt. I knew well enough—she never let me forget—what a burden I was, not that she didn't kiss me and make a great to-do when I was dressed up for church or had done something nice for her, dust-mopping the bedrooms without being told to, or helping her find her brass thimble. (She was a great mislayer of things. It made my father sigh deeply and shake his head.) I was, in general, as good a child as I knew how to be, but it's true, I was sometimes a trouble. I justified her existence, I realize now: living with my parents, too old and poor to live alone, she didn't have to think herself a nuisance to the world. As my babysitter, she made it possible for my mother to teach school and for my father to work in the fields all day. All the same, I'm sure I ran her ragged, and there were times—especially when my parents had somewhere to go after dark—when I was as much trouble as I dared to be.

I hated those nights when my parents left me—for a Grange meeting, at home, or for a sing when we were in Remsen. I'd live through them, I knew—I might even enjoy myself, after a fashion—but the night would be darker than usual, outside the big old Remsen house when my parents and grandmother weren't somewhere within call, upstairs, or in the elegant, dimly lit livingroom. The mill, much as I loved it by day, looked ominous from Uncle Ed's kitchen window after dark. It would seem to have moved closer, blocking out the starlight like an immense black tombstone. I would hear the clock on the kitchen wall solemnly knocking the seconds off—*tock . . . tock*—the silence so deep I could also hear the clock on the desk in the livingroom, hurrying as if in panic—*tick-tick-tick-tick!* The sunflowers at the end of the garden would be gray now, staring back at me like motionless ghosts, and the blacksmith's shop across the road, a darker blot in the surrounding darkness—weeds all around it, hushed as if listening to the clatter of the creek—was transformed in my mind to a terrible place, the overgrown hovel of a cum-witch.

I would whine, hanging around, clinging to the white porcelain doorknob as my parents dressed. "Why can't I come with you?" I'd say. My mother's eyes would remain on the mirror, concentrating hard on the eyebrow pencil. Though she was fat, I thought she was amazingly beautiful. Her hair was dark red. "You can, when you're bigger," my father would say, standing behind my mother, chin lifted, putting on his tie. In the bathroom my grandmother would be singing, loosening up her voice. She *did* sound like a bird, I thought grimly. Like a chicken.

In the end, knowing I had no chance of winning, I would pretend to be seduced by Aunt Kate's molasses cookies and the promise that Uncle Ed would tell me stories. Sulking a little, to show them I didn't intend to forget this, I'd walk with my parents as far as the door, keeping an eye on their red, beaming faces and listening, full of disapproval, to their loud, cheerful talk as they took leave of my uncles and aunt and went down the wooden steps between the house and the big, dark mill to greet the relatives who'd come for them in their car. The inside lights of the car would go on as the car doors opened, and in that little, square-windowed island of light I'd see grown-up cousins and children cousins just a little more than my age squeezing over, climbing onto other cousins' laps. The alley between the mill and the house would fill up like a pool with laughter and shouts of "Watch your elbows!" and sometimes my father's voice, carefully patient, "That's all right, Mother. Take your time." Then the doors would close, leaving only the headlights, and the car would *chuff-chuff-chuff* past the mill and, listing like a carriage, would go around the corner at the end of the garden, then, listing again, taillights like two garnets, would veer out onto the road, briefly lighting up trees. When the taillights were out of sight I would turn, trying not to cry, to Uncle Ed, who would lift me and carry me on his shoulder like a feedsack to the kitchen. "*So,*" he would say, "I guess you didn't know I used to work for a bear!"

"I don't believe it," I would say, though I did, in fact.

"Big old black bear name of Herman. Used to live up by Blue Mountain Lake."

He often set his stories on Blue Mountain Lake, or on nearby Black River, where his camp was (he would take us there sometimes, to my grandmother's dismay)—an immense log-and-stone lodge filled with stuffed lynxes, wolves, and owls, Japanese lanterns overhead, and on the rustic tables a whole museum's worth of strange objects Aunt Kate had collected—little models of birch canoes, carved figures, a stereopticon with pictures of Paris long ago. The lodge was set in among trees, all but inaccessible, a wooden dock below it, where Uncle Ed's guideboat was tied during the day. The water on the river, shallow and clear as glass, seemed hardly to move, though when you dropped a leaf on it it quickly sped away. Fish poked thoughtfully in and out among the shadows of underwater weeds, and when you looked up you saw a world almost equally strange—pinewoods and mountains, large hurrying clouds of the kind I thought angels lived on, huge white mounds full of sunlight. Whenever Uncle Ed began to speak of the Adirondacks, you knew that in a minute he'd be telling of his childhood in Wales, where people lived in cottages on dark green hills with their sheep and collie dogs, and nothing ever changed.

All through supper Uncle Ed would tell me stories, Aunt Kate tisk-tisking, moving back and forth between the table and the stove, patting my head sometimes, telling me not to believe a word of it. Uncle Charley would sit grinning as if sheepishly, sometimes throwing me a wink, sometimes saying a few words in a high-pitched voice, trying to make me think it was the parrot, Bobby Watson, who stood watching and pecking at lettuce in his cage in the corner. Uncle Charley was as small-boned as a sparrow and had startling eyes, one brown, one blue. Though he was almost as old as Uncle Ed, he had light brown hair and a brown moustache—a shiny, soft brown with hardly any gray in it. Perhaps it was partly the way he sat, head forward, eyes lowered, his hands on his knees except when he raised his fork or spoon: he seemed, even with all his wrinkles, just a boy, no bigger around than Uncle Ed's right arm. People who didn't know them thought Uncle Charley was Aunt Kate's brother, not Uncle Ed's. She too was, she liked to say, petite. After supper, while Aunt Kate washed dishes and the two old men went out to the mill to "catch up"—really to smoke cigars—I would bang on Aunt Kate's piano in the livingroom. The piano was a good one, a Storey & Clark upright. In the tiffanied dimness of the livingroom, its coal-black surfaces shone like mirrors, or like Black River at night, and everything I played on it sounded to me like real music. I would lose all track of time, closing my eyes and tipping my head to the piano sound, dark, sustained chords that in my mind made a shadowy place you could move around in, explore like an old-time Indian. When my uncles and aunt came together again, after the dishes and cigar smoking, they'd call me back and we'd play dominoes at the kitchen table. After an hour or so, Uncle Charley would say, grinning, not meeting anyone's eyes, "Well, time to turn in by gol, ant-it?" and he'd go down to his narrow, yellow-wallpapered room in the basement.

I'd sit a little longer with Uncle Ed and Aunt Kate. They must have known how I hated to go upstairs alone in that big, quiet house; but it was Aunt Kate's habit to listen to her records—some of them old, thick Edison records, most of them opera—and sew for a while before going up to bed, and it was Uncle Ed's habit to settle down across from her, heavy and comfortable as an old gray cat, draw on his steel-rimmed spectacles, and read. They were both too old to go climbing that narrow back stairway twice. (The front-hallway stairs were wide and glossy, with a runner down the steps; I don't remember anyone's ever using them much except my cousins and me, playing Chinese School.) Aunt Kate was brittle and climbed steps one at a time. As for Uncle Ed, he was huge, for a Welshman, with hair as white as snow. When I began to nod, he'd say, looking at me over the spectacle rims, "You run and put your pajamas on, Buddy. We'll be up in a jiffy." As I think back to it, it surprises me that I didn't make a fuss; but I obeyed without protest, knowing I'd be long asleep before they got there.

Once in a while I'd wake up for a minute when they came, and I'd see them in their white flannel nightgowns, kneeling beside the bed. Pretending to be asleep—I slept on a cot across the room from them—I'd watch them bow their heads, side by side, and press their hands together just below their chins, and I'd listen to their whisperings in Welsh. Uncle Ed had three stubbed fingers, cut off in a gristmill when he was young. His rounded shoulders were enormous. In my memory, no doubt inaccurate, they went a third the length of the bed. In the mill, during the day, Uncle Ed was like a king, lifting heavy feedsacks as if they were nothing, chattering lightly past his dead cigar, mostly in that clicking, lilting gibberish he spoke; but now, for all his size, he was as subdued and meek as Uncle Charley, or Aunt Kate there beside him. The only light in the room was the dim one on the table beside the bed. It made his hair look soft, like a baby's. Aunt Kate's hair was like fine silver wire.

One time when we were visiting, Uncle Charley took what they all called later "a tumble." I'm not sure how much of it I actually saw. I was, as I've said, only five or six. A few sharp images have stayed with me all these years, but for the rest I must trust imagination and family stories. I remember sitting in the office at the mill—that time or some other time—draw-

ing on one of the yellow, legal-sized notepads Uncle Ed used
for figuring and keeping records, the pot-bellied stove unlit in
the corner. It was August; I know because farmers were bringing their wheat in. All around the stove stood pale, bluish
saltblocks, the slippery blue-white of bone in a butchershop,
and stacked around the saltblocks there were bales of twine
and barbed wire, kerosene lanterns, and zinc-coated buckets
set one inside the other, the top bucket filled with nails. Outside the window I could see Aunt Kate's garden, aglow at that
time of year with roses, zinnias, and sunflowers, vegetables
down the middle, at one end a scarecrow in a washed-out,
ragged coat and straw hat that had once been, no doubt, Uncle
Charley's. There were farmers in the room with me, ritched
back on their round-backed wooden chairs, talking and joking
as they always did while they waited for Uncle Ed to grind
their grist and then for Uncle Charley to load the bags on the
two-wheeled feedtruck and roll them to the dock, then lift
them down a foot or two onto the wagon. No doubt I'd been
running back and forth with Uncle Charley for most of the
morning, since that's what I usually did, neither of us talking
—Uncle Charley almost never talked, except when he pretended to be the parrot in the kitchen—I, for my part, trying
to be of help: snatching an empty feedsack from his path,
though in fact there was plenty of room; trying to push a
heavy door open further. But now I was in the office, weary of
the game, half listening to the singing of the wooden walls as
they resounded to the mill-wheels, and drawing rabbits so
much like those my father drew (rabbits were all he knew how
to draw) that if you'd asked him later, he couldn't have told
you for sure which one of us had done them.

I heard no shout, no noise of any kind, but suddenly the
farmers were up out of their chairs, running in their heavy
boots from the office into the mill, and as fast as I could get
down out of my chair I was after them. Where the wooden
machinery thudded and sang, sending up white powder, noth-

ing was wrong. Uncle Ed stood blinking as the farmers ran up to him and past him; then he pushed the worn-smooth wooden lever that made the rumbling stop, caught me up in his arms, and ran after the farmers. When we came into the sunlight beyond the open door, we found Uncle Charley climbing up from between the loading dock and one of the farmers' wagons, furiously shouting and wiping dirt from his mouth and moustache. The wagon had been carelessly parked, a three-foot gap between the dock and the wagonbed. On the wagon, where Uncle Charley had dropped it when he stepped into the gap and fell, a sack lay split open, slowly drizzling grist down through the slats onto the ground. He shouted louder than before, no doubt swearing in Welsh—an amazing sound from a man always so quiet—and with a look half enraged, half guilty, he tried to get up on his feet and save the grain. Then another look came over him—surprise, indignation—and one leg, cocked like a corn-knife, flipped out from under him. Uncle Ed set me down, almost threw me from him, and jumped onto the wagon, holding out his arms as if to pick up Uncle Charley, then thought better of it, or got confused. He just stood there, bent at the waist, arms thrown forward, like a child playing catch.

At the top of the stairs across the way, the back door of the house opened, and my grandmother came out in her knitted black shawl. "Land of Goshen!" she cried in a loud, angry voice. "*Now* look what you've done!" My father came out behind her, looking baffled and apologetic, as if if he hadn't been taking a nap he could have prevented it. "Now stop that," he said to my grandmother, almost absentmindedly, and instantly she stopped. Tears ran down the sides of Uncle Charley's moustache and he clung to his leg with both hands, not shouting now, clamping his lips together and whimpering. Then Aunt Kate was there with them, near-sightedly bending forward. "I'll call the doctor," she said, turning, and went back into the house.

"It's all my fault," one of the farmers said, shaking his head and working his jaw as if in a minute he meant to hit himself.

"Here now," Uncle Ed said, "let's get you inside," and carefully fitting his arms under Uncle Charley, taking pains to support the broken leg, he lifted him like a child or a newborn calf and carried him up onto the loading platform, over to the steps at the far end, then down and across the way and up the wooden stairs toward the kitchen.

"Mercy!" my grandmother said, unable to control herself, her eyes as bright as when she went out with a hoe to kill snakes. My mother took her arm and patted it.

I was of course not aware at the time that they all felt as guilty as I did. Even my grandmother, I realize now, must have felt guilty, shouting at us all as if she secretly believed she should have taken better care of us. But whatever they were feeling, they soon got over it, once Uncle Charley was inside, on the couch in the livingroom. I myself took longer. It was a matter of fact to me that if I'd been doing my job, running along with Uncle Charley and his feedtruck, keeping his way clear and watching out for trouble, he'd never have fallen down and broken his leg. The doctor, when he came, was professionally grave. Aunt Kate wrung her hands in her apron. I offered, bursting into tears as I did so, to pay Uncle Charley's doctor bills. Uncle Ed just looked at me, lips puckered in surprise. None of the others seemed to have noticed what I'd said. "I really will," I bawled, clinging to his leg.

"Here now," Uncle Ed said. "Katy, get this boy a cookie!" And then: "Go on, now. Away with you both!"

I went with her, looking over my shoulder at Uncle Charley, gray-faced on the couch, the doctor in his black suit bending down beside him. They were all smiling now, even Uncle Charley, all of them describing what had happened as "a tumble"—or all except my grandmother, who always took, according to my father, the darkest possible view of things. My mother and father had a fight that night, when they

thought I was asleep. My father said my grandmother was an Angel of Death. (His anger may have made him unusually poetic—though now that I think of it, he said the phrase as if he'd used it against her many times.) "If you hate her so," my mother said, "why don't you just send her to the old folks' home?" Thus my mother won, as she always did. When it was clear to them both that she'd won, she said, "Oh, Bill, she's just worried. You know that. She's like a child." I lay in the darkness with my eyes open, trying to make sense of the queer idea.

It wasn't until the following summer that my family visited Remsen again. Letters passed back and forth two or three a week in the meantime, Aunt Kate telling us of, among other things, Uncle Charley's gradual recovery—not as quick as it should be, she let us know—my mother sending back our family's encouragement and sometimes inspirational poems from my grandmother's magazines. When we finally went to visit it was partly because a Cymanfa Ganu—a singing festival—was to be held nearby, in Utica. At Uncle Ed's I learned to my surprise and dismay—since I disliked change, hated to see any slightest hint that the universe might not be orderly to the core, as smooth in its operations as an immense old mill—that my uncles and aunt, though they'd never before shown much interest in such things, were planning to go to the festival with my parents and grandmother. I learned it by eavesdropping. When I was supposed to be asleep—as Uncle Charley was, down in his basement room, snoring with his mouth open (I'd sneaked down earlier and seen him there, lying with one arm hanging over the bedside)—I crept without a sound down the front-hallway stairs and settled near the bottom to listen to the voices in the livingroom, just to my left.

Aunt Kate was saying, speaking more softly than usual, "He could do with the lift."

"He's still down, isn't he," my mother said.

"Oh, Cholly'll be fine," Uncle Ed said, hearty as ever, and gave a laugh.

I listened, uneasy, for what my grandmother would say. When she said nothing, I let myself believe she'd fallen asleep over her sewing.

"He keeps in too much, that's all," Aunt Kate said, as if shyly, embarrassed that Uncle Ed hadn't agreed with her.

"So anyway, we'll all go," my father said, settling things. "Take Buddy too. He's never been to a Cymanfa Ganu yet. High time he went!"

"Heavens to Betsy!" my grandmother burst out. "You'd let that poor whippersnapper stay out till midnight with a bunch of wild lunatics howling their miserable heads off?"

A shiver went up my back. I was much too literal-minded a child to fit her description with any kind of singing I'd ever heard of, much less any I'd been in on. I remembered stories my uncle Ed had told me of how the Welsh were all witches in olden times—how they used to fly around like birds at night, and make magic circles among trees and stones.

The following day I was so filled with anxious anticipation I could hardly breathe. Out in the mill I kept close to Uncle Charley, trying to guess every move he was about to make and help with it. He seemed smaller all over, since the accident. Though he wore arm-elastics, his cuffs hung low, as did the crotch of his overalls. His hands trembled, and he no longer bothered to put his teeth in. In the past he'd pretended to appreciate my help. Now, as I gradually made out, it annoyed him. "I'll get that," he'd say, kicking a twine-bale from the aisle as I reached for it. Or as I ran to push a heavy door open further, he'd say, "Leave it be, boy. It's open far enough." In the end I did nothing for him, simply stayed with him because I was ashamed to leave him and go look for Uncle Ed.

He no longer did the kinds of work he'd done before. The hundred-pound sacks were too heavy for him—he wasn't much heavier than the sacks himself—and when he pushed the feed-truck, after Uncle Ed had loaded it, both Uncle Ed and I would watch him in distress, afraid it would tilt too far back, off balance, and fall on him. Mostly, Uncle Ed had taken over the pushing of the feedtruck. "Go ahead, then," Uncle Charley said crossly. "It's your mill." To keep busy, Uncle Charley set rat traps, wound wire around old ladder rungs, swiped down cobwebs, swept the floors. He still joked with farmers, as he'd always done, but it seemed to me the lightness was gone from his voice, and his eyes had a mean look, as if he didn't really think the jokes were funny or the farmers his friends. Sometimes in the office, when the farmers were alone with Uncle Ed and me, one of the farmers would say something like, "Cholly's gettin better every day, looks like," and I would know by their smiles that none of them believed it. I would stand by the heavy old desk full of pigeonholes and secret compartments—Uncle Charley had once shown me how to work them all—trying to guess what Uncle Ed might need: his pocket-sized notebook, one of his yellow pads, or one of the big white pencils that said "E. L. Hughes" in red—but I could never guess which object he'd want next, so I could serve no useful purpose except if he happened to look over and say, "Buddy, hand me that calendar there." Then I'd leap. Out in the mill Uncle Charley moved slowly back and forth with a pushbroom, needlessly sweeping white dust from the aisles, or hammered nails into loosened bin-boards, or mended burlap sacks not yet bad enough to leak. Now and then he'd poke his head in, the buttoned collar much too large for his neck, and would ask Uncle Ed if he'd gotten to Bill Williams' oats yet. "I'll get to it, Cholly," Uncle Ed would say, waving his cigar. Uncle Charley would frown, shaking his head, then disappear, going about his business.

Sometime after lunch I found Uncle Charley sitting on the floor beside one of the bins, nailing a round piece of tin—the top of a coffeecan—over a hole where bits of grain leaked out.

I stood awhile watching him. His hand, when he reached to his mouth for a nail, shook badly. He pretended not to notice me. After a while I went over and hunkered down beside him, thinking I might hand him nails from the zinc-coated bucket beside his knee, though at the moment his mouth was as full as a pincushion. When he said nothing, I asked, "What's a Cymanfa Ganu, Uncle Charley?"

"Welsh word," he brought out through the nails, and carefully finished driving the nail between his fingers through the tin. Then he glanced at me guiltily, took the nails from his mouth and laid them on the floor between us. "Means 'Come on back,'" he said, then suddenly—his heart not in it—grinned. "'Come on back to Wales,' that is. That's what all the Welshmen want, or so they think."

He tipped his head back, as if he were listening. The way the sunlight came slanting through the mill—great generous shafts full of floating white specks all whirling and swirling in patterns too complex for the eye to comprehend—it was like being in church. Even better than church. I thought of the trees where Uncle Ed had told me the Welshmen used to worship their peculiar bug-eyed gods—"River gods, tree gods, pig gods, Lord knows what," he'd said. (My grandmother wouldn't speak of it. "Your uncle Ed," she said, "has peculiar ideas.") Abruptly, Uncle Charley dropped his head back down, snatched up a nail, cocked it between two fingers over the tin, and started hammering. "Damn fools," he said, then glanced at me and frowned, then winked.

"Tell me something else in Welsh," I said.

He thought about it, placing another nail. At last he said, squinting, "You know what 'Buddy' means?" Before I could answer, he said, "Means 'the poet.' They used to set great store by poets, back in Wales. Only second to kings—maybe not even second. Same thing, kings and poets. Different kinds of liars." He looked solemn, his face ash-gray under the age-spots. I studied him, perturbed—no more perturbed than he was, I realize now; but at six I knew nothing of the confusion of adults. All I knew was that his eyes were screwed up tight, one brown, one blue, and his moustache half covered the black hole of his mouth like a sharp-gabled roof of old straw.

I asked, "Are we *all* going to the Cymanfa Ganu?"

His eyes slipped off axis, then abruptly he reached for another nail. "Course we are," he said. He lined up the nail and with two angry raps drove it home. "Don't worry," he said, "it don't hurt much."

I remember only the inside of the building where the song-fest was held. It must have been a church, very large, with wooden walls, as yellow-gray as the walls of a new barn. It was brightly lighted, the walls and overhead beams high above us all glowing as if waxed. Everyone my parents had ever known was there, it looked like. The people milled around for what seemed to me hours, shouting and talking, pressing tightly together, my father moving behind my mother from group to group, carrying me on his shoulders. My grandmother, wearing a light black coat and helping herself along on two brown canes—it was only that winter that she'd begun to need them —went from one old white-haired Welshwoman to another, talking and nodding and laughing till she cried, sometimes pointing a bony, crooked finger across the room and gleefully shouting out a name, though no one could possibly have heard her in all that uproar.

Then somehow we got to seats, all of us together, me wedged in between my father and Uncle Charley. A man got up in the front of the room—he looked like a congressman or a well-to-do minister—and said something. Everyone laughed. He said something more, they laughed some more, and then from somewhere, booming around us, came organ music. Uncle Charley was jerking at my elbow, making me look down. He held a small Bible-like book with writing in it—no music, as in the hymnbooks in our church at home (I hadn't yet seen the ones my grandfather left my mother), just writing, and not a word anywhere that I could read. "You know your *do re mi*?" he asked, looking at me sternly, his face very bright. I shook my head, noticing only now that above the hymn words, all in Welsh, there were little words—*do*, *re*, *mi*, and so on—as meaningless to me at the time as all the others. Uncle Charley looked up at my father as if in alarm, then grinned, looking back at me. "Never mind," he said, "you sing what *I* sing." On every side of us people were standing up now, a few of them beginning to tap their feet, just barely moving the toes of their lumpy shoes. My father and Uncle Charley helped me stand up on my chair. Suddenly, like a shock of thunder that made the whole room shake, they began to sing.

Most of them seemed to have no need of the hymnbooks and couldn't have used them anyway, singing as they did with their heads lifted, mouths wide as fishmouths, proclaiming whatever it was they proclaimed not so much to the front of the hall as to the gleaming roof. They sang, as Welsh choruses always do, in numerous parts, each as clearly defined as cold, individual currents in a wide, bright river. There were no weak voices, though some, like Uncle Charley's, were reedy and harsh—not that it mattered; the river of sound could use it all. They sang as if the music were singing itself through them— sang out boldly, no uncertainties or hesitations; and I, as if by magic, sang with them, as sure of myself every note of the way as the wisest and heartiest in the room. Though I was astonished by my powers, I know, thinking back, that it was not as miraculous as I imagined. Borne along by those powerful voices, the music's ancient structure, only a very good musician could have sung off key. And yet it did seem miraculous. It seemed our bones and blood that sang, all heaven and earth singing harmony lines, and when the music broke off on the final chord, the echo that rang on the walls around us was like a roaring Amen.

Hymn after hymn we sang—old people, children, people my parents' age—ancient tunes invented before the major mode was thought of, tunes like hugely breathing creatures. We were outside ourselves, caught up in a *hwell*, as the Welsh say. It really did seem to me, once or twice, that I looked down on all the congregation from the beams above our heads. My father's hand was closed hard on mine; Uncle Charley held my other hand, squeezing it just as tightly. Tears streamed from his brown eye and blue eye, washing his cheeks, dripping from his moustache, making his whole face shine. Afterward, when we were leaving, I saw that Aunt Kate and my mother had been crying too, even my grandmother, though not my father or Uncle Ed. On the steps outside, lighting his cigar, Uncle Ed said, "Good sing." My father nodded and hitched up his pants, then turned to look back at the door as if sorry to leave. "Good turn-out." Uncle Charley, with his hands in his pockets, staring at the ground, said nothing.

The following night Uncle Charley didn't come in for supper, though they called and called. I watched through the kitchen window as Uncle Ed and my father, gray as ghosts in the moonlit garden, shouted toward the trees across the road, the glittering creek, the blacksmith's shop, then turned and moved heavily, as if gravity had changed and the air had grown thick, toward the mill. Later, Uncle Ed, in the wooden armchair in the kitchen, holding his cigar in the hand that had three fingers missing, stared into space and said, "Poor Cholly. I wonder what's got into him."

Aunt Kate stood over by the sink with her head bowed, thinking, folding the dishtowel, then unfolding it, then folding it again. "I guess we better phone the police," she said at last.

"No, don't do that!" Uncle Ed said suddenly, as if she'd startled him out of a daydream. He leaned his forearms on the arms of the chair and hefted himself up out of it. "I'll run out to the office and phone around among the neighbors a bit," he said, and at once went to the door.

"Why not phone from here?" Aunt Kate said, or began to say, then glanced at me and stopped.

"Here, let me give you a hand," my father said. The two of them went out, bent forward like shy boys, and closed the door quietly behind them.

"I'll give Buddy his supper," my mother said. "I suppose it won't hurt for the rest of us to wait."

"That's fine," Aunt Kate said, still folding and unfolding the dishtowel.

"We should never have taken him to the songfest," my grandmother said. "I *told* you it wouldn't be good for him!"

My mother, herding me over to my chair, said, "Mother, you never said any such thing!"

"Well, I meant to," my grandmother said, and firmly clamped her mouth shut.

Toward morning they found him, I learned much later, right across the road in the creek behind the blacksmith's shop. I still occasionally dream of it, though of course I never saw it, Uncle Charley lying face up below the moonlit, glass-clear surface, staring, emotionless, at the perfectly quiet stars.

Aunt Kate, it turned out, had known all along that he'd gone off to take his own life, though she'd refused to believe it and had therefore told no one. She'd found his clothes that afternoon, just a little after sunset, neatly folded and stacked on the chair beside his bed in the room they let him live in downstairs. He'd left them as a message, my grandmother said: for what they were worth, the world could have them back. ("Now that's enough of that," my father said sharply.) Aunt Kate had told herself one foolish lie after another, she explained to us, her hands over her eyes, her glasses on the table in front of her. Perhaps he'd found a lady-friend, she'd said to herself, and had gone out and bought himself new clothes, even new socks and shoes.

The following night, when everyone knew Uncle Charley was dead, though no one was admitting it was suicide (they never did admit that), Uncle Ed's livingroom was filled with people. All the chairs were occupied, even the arms of them, where boys or young women sat, most of them cousins, and there were people on the chairs my father had brought in from the diningroom and kitchen, too. The people were all talking in low voices and sniffling, their eyes wet and red. I sat on one of my father's legs, watching.

They talked of the singer Uncle Charley had been; the festivals would never be the same without him. They spoke of what a shame it was that he'd never had a wife and children; it would have made all the difference. Then for a while, since sad talk made them ill at ease, they talked about other things— crops and the weather, marriages, politics. Sometimes they talked now in groups of three or four, sometimes all as one group. Aunt Kate served tea. Some of the men had whiskey with them, which Aunt Kate didn't approve of, but she looked at the carpet and said nothing. The clock on the mahogany desk ticked on and on, but neither in the darkness outside nor in the dimly lit livingroom was anything changing. People stirred a little, now and then, shifting position, moving just an arm or a foot, sometimes blowing their noses, but no one got up yet, no one left for home. Slowly the whole conversation died out like embers in a fireplace, and as the stillness deepened, settling in like winter or an old magic spell, it began to seem that the silence was unbreakable, our final say.

Then an old farmer named Sy Thomas, sitting in the corner with his hands folded, twine around his pants cuffs, cleared his throat, pushed his chin out, face reddening, eyes evasive, and began to sing. Tentatively, then more boldly, others joined in with him. Aunt Kate, with an expression half timid, half cunning, went to the piano and, after a minute, sat down, took off her glasses, and began to play. They were singing in parts now, their heads slightly lifted. On the carpet, one after another, as if coming to life, their shoes began to move.

THE ART
OF LIVING

There used to be a cook in our town, a "chef" he was called in the restaurant where he worked—one of those big, dark Italian places with red fake-leather seat cushions, fake paintings on the walls, and on every table a Chianti bottle with a candle in it—but he preferred to think of himself as simply a cook, since he'd never been comfortable with high-falutin pretense, or so he claimed, though heaven knew the world was full of it, and since, whereas he knew what cooking was, all he knew for sure about chefs, he said, was that they wore those big, obscene-looking hats, which he himself wouldn't be caught dead in. In all this he was a little disingenuous, not to mention out of date, since everybody knew that, in the second-floor apartment over Custus's Sweet Shop, Newsstand, & Drugstore, where he and his family lived, he had hundreds of books and magazines about cooking, as well as books and magazines about everything else, even a couple of those San Francisco comic books, and all his talk about being an ordinary cook, not a chef, was just another pretense, in this case low-falutin, an attempt to seem what he would never be in a hundred years, just one of the folks. His talk about chefs' hats was just empty chatter, maybe something he'd thought up years ago and had never thought better of. He did a lot of empty chattering, especially after his son died in the war. He could get all emotional about things not even locked-up crazy people cared about. At the time of this story there weren't many chefs' hats in the town where I lived, up in the northern part of New York State, but they were standard garb in the pancake houses, hamburger islands, and diners of the larger cities, like Rome or Utica. The cook's name, I forgot to mention, was Arnold Deller.

Cooks are notoriously cranky people, but Arnold was an exception. Why he should have been so even-tempered seems a mystery, now that I think about it—especially given his fondness for rant and given the fact that, as we all found out, he was as full of pent-up violence as anybody else at that time. Nevertheless, even-tempered he was. Sometimes when certain kinds of subjects came up, his eyes would fill with tears; but he never swore, or hardly ever, never hit anybody, never quit his job in a huff.

He had it easy, I suppose, in some ways at least. He'd worked in the same place for twenty-some years, almost one of the family, and the working conditions weren't bad, as such things go. The place was respectable. If you got out a joint, just held it between your fingers, the next thing you knew you were out in the alley on your back, looking up at garbage cans and waste bins. And the kitchen he worked in was large and sufficiently well designed that he didn't have to run his fat legs off all the time. He'd gotten them to copy it from a restaurant he'd seen in San Francisco or someplace, some convention he'd gone to on saving the endangered species. He and his daughters were big on things like that, also politics and the Threat of Drug Abuse, the same things everybody else was into, except that Arnold and his daughters were more serious. When people wore fur coats, Arnold's daughters would practically cry. Arnold's wife mostly slept and watched TV. After their son's death, she hardly ever left the apartment.

As I say, it was a good job for Arnold. He had a helper, part cook, part dishwasher, a half-Indian, half-Italian kid named

Ellis. And all across one wall of the kitchen there were windows, which Arnold and Ellis could open if they wanted to, summer or winter, so the heat was only slightly worse than elsewhere. But above all, the job was ideal for a person of Arnold's inclination and temperament because the owner, an old man named Frank Dellapicallo—a gray-headed, gloomy man we hardly ever saw—would let Arnold cook anything he wanted, so long as the ingredients could be found and weren't wildly expensive and the customers would eat it so the old man, Dellapicallo himself, didn't have to. All he ever ate was spaghetti.

Granting Arnold Deller this freedom was no big risk on Dellapicallo's part. Though he could talk like a congressman or a holy-roller preacher, Arnold was never outrageous when it came to cuisine—or anyway almost never. It had all started a long time ago, when he'd gone to Paris as a soldier at the end of World War II—he was an army cook—and had eaten in a couple of relatively fancy restaurants (considering the times), which he'd enjoyed a good deal and could still talk about in tiresome detail to anyone who'd listen. Since then, of course, he'd visited other good restaurants. It wasn't that, discovering fine food, he'd lost all perspective. The first times, in Paris, had taught him that food could be "art," a fact he never tired of mentioning; but it hadn't turned his heart to exotic dishes, in spite of what you may think when I come to the event this story must eventually lead to. What he'd ordered in Paris, both times, was steak, which turned out to be *bifteck au poivre*, and it had taught him that food should be wonderful, not necessarily outlandish. Both times, he said, he'd praised the food, the waiter, and the chef so lavishly that in the end they'd insisted he had to be Canadian. That too was a revelation, that food made peace between nations.

So now, every other week or so, Arnold would come up with a new "Friday night chef's special"—Peking duck, beef Wellington, rack of lamb, salmon mousse—which always ran

out before the evening was half over and which gradually made Dellapicallo's restaurant somewhat famous in and around our town, so that if somebody came home from Viet Nam, or cousins came in from Syracuse or somewhere, or a bunch of old ladies wanted a nice place to go, Dellapicallo's was the first place they thought of.

I know now, looking back, that the food was more or less ordinary, at least by big-city standards. But our town, in those days, had only twenty thousand people, give or take a few thousand, depending on the weather and conditions on the lake, and so it didn't really seem to us pretentious or deep-down stupid when Arnold began to describe himself as "an artist." For one thing, it came on him gradually, so that none of us really noticed, except in passing. And for another, Arnold had a bookish way of speaking—he read a lot, as I've said; not just cookbooks but anything that fell into his hands. Any kind of print that came in front of his steel-rimmed spectacles he would read—license plates, the numbers on wallpaper seams —and a lot of times with a person like that, especially if the Beatles or the Jefferson Airplane are wailing in the background, you don't really notice when what the person is saying has gotten odder. Anyway, the "we" I'm talking about now is the Scavengers gang, motorcycle hoods, or so we liked to think, really just a bunch of greaser kids in second-hand black jackets, fighting pimples, hanging around, waiting to get drafted and shot at. We weren't exactly unaware that that was how it stood with us. Some of the kids in our town enlisted, ran out and joined up as quick as they could with the United States Marines; others went to college and tried to get out of it. We were the poor stupid animals in between: too smart to enlist, too dumb to run and hide in the revolution. "A pox on all your houses!" was our motto, or would have been if the phrase were one we'd ever heard. Our bikes bore no peace signs, no American flags, no LSD rainbows, Nazi swastikas or iron crosses. Their only symbolism was their dull black paint.

For Romantic despair, invisibility. We drove third- or fourth-hand Harleys, mostly old flatheads with the pipes opened up—drove them or, more often, pushed them. Nonetheless Kings of the Road we were, with muscular grins. For the most part, whatever our anarchist dreams, we had to be good honest laboring citizens to keep our hogs rolling.

Usually it was sometime in the early afternoon that we'd drop in to rap with old Arnold. "Hey, let's go rap with old Arnold," one of us would say, maybe Tony Petrillo, making a kind of joke of it. The last thing anyone in the gang would have admitted was that it was actually interesting to hear Arnold talk. So far as I remember, nobody even admitted that it was interesting to sit in the terrible proximity of old Dellapicallo's granddaughter Angelina. In the early afternoon Arnold the cook had nothing much to do. He'd have a pot or two simmering, things he'd go back into the kitchen to check on, from time to time; but at that time of day there was nothing urgent, nothing Ellis couldn't have handled fine if Arnold had temporarily dropped dead. So Arnold would settle himself at one of the dark, round tables near the bar (the restaurant was separate) where Joe Dellapicallo, the owner's son, was bartender and where sometimes, if we were lucky, Joe's daughter Angelina worked as waitress. Arnold drank sherry; he'd pick up the glass with just his thumb and first finger and let the others sort of float. He allowed himself only one large glass all afternoon, though it was said that after work, when he went home, around midnight, he often got smashed, reading books and sipping whiskey while his wife and three daughters snored. It was dark in the bar, blurry with TV noise and the music of the juke that was fixed so it never shut off. We'd get ourselves draught beers and go to his table, turn the chairs around, and sit.

"Hey, Arnold."

" 'Lo, boys." He spoke with what he no doubt intended to seem dignified reserve, voice from the mountaintop, like Lyndon

Baines Johnson when he talked on TV about controlled response; but Arnold's voice never quite made it. He was fat and pink, the steel-rimmed glasses on his nose slightly steamy, the eyes behind them tiny and light blue, and even here, where it was dark and cool, his forehead and throat always glistened with a thin wash of sweat. The smell that came off him, if you sat downwind, was awesome. His hair was light reddish-brown, partly gray, and cut short, old-time army-style but with longish golden sideburns, which made him an anomaly at Dellapicallo's, where just about everybody—at least until the dinner crowd arrived—was Italian. I too was, to some extent, exceptional: half-Irish.

"How's the stock market?" one of us would say, maybe Benny Russo; years later he'd become a computer expert. Or maybe one of us would say, "Hey, what's the secret of happiness, Arnold?" That would be Lenny the Shadow. He was into sensation—mired in it, I guess. In Viet Nam, he'd learn about drugs, and he'd be wasted from an overdose at twenty. It didn't much matter what you said, it would get Arnold Deller rolling. Whatever we asked him, he always assumed we were more or less serious. Hippy sincerity was in, in those days, at least in certain circles, and that was more or less the tone we took, with just sufficient ironic edge that nobody could really pin us down, prove we actually existed.

"Ha, you punklets," Arnold would say, just lifting the corners of his mouth and eyebrows, as if drawing his head back in disdain were too much work; but it wasn't unfriendly. He knew us. Everybody knew us. Most of the people in town even liked us, I learned years later, though they hated the damn noise. "Listen, kid," he said the afternoon this story begins. His eyes were narrowed more than usual and his voice was edgy. "Listen, kid, you're talking to an artist, see? What does an artist know about a thing like that? You know what's the matter with the world today? People are always asking the wrong people the big important questions. Like a football player, they want him to tell 'em about politics. Or a famous minister like Billy Graham, they want him to predict who'll win the Super Bowl." He shook his head, as if the whole thing depressed him more than words could say. "You kids had any brains, you'd ask me what to do with oregano. Educate yourself, learn a good honest trade, or, rather, art." He smiled, big-chinned. His chin was like a big pink softball with two or three whiskers. "But I'll tell you one thing. Better to ask *me* these grandiose questions than ask somebody thinks he knows the answers." He looked over at Joe at the bar, as if that was who he meant.

Joe went on as always, wiping things with his cloth—bar-top, faucets, ashtrays, anything he couldn't remember having wiped just a minute ago. The television was on above him, the latest news of who'd killed who, demonstrations, riots, helicopters hovering over Viet Nam or Berkeley, it was all the same. Lot of shouting, bearded commies, bearded Green Berets, one with a piece of Scotch tape on his glasses. It was hard to believe that outside the restaurant the sun was shining and dogs lay asleep on the sidewalk.

Joe never looked at the television. He had his own wars, undeclared, like the big one; mainly with Angelina. He had quick, nervous hands like a card player's, and his black hair was slicked back so smooth you might have thought it was paint. Like Arnold, he was resisting the longer-locks look. Sometimes when his eye accidentally fell on my hair, which hung pretty far down my back in those days, his face would freeze out and for a minute or two it would look like he'd given up breathing. Of those who admired my ambling indifference to the world's imperatives, Joe Dellapicallo, Angelina's father, was not one. Sometimes today he would suddenly grin a little crossly, like a man hearing voices, but he was careful never to let on that he was hearing Arnold's voice, or ours.

Then the front door opened, letting in a blast of light, and Angelina came in. School had let out. She was a senior. Joe glanced up and noticed, that was all. He was always like that, so cool he was ice. You'd have thought he hated her or didn't know her, but if anybody'd touched her on one of those beautiful brown bare-naked legs he'd've been out from behind that bar like a shot, and for the man with the traveling fingers it would have been Doomsday. I thought a lot about that, usually lying on my back with my hands behind my head, in my bed at my parents' house at night. It was supposed to be the age of the sexual revolution, love for free, just ask—it was in all the magazines, and sometimes I was sure it was happening all around me, every party I didn't get to, every lighted-up farmhouse. It probably was, in fact, even in our town—people painting flowers on one another's bodies, giving gang-bang massages, one eye cocked over toward the instruction book; but it wasn't happening where I was or, apparently, where Angelina was. I was fairly sure of that. I had a habit, to tell the truth, of checking up on her nights. I'd idle past her house, sort of coasting, almost silent, to see if the light in her room was on, and if it wasn't, and I couldn't catch a glimpse of her downstairs, I'd tool around checking out parties from a distance. Once for something like an hour and a half, I followed a car she was riding in, I thought—hanging back with my lights out, keeping down the noise—but when they finally got up their nerve and pulled under some trees down by the lake, and I zoomed in and zapped the headlights on, all three of them at once, on high-beam, the terrified face that looked out at me wasn't Angelina's; some girl with blond hair. I beeped and waved, let 'em know I was a friendly. Suffice it to say that, between her father's watchfulness and mine, Angelina could hardly move a finger.

She came in walking fast, long-legged, sailing, her expression intense, as if expecting a fight and hoping this once she might get out of it. "Hi, Pop," she said, chewing gum, not meeting his eyes, pulling her coat off. She had her outfit on, black with white around the collar and the hem of the skirt.

She wore these push-up bras, and the collar was as low as the skirt was high. She couldn't be blamed for it, that was what waitresses wore in such places; but when she came to your table she liked to lean way over and make you nervous, and that I did blame her for, a little—as did her father, watching—not that I wanted her to stop. It didn't mean a thing, though, or meant the opposite from what it said. I'd figured out long since that in her heart of hearts she was a nun, maybe a physicist. I guess the real truth is, Angelina hardly knew what she wanted herself. She was a straight-A student, a virgin, a tease —church-scared, father-scared; the usual business. In the days of *Playboys* right out in the livingroom, she might as well have been back in Calabria, winking at goatherds, warning them back with a knife.

"Hi, Arnold," she'd always say, smiling. Not a word to us.

He would smile back, blissful, squeezing his eyes shut. "Hi, Angelina." It was obscene. But he'd known her since she was zero, of course. He had uncle's rights.

She would say, jabbing out at us with the filthy wet rag she wiped the table with and maybe tossing a quick look at her father, "You guys should pay rent. You ever try walking around outside in the sunshine?" Big smile, eyes like dark jade. I used to wonder if it ever occurred to her that one of these days, for all her glory, she'd have to marry one of us and have babies and get fat. I took it for granted that that was how it would end. Who could have believed, in a town like ours, that a little more than a year from then, Angelina would be trying to close down Cornell University, shouting angry slogans in doggerel verse, and firing windy, ranting letters at me—"Dear Finnegan"—in some Asian swamp?

As soon as she'd left us, Arnold would wipe his forehead and start up again, folding his pink hands on the tabletop, smiling like a pink-faced priest in the direction of Angelina.

This day he said, "You wonder why she's so attracted to me,

right? Maturity, boys. Maybe I can give you some pointers."
He tapped the tips of his fingers together.

"Hey, Mr. Deller, *do* that," Lenny Cervone said, holding
his hands out to Arnold and wiggling the fingers as if to lure
out words. Lenny—Lenny the Shadow—was the toughest of
us, at least he looked it. Even right after he shaved, before he
stopped doing that, he had five-o'clock shadow. We all leered
and waited.

Arnold smiled and stretched his chin. "Your trouble is,"
he said, "you just circle. That's for goldfish. No offense! Listen,
the world's in chaos, right?" He leaned forward over his elbows, eyebrows lowered, wincing a little, as if thinking hard
made his head ache. "War, revolution, students rioting, police
rioting, drugs and promiscuity . . . Let me tell you something:
it will pass. Nobody believes that, nobody thinks about afterward—hell no!—but let me tell you, *it will pass!* After the
world-wide glorious high there's going to be a crash like the
world never dreamed of. Things will be changed, even here, in
a backwater hick-town like this one, but whatever the world's
like afterward, we're gonna be stuck with ourselves again—
ourselves! It's a gloomy prospect. A person could go crazy!" He
smiled and pushed out his chin in the direction of Tony Petrillo. "It's easy to throw yourself at grand ideals, and it's also
easy to cut out, call everything nonsense. It's even natural,
right now: the world's in the middle of a big noisy party; but
eventually the party will be over, you mark my words. All this
wild scrambling, all this floundering and screaming, people
killing each other, making love in the street—one of these days
you'll wake up and it's gonna be quiet out. Maybe a few storm-
troopers or black-suited businessmen keeping order. But quiet,
everywhere. Nothing moving. People will be stuck with themselves again." He drew back and wiped his mouth. His hands
were shaking, though he grinned and tried to hide it. "It's no
good, this backing off from things. Don't worry, I know what

you're up to, you guys. I know what everybody's up to." He
looked over at Joe. "You think *I'm* not tempted to back off, just
throw up my hands and say the hell with it? But it's no good,
leads straight into craziness. The thing a person's gotta have—
a human being—is some kind of center to his life, some one
thing he's good at that other people need from him, like, for
instance, shoemaking. I mean something ordinary but at the
same time holy, if you know what I mean. Very special. Something *ritual*—like, better yet, cooking!" He stretched back his
lips—no doubt he meant it for a smile—and closed his eyes.

It made us all uneasy, the way he'd plunged straight into it,
no fooling around, no glancing back. Then Lenny the Shadow
snapped his fingers and said, "That's it! Pass me the stove!"

We all pretended it was funnier than it was, hitting each
other on the shoulders lightly, saying "Hoo!" and "Shit!"
(Sometimes it was a lot of work, just hanging around.) Angelina glanced at us from her barstool, letting us know we
were deep-down boring. Joe went on mechanically wiping
things, one small muscle in his jaw working. Only the cook
showed any mercy. He looked away from Lenny and, without
raising the heel of his hand from the tabletop, pointed at
Benny the Butcher—that was what we called him, nobody
remembers why. He had a bushy long black beard, Indian
headband, little gold-rimmed glasses.

"You smile," the cook said, mostly for rhetoric, since Benny
the Butcher was always smiling, his look faintly rueful, staring
at the table or the wall or the floor, slightly moving his head as
if slowly and thoughtfully saying "No." He had something a
little bit wrong with his eyes. "You smile," Arnold said, "but
you'll see, believe me! People can get the idea life's just instinct, no trick to it. But we're not animals, that's our great
virtue and our terrible dilemma." He raised one finger, solemn,
a kind of ironic apology for the super-fancy talk. "We've got to
think things out, understand our human nature, figure out how
to become what we are."

"Plan a *head*," Tony Petrillo broke in. "Plan a *head!*" He smacked his right fist into his left hand, almost missing though he was watching so hard his eyes crossed. Nobody paid any attention to him. Nothing Tony ever said made any sense. He claimed he'd gone crazy from watching Walter Cronkite. He always tried to get the channel turned before Cronkite said, "That's the way it is." Tony was gangly-armed, swing-headed, clumsy. He was so out of it that one time when we stopped for a redlight he forgot to put his feet down and tipped over, damn near caught the bike on fire. His ambition in life was to run a skull-crusher in some big city. It was a scary idea. Actually he ended up working in a V.A. hospital.

"What are we?" Arnold said, moving his hands across the tabletop, palms up, toward me. I was always the one that paid the closest attention and made the fewest jokes. I don't brag about it. I was just never very funny. "Big super-apes with enormous brains," Arnold said. He suddenly looked angry, as if it were the fault of the Scavengers gang that people were just apes. "Enormous brains relatively speaking, I mean," he said. "Half-wit morons compared to whales, but never mind. Big brains relatively—anyway big enough that they've tuned out the body, if you know what I mean. What animals know by instinct has a hard time getting through to us, except for the really big instincts, the ones that knock your block off. So what are we? What can we deduce about, to coin a phrase, the Art of Living?" His lips shook.

Angelina was half sitting, half leaning on the barstool, one leg bent at the knee, as in a movie-ad, mocking by her very existence the enormous human brain. It came to me that she was listening, as interested as any of the rest of us, though she pretended not to be, and then it came to me that Arnold Deller knew it. I wondered if her father did.

The cook started counting things off on his fingers, never looking for as much as a second at Angelina. He sat mounded forward over the table, leaning on his elbows, urgent. "We're social animals. We're no good if we don't run in packs, like you guys. Take one of you alone—even Benny the Butcher here— why a half-starved alleycat could knock him over! But it's not only that. Even when we pretend to be otherwise—like you, Finnegan." He pointed at me and closed one eye, very grim, lips trembling. "Even if we pretend it's otherwise, we *like* to run in packs. We get lonely. We want something to love and protect." He wagged his head toward Angelina and winked, not humorously, as he no doubt intended it, but somehow horribly, the way a severed head might wink. I shot a glance at her father, then another one at Arnold, startled. He raised his hand, palm out, all innocence. "Okay," he said, "so, *one*, we're social animals. We gotta live with that. It's one of those big instincts you can't get away from—comes of having babies that can't fend for themselves. Parents gotta stick with 'em enough to take care of 'em, so little by little, through the centuries, as Mr. Darwin says—you should get somebody to read him to you, Finnegan—ha ha! ha ha!—little by little through the centuries human beings got more and more loving until now, the way we are, it's almost like a sickness, all that anguish of love—but cheer up, it's even worse with whales. Okay, so where was I? Okay." Suddenly, like a fist closing, his face closed into a frown.

Benny the Butcher looked at me, suspecting something, then went back to looking at the table and shaking his head. There was nothing I could tell him. I wasn't sure what was happening myself. The cook was always a little crazy, a little rhetorical and preachy, but something was going on that wasn't quite usual, that was clear. The room was building up a charge, as if it were the furniture, the dark red walls that had slipped toward not-quite-sane. I felt restless, in need of space and air, but also I wanted Arnold Deller to keep talking. Even if he was making some kind of play for Angelina—it was a weird idea, but it crossed my mind—I had a feeling the talk was in some strange way getting at something. Angelina sat aloof, poised like a bird on a wire. Her father stood with his back to her, only his arms moving, mechanically washing glasses.

"Okay," Arnold said, "but what else we know is, *two*, we got a *war* instinct, also on account of the baby." He aimed a finger at me like a gun. "Any animal can fight—duck, wolf, bear—but human beings are serious about it. You ever wonder about that? It's all on account of those babies, that's what I figure. Ordinary mating fight, usually sooner or later one of the males will back off, except horses. Horses are nuts. But human babies, that changes things. You gotta protect the nest till the baby can walk and talk, learn to make fire, hunt and cook. That takes a long time. Ten years? Twelve? It's no good just knocking off an enemy now and then. You gotta clean out that forest, make the whole place safe. So the baby that survives is the one with the parents that are the best at holding grudges, the ones that are *implacable*." He looked at Lenny the Shadow, who had his mouth open, ready to break in. "Look it up, kid," Arnold said. "Ask your priest."

Lenny raised his eyebrows and his hands and looked at me, innocent and injured, surprised by the attack. "Is there no *justice*?" his look said. There was no justice.

Arnold was digging in, cutting rock. He leaned forward on his elbows again, sweat shining on his face, and looked straight at me as if he'd forgotten the others were there. "But ah," he said, "that's where the trouble starts, you can see that yourself! The parents love the baby, and love each other, of course, or they wouldn't stay together and protect the baby, and pretty soon they learn to love their relatives and neighbors, since that also helps survival, and after a while, after centuries and centuries, they learn to love dead relatives and whatever bits of wisdom they may have scratched on pieces of wood or stone before they died. What a conspiracy! The family and neighbors both living and dead, all standing guard over the poor helpless baby! But they hate—repeat, *hate*—the enemy, the stranger." He threw a sharp look at Joe behind the bar—Angelina looked at him too—but Joe, it seemed, noticed none of it.

"All very well," Arnold said, "as long as people stay in tight little groups. But what happens when Italians and Irishmen start trying to live in the same town? Or Englishmen and Welshmen, Germans, Jews, Chinamen, black men? When that begins to happen we've gotta expand our horizons, retrain our instincts a little." He lowered his head and pointed at my nose. "We invent civilization and law courts, even figure out ways of loving the dead relatives of those other guys—dead relatives who said terrible things about our own dead relatives. That's when you've gotta use your head—you see? Love by policy, not just instinct. That's the Art of Living. Not just instinct; something you do on purpose. Art!" He was practically shouting.

It may be clear to you by now what was happening, part of it anyway, but it wasn't clear to me. My heart was pounding and I could feel the blood rushing up, stinging my cheeks, though I managed to keep my cool muscle-smile. It didn't quite seem to me that the cook had gone really, literally insane, and I was sure he wasn't drunk, but why he was yelling at me, apparently trying to make a fool of me, I was in too much of a panic to understand. Even the weird things Tony Petrillo said seemed to make more sense.

"You got it all figured out," I said. "I gotta hand it to you, Arnold." Smiling; voice soft, as if I weren't actually there, just a projection beamed down from a spaceship. I had a feeling Angelina was looking at me, but when I glanced over at her, she wasn't. Her partly turned-away face was dark, as if she too were blushing.

It must finally have occurred to Arnold Deller that none of us was getting it, with the possible exception of Joe, behind the bar. Arnold suddenly grinned and drew back. "Crazy talk from a cook, eh?" he said, and gave a laugh.

"Hey, listen, man," Lenny the Shadow began, but then, whatever he'd meant to say, he forgot it, just sort of faded back into the darkness.

"I'll tell you this," the cook said. "Art's where it all comes together, that's what we're talking about. You take a good Chinese dinner, something very special." He shot a quick nervous look over at Joe and Angelina. The way he was rolling his eyes, it was like one of those old-time Eisenstein movies. "My boy Rinehart, over there in Viet Nam—"

Quickly, we all nailed our eyes to the table. It was the worst trick he had, that way of talking about his son as if everything were fine. He'd always fake a smile and raise his eyebrows—he didn't even know he was doing it—and his lips would tremble and his voice would cloud over and more often than not his eyes would fill with tears. It should have made us sad, theoretically, but I guess the truth is it made us feel creepy, crowded in on, a little disgusted. If he'd done it any oftener, we'd have quit going by.

"My boy Rinehart had a certain dish over there in Asia, a certain dish you might think no American would touch, given our prejudices. But it was made so perfectly, it was so downright outstanding, sooner or later you just had to give in to it. That's what he wrote. I've got the letter. It wasn't just food, it was an *occasion*. It was one of the oldest dishes known in Asia. Sit down to that dinner—this is what he wrote, and he was right, dead right—you could imagine you were eating with the earliest wisemen in the world."

We went on staring at the table, maybe all of us thinking about that slip, "dead right."

Arnold said, talking more quietly all at once, "Art, ya see, art stirs up emotion that people can get together on. Universal humanness, you know what I mean? It's one of those centers of order I was talking about. It doesn't matter whether you're the artist or one of the serious appreciators, one of those people that gets a big crowd together and goes to listen to, ha ha, Ol'

Blue Eyes every time he comes to town. Life's full of drift. Everything. Drift." His voice was shaky. We all breathed shallowly, as if to steady the room, keep him from breaking out in sobs. I was thinking dark thoughts—I suspect we all were. I was sorry for him, sure, and I knew you couldn't blame him; but I wished he'd get the hell ahold of himself. No doubt that was programmed too, I thought—the inclination to pull away, leaving the dying to the wolves.

"Listen," I said, "nobody's down on art, okay? Artists are beautiful."

Angelina was staring into the mirror, no doubt thinking, correctly, that she was art. Accidentally, our eyes met.

The cook was wringing his hands, moving his shoulders back and forth as if his back ached. Instead of taking the out I'd offered him, he felt, apparently, a compulsion to be honest and exact. "It may not be they *all* are," he said, sort of whining. "I guess there are some that cut their ears off and shoot themselves, maybe even a few that shoot other people." He jerked his mouth, then leaned forward, quickly and guiltily licking his lips. His cheeks were wet, tears oozing out in a thin wash below the steel-rimmed glasses. I agreed with Benny the Butcher, shaking his head. There wasn't much hope. Maybe the floor would open up and the cook would vanish.

He brushed at the wetness on his cheeks with both hands, then bent his head and rolled his eyes up, still guilty but also cross now, damned annoyed at our daring to pull away on him. Maybe he sensed that his talking of himself as an artist was beginning to grate. His tone became stubborn, petulant. "But it's not as artists they do those things," he said, "or anyway the crazy things aren't what makes 'em artists, though maybe it all goes together, maybe artists are children, impractical and so on." He stretched his chin out, warning us not to agree with him too boldly. "But you gotta consider the end result," he said. He poked the table, hard, with his finger. "If he's an artist, what a man does, or a woman, is make things—objects which nobody asked him to make or even wanted him to make, in fact maybe they wanted him *not* to. But he makes them, and once people have them in their hands or standing there in front of them, people for some reason feel they would like to take them home with them or eat them, or if the object's too big to take home or eat, have it hauled to some museum. That's what it's all about. Making life startling and interesting again, bringing families together, or lovers, what-not."

Suddenly Joe leaned over the bar, hands out to each side on the bartop, eyebrows arching out like blackbird wings. "No!" he shouted, apparently at Arnold. "I don't give a damn about all your crazy talk. *No, black, dog!*"

Angelina's face went pale with anger. She glanced at her father, then came over and put her hands on the table and said, "Why don't you hoods get out of here? Why don't you just beat it and leave him alone?"

"Jesus Christ, Angelina!" Lenny said. He looked like he might fall over from purest amazement.

"It's all right, Angie," the cook said. His face was dark red, his eyes murderous. "I gotta go back and check on things." He pushed back from the table, then leaned forward and stood up—big as a house, tattoo of a blue-and-red dragon on his arm. He grinned, lips trembling. "It's not you guys. Don't worry." He pointed at me. "What I said, Finnegan. Take it to heart!"

With our mouths open, we watched him waddle to the kitchen, then we got the hell out.

After we left Dellapicallo's we cruised awhile, as usual. With the wind in my ears and hair, right away my head felt clearer, though what had happened was as baffling as ever. The others had no more understood it than I did. "What the fuck did *we* do, man?" Crazy Tony said as soon as we were out on the sidewalk, blinking in the light. "Yeah, what did *we* do?" the others said. We threw our arms out to the sides and jerked our heads as if to shake off dizziness, all the age-old gestures of the falsely accused poor misunderstood hood, but this time it was for real. So now we rode in somewhat closer formation than we usually did, geared down, making all the noise we could.

Despite my feelings of guilt and confusion, riding with the pack felt beautiful, maybe more so that afternoon than at other times, since the ride was charged—must have been charged—with the poignancy of things one has intuited to be passing. It was good hearing that deep *chug-chug* only Harleys make, or used to make, and looking at Benny the Butcher's black-jacketed back, solid as a wall there in front of me, Lenny the Shadow to the left of him, both hogs fat-wheeled, borne down by taillights, big-piped as classy small-town whores. Tony Petrillo rode to the left of me, old-time coontails streaming from his handgrips. When I glanced at him he raised a black gauntlet, with such elegance I wondered if all the spastic clumsiness was just play. I grinned and gave him back his sign.

Ah, that too was love, of course; part of the vastly complex genetic plan. Kings of the Road we were, vrooming the throttle, backing down the spark to shoot a fart at the ladies and gentlemen on the curb. We came to the edge of town and we began to lean in, cut rock. Twilight was upon us. Benny, then Lenny, turned his lights on, bank on bank of them. The lake was still, as smooth as a mirror, every corner from end to echoing end accepting our wild young animal racket as if pleased that we'd swung by.

I was still feeling aftershocks of guilt and confusion—though also I was beginning to incline toward a theory—when I went out to the garage that night and hunkered down to work on my motorcycle, trying to get it fine-tuned. Part of the anguish I was feeling was hope. At supper my mother had told me I

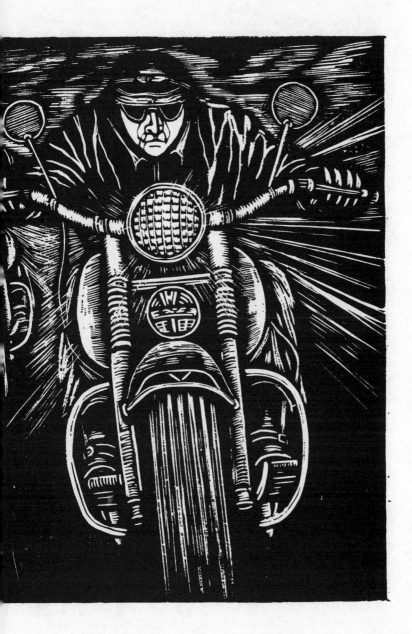

looked sick, and my sister had said as if stating a fact, "Finnegan's in love."

"Don't talk with your mouth full!" I'd told her—just the helpful big brother.

"Oh, Finnegan's always in love," my mother said, and waved it away.

But my father the sly one, crafty old Calabrian, looked over at me, his head down near his plate, level with the hurrying fork, and grinned. "Can she cook?" he said. The innuendo was faint, but when I saw my mother and father exchange looks, I knew they were on to me. Suddenly—three or four seconds had passed—Shannon, my sister, got the joke and cackled, both hands up to her mouth.

"Finnegan's in love with Angeleeena!" she sang.

"Shannon, stop teasing your brother," my mother said. She turned to me, reaching for my plate to heap on more food. "You should invite her over sometime, Finnegan."

"She wouldn't come," I said.

"Don't be silly," she said. She said it with such instant and absolute conviction that I suddenly got a whole new vision of what had happened at Dellapicallo's—what was happening every minute, everywhere in the world.

When I'd been working on my bike for an hour or so, I heard a knock at the door behind me—a knock merely of politeness, since the door was wide open, looking out at the street. I turned but at first saw nothing, just a blurry outline, my eyes loosened by the glare of the trouble-light. Then the blur, like an image through heat-waves, settled down, and I saw that it was, as I'd thought it just might possibly be, Angelina. I looked at my watch: 10 p.m. She should still be at the restaurant.

"Hey, Angelina," I said.

She looked small, as if huddled against cold, though it wasn't cold. She didn't even look all that pretty, just tired,

though my heart was whamming. She stayed by the door, leaning against the frame.

"Hi," she said. Then, after a moment, "Finnegan, could I
talk to you?"

"Sure. Why not?" I couldn't decide whether or not to stand
up. If I stood up, that would be nice, a sign of welcome; but it
might seem aggressive or threatening or something, and anyway maybe I looked better hunkered down by my bike. Nor
could I think what to say. "You look terrific," I might have
said, which was true and not true. No matter what I said, even
if I said something honest, she'd catch me out. I knew her. She
hadn't even apologized for yelling at us, like she was the
Queen and she had the right.

"That's a beautiful motorcycle," she said. She pronounced
it "sigh-kull," not as we did, "sickle." It was glorious that she
did that. Don't ask me why.

"Yeah. It doesn't always run so good," I said.

"Is something wrong with it?"

The question seemed thoughtful, loaded with overtones, as
if maybe she were making fine distinctions too complex for me
to dream of working out. My heart soared. What a face! What
eyes! It was true, as I've said, that she was supposed to be
smart in school.

"Well, it just doesn't work so good," I said, and shrugged.
"I'm sort of tuning it." I smiled. "Like a piano." Now I did
stand up, but stoop-shouldered and loose, so anybody could
see I wasn't dangerous. I wiped my hands on the rag over the
seat.

"Like a piano," she said, almost but not quite smiling, looking for just an instant into my eyes, then away. After a minute
she came a few feet into the garage, sort of looking at the
machine, not me, and leaned on the workbench. Hesitantly,
carefully, she raised one foot onto the grease-can I kept oil and
parts in. It struck me that the pose was the same one she'd
got into when she was leaning on the barstool, one foot raised

on a rung, but it didn't look like a movie-ad pose now, just tired and natural. I said, "What did you want to talk about?"

I thought how far it was from her house to mine, then remembered she had a car, a red convertible. When I turned I found I could see it, shiny under the streetlight.

"You won't be mad if it seems a little . . . funny?"

"Me?" I suddenly grinned, forgetting myself. "I don't think so."

She thought about it, getting up her nerve, once or twice glancing up at me. At last she said, "Did you ever hear of something called 'Imperial Dog'?"

I pursed my lips, making myself look thoughtful, then shook my head.

She pushed off from the bench and walked to the narrow back door of the garage. She opened it to look out. She could see the lake from there, I knew, very still in the moonlight, maybe two miles away, though it looked a lot nearer. I thought of going to stand with her, but I didn't. "There's this ancient Chinese recipe Arnold found, called 'Imperial Dog,' " she said. She spoke as if to the darkness, the lake. "According to the book, it's supposed to be the absolutely most elegant dish in the world." She half turned her head, checking my reaction.

"Oh?" I said.

She turned around more now, and looked not at me but at my boots. "It has to be completely black—the dog. It has to be killed just a minute before it's cooked. And—"

I said, "Is that why he was yelling at me?"

"He was yelling at my father." She avoided my eyes, then relented, and when she saw that I was waiting, hoping she'd see fit to explain, she said, "I guess he was yelling about a lot of things, not just that my father didn't want him to cook it at the restaurant. We had this big fight last night, my father and I. About school and . . . things."

"Boys?" I asked.

"Boys! What boys do *I* ever see?"

But I was on to her. "Oh, I guess there are those that hang around. Too love-sick to go out in the sunshine."

She studied me, guarded. "You think you're pretty smart, don't you."

"Nah. Not at all, really." Again I picked up the rag to wipe my hands. "So he was yelling at your father. Defending you?"

Her expression was exactly that of someone suddenly catching on to a new game, figuring out all at once how to play it. "I guess you'd have to say he was yelling at the whole world. I mean, Death and everything. By pure chance he found this recipe—I mean, I *guess* it was chance—and it was something Rinehart had eaten over there. . . ."

"So now he wants to cook it. At the restaurant. A dog."

She nodded.

"Well, well," I said.

She waited, watching me. I folded the rag and tossed it over on the workbench, then switched off the trouble-light, unplugged it, and began to loop the cord.

At last I said, "So what is it you want me to do?"

For the first time all night, she looked straight and steady into my eyes, cranking up the nerve to say what she'd come to say. "Get him the dog, Finnegan." She paused. "Please."

I laughed.

She looked astonished, then furious. I realized only later that probably a lot of what she was feeling that instant was embarrassment, even shame. She knew as well as I did what a thing it was she was asking of me. If I'd been smart I would've been indignant at her thinking I'd do it. But I just laughed. Her eyes widened, then narrowed again, and she started toward me—from the back door she had to get past me to leave. Though I was still laughing, I reached out and grabbed her arm. She tried to shake free, jerking away hard, half turning, about to swing at me, but I held on and suddenly I saw her change her mind. She stopped struggling. Her face was still angry, but the quiet elbow was a dead giveaway. My mother was right. Arnold Deller believed it too, I knew now. That was why in his crazy way he'd played matchmaker, though for his own purposes. It made me laugh harder, remembering his talk about Chinese cooking, how it brought people together.

"I'm sorry," I said. "Look, *anybody'd* laugh. It's like those fairytales, you know? Where the princess gives her lover this quest—'Go kill the dragon!' or, 'Find me the magic golden duck!'"

Her eyes flashed. "What do you mean, *lover?*"

"I just mean it's *like* that," I said.

"If you get any ideas—"

"No ideas!" I let go of her arm and raised both hands in surrender. "So what you want is, I'm to go rip off some kid's black dog."

"Of course not! Jesus, Finnegan, what's the matter with you? But we do need a black dog from somewhere, *somehow*." Her face was tipped up toward mine, the scent of her endangering my heart. She looked troubled, as if she had still worse to say, then said it. "It has to be completely black. And we need it tonight."

"Tonight! Hey, *listen!*"

"I promised Arnold. Look, he can't cook it at *home*, Finnegan—he hasn't got the right kinds of pots and *pans* and things, or the right kind of stove, whatever." There were suddenly tears in her eyes. "He *has* to cook it at the restaurant. *You* understand that."

"I don't understand why he's got to cook a goddamn dog at all."

"Well, he does," she said. I don't think she knew until this minute, when she said it, how firmly she believed it.

I backed away a little, not giving up exactly but trying to

come at it more from the side. "Your father says it's okay, if we can get the thing tonight?"

"He didn't say anything. He doesn't think we can do it."

I thought about that *we*. I also had questions of a philosophical nature. Arnold Deller had claimed to us, this afternoon, that the artist was the great servant of humanity, even that the artist was some kind of model for humanity, someone whose process could teach people the process of a higher art, the to-coin-a-phrase Art of Living. Now, for his alleged art, his childish faith in life's unstainable goodness, his chopped-off-ear innocence—really for his fanatical artist's ego, his cook's dementia—I was supposed to steal some dog.

"Dogs," I said, "are practically human."

"Not to the Chinese."

Reasoning with her, I saw, was useless. "Angelina," I asked, "what's all this to you? How come you're helping him?"

"My grandfather made a promise," she said. "Arnold can cook anything he wants."

"That's not the reason."

"My father has no *right*," she said.

"Ah!" I said. "Ah *so!*"

"That's Japanese," she snapped, "not Chinese."

"Same thing," I said.

"Finnegan," she said, "you are so *stupid*."

The scorn was partly faked, that old Calabrian play; but it was sufficiently real that I knew I wasn't being fair to her. It wasn't only to oppose her father's power that Angelina was doing this. Maybe it had to do with Rinehart, how he'd carried her around on his shoulders when she was five and he was nine; had to do with Arnold Deller's immense, exasperating sorrow.

"Angelina," I said, "it's wrong. It's unbalanced."

She considered it, then shook her head. "No, it's not," she said. "Not wrong, anyway."

I rubbed my nose with my index finger. "Well," I said, "maybe I'll see if I can round up the gang."

So we went out. First we phoned dog pounds for forty miles around—Benny the Butcher had this trick he could do with payphones—but everyplace was closed. Then, though we all had our doubts and misgivings, we cruised, watching for, for instance, black Labs. You'd think, if you weren't looking for one, that practically everybody's got one, but not so. Each of us knew, somewhere far or near, some friend who had a black Lab, or a black poodle, something. But when it comes right down to it, it's hard to steal a dog from a friend. Then we found one: a black something-or-other playing in a yard with a kid. We sat looking through the wire-mesh fence—it was one of those big places down by the lake, people that come up for the summer from New York City—and Tony Petrillo said the first flat-out uncrazy thing I'd ever heard him say. "Let's not do it. Let's just break into a pet store."

So we did.

It was a little after midnight when we vroomed up with the dog, a medium-sized all black one of indeterminate breed—there'd been no sign on the cage, and none of us knew. We packed it in a heavy cardboard box we'd poked air-holes in and roped it to the rack on Benny the Butcher's back fender. Tony got bit, also Lenny the Shadow, but nothing bad; anyway, we made it. Arnold was waiting, actually expecting us. So was Angelina. Arnold was crazy-serious, bent over, rubbing his fat hands and muttering what was probably little pieces of the recipe he was afraid he might forget. He had the book open over on the worktable, right under the light. When we carried the dog into the kitchen from the alley, Joe came in from the bar and stood watching us, the muscle on his jaw moving like a guitar string. Arnold ignored him, petting the dog, feeding him, talking fast to Ellis, telling him what he needed, getting everything ready, exactly according to the book. Ellis moved around with his head ducked, not making a sound, walking very fast, as if he thought somebody might jump out from behind a refrigerator and shoot him. Then Joe turned on his heel and left us, and after a second Angelina followed. We just hung around, trying to stay out of the way, watching, probably feeling a little sick—all but Tony Petrillo, who hunted around through the refrigerators and worktables, whistling, and fixed himself a ham-and-cheese sandwich. When Angelina came back she told us her father had phoned her grandfather.

"Whattya think," Lenny the Shadow said. "You think ole Arnold's really gonna do it? Kill the doggy?"

"I don't know," I said. "Maybe now that he's beginning to be friends with it—"

"He'll do it," Benny the Butcher said. His head drifted thoughtfully from side to side.

Arnold killed the dog. It was something. I could hardly believe it. Angelina, watching, reached out without thinking and touched my arm. "I'm gonna puke," Lenny said, and left the room.

Maybe it was because he felt guilty that Arnold began to chatter. He'd poured himself whiskey, I noticed. "People live too easy, that's the trouble with the world," he said. He wiped the bloody knife again and again on his apron. "They watch the stupid TV, they read the stupid *Reader's Digest* and the stupid best-sellers, they eat trucker tomatoes that got no taste and no color, no value in the world except they're easy to ship, they go to work, go home again, just like cows to the milking—" He picked out another knife, a long one with a blade eight inches wide, raised it, and brought it down once—very hard, *WHUMP!*—and the dog's head fell off, blood splashing. Angelina's hands flew to her white, white face. He raised the knife again, his left hand quickly shifting the body. Sweat soaked his T-shirt and ran down over the dragon on his arm. He shouted past his shoulder, "They go to their churches where all they ever do is sit still with their knees together, they even got people they pay to sing hymns for 'em, and then Monday they go to the dentist who makes them a sculpture of their teeth, with a fine big wooden stand and a fine gold plate with their very own name on it, and they hand him a credit card—not money, never a sack of new potatoes—and the dentist makes them as pretty as Joan Baez—" *WHUMP! WHUMP! WHUMP!*

Blood was spattered everywhere, all over the floor and on his apron and T-shirt, even on the side of his nose. The dog's head looked up at me with the tongue hanging out through the big, still teeth, an expression of absolute disbelief. Nobody looked away, Angelina or the rest of us, except for Lenny, who was gone. The horror was too solidly there to look away from. You can look away from someone squishing a bug, or something sick in a movie, but not this—blood, hair, teeth, and that slaughter-house smell that blanked out even the sweat smell of Arnold the cook. All you could do was, like Arnold, drink, not that I mean to suggest he wasn't facing it. As a matter of fact he was revelling in it, bug-eyed as a Satanist, the blue-and-red dragon on his big pink bicep dancing.

He said, sweat streaming down his face, sweat and maybe tears, his whole face awash, the useless, wet glasses up on his forehead, "Everything's easy, easy as pie!—TV dinners of chicken that never in its life felt the ground under its toes, instant potatoes, lettuce that's been put in some stuff to make it fresh till the day of the Antichrist—and what's the result? All humanity begins to be like sheep. That's right! They baby themselves till they don't *care* about themselves. They accept first little things like trucker tomatoes and eternal lettuce, then they begin to accept no-good houses, and cars made of plastic, engineered to kill, then it's Pentagon budgets in the multi-

multi-billions and commercial nukes built on earthquake faults, not to mention your snap-of-the-finger divorces—why stay married if it's trouble, right? To all of which I say—"

He sucked in breath and threw the dog, now gutted and hairless except for the tip of the tail, into boiling water, then turned quickly and started shaking sauces into a pan. Ellis was cutting fruit and pouring strange lumpy things out of cans, his face perfectly solemn, black hair falling over it. His apron came almost to the floor, falling all around him like a skirt.

"Arnold," I broke in, "you're crazy!" I shouted it at him as if all at once the realization had made me furious. It wasn't really that. I was thinking of Rinehart. It had suddenly come back to me how when he'd sat down to that dinner of Chinese black dog he'd felt one with centuries and centuries of dead Asians, people that would probably have slit his throat on sight and put the pages of his Bible inside their shoes to keep their feet warm and at the same time tromp on the writings of the infidel; and now Arnold too had to be one with all those thousands and thousands of dead Asians, so he could be one with his son; and it was all pure bullshit: Rinehart was dead, and soon we'd all be, two years or seventy, though the programmed anguish would go on and on for centuries, like a heatwave around the planet, until at last the sun went out, or some scheme from the Pentagon knocked it out, and there would be no more babies, no more sorrow or misuse of the gift of life, just a big, dark, wheeling stone. It was pity that made me yell, pity for the innocent tables and chairs that would be left, afterward, and couldn't so much as move an inch unless human beings helped them.

"Not crazy," he shouted, turning on me, red-faced and wide-eyed, brandishing a bottle with Chinese writing on it, shaking it at me like it was blackish holy water.

"You're a child molester," I shouted back.

"What?" he said, surprised.

"Well, something like that," I said. "I forget the word. You corrupted Angelina and you corrupted us—made us perfectly good citizens steal a dog and kill it for somebody to eat, which is practically cannibalism, and yet on you babble about people accepting things, not caring about themselves, not daring to stand up!"

Arnold held out his hands, pleading for a little justice, a little common sense. "You think I condone your lawless acts?" he asked. "But at least you had a reason. You actually *felt* something." He glanced at Angelina, then quickly away again. He picked up a pair of tong-like things. "You *felt* whatever it was that made you do it, and you felt something when you did it, I'll bet. Felt something. Right? For a minute you existed! How do you feel about the packaged, drugged-up meat at your supermarket, or airplanes dropping bombs from so high up they don't know there's people down there—they never have to see it—or the Japanese and Russians out murdering the kings of the sea? Do you feel anything at all about such matters, my hot Irish friend? Not likely! Most people don't. If you can't feel anything about things near at hand, how can you feel for things more distant and abstract? Ponder it! Ponder it!"

"You're nuts," Lenny the Shadow said. It was the first I knew that he'd come back. "You shouldda been a man-eating tiger."

"More like he shouldda been napalm," Benny the Butcher said. "*Fsssss!*"

"*Not* nuts!" Arnold yelled, whirling and pointing at Lenny with the tongs. "Similar but different! I got centuries of tradition controlling my craziness. I got ideals, I got standards!"

He didn't seem to notice that the old man, Frank, the owner, was in the doorway, shrunken, morose, leaning hard on two canes. The bags under his eyes were like toadskin. The eyes, above the bags and under the gray eyebrows, were filmy. Joe stood a little behind him, in the shadows.

Arnold was raving, "I'm an artist, you understand that? What's an artist? How's he different from an *ordinary* nut? An artist is a man who makes a covenant with tradition. Not just dreams, grand hopes and abstractions—no, *hell* no—a covenant with something that's *there*, pots and paintings, recipes: the specific that makes things indefinite come alive—assuming you don't get lost in 'em, the specifics, I mean. Salt, for instance. A man can get lost in the idea of salt—too much, too little, what the ancients thought of it, whether you should shake it with the left hand or the right— No! *That's* not art! *Dead* art! *Cancel!*" He gasped, jumped in again, swinging his left arm in front of him as if driving back hordes. "The artist's contract is, come hell or high water he won't go cheap, he'll never quit trying for the best. Maybe he fails, maybe he sells out and hates himself. You know it can happen just like you know you can stop loving your wife, but all the same you make the promise. Otherwise you have to go with ordinary craziness, which is disgusting." He spit. Forgot himself and spit right on the floor.

Then he turned with a flourish, reached into the pot two-handed with the tongs, and raised up the dog to look at it. He was bent forward like a wrestler, his expression fierce, arm and shoulder muscles swollen. Whether he was pleased or disappointed we couldn't tell. He swung around and held the carcass toward us, high, dripping pink water—raised it and held it up like some old-time sacrifice the gods were supposed to come sniff.

In the doorway old Frank Dellapicallo said, gravel-voiced, black as doom, "If you cooked that thing you better serve it, mister."

Arnold swung his head around to look at him. Automatically he lowered the dog into the pot. "What's that?"

"You heard me," Frank growled. "If that's your chef's special, you better find customers to feed it to."

"I'll eat it, don't worry," Arnold said.

"Not you," Frank said. "*People*. Otherwise"—he jerked one cane toward the hallway behind him—"out!"

Joe came into the light now, arms folded, white sleeves

sharply outlined over the black of his vest. He was grinning. You couldn't really blame him, even though Arnold had been more or less a friend. There were blood marks all over the floor, though not as bad as earlier. Ellis had mopped some of it up. Angelina was leaning forward, stretching out her arms toward the old man, whining at him, "*Gram*-pa . . ."

"Shut up," Frank said—just like that, exactly as you'd speak to a three-year-old child, or a dog. "He knows the agreement."

Mechanically, because it was time, according to the recipe in the book, Arnold took the dog out of the pot and laid it in the pan where Ellis had put the fruit and things, arranged it so the pawless feet were tucked under the body and the black cap of hair on the tail could be seen, then carried the whole thing to the oven. Ellis held open the oven door for him while he slid in the pan.

Then everybody just stood there. Arnold poured himself more whiskey.

"Well," Arnold said, squinting his little pig-eyes and rubbing his hands on his apron, "there's a lesson in this." He didn't go on. According to the clock over the counter it was 3 a.m.

Just then a knock came at the kitchen's back door. We all jumped, and then after a minute Benny went over and opened the door a few inches to look out. He opened the door wider. Arnold's three daughters stood there, homely and scared-looking, their skin the color of old ashes. The oldest one was eighteen, though she looked more like fourteen or fifteen. The youngest was ten. I knew her a little; she was in my sister Shannon's class at school. All three of them looked like orphans—little glasses like Arnold's and washed-out hand-me-down clothes—but if they looked pitiful it was mostly just the hour and their shyness, maybe a fear, not fully admitted, that their father had had some accident, or had shot himself. They came in sideways, like refugees, looking at Arnold and saying nothing, their expressions meek, timidly friendly, as if they were hoping no one would yell at them. I was aware again of the room's thick blood smell. Arnold stared at the three girls, saying nothing, no doubt trying to figure out how he felt. At last he gave an abrupt nod, freeing them to smile and shyly nod back—they stretched out the nod to make it do for all of us—then they faded as well as they could into the walls.

Arnold began cleaning things up, putting condiments and spices away, carrying knives and pots and pans over to the sink, throwing out his waste. Angelina moved over closer to her grandfather, probably so that when she spoke Arnold's daughters wouldn't hear her.

"How can you fire him, Grandpa?" she asked. "He made us *famous*."

She knew well enough why Frank could fire him. He'd challenged Joe; he'd made us steal the dog; he was crazy.

But the old man was too tired and impatient for the complicated reasons. "We had an agreement."

We stood and waited. A strange, mysteriously sweet smell began to fill the kitchen. Tony Petrillo opened a bottle of wine from the bar, just walked in and got it. Awkwardly, spilling a little, he poured a glass for Arnold, leaning on the counter, standing with his feet crossed, big bags under his eyes. Arnold accepted the wine without even noticing, though he had whiskey in the other hand. Tony poured another glass of wine for Angelina, then one for me, one for Benny, one for Lenny, and one for each of the girls. When he held a glass up for Frank, the old man waved him away in disgust. He didn't offer one to Joe.

The three daughters edged over to the sink where Ellis was washing pots and pans and stood watching as if it were fascinating work or he was unusually good at it. They still hadn't said a word to anyone, even to ask what was happening. They put down their wineglasses and began stacking dishes from the dryer. The way they worked—smoothly, silently—you'd've thought they'd been there for hours. They were nice girls, it suddenly struck me. It was funny no one ever noticed them. Maybe the same thought occurred to Angelina. She went over and joined them. She looked the way she had in my father's garage. Small and tired. I was reminded, watching her, that I was going to have to help eat that dog.

"Hey, Arnold," I said, "how much you figure on charging for that dog?"

He looked at Joe, then me. "Two-fifty sound fair?"

"Hey," Lenny the Shadow said, "I just had supper." He put his hand on his stomach. The oldest of the daughters smiled, then looked puzzled.

"Me too," Benny the Butcher said, and grinned.

Crazy Tony said, "How much for the child's plate, Arnold?"

Angelina turned her face a little to glance at me.

"Child's plate! That might change the picture," Lenny said. He wrapped his hand around his jaw, thinking.

"Dollar-fifty?" Arnold asked.

So we did it.

We ate by candlelight, out in the restaurant, old man Dellapicallo at the end of the table leaning on his elbows, no plate in front of him. Joe had gone home. When he went out the door he looked smaller than Angelina. I was sorry for him. He was the one who'd been right—sane and civilized from the beginning. But also his walk was oddly mechanical, and the way he shook his head when he looked back at us from the door, it was as if under his hair he had springs and gears.

Angelina sat by me, the others spread around us, close enough to come to the rescue just in case, in this strange world where anything could happen, the dog should wake up. There was no sign of the thousands and thousands of dead Asians, or of Rinehart either, but it felt like they were there—maybe even more there if there's no such thing in the world as ghosts, no life after death, no one there at the candlelit table but the few of us able to throw shadows on the wall. Say that being alive was the dinner candles, and say they burned forever over this everlasting meal of Imperial Dog. Then we were the diners there now, this instant, sent as distinguished representatives of all who couldn't make it this evening, the dead and the unborn. Everybody was feeling it, the importance of what we were doing—though it wasn't *what* we were doing that was important. We could've been, I don't know, planting a tree. The dog was terrific, by the way, once you talked your stomach past the idea. The wine was also terrific. Angelina, as if by accident, put her hand on mine.

"To the future of Ancient China!" Benny the Butcher said, raising his wineglass.

"To the Kings of the Road," Arnold said, and raised his.

"Hear, hear," the three daughters said softly, smiling and blushing as if they understood.

Tony Petrillo said thoughtfully, almost so no one could hear him, "To grasshoppers and mice."

"To Angelina!" Angelina cried, eyes sparkling.

We were all, even Arnold, a little shocked, but in the darkness beyond where the candles reached, Rinehart nodded, and a thousand thousand Asians bowed from the waist.

ABOUT THE AUTHOR

John Gardner received wide acclaim for his novels, his collections of short stories and his critical works. He was born in Batavia, New York, in 1933 and taught English, Anglo-Saxon and creative writing at Oberlin, Chico State College, San Francisco State, Southern Illinois, Bennington, and SUNY-Binghamton. His books include *The Art of Fiction*, *The Art of Living*, *Grendel*, *Jason and Medeia*, *The Life and Times of Chaucer*, *Mickelsson's Ghosts*, *Nickel Mountain*, *October Light*, *The Resurrection*, *The Sunlight Dialogues*, *Stillness and Shadows*, and various books for children. He died in a motorcycle accident in 1982.